Reality Principles

Reality Principles

From the Absurd to the Virtual

Herbert Blau

The University of Michigan Press
Ann Arbor

Published in the United States of America by
The University of Michigan Press
Manufactured in the United States of America
♾ Printed on acid-free paper

2014 2013 2012 2011 4 3 2 1

A CIP catalog record for this book is available from the British Library.

Library of Congress Cataloging-in-Publication Data

Blau, Herbert.
Reality principles : from the absurd to the virtual / Herbert Blau.
p. cm.
Includes index.
ISBN 978-0-472-07151-7 (cloth : acid-free paper) — ISBN 978-0-472-05151-9 (pbk. : acid-free paper)
1. Theater—Philosophy. I. Title.
PN2039.B5775 2010
792'.01—dc22 2010047518

ISBN 978-0-472-02790-3 (e-book)

To my son Dick

Contents

Introduction

ALL OF THESE ESSAYS, with one exception, were written just before or after the millennium, and while they reflect upon each other, that earlier essay does, not only across the years, but from so long ago that I might have forgotten what it was about. It would seem to have been an irrelevance until, working on an autobiography, I happened to read it again, while remembering the dissident 1960s, spilling into the 70s, when classrooms were invaded, students were lecturing teachers, and *relevance* was a watchword. That my view of it all then, as a rather chastening lesson, is still germane today was confirmed by my wife Kathleen Woodward, when she was recently asked to contribute to a special issue of *Daedalus,* where my essay was published over forty years ago, after a rather high-powered conference, sponsored by the American Academy of Arts and Science, "The Future of the Humanities." That the future is still in question—and with the economy reeling, the job market worse than ever—is what Kathy was writing about.[1] Much involved as she is with the digital humanities, a possible source of salvation, about which I know very little, she nevertheless quoted me in her essay (without saying I was her husband), because "Relevance: The Shadow of a Magnitude" had apparently left a reproachful shadow on what, in the academy today, remains misguided, unthought, or knowingly hypocritical. And though I had serious misgivings, in those performative days of protest, about my alignment with the students, their insurrectionary fervor, I felt we had to come to terms not only with what they were demanding, but what we had been evading, with a repressed blush, as if the books we were teaching and analyzing—the sometimes forbidding subtext or darkling indirections, myths of otherness, love's body, their implicit bearing on life, ethically, kinesthetically, never mind psychedelically—were telling us we were lying, even as the universities were being corporatized.

What I said at the conference, and what I wrote, apparently had sufficient fervor of its own, which caused James Ackerman—the distinguished art historian, in his introduction to the essays—to describe it as an "apocalyptic message" that had "the most radical implications of any in the issue."[2] If the message was partially determined by my radical work in the theater, which had produced a scathing manifesto a few years before,[3] the more immediate site of provocation was my being at California Institute of the Arts, where as founding provost I was responsible for its conception as an implosive scene of learning, a sort of mixed-media merger of the Bauhaus and Black Mountain. With a faculty of major artists interacting with students, and the avant-garde as second nature—first in beautiful downtown Burbank, that right-wing wasteland, scandalized by it all, then with happenings and installations all over the landscape of the San Fernando Valley—CalArts became the exemplary model of the antiacademy. And while there were wild and whirling dilemmas in its uncensored beginnings, with an escalation of controversy (up to the Disney-world board) that eventually caused me to leave, there hasn't been in my lifetime, except maybe for Black Mountain, a pedagogical dynamic even remotely like it.

How all of this came about is rehearsed in a miniature autobiography, called an "Auto Archive," which I was asked to write for *Theater Journal,* explaining how I came to theater, and why, since I left it, I'm doing what I'm doing now. If much of that is theoretical, it's with a haunted materiality, what I first tried to define in *Take Up the Bodies: Theater at the Vanishing Point*—with the ghostings of (dis)appearance, "the body's long initiation in the mystery of its vanishings,"[4] and the shadowy magnitudes there. As for the order of things here, with "Relevance" at the beginning, in an ambience of the Absurd, its manic, non sequitur theater, the "Auto-Archive" is at the end, as an appendix of remembrance, in the encroaching world of the virtual, with the "liveness" of bots and bytes, and mediatization setting the standard for what we take to be "real" in performance. Or with the body immaterial, so it would seem: the appearance of mere appearance, a techno-mimicry of mimesis. About the nostalgia of virtuality—liveness abolishing presence in a facsimile of *life*—there's a brief reflection here in "The Human Nature of the Bot," which was solicited actually for a debate online.[5] The repercussions were such that I was asked to extend the essay for an updated anthology, *Critical Theory and Performance,* where I had written previously on the psychopathology of the actor and, from Brechtian Alienation to the hegemony of cultural studies, ideological vigilance and the illusions of *de*mystification.[6] As for the resources of mystification in the electronic age, from neural stimuli to info-phantoms of the brain, the programs proliferate, but despite the "body electric," the byte encoding of Whitman's dream, "*the subtext of the virtual is that it really wants to be real.*" Thus, I raised a jaundiced eyebrow over the performative allure of cyberspace and, without the smell of mortality,[7] the empty staginess of its digital seeming. The title of the revised essay, "Virtually Yours: Presence, Liveness, Lessness," is a simulated sign-off on the devolution of it all. Which also suggests Beckett, who in the abbreviations of being, its synaptic circulation, made a commodius virtue of "Lessness," as with the Fizzles and *Texts for Nothing,* or in his shortest play, that "faint, brief cry," the plaintive "vagitus" of *Breath.*[8]

As for mortality itself, that difficult birth astride of a grave,[9] it's to be seen from another perspective, seemingly transcendent, in "The Faith-Based Initiative of the Theater of the Absurd." A symptomatic image there, unconscionable in its excess, out the window and to the stars, is "*the long, long body . . . winding,*" in Ionesco's *Amédée or How to Get Rid of It,* floating amid the supernal, an ever-ballooning corpse. The essay was originally commissioned as one of two keynotes for a symposium at Stanford, a retrospective on the Absurd, from that existential period when all values were up for grabs, or seemed to have disappeared, even in celestial regions, into a black hole, where gravity is so impacted that nothing, not even light, can escape its relentless pull. How to think about that, or if value exists at all, might require "complexity theory," as with the fractals of disordered systems. If that seems, systemically, cosmically, an overview of absurdist dramaturgy, the invitation came with a cautionary note to me, about how things should be said, not said, for a not entirely academic, rather hypothetical audience, the "educated public." With an apology, then, in advance, and "chronometrably" in submission, I abided by "the game of the rule," taking my cues from Ionesco, with a hyperawareness of words, wearisome, slippery words, the crimes committed in their name. That didn't prevent me, alas, with a disposition to theory and subjunctive habits of mind, from doing precisely, criminally, what I was warned against, making things difficult, in appraising the theatricality that, with every inconsequent gesture or conscious incoherence, "inevitably returns to the tortuous question of whether or not there is meaning in the world, or whether we were merely born deceived into a reality that is incurable."

The other keynote was by Martin Esslin, whose book *The Theater of the Absurd* (published in 1961), began with an account of that now-legendary performance of *Waiting for Godot* at San Quentin Prison (1957), where we weren't quite sure, as the convicts assembled, the actors nervous, there'd be an educated public, or what kind of education. As for sophisticated San Francisco, when I first directed that production at The Actor's Workshop, and the now-canonical Beckett just about unknown, there was not only in the audience, but even in our company—the knowledgeable ones, of course, really experienced in theater—much resistance to our doing that gratuitously unintelligible, pointless nondrama. I'd given various talks at Stanford over the years, but if it was a pleasure to be there with Martin, by then an old friend, it was like a pleasure postponed, amusingly ironic, to find myself this time on the stage of the Little Theater, where there'd been (in 1949) the first-ever production of any play of mine, then several others, written there at Stanford, to which I came by an almost capricious series of accidents, with a graduate fellowship in drama, as a temporary diversion from a career in chemical engineering (about which, again, see the "Auto-Archive"). It took some time, even while working in theater, before I really put the periodic table and fluid mechanics behind, but out of old reflex, ideas from the sciences, subatomic or astrophysical, will turn up in these essays, and another one in a moment on the selvage of the Absurd—now, but not then, linked to "chaos theory."

Meanwhile, unfortunately, back to the incurable. It may have been up in the air, like that corpse in the Milky Way, but mortality came down to earth, as if through the retrospective. And we even saw it on stage, in the course of the other keynote, the quivering immanence of it. With no discernible change in an encyclopedic mind, but his whole body shaking from an advanced case of Parkinson's, the sad aftermath of the occasion was the death of Martin Esslin. Thinking of it now, I remember another symposium (back in 1969), when the two of us were together in western Canada. At the hotel, Martin and I were having breakfast, when we heard over a radio that Beckett had won the Nobel Prize. We tried to call him in Paris, but to avoid reporters and unwanted attention he'd already gone into hiding, somewhere in Tangiers, and he didn't show up in Stockholm to receive the prize. The morning after the talks at Stanford, when Martin was about to return to London, we again had breakfast together, and were reminiscing about that, when I saw his hands trembling, and asked about the prognosis. He said it wasn't good, nothing the doctors could do . . . That, to be sure, was the wrong kind of *nothing,* which in Beckett has to be *done,* as in the waiting for Godot. More to be said about that, and in the tribulations of Beckett, "the science of affliction," or with the apnea we shared, its suffocating perspective.

There are three pieces on Beckett here, but it was the faith-based irony of my essay on the Absurd that caused me to return, out of a "vertigo of nothingness," to when I was studying thermodynamics and became fascinated with entropy—a measure of the unavailable energy of the universe, which seemed, as I say at the end of the essay, a datum of the Absurd, "with its law of increasing disorder and commitment to evanescence," sneaking up in "a dizzying anguish on whatever made it available." Along with the dizzying anguish, what made it available, too, was what I called in the following essay "The Soul-Complex of Strindberg," which like complexity at the edge of chaos, disorderly, but adaptive, inclined to something rather than nothing—though we're never quite sure what it is, since it came, as in *A Dream Play,* through an illusory "triplex cosmos," and with "occulted symbols." Or worse, what we'd rather forget, like "an anxiety dream that becomes increasingly nightmarish," while the nightmare itself, in its seepage from the unconscious to the unspeakable in the world, brutally implacable, garishly banal, becomes reality principle. If there is, in the preface to *Miss Julie,* a provision of technique which anticipates Brecht, that effect of alienation is only momentary in the mind. Whether naturalism or symbolism, there's still a double bind: in the penumbra of representation, from the materialist to the sublime, no escape by illusion from the oppressiveness of it all.

For in Strindberg, ultimately, whether in "vulvous grottoes" or whatever idyllic residues of the biblical garden, the world into which we've fallen is a time-induced pollution of ignominious lessness, making it hard to breath. In this suffocating regard, the soul-complex foreshadows, with its mordantly longing vision of a world outside this world, the lingering affliction in Beckett—that too, incurable, with its earthbound outbursts of rage, all the more because of nostalgia for what, "having terminated my humanities," as Beckett says, but says in vain, with maybe "a new no to cancel all the others,"[10] unnamably never existed. Not so for the early Strindberg, influenced by Swedenborg, who in his spiritual awakening could visit heaven and hell, to consult with angels and demons, charged by the Lord with parsing out holy doctrine. But for the dispirited Strindberg, nothing that ever lived was holy—no world but this world, no good, no truth, no meaning, there's only hell on earth, a Swedenborgian "vastation," where misery prevails. Thus with the Student in *The Ghost Sonata,* well tutored in disenchantment, a far miserable cry from the students we started with here, who in those cold war days of relevance, presumably telling it like it is, countered the threat of MAD (Mutually Assured Destruction) with the promissory note of a counterculture claiming to change the world. Strindberg's unappeasable Student would probably have laughed at that, with a raging desire to say what he thinks, though if he did, and people were honest, he's sure the world would collapse. As I say in the essay, however (as true now as it was then), "the horror may be that it wouldn't"—which is the news that Indra's Daughter, having descended to earth, brings to the Throne above. And then there's the Captain in *The Dance of Death,* who, mortified, impotent—and without the magniloquence of Hamm in *Endgame,* even if self-deflating, the saving grace of his histrionics—can only shake his fists!

In the drama of modern Austria, historical site of one of the essays, the worlding is still demoralizing, as with the imprisoned Sigismund in Hofmannsthal's *The Tower,* "not sure he is in the world, or [*pace* Heidegger] where the world *is,*" with boundaries blurred, too, in a chimeric subjectivity, between within and without. (To return again to the virtual: that chimeric subjectivity may be even more so today, with split-screen attention to a world that is an elsewhere, with Googling, linkage, WinZip, and instant access to multiple selves, by merely the click of a mouse.) As for those words, words, words, and the crimes committed in their name, there's a logorrheic archive in Peter Handke's *Sprechstücke,* particularly *Offending the Audience,* and a magisterial indictment in Karl Kraus's massive drama, *The Last Days of Mankind,* which in no uncertain terms, and a corrosively assured omnipotence, is meant to be the last Word. "Where are all these corpses from?" asks the bewildered tramp in *Godot,*[11] who might very well be referring—after two world wars, by then in their ghostly presence—to the rotting horde of unburied corpses at the end of Kraus's play. Though he was not at all Marxist, what Kraus said with millennial scorn of post-Secessionist Austria would seem to be the fulfilment of what Marx once demanded, in an early letter to the Young Hegelians: "a *ruthless criticism of everything existing.*"[12] Such a criticism was actually initiated—about the time of that letter, and years before the Young Vienna, who just before the Secession met in the coffeehouses—in the satires of Johann Nestroy, whose wordplay buffoonery and redheaded mockery also took on the censors, that religiously endorsed surveillance, a refined dynastic tradition, covering up the scandals of imperial power, and its trickle-down hypocrisies, not only in highbrow Vienna, but at the city limits, among the theatergoers of an emerging middle class.

Nestroy stuck it to them, his insults making them laugh, but then was long-neglected, until rediscovered by Kraus, and then again neglected, not only in the Austrian theater, his plays rarely produced anywhere, but even by those of us who had studied European drama. Having read him last I don't know when, I rediscovered Nestroy myself, in wondering how to approach the keynote for an international symposium, here at the University of Washington, "Cultures of Performance in Modern Austria." It wasn't only Nestroy I had to catch up with, but Kraus and others, and the Secession too, since I was hardly familiar with what had happened under the Hapsburgs, or onstage, backstage, or the inner circles of waltzing Vienna, when I was asked by my Germanic colleagues to give that talk. I hesitated to do it, but they persisted, because of my background in theater and writings on performance. Even so, there would be scholars from here and abroad, who knew modern Austria and its heritage as I didn't, and all of whom read and spoke German (indeed, many of the papers were in German, and when mine was published in a collection from the conference, all quotations I'd made in translation were restored to the original.) Aside from that delinquency—next to no memory of the language, studied for my doctorate, but unused then and since—my major immersion in Austrian culture was at a rather remote scholarly haven, when I taught at the Salzburg Seminar, in the Schloss Leopoldskron, redesigned by Max Reinhardt as a sumptuous salon for artists, across the lake from the mountaintop castle where the aged Kokoschka had a workshop for painters, and might have been teaching then. I follow him here, however, through his wilder years when, as with the blasphemous erotics of *Murderer, Hope of Women,* he shaved his head, bloodied his actors, to make the theater outrageous, and through a propensity for derangement, became in the café scene of Vienna a spectacle himself. At Salzburg, much cultural history all around, but my seminar, for the equivalent of postdocs from all over western Europe, was on American drama. When I thought it over, however, what made me eminently qualified, as I said jokingly before the talk, as in accepting the invitation, was the fact that one of my immigrant grandfathers, an illiterate tailor, came from somewhere in Austria; hence, the name Blau. Actually, too, as can be seen in the essay, I had some direct experience at the more contemporary end of modern Austria, with Viennese Actionism; and in another context, with one of those affiliated, the versatile Valie Export (body art / cinema / video / mixed-media installations), with whom I had coedited an issue on performance in the journal *Discourse.*[13]

Recurrently in these essays, as in a previous collection, *The Dubious Spectacle: Extremities of Theater,* the thought of performance is not only confronting some limiting condition, but as with the Actionists, their self-abusive performances, extremities at the extreme, often hard to watch. Or, as with other body artists, such as Stelarc (with fishhooks through his flesh) and Orlan (with multiple surgeries on her face), even a photograph might make you wince. This would seem to be, however, the desirable state of things within the "*trajectories and becomings*" on the thousand plateaus of Gilles Deleuze, with its "rhizomatics of theatricality," where the repertoire is endless, each of us many others, all roles insufficient, in the assayings of nonidentity. In that period of demystifications, when theory was exposing systems of power, the anti-identity politics had to do with a pretentious subjectivity or the bogus individualism imposed upon us by capitalism. As for the anti-Oedipal dispensation of Deleuzean performance, where the desirable state is desire, the incessant production of which is assured by lubricious desiring-machines, when I wrote that "the autoerotic [is] on automatic in runaway machines, given over to pure expenditure in the libidinal economy," it still made sense to compare that to Wall Street, which wasn't much concerned then "with the prospect of recession, or stagflation," no less a Great Depression. That was, of course, before the enlightenment of the economic collapse.

Whatever the stimulus now, there's nothing like deficit spending in the superfluity of Deleuze, the incorrigible excess of its plateauing evanescence. In the early writings with Guattari, that excess was indebted—the instabilities and fluctuations, free of all normal causalities—to the utopian anarchy of May '68. They concede about the dissidence (as I did about relevance) that there were agitations, slogans, idiocies, but despite all absurd illusions, there was an opening to the possible, a visionary phenomenon, throwing off the nightmare of cultural suffocation. And in the dream of a new existence, eventually betrayed, what appeared was a "spectral cosmos" that "superseded the world." Chance was admissible too, but the betrayal, however, was always in the cards. For there was, at the outset, in the schizoanalysis of capitalism, a reversing, anomalous logic; even in boundless speculation the codes of capitalism determined semiotically the vaunted exposures of critical theory. Or given the law of value, with a marketable equivalence: "*floating theories,* . . . floating money," as Jean Baudrillard concluded in an early book on symbolic exchange.[14]

With a momentum, nevertheless, overriding contradiction, Deleuze's spinning circuitry spawned (all verbal, no object), in a profusion of instantaneity or haphazard of signs, as it might on the Internet. And with the libidinal inexhaustible, pure expenditure continued, neither mere data, nor pixelated, rather replenished in whatever becomings by an "energy-source machine," which in rejecting the Oedipal structure had nothing to do with the Freudian unconscious, or the inadequacy of an Id. The machinic fact of the matter is that with all value going at once, into and out of all the bodily orifices, despoiling from ass to mouth the fiction of a natural function, the deterritorialized flows became, in a redundancy of irrelevance, the spaced-out apotheosis of the polymorphous sixties, with its perversity in regression. As prefigured by infant autism, the yammering, stuttering tantrums, and with chiliastic dimensions, by the sonorous organless body in the alchemical theater of Artaud, the "vitalism"[15] is examined here, in "Performing in the Chaosmos: Farts, Follicles, Mathematics, and Delirium in Deleuze." Which will not be the first time, and I say this with no bias against it, we'll encounter a lot of shit—though in other respects, unexcremental, I do take issue with Deleuze.

Given his long hostility to bourgeois theater, overburdened by representation, there's a deep affinity with the "operations" of subtraction in the "minor" stagings of Carmelo Bene, who refused to think of himself as a director.[16] Insufficiency the heart doth sway, as Shakespeare says in a sonnet,[17] maybe releasing other prospects, but otherwise—and it may be the inversion of a reductio ad absurdum—Deleuze's antitheatrical prejudice is dispersed through the rigors and excess of excess, though with insufficient deference to the future of illusion, which appears to be, as I think it (or is it thinking me? as I've also asked about history) the only future before us, and thus a reality principle. This rather unnerving thought is more than implicit in the balancing act of the prejudice, between *more* theater and *less* theater, which has varied through historical periods, but leads to the age-old question, *Why theater at all?* With history blurring, however, in a dromoscopic, simulacral, hyperdigitized world, given over to speed in the furore of information, theater would seem to be left behind, with the body as an encumbrance, no less the mortal body performing, arousing thoughts of death and dying, which can't be outsourced, except into tragic vision. As to what death *is,* as Montaigne once remarked, it is a scene with one character. An unseeable scene, perhaps. To what extent, we might ask, is it related to stage fright?—which nobody can avoid, even the best of actors, but as covered up in performance, or from the body's specific gravity working up a sweat, the dark energy of theater, what really activates acting. Meanwhile, there's something other than mere liveness in new modes of genetic and molecular art, which suggest, however (if at all a knowable truth), that death may be dying, even as antitheater appears to be obsolete, its inexistence explored, with the perceptual permutations of that always reversing conundrum—reality of appearance? appearance of reality?—in "Seeming, Seeming: The Illusion of Enough."

And when we speak of the future before us, there's always the correlative question, what constitutes that *us*? which I've asked before in *The Audience,* and here with some afterthoughts, in "'Who's There?'—Community of the Question." The issue is unavoidable in an ontology of theater, which is more than implicit through this entire book, though not very characteristic of performance studies, which tends to be, while crossing nations and cultures, ethnographical or anthropological, and when merging with race and gender, ideological too—which, theoretically, just about everything is, but that predictably so. Wherever the theater comes from, and whether more or less, that essay was crossing borders for another international symposium, which in its conception was influenced by *The Audience.* What was in question there, in Zurich, Switzerland—where the floating money usually floats (through declared transparency now) in labyrinthine vaults—is the nature and status of the spectator in a globalized, migratory, mediatized world. As if resisting dissemination, there had actually been, several years before, a similar conference in Lisbon, Portugal, once politically isolated, but about to become, with Expo '98 scheduled a few weeks after, the cultural capital of the world. With a festival of performances already around the city, it seemed an ideal setting for a lively dialogue, between European Americanists and American scholars, about "Ceremonies and Spectacles, and the Staging of Collective Identities."

What contributed to the festive atmosphere, for those of us giving keynotes, was our being taken for lunch and dinner to the finest Portuguese restaurants, where there was in the background, unbeknownst to me, the plaintive irony of a collective identity out of the city's past, and probably still in the barrios we weren't taken to see. I heard it, but nobody explained it, so far as I recall, but in the slow, lingering sadness of fado guitars and song, there was an unobtrusive staging of poverty and dispossession, what in newly prosperous Lisbon was better unremembered. As for the worldly scholars at the conference, what seemed to have been forgotten, in the acceleration of history, is that with the accumulation of capital into a Society of the Spectacle (what Guy Debord had called "Separation Perfected" or "an *abundance of dispossession*"),[18] there was reason to be skeptical about the communitarian theme—which, though I took issue with it, provided the title for *The Dubious Spectacle.* To begin with in my talk, I confessed that I might be there under false pretenses, since after many years of directing, in multiple kinds of theater, conventional or open spaces, with distance or intimacy—even actors within the audience or the audience becoming actors—I'd come to think of the staging of collective identities "as a rather vain enterprise," or a leftover platitude from the participatory mystique. Nor, since the more contentious days of The Actor's Workshop, and *The Impossible Theater,* could I buy into the tedious notion that the theater is at its best when it does what the audience wants—as just last week, praising a production, a critic said in *The New York Times.*

As for "the semblance of a gathered public," I won't belabor it here, nor elaborate as in *The Audience,* but as I'd written in its first paragraph, "Such an audience seems like the merest facsimile of remembered community paying its respects not so much to the still-echoing signals of a common set of values but to the better forgotten remains of the most exhausted illusions."[19] And so, too, those attending or watching being set up for participation, the audience becoming actors, and not only entertained, but edified by that. Whatever the identities among the sizable group in Lisbon, there was some discomfiture when I said, "As for the scholarship that takes for granted that theater is the site of the social, or an affirmation of community, that appears to me now—though I believed it when I was younger—an academic ceremony of innocence, assuming as a reality what is, perhaps, the theater's primary illusion."[20] Those few years later in Zurich, among the others there, it certainly seemed that the dubiousness was more advanced, as in the cadenced title of the conference, which was—with globalization speeding up, and the nervous European Union—phrased in three languages: "*Zushchauen* / *Quel* Public? / *As You Like It.*"

Have it anyway you like it—with everywhere linked to elsewhere in a computerized cursor(y) life, with Facebook, Twitter, doyouQ, the scrolling identities there—community *is* the question, and surely we know that the early-on autotexted, bitlet generation, growing up at the keyboard, gaming, with infinities of data, hardly goes to the theater. "Who's there?" At the two major theaters in this city, the Seattle Repertory and Intiman, if you look around the audience, a large number are elderly, and the youngest in attendance are usually the baby boomers. And indeed, what's up on stage is what that audience wants, invariably so familiar that, sitting on the aisle, I'm ready to leave after ten minutes, except that my polite, forbearing wife presses down on my arm, keeping me there until we slip away at intermission. Just last night, at dinner, an artist friend who works in a gallery literally asked what I was often asked when I was still doing theater, especially the more inquisitional, long-rehearsed, encrypted work of the KRAKEN group: "What kind of audience did you have in mind?" What I said—and he couldn't believe it—is what I used to say then (often in stronger language), that I couldn't care less about the audience. What I did care about is precisely what we were doing, on the premise that theater is *thought,* and whether verbal or ideographic, at its best when self-conflicted, or this one's quarrel, that one's pulse, or some last will and testament, stubborn but indecisive, which to believe it would make you bleed. And even then, with afterthought in the grain of the voice, as if the "geno-text" in Barthes[21] came from the orifices in Deleuze, there'd be the spittle, sputtering, stammering, or at some extremity of a scream, shattered words becoming gesture—glottal stops, rasps, plosives, fricatives piercing the body—and we'd rehearse it all over again.

The method was psychophysical, in a process we called *ghosting,* but whatever it is we were after, it was impassioned by the necessity of understanding *that,* however inaccessible its meaning might be—or at some periphery of estrangement, as if the thinking had never started, and there you are confounded by the ghostly thing itself. So: "Who's there?" No wonder that voice on the ramparts has been like a light in the dark, though it's the wrong one making the challenge. Of course, as with everything in *Hamlet,* you won't see it if you're not listening. Then, that other voice out of the dark: "Nay, answer me. Stand and unfold yourself." Who exactly is being addressed? Onstage, sure, but offstage? They can be in their seats, watching, as in the play within the play, watching and being watched, but there in the unfolding the audience is *what happens.* Or it does and it doesn't, depending on who's there. Some are there for entertainment, but there's a second meaning of the word, as when one says, "I'll entertain that question." But how to entertain it when you don't know what it is, or in the Hamletic vein, nothing either good or bad, but thinking makes it so.

Maybe so, maybe not, like to be or not to be—and is that really the question? If that exasperates the thinking, what may complicate the unfolding is some confusion of the senses, those lower bodily senses, which also inhabit performance: touch, taste, smell, breathing and being breathed. Thus, if there is a nuance there onstage—more or less discernible, sometimes unacknowledged—when two actors are kissing or making love, there are similar effects offstage, not always negligible, when somebody rustles a program, sneezes, shifts in a seat, whispers, puts a hand on a knee, or digesting a meal, has bad breath. Those fine distinctions kept in mind, there was a time, too, as in the novels of Henry James, when one could say s/he went to *hear* a play (and with Shakespeare spoken correctly, as now, indeed, some demand for Beckett). We've heard from Hamlet, too, about an interiority, that within which passeth show, but any way you look at it—the eyes with gazing fed, deconstruct it as you will—theater is specularity. What's there, not there, you really have to *see* it, in that elision of seeing and knowing, whatever it is that escapes you, which is what keeps us thinking, and has caused me to say, too, that theater *is* theory, or a shadow of it. Or if only the shadow's shadow, it's no mere social construction (the shibboleth of cultural studies), and something other than virtuality.[22]

Which goes to the heart of directing, or it eventually did for me, as in the most searching rehearsals, where sometimes manic obsessively, testing the limits of theater, its capacities, incapacities, and what it was meant to be, I was already doing theory. And though I came to theater belatedly, I was still wondering—after many years of directing, achievement recognized—what I was doing there, and why at recurring critical moments I also threatened to leave. That questioning was resumed at a conference on directing in St. Petersburg, Russia, appropriately enough at the Alexandrinsky, which had once been Meyerhold's theater. What I talked about, however, "The Emotional Memory of Directing," was cued in by Stanislavski, and my earliest reading of *An Actor Prepares.* At the time, if there was any technique among American actors, much of it was patchwork, but with a character's actions divided into units and objectives, and emotion turning inward, psychology was the going thing. Yet, from private moments to public solitude, with superobjective defined, and affective memory focused for access to the unconscious, there were indeterminate feelings, and feelings about feelings (some projected on the director, who has to decipher, deflect, turn back, get the actor to use them), and a maybe stressful subtext of "emotions *about* memory"—of which I've been particularly conscious, at an advanced age, in the writing of an autobiography.

The unconscious, according to Freud, is our oldest mental faculty. It is also, however imaged, whether as writing or mise-en-scène, the deepest form of memory, though what seems most deeply remembered, and no illusion of aging, is what you'd rather forget, so painful to even think it, it's never sufficiently thought, as with the egregious lessness of Beckett, where "the brain still . . . still . . . in a way" is still propulsively thinking. Indeed, it was a spasm of derangement, from a transient ischemic attack—brain fever? no painkillers?—that initiated the essay "Apnea and True Illusion: Breath(less) in Beckett," his thought, my thought, conflating his pain with mine, which in its empathic way, along with remembered amnesia, blurs into acting method. True, the methods may radically differ, but in the most powerful acting, whether subjective, from the unconscious, or before the Brechtian *gestus,* Meyerhold's biomechanics, or masking what it reveals, the "mathematical meticulousness"[23] of Artaud's naked life, there's some propulsion there, which like dark matter, unseeable or unseen, turns each thought in its thingness into a condition of possibility—or, as with high energies in particle physics, an "asymptotic freedom."

As for Stanislavski's injunction to make a life in art, it was not very long after I began to direct that I was trying to literalize that, by bringing art, so far as I could, into my life in theater. This came about as I realized, after reading everything, seeing everything, to prepare myself for directing, that the high energies were elsewhere, and there was more to be learned about doing theater, and what might be done, from the other arts, whether visual, sonic, conceptual, or what was on the scene then, happenings and action events, or performative risks with the body. Not quite body art, but some approximation of it showed up in our stagings, as with the cataracts of madness in the storm of *King Lear,* and the self-shattering corporeality of its "thought-executing fires";[24] or in the Grand Brothel of *The Balcony,* from masturbation to necrophilia, its carnal repertoire of perversion; or finished, nearly finished, the algorithmic steps of Clov's opening walk in *Endgame,* the spastic immediacy of it, visceral, its *thingness,* which was also an act of mind. As for those extremities of performance that, at some limit almost illicit, can drive you out of your mind, there were times in directing when, urging the actor to *let it happen,* whatever it is, wherever it goes, latent violence, self-abuse, or at some perilous edge of the psyche, I seemed possessed myself. What made it next to immoral is that the actor could really get hurt, but if it were done as it might be done, in its asymptotic freedom, almost beyond acting, the performance would be out of sight.

Which doesn't guarantee that it would happen again, nor that the emotion that went with it, ephemeral, uncertain, would even be remembered. And meanwhile, too, the question persists as to what constitutes *truth* in acting. Stanislavski required it, and believed he knew, but as you think through the possible forms of theater, across cultural distance, how do you ascertain it, truth in respect to what? and what kind of acting? *where? how? what for?*—is it meant to be spontaneous? or as with Brecht, ideologically constrained? or stylized by inheritance, as in the Japanese Noh? Despite early resistance—to the plays we did, and how we did them—experiment made the reputation of our theater in San Francisco, but whatever the gratifications of my work with the actors there, it wasn't until the uncertainty principle in the evolution of the KRAKEN group, its "*methodical indeterminacy,*" that those elemental questions about acting were really explored, which taught me a lot more about what it means to be a director. That was the real substance of what I talked about in St. Petersburg, while returning to the emotional memory that, despite the anti-Oedipal, continues to haunt the theater, "ghosting its greatest drama, the ineliminable riddle, the riddle of self-doubt."

There's all the more reason for doubt when, with the uncertainty of riddling ambition, artists "try to go beyond the limits of what is feasible and conceivable, so that we wake up, so that we open ourselves to another world."[25] This desire to go beyond is not exactly mine, but from the notorious response by the composer Karlheinz Stockhausen to another extremity of performance, which seemed to come out of nowhere, with the most formidable, theatrically stunning dimensions, and for all the traumatized world to see, its mesmerically repeated, televised images. The phantasmic aureole of smoke and flame, the crumbling towers, the falling bodies, the horrific aesthetic of it—as if, indeed, a post-postmodern perverse sublime, though many were scandalized when Stockhausen proclaimed it the greatest work of art that has ever been. What art could follow after—whether for solace, testament, outrage, no less an impossible closure—became a distressing question, as when Theodor Adorno remarked that there could be no poetry after Auschwitz. But as if to alleviate 9/11, several faculty from the UW School of Drama and Dance initiated a yearlong project in honor of Myra Hess, the British pianist, who during the Nazi bombings of London tried to avert a cultural blackout, and overcome wartime stress, by bringing the foremost concert musicians to perform in the empty National Gallery. With another vast emptiness, Ground Zero, still awaiting a memorial, the Myra project, or *Myra's War,* was meant to demonstrate, in a series of performance events, that "in the midst of crisis art remains a vital and buoyant force in our lives."[26] Whether it was adequate, however, to an era of insidious prospects, on color-coded alert, with a virtually invisible jihad, and "the foreboding infinity of the undeclared," were issues I raised in a lecture, which was not the keynote this time, but the endnote to the project, "Art and Crisis: Homeland Security and the Noble Savage."

Given his wealth from Saudi Arabia, and elitist family there, Osama bin Laden might have been the Noble Savage, that figure defined by Rousseau as having a mythic purity upheld by natural law, which for the Wahhabi bin Laden would be the sharia. The reference, however, was to a journal coedited by Saul Bellow, in which I'd published years before an essay on the cold war, and its Balance of Terror, called "The Public Art of Crisis in the Suburbs of Hell." If hell is other people, as Jean-Paul Sartre once declared, the suburbs have certainly widened, way beyond the Paris *banlieues,* with indescribable legions of others, dispossessed, futureless, or fanatically fundamentalist, who were then, and no less now, ready and willing to kill us. And I say that still, for all the explanations about Islam, and cautions about categorizing Muslims, that go with the proliferating discourse on terrorism (what they're calling "terrorology"), including reminders that the United States has to be held accountable for an exploitative capitalism, and with an eye on oil in the Middle East, sponsoring Israel in oppressing the Palestinians. As for the real "Axis of Evil"—according to revelations by counterconspiracy theorists—that consists of government officials, FBI agents, and military tacticians, who by creating war games and disaster drills that were supposed to avoid it, covered up "the fact" that 9/11 was conceived for the Bush administration, as a pretext for invasions in Afghanistan and Iraq, with a scenario written by the CIA.

Meanwhile, it's not exactly to augment homeland security when, amid debates about health care, jobs, bankruptcy, and failing mortgages, there's impatience about getting our troops out of a debacle, with insurgents, that has been reminding us of Vietnam. Should there be, however, with growing animosity in the Muslim world—whether exacerbated by our policies, poverty, madrassas and mullahs—another sudden attack, not at the L.A. airport or Times Square, or toppling the Space Needle in Seattle, but by a suicide bomber at University Village, between my house and the campus, followed by another in Tacoma, at a suburban shopping mall, and still another at a supermarket in Idaho, and in the serial terror, a magnetic bomb attached to a bus in North Dakota, we'd be ready for the return of Dick Cheney as national security advisor. It was Ronald Reagan that I always considered our most repellently hypocritical president, and I was certainly no supporter of the born-again George Bush. But when I suggested in the talk some tolerance for decisions that, with a globalized plague of "venomous hatred," his suspect administration had to make, I could see that leftist colleagues in the audience were disgruntled, and at one point in discussion afterward, a woman who apparently knew just about everything I ever wrote stood up to say that she couldn't believe, given my radical views in the theater, that I would ever justify what that crowd of thugs in the White House was doing.

Whereupon I said what I still believe, that until you've had some experience of power, it's hard to know how to judge it, and while I haven't been president of the United States, I've held some fairly responsible positions—on or over the edge of controversy, not only in the theater, but academically, as a dean (twice) and a provost—where you're often confronted with decisions that, with all the advice you can get from those presumably best informed, are still a matter of guesswork. We can certainly see that now, with public advice from his generals, about President Obama's delay in getting out of Afghanistan, and in the discrepancy between what he promised during the elections and—aside from those compromises that antagonize his leftist following—

his often discretionary hesitancies in office. Which for the thugs really there on the right, who question where Barack Hussein was born, confirm that he's hypocritical.

Hypocrisy, too, has its own ambiguities, and sometimes you're not sure you're doing the right thing when you *are* standing on principle. And while I spoke of it earlier as the most extraordinary site of learning in my lifetime, my experience at CalArts, coming and going, was a lesson in that regard, testing ambition and possibility, and at the end, the willingness in principle to leave it all behind, though I might very well have stayed. When I was first invited to become provost, with an opportunity to conceive California Institute of the Arts (what we abbreviated first as CIA), I hesitated, because it was financed by money from Walt Disney's will, and while I grew up with Mickey Mouse, I remembered my father, a plumber, saying Disney was a union-buster in the 1930s, and anti-Semitic too. The family was right-wing, and the board consisted of those who became Richard Nixon's, and then Reagan's, kitchen cabinet. Watergate came later, of course, but the head of the board who actually hired me was H. R. Haldeman, who was an executive then in Hollywood with the J. Walter Thompson advertising agency. Haldeman and I hit it off, despite total political difference, and I could level with him, too, about what I thought of Nixon. As for the controversy that caused me to leave, that might have seemed inevitable, though it was my choice at the end, because that reactionary board was reasonable at first, willing to put up with a lot that offended or confused them. But because it was hard to believe where the money came from for this contentious, polemical, leading-edge institution, there were faculty and students who escalated conflict, always testing the Disneys—until their board eventually wanted me to do what I wouldn't do, fire certain people and alter the governance structure. That, too, was experimental, participatory, leveling out authority, in the mystique of the sixties, yet with a disciplinary consciousness among the artists on the faculty, which was with all the dissidence passed on to the students.

When I left CalArts, nearly forty years ago, I never expected to return, but a couple of years ago I received a call from Steven Lavine, current president there, who said they wanted to give me an honorary degree at graduation. When I was silent for a moment over the phone, Lavine asked a little nervously if I would accept, and I said I would, if it was offered "as a form of penance." If you look at the webpage of CalArts today, it still uses language from the original prospectus, which I wrote back then, defining that atmosphere of experiment, always open to risk. The graduation itself was spectacular, with everybody performing, dancing and singing through the awarding of degrees, and an ensemble of bongo drummers accompanied me to the stage. And I went up there, arms swaying, shuffling to the rhythm. With a laughing crowd and a Dada backdrop, it was hardly a scene for getting serious, but what Lavine had asked me to talk about, after receiving my Doctor of the Arts: *Honoris Causa,* was "the original vision," which he has tried to revive against some resistance. The text of what I said, which is included here, relates the state of the arts then to what's happening now, with reflections upon what, at Ground Zero, "challenged the powers, the significance, and dimensions of the arts." The other honorary degrees were awarded to the singer/activist Harry Belafonte and the electronic, mixed with Buddha, composer Terry Riley, both of whom, with contrasting dimensions, took their own risks.

Another short piece that I've included was written for a controversy that I was asked to mediate at the University of Minnesota, having to do with the playwright Dario Fo, whose proletarian activism received a Nobel Prize, though he was twice denied visas to enter the United States, under a law excluding aliens with anarchist, communist, or terrorist inclinations. No doubt whatsoever, the anarchism was there in the off-the-Vatican-wall zaniness of *The Pope and the Witch,* really arousing outrage in the Catholic community of Minneapolis–St. Paul, because of what they considered its abusive ridicule, even hatred, of the church. What Fo intended to expose, in the pious idiocies of his agitprop farce, was the injury done to the impoverished people of Third World countries because of the Vatican's teachings on contraception and abortion, and the strictures enforced by the present pope. When the production was announced, there were denunciations in the Catholic press, and the archbishop of Minneapolis petitioned the university president to cancel the play. There were also threats by wealthy Catholics in the city, and on the university board, to withhold money promised to endowments, or for new buildings on the campus. With the support of the university administration, on behalf of academic freedom, the production was going ahead, but Michal Kobialka, chair of the Theater Department, who knew of my background in controversy, asked if I would come to Minneapolis to address the conflict before the first performance, and then participate in an open forum, at which there were Catholics and anti-Catholics, and liberal Catholics who were not for censorship. With the student cast listening, and apprehensive, there was quite a rabid discussion, by panelists on stage, by others shouting out from the audience, but the show did go on, with my "Blessings to *The Pope and the Witch*"—which came in part from old relations with Jesuits at the University of San Francisco, who were faithful admirers of The Actor's Workshop, despite our rather frequent anticlerical plays, which they religiously attended.

If there was a lively dialogue over the play, that really took some doing, quieting some, letting others speak, shouting down the shouters, and one wonders still how many change their minds. When the words are flowing in public, as in a political debate on television, they're likely to be self-serving, specious, even vacuous words, and without going on at length about the entire repertoire of free-enterprising evasion, I did refer to the slippery signifiers in another short essay, "The Pathos of Dialogue: Unable to Speak a Word." A solicited contribution to an anniversary issue of the Polish journal *Dialog,* it was not quite what the editors expected, which was, I gather, some encomium to dramatic theater as a form of verbal exchange. What I wrote was actually published in translation, and though my grandmother was from Kraków, I don't read Polish, so I have no idea to what extent those words were my words, with the caustic disposition of the essay here. As for being unable to speak a word, we've seen in the academic world, through the era of political correctness into cultural studies, that there isn't much to say—not what you'd think of as dialogue—unless within the spectrum of race, gender, ethnicity, and regarding facts of the past, properly historicized, which is to say, with some revisionist Marxist view of what constitutes history. Or as it tends to be registered now, with suspect facticity, as a matter of social construction.

What of reality then, or reality principle? Or from the absurd to the virtual, is there nothing but metahistory? Whether what happened happened, and how we'd know it, that's a major concern of the last pair of essays, the first of which was for a special issue of *Theater Survey,* "Theater History in the New Millennium"; and the second was the introduction to the conference "Performance and History: *WHAT* History?"—which became another special issue, of *Modern Language Quarterly.* It was Marshall Brown, editor of *MLQ,* who persuaded me to put the conference together, after he'd read the first essay, "Thinking History, History Thinking," and that big red *WHAT* in the conference poster, italicized, capitalized, was there as a challenging reminder that there are variant ideas of history, and that the cultural materialism, and its reductive new historicism, which had dominated performance studies, was inevitably being rethought, as if history were doing the thinking. As for an interactive discourse on history, there isn't likely to be much in what passes for collegiality in academic life, where faculty for the most part don't know each other's writings, and at department meetings, instead of engaged ideas, bureaucracy takes over, that spirit of corporatization.

Unlike Beckett, in his *Text for Nothing,* my humanities are not over, but with digitalized capitalism diversifying the world, in "a sort of corporate takeover of morphological flux," the question persists "about the reality of the world, and how in the world we'd know it through the free trade of appearance," which would seem to have purged history of anything teleological, while scattering remembrance with those seeds upon the ground. Or after the collapsing towers, in the accretions of dust. If what's written there is terror, I've felt obliged to teach it, as in a seminar coming up, that is, the almost ceaseless discourse since 9/11, discourse producing discourse, if not, as some books claim, terror(ism) itself. Or in mortifying detail, with impartial documentation, we may see the compounded irony: that Americanization of the world, or its mediated appearance, corresponded with the renewed dream of a caliphate and, under the Prophet's banner, an Islamic imperialism, with inevitable global jihad and apocalypse for the West. If that sounds melodramatic, or once again about Muslims, politically insensitive, it may also be what's otherwise repressed, a more tragic view of history—what Secretary of Defense Gates seemed to suggest, in this morning's news, when asked by a soldier in Kirkuk why, and how long, we'll remain in Afghanistan. The repercussions of what I wrote in "Thinking History, History Thinking" are complicated every day, as when shortly after the Fort Hood massacre, by a crazed Muslim psychiatrist, the decision was made by the attorney general to prosecute Khalid Shaihk Mohammed, self-proclaimed mastermind of the 9/11 attacks, in a Manhattan federal courtroom just blocks away from where the World Trade Center was. And meanwhile the debate continues as to the propriety of that location, under civil jurisdiction, or whether it should be in a military court.

While all of this would seem to antiquate the once-influential critique of Orientalism, there are certainly residues of colonialism in various aspects of foreign policy, especially in assessing and acting, or mostly failing to act, on atrocities in the Congo, Darfur, Zimbabwe, or immeasurably elsewhere in the underdeveloped world. What remains undeveloped in the academic world is, as I've said, our attitudes toward history, and whether or not what happened can be perceived, no less authenticated, through the attritions of time—whether in the vanished immediacy of the living moment or over *la longue durée,* or extending to outer space, that realm of dark matter or "stupefyingly empty voids." But I've now taken considerable time rehearsing the interwoven thematics, or possible empty voids, of these various essays, in which, though I'm not a historian, there is an emergent idea of history. As to

WHAT history? whether guided by vanities or "supple confusions," failing memory or contradictions, it may very well escape me, but—conscious again, as in theater, of the ghostings of (dis)appearance—I'll leave that now to be thought.

NOTES

Quotations in this introduction, without any superscript, and not annotated here, are either from what I've written in the essays that follow, or if quoted there, with references in the endnotes.

1. Kathleen Woodward, "The Future of the Humanities—in the Present and in Public," *Daedalus* 138.1 (2009): 110–23.

2. James S. Ackerman, introduction to the issue "The Future of the Humanities," *Daedalus* 98.3 (1969): 609.

3. *The Impossible Theater: A Manifesto* (New York: Macmillan, 1964).

4. *Take Up the Bodies: Theater at the Vanishing Point* (Urbana: University of Illinois Press, 1982) 299.

5. The debate was with Philip Auslander, who some years before had organized a session on my work at the American Educational Theatre Association convention. In an inscription to his book, *Liveness: Performance in Mediated Culture,* he acknowledged me as a "mentor," but differed with me, nevertheless, as I did with him, as to what was mediating what.

6. "Ideology, Performance, and the Illusions of Demystification," in *Critical Theory and Performance,* ed. Janelle G. Reinelt and Joseph R. Roach (Ann Arbor: University of Michigan Press, 1992) 430–45.

7. Lear to the blinded Gloucester on the heath, when he tries to kiss the mad king's hand: "Let me wipe it first. It smells of mortality" (*King Lear* 3.7.132).

8. Samuel Beckett, *Collected Shorter Plays* (New York: Grove, 1984) 211.

9. Samuel Beckett, *Waiting for Godot* (New York: Grove, 1954) 58: "Astride of a grave and a difficult birth."

10. Samuel Beckett, *Texts for Nothing 11,* in *The Complete Short Prose, 1929–89,* ed. S. E. Gontarski (New York: Grove, 1995) 145, 147.

11. *Waiting for Godot* 41.

12. Karl Marx, "For a Ruthless Criticism of Everything Existing," in *The Marx-Engels Reader,* ed. Robert C. Tucker (New York: Norton, 1978) 13.

13. Valie Export and Herbert Blau, eds., "Performance Issue(s): Happenings, Body, Spectacle, Virtual Reality," special issue of *Discourse* 14.2 (1992).

14. Jean Baudrillard, *Symbolic Exchange and Death,* trans. Mike Gane (London: Sage, 1993) 44.

15. "Everything I've written is vitalistic, at least I hope it is" (Gilles Deleuze, "On Philosophy," in *Negotiations: 1972–1990,* trans. Martin Joughin [New York: Columbia University Press, 1995] 143).

16. Bene's work has been contrasted with mine, by Mark Fortier, in "Shakespeare as 'Minor Theater': Deleuze and Guattari and the Aims of Adaptation," *Mosaic* 29.1 (1996): 1–18.

17. "O, from what pow'r hast thou this pow'rful might / With insufficiency my heart to sway?" (Shakespeare, Sonnet 150).

18. Guy Debord, *Society of the Spectacle,* trans. unnamed (Detroit: Black & Red, 1983), part 1, sec. 31, n.p.

19. *The Audience* (Baltimore: Johns Hopkins University Press, 1990) 1.

20. *The Dubious Spectacle: Extremities of Theater, 1976–2000* (Minneapolis: University of Minnesota Press, 2002) 137.

21. Roland Barthes, "The Grain of the Voice," in *Image-Music-Text,* trans. Stephen Heath (New York: Hill and Wang, 1977) 179–89.

22. That it's possible to think, however, through various meanings of the word, "across the fields of moral philosophy, optics, physics, and ontology," of virtual worlds on stage—or in diverse modes of performance, as a movement from science to spiritualism—one can see in an imaginative critique of the rites and strategies of representation, in Sue-Ellen Case, *Performing Science and the Virtual* (New York: Routledge, 2007). There's an overview of it all in the introduction and prologue, 1–14. What Case says of the virtual is not the rites we're concerned with here, nor is there any assent to what others have aspired to, the abolition of representation, which is, however theorized, as with Derrida on Artaud or the desirings of Deleuze, nevertheless wishful thinking.

23. Antonin Artaud, "On the Balinese Theater," in *The Theater and Its Double,* trans. Mary Caroline Richards (New York: Grove, 1958) 57.

24. *King Lear* 3.2.4.

25. "Documentation of Stockhausen's Comments re: 9/11," http://www.osborne-conant.org/documentation_stockhausen.htm (visited September 24, 2010).

26. "Innovative Projects in the Humanities," Walter Chapin Simpson Center for the Humanities, University of Washington, newsletter, vol. 6 (November 2003): 6.

ONE

Relevance

The Shadow of a Magnitude

I got undressed and I looked at myself, and began to cry.
Hush, Luster said. Looking for them ain't going to do
no good. They're gone.
—BENJY, in *The Sound and the Fury*

IN ONE OF THE CHAPELS OF Peterborough Cathedral, there is a panel that shows an ass playing a harp. One doesn't know whether to laugh or pray. Is it a supreme expression of faith in man, to waft him to heaven as a dumb beast? Or was that twelfth-century craftsman anticipating Rabelais, who stripped man to his behind and gave him a comic beating for his pains? One may feel it both ways: adoration and a secret skepticism below the altar. It was the same in medieval drama. God was the hero, magniloquent and vast, but most of the energy came from the Devil. In the iconography of the alchemists there is an image related to the panel at Peterborough. It shows the Devil as a donkey circled by dancers, braying a tune out of a horn up his ass. It's not entirely clear that the joke is on him. Actually, there's no point in hedging our bets—all ambiguities registered, the comedy is obviously leaning the other way. In virtually the same circle where Death the antic sat, grinning over his court, irreverence is presiding over life.

It's the same in Rabelais, in whom there's the barest syllable's difference between the scatology and eschatology. He was a physician and committed to healing. "Without health," he said, "life is not life, life is no longer livable." In his considered opinion, there was little health in Paris, which resembled an open drain, a cesspool, a running sore—pollution so rampant there was only one cure. He sent Gargantua to the top of Notre Dame and had him piss all over the city, drowning thousands. It was an act of moral edification and civic improvement, medicinal, a prodigy of nature. It was also educational, the basis of a reconstruction of learning in the Abbey of Thélème, a radical institution in the history of humanism. Instead of the cautionary "Nothing in excess," the heuristic "Do What Thou Wouldst" was inscribed over the portal. There's a long subterranean torment between that mandate and the nihilist's "All is permitted," but when Pantagruel is born he breaks the cradle to signify there's no turning back. Or rather, in that revolution there is a turning back—an audaciously selective attitude about the past. The Hippocratic oath is leveled against the hypocrites, and the Delphic "Know thyself"—the other inscription on the ancient portal—becomes "Physician, heal thyself." Personal hygiene is public therapy. The beginning of healing is in exposing the hidden. Is it true or is it not true that the unexamined life is not worth living? Socrates thought so, and the scholars at the Abbey of Thélème are told, "Let nothing be unknown to you."

If there is anything novel in the gesture of Pantagruel, it is a lust for totally expanded consciousness and the demand for suffrage at the instant of birth that we are still trying to redeem. In the calls for Black Power and Flower Power and Student Power, there is a similar irreverence and a comparable rage, coming out of the feeling that a birthright has been violated and a significant part of our human legacy lost. In the act of salvage, there is an impatience with half-measures. When the students, demanding relevance, are charged with being heedless of the past, the case is being misrepresented. What they are doing is choosing from the parallel and countervailing traditions in the available lore. The doctrine of Black Power is not solely a matter of civil rights but of claims upon the psyche from the vasty deep. There is no politics of joy that doesn't somehow respond to those claims. The rest is mere legislation, curriculum shift, and tedious lying. We needn't overestimate the percentage of students agitating to admit the potency of their quest for power. The quieter criticism of the moderates is affected by it. And only the grossest moral inattention would be consoled by the careerism and daily acquiescence of a majority. What's at stake is hardly a game of numbers. Seizing on traditions that have been denied has released both energy and moral fervor, and shaped the logistics of protest as well. High on the ledge of the library at Columbia was the shadow of Gargantua, and it was the spirit of Pantagruel which advanced at Chicago the disruptive candidacy of the obscene Pig.

No matter what the media make of it, we get the message. As they chanted over television, the whole world was watching—and neither backlash, tear gas, decrepit electoral process, nor the return of Richard Nixon on a platform of law and order could reverse the inevitable "return of the repressed." Both presidential candidates of the major parties were already undermined by a rhetoric they couldn't master as they constantly assured us they were socking it to us and telling it like it is. What is happening to our institutions is providential and irresistible.

It is part of a *novus ordo saeclorum* that is no mere fantasy of the radical left but the existential recurrence of a venerable dream. Fantasies, like politicians, find their time, or make a comeback. In the humanities, it is already second nature to defend—with the most formidable cerebration and passion for form—the demands of the instinctual life, subjectivism, love's body, *homo ludens,* and the primacy of personal vision, down to the most perverse mutation of our most singular monsters. With nearly incredible technique we scanned the uncontrollable mystery on the bestial floor. ("Behaviour, what were thou / Till this madman showed thee?") All through the twentieth century we've been studying the comic mortification or outright retribution of repressed Energy seeking its Other. There we were gaping with our marvelous craft, when the rebellions came along to say look how little of such vision you're getting into your programs.

Surely our disciplines have only a sad drained remote affinity to that joyous exercise of spirit in pursuit of knowledge that Rabelais proclaimed at the Abbey of Thélème. With immaculate methodology we've sucked "the substantific marrow" and ended up, self-deluded masters of our areas of "responsible knowledge," gnawing on an old bone. What the student rebellions turned up was news to the students, but it was hardly news to us. We all knew the ways in which the humanities had broken faith. The forms we teach have hit upon a void. If our teaching has any contemporary substance, we have pronounced our own judgment. The books we taught are used against us—Plato, Sartre, Buber, Blake. The demand of the students is not for dilution of knowledge or the abandonment of discipline, but that we be there, *present* in our knowledge—and not some bifurcated portion of what we are, but the whole man whose body is the book, else a great Prince in prison lies. The great rediscoveries of this period—in civil rights, action projects, encounter psychology, and the war resistance—have to do with what Polanyi calls personal knowledge. If criticism has emerged as a surrogate for moral philosophy, the drive is to reduce the distance between philosophy and action.

I remember teaching Kafka's *The Trial* on a day when some tractors appeared on campus to knock down some trees in order to put up some huts. We were talking about the ambiguities of power. There's nothing ambiguous about it, one of my students said. There's that tractor, here's my body, there's that tree. Too simple? Perhaps. We've seen enough of it, however, to know there's a moral to be drawn. The moral is *authenticity.* All the anxieties of humanistic scholars about the idea of relevance have to do with the failure to face up to this issue. In defense, we accuse the students of simplifying or wanting a sense of history; but that charge is stupefyingly evasive. We answer the call for relevance with proliferating pseudoknowledge as the monographs stockpile like Overkill, and we stiffen above the burden of stack-dust like the Duc of Guermantes above his years in *À la recherche,* as if perched grotesquely on giant stilts taller than church spires.

If the students are delinquent about the prose of history, their consciousness of its bloody poetry is impacted beyond tolerance. Where they stress what happened, they don't want it to happen again. When the student protest is countered by saying we've seen it before, we are telling a truth and missing its meaning. The analogies fail under the duress of history. If similar motives were operating, say, in 1848, the solution then seemed to be the acquisition of historical consciousness amid the facts of history that went along with it. Today humanistic scholars must ask why, pondering civilization and its discontents, protest among the students takes the form of historical consciousness that is impatient with the facts or an obsession with the facts that have simply been left out of history, as with the blacks. I take it that the escalation of protest into anarchy is both inevitable and provisional. There is something Tolstoyan in the tactics: "Why talk in subtleties," Tolstoy wrote when criticized for abandoning the complexity of art for the bluntness of polemic, "when there are so many flagrant truths to be told." This is not to say the students aren't contributing their share to the credibility gap exposed. In the revolutionary process they have learned to lie, blackmail, and brutalize themselves in the provocation of the brutality they wanted to remove. No matter that they proved it. The veil falls, the beast is exposed, and one sees his double. It happens even to people under thirty. The wrench thrown into the machine to curb an insane momentum has released a brainless violence no better than brainless authority. If it's not yet equivalent to the subtler violence of our educational system, with its illicit connection to the technostructure and its distant reflection in Vietnam, there's no reward in waiting for an escalation of inhumanities to make a balance. I can't pretend to measure the point of no return, but the students who have been resisting force-feeding by the system must eventually see there is only so much of a lesson the university can learn by force. When the university retaliates, nobody is learning anything. The university's survival depends on refusal of the means of violence even to protect itself against outrage. The students' cause depends on recognition of the difference between confrontation politics and a confrontation.

All outrage admitted, what the students have done beyond

reproach is to make us question the wholeness and accuracy of our teaching and to measure our precious values not dispassionately against one another but in real-life situations, urgently, against ourselves. They are also reminding us of what gets lost in the rationalistic jostling of values in our most resourceful habits of thought—that the deepest agreements with life are made below the structures by which we are bound. The true social contract is written in invisible ink. It represents a consensus of the inviolable. I am speaking of what is sovereign in ourselves that is the basis of any polity, and of which we are forever trying to understand the terms. The archives are full of preliminary drafts of which the humanities are the guardian, our Central Intelligence Agency. When impotency looks imminent, we are theoretically prepared. The task of the humanities, all fine print read, is to support the resistance and protect our private property by summoning up the imagination of power. It would be pitiful if the humanities, foolishly arguing the validity of relevance, couldn't hear the message or read the handwriting on the wall, for it's all been lifted from some of our sacred texts.

The trouble is, as the graffiti said during the May rebellion in Paris, "Ears have walls." That wasn't all the graffiti said. For Herbert Marcuse, what was written on the walls in Paris defined the nature of the insurrection. He saw in the graffiti a coming together of Karl Marx and André Breton (there was also the coming together of students and workers, which General de Gaulle has neatly contained and to which we have no real parallel in America, the blacks notwithstanding). "Imagination in power: that is truly revolutionary. It is new and revolutionary to translate into reality the most advanced ideas and values of the imagination." One thinks of Shelley, proclaiming the poet the unacknowledged legislator of mankind, handing out pamphlets on the street corners of Dublin. It was a lonely operation in the white radiance of eternity. Over the millennium settled the factory dust. For both Marx and the surrealists—and now the students—history is the nightmare from which we are trying to awaken, like Gargantua from "Gothic night." Since the atomic dust, history has entered the biological cycle. For students weaned between fallout and dropout, going into the Underground or the New Politics, the marriage of the Dialectic and the Unconscious is a consummation as devoutly to be wished as the marriage of heaven and hell. The marriage has been expected since that time in the old town of Zurich when Lenin moved into the house at No. 8 Spiegelgasse directly across from the Cabaret Voltaire at No. 1, where Dada was issuing its manifestos. Samuel Beckett, to whom activism is irrelevant and social solutions insane, nevertheless gave us a description of the oscillating ideology that brought the Pig to Chicago and the son of Ubu Roi, screaming *merdre!,* onto the barricades at the Sorbonne. "But he had hardly felt the absurdity of those things, on the one hand, and the necessity of those others, on the other (for it is rare that the feeling of absurdity is not followed by the feeling of necessity), when he felt the absurdity of those things of which he had just felt the necessity (for it is rare that the feeling of necessity is not followed by the feeling of absurdity)."

When, to avoid vertigo, the Theater of the Absurd moves out to the streets, we have one of the dizzier and more demoralizing aspects of the student rebellions. But the motives can hardly be discounted, and they are by no means academically disreputable. The students have learned their lessons intolerably well. The reign of the critical intelligence during the stasis of the cold war is reaping poetic justice. The logic of an art form has reached its bitter end. There is a creative disequilibrium in the polymorphous perversity. We speak of infantile or adolescent behavior, but that's partially a response to the unnerving threat of childlike questions: We hold these truths to be self-evident—why? We hold these truths to be self-evident—why not? Are the students alienated? No, it's not really the students who are alienated, since they are the atomized reflectors of profound cultural disorder, performing for us now like the mechanisms of dream, telling us more perhaps than we want to know. They inherit our contradictions with our guilt, and they are acting them out objectively for us to see. It's as if the young were doing therapy for us. The psychodrama reveals that we are the alienated, since we are the ones who insist, with injury to ourselves, on a critical distance between what we profess and what we do.

The process of revelation is painful, and it has opened up real issues of matter and methodology in education. Making learning relevant has little to do with mere topicality or immediacy or politicization or the updating of accepted knowledge or denial of the past or the abrogation of discipline; rather our disciplines are being pressed back to first principles and reinvested with a passion for the elemental. Like the gas man playing the Bishop in Genet's *The Balcony,* those of us who teach are being asked whether we dare go to the limit of our self-conceptions. Choose a role and there are frightening implications—in text, subtext, and shadow text too, what is mirrored in the mirror behind the words; or to put it in the classroom, what remains in the mind's eye when the blackboard's erased.

The issues are explored in the contest of alter egos in Peter Weiss's play on Marat and the Marquis de Sade. In the entertainment designed for the madhouse, in which the madmen play historical parts, the man of detachment is poised against the violent revolutionary whom he has created for the occasion. As he examines his own incapacity for action, Sade resembles the humanist brought to the highest equivocating pitch of analytical introspection. The problem of identity is given priority over the need for action. But self-definition follows a truthless path to a limitless and metamorphic bottom. All we can do as we descend is try to dig the criminal out of ourselves. That criminal is the shadow of a criminal society, in which "What we do is just a shadow of what we want to do." The reflections of Sade, who distrusts revolutionary extremism, are attacked with scorn by Marat, who has had enough of the politics of despair:

> If I am extreme I am not extreme in the same way as you
> Against Nature's silence I use action
> In the vast indifference I invent a meaning
> I don't watch unmoved I intervene
> and say that this and this are wrong
> and I work to alter and improve them.

At the bottom of their respective obsessions, the activist Marat and the uncommitted Sade are allies, similarly demonic. Either one might have said this:

> The important thing
> is to pull yourself up by your own hair to turn yourself
>   inside out
> and see the whole world with fresh eyes.

And as the chorus chants, "We want our rights and we don't care how / We want our revolution NOW," the decisive voice is that of the former priest and radical socialist Jacques Roux, straitjacketed by the Establishment, who says of the conflict between Marat and Sade to the audience that is impassively watching: "When will you learn to see / When will you learn to take sides." Of course we must remember, in this whirligig of identities in a no-man's-land first explored by Pirandello, that Roux is an actor playing a madman playing a defrocked priest. The cast applauds with catatonic derision at the end of the play, as the audience backs nervously into the streets. Fortunately, the distractions of the boulevard are available to relieve the hazards of pulling oneself up by one's own hair.

But that's not entirely true in a university. Our commitment to truth confounds us there. Who was it that was dragged screaming into the twentieth century? It's not the reform of our institutions that disturbs us so much, it goes deeper than that. As in Genet's play, we are being forced back, naked, into that clearing where all values are in jeopardy and we're no longer sure we have anything to put in their place. "We discover that we do not know our own role," as Rilke observed in *The Notebooks of Malte Laurids Brigge;* "we look for a mirror; we want to remove our makeup and take off what is false and be real. But somewhere a piece of disguise that we forgot still sticks to us. A trace of exaggeration remains in our eyebrows, we do not notice the corners of our mouth are bent. And so we walk around a mockery and a mere half: neither having achieved being nor actors." Nietzsche anticipated this condition in *The Genealogy of Morals* and put the question we are forced with all scholarly scruple to put to ourselves: "We knowers are unknown to ourselves, and for good reason: how can we ever hope to find what we have never looked for? We are perpetually on our way thither, being by nature winged insects and honey gatherers of the mind. The only thing that lies close to the mind is the desire to bring something home to the hive. As for the rest of life—so-called 'experience'—who among us is serious enough for that?" He speaks of seriousness, but his end is lightheartedness, a "gay science" that "is the reward of a long, courageous, painstaking, inward seriousness, which to be sure is not within every man's compass." Looking back over the wild and dangerous territory of his mind, where all value is shattered by the intensity of exposure, Nietzsche adds, "On the day when we can honestly exclaim, 'let's get on with the comedy!' . . . we shall have given a new turn to the Dionysian drama of man's destiny."

In the presence of Dionysus we are quick to invoke Apollo. But the comedy won't be satisfied until the laugh laughing at the laugh deflates pretension and drives men and institutions back to their source, to the "radical innocence" that Yeats sought or the ecstasy of the elemental that Hart Crane was desperate for in *The Bridge* when he cried out, "dance us back the tribal morn!" Lévi-Strauss, whose investigations of the mind of the savage inform us about the savagery of mind, developed a vast cerebral system after eating the pullulating sap of the white *kouro* worm. We have lain in the soil, T. S. Eliot told us some time ago, and criticized the worm. When the worm turned, all the old dualisms were up for grabs. We are expert in the ambiguities. Confronting the inseparability of reality and illusion, action and passion, identity and character, sin and sensibility, being and becoming, art and life, we have warned ourselves about no irritable reaching after fact or reason. Now all the barriers are down, and the scenarios being acted out by the young contain imperatives prepared for in our research.

What is it that really disturbs us in the new generation, if it is not a shift into the abyss as normative, the aim being an extension of sensory capacity by immersion in the undifferentiated? They are committed to the art of flux. What we once studied in Rimbaud and Mallarmé as a calculated derangement of the senses has become an habitual way of life. In a strange consortium of powers, technology has come to the aid of art. They think cinematically, feel spatially, perceive by montage. Synesthesia is second nature. They live in a mystique of depth involvement. At the end of ideology was tribalism, the new communes, participatory democracy. Teleology is replaced by simultaneity, time is scanned topographically, narrative structure gives way to cyclical structure, since it's always the same story being told without end. "Sucked within the Maelstrom, man must go round." Coherence is a continuum of succeeding vacancies into which rushes at every instant the outside possibility of a causeless being, revised, travestied, and birthed by recapitulations of a future hopelessly out of reach.

According to Marx, the revolutions of 1848 were the beginning of the end of the disguises of history. More than a century later, we still find ourselves acting out a costume drama. The difference now is that the students, revising Marx, have accepted the inevitability of the costumes. Metamorphosis is at the heart of things; behavior is masked. Revolution is a performance. What distresses us is that they accept in dead earnest what our greatest literature implies: life is a dream, an insubstantial pageant. Our affairs are being conducted on the great wobbling pivot of permanent change. If there is coherence in our passing, there is no final proof—only sensation and guesswork. The ego, as Hesse explores it in *Steppenwolf,* is a manifold entity whose nature is lost in the optical illusion of a single undeniable body. Only the fictions are inexhaustible. The experimentalism of the students in the playing out of roles is an effort to recover the lost repertoire. *L'acte gratuit,* the existential moment, making the scene, the thing itself—they are all trial balloons, improvisations.

It may seem at times like radical nonsense, but who can deny that they have redeemed in the process old theoretic modes of behavior—including concrete purpose, commitment, sacrifice, martyrdom, and heroism. Like Yeats, who thought Cuchulain till Cuchulain stood where he stood, they have converted fantasy into possibilities of action. In accepting the fundamental theatricality of being, they have told those of us protecting our disciplines something about the renewal of discipline. As Yeats put it, "There is a relation between discipline and the theatrical sense. If we cannot imagine ourselves as different from what we are and assume that second self, we cannot impose a discipline upon ourselves. . . . Active virtue as distinguished from a passive acceptance of a current code is, therefore, consciously dramatic, the wearing of a mask." In the French Revolution, bourgeois businessmen wore the mask of Romans; in the American Revolution, Boston patriots were disguised as Indians; and today rebels wear motley borrowed from the rag and boneshop of the heart.

"We are all under the influence of a collective historical unconsciousness," says one of the student leaders. "We want a communal world where the imagination runs supreme, and where human institutions respond to human needs." If there is a mockery of history in the disguises taken from the *anima mundi,* there is also the historical courage to choose not only a second self, but to play out selfhood in its metamorphoses. "We are Instant Theater," proclaims another militant, "we create our own roles. The humanities are dead in our institutions, alive in ourselves alone." If Instant Theater looks through its more sweeping existentialism like another manifestation of the Instant Culture it is trying to subvert, we are only fooling ourselves when we dismiss too lightly the substance in the presumption. Bad faith is not only limited to politics, but ingrained in every aspect of the systems and techniques by which men live. "Lie, copulate and die," wrote Céline in *Journey to the End of the Night.* The line is a litany in modern literature. "One wasn't allowed to do anything else. People lied fiercely and beyond belief, ridiculously, beyond the limits of absurdity. . . . Everything you touched was faked in some way—the sugar, the aeroplanes, shoe leather, jam, photographs; everything you read, swallowed, sucked, admired, proclaimed, refuted or upheld—it was all an evil myth and masquerade." Certainly the condition has been compounded by technology, which proliferates the resources of mystification: food substitutes, organ transplants, new techniques of replication, and, by the year 2000 if the technocrats are right, gene modification and programmed dreams. While energy from the nerves may be used to actuate exoskeleton power devices, the nervous system may be virtually imitated by miniaturized electronic components. Every breakthrough in science and social engineering contributes to the intensity of the masquerade. Every channel of information contributes to the plethora of pseudoimage and illusion, escalating distrust into a sense of conspiracy. The killing of Lee Harvey Oswald occurred on television like a demented fantasy.

According to the ancient drama, Destiny moves in mysterious ways. In the vitiated pageantry of things, we add irreality to inscrutability. The mystifications to be removed are far beyond the imaginings of Marx. If we accept the notion that all the world is a stage, we are in danger of adding theater to theater till nothing but illusion reigns. Here we are, perhaps, at the self-defeating end of the active virtue of the students; or at a conceptual impasse where we can see, from another point of view, what we have released in their behavior. In the theater's terms, too much theater is melodrama. Like farce, melodrama is an agency of the Absurd. It is also the expression of a persecution complex, with all the distortions of childhood fantasy and neurotic dream. The power of melodrama is its instinct for the primitive and the uninhibited. It is an exposure of the repressed life; it gives us the power to play out what we didn't dare. As the bland world of affluence is rejected, it caters to a desire for risk and adventure. On the other side, melodrama is also the realm of the grotesque, the dreadful, and the unassimilable. We have only come to respect it again since World War II, with its mutilations and desecrations, the Buchenwald lampshades and radioactively peeling skin, indiscriminate slaughter on a gigantic scale. As we can see in the plays of Sartre, melodrama is the realism of atrocity. Just as any horror is imaginable, so is any sequence of impossibility—as in the novels of Burroughs, form following function like a razor blade. Perversion, magnification, barbarity are the conventions of the melodramatist who, in our own day as in Jacobean drama, may insist he is merely ordering it as it is.

Yet who can really argue that it is telling the whole story? In our ardor for the elemental, we have renewed, and necessarily, absurdly, the truths of childhood, neurosis, and savagery—opposing the apprehensions of myth and magic to the misapprehensions of rationalism. But the melodramatic point of view, seen from anywhere but inside itself, is ultimately paranoid. Inside melodrama, reality is villainous and unnegotiable, and the only way to transcend it is to make one's own being the indisputable center of all integrity. The melodramatic hero is Faust without Mephistopheles, undeterred will without limit, Gargantua disguised as the hunchback of Notre Dame.

To describe the melodramatic vision is not to dispel it. So with the behavior of the students, when demands are escalated into the intense inane. The generation that grew up affluently with a sense of powerlessness is now, quite powerfully, in the center of the stage. Ruthlessly sure they will overcome, they are still insisting that nobody is listening. The fact is, certainly since Chicago, everybody is listening—though that fact alone may not alter social process or the mechanisms set in motion long before our military-industrial complex. It may even be that we are dealing with forces that are by now irreversible, and hence really unnegotiable. Given the forces that none of us understand, the human mystery, protest can only be posture. It is at this point in the theater that we return to the tragic vision.

Still, we have lived through a period, the decade after World War II, when a facile sense of tragedy was a pretext for silence and evasion. In tragic drama, the emotional life and history of the individual are organized to earn his fate. It may be similarly so in life, but we don't always believe it. It's good that we don't believe it. If life is tragic, there's no reason to live *as if* it were tragic—that's also adding theater to theater. The result is a fake pathos. The activism of the sixties grew out of impatience with that pathos—a kind of sentimental melodrama. It began by finding power in a negative capability, by a refusal to relinquish the power it had almost no reason to believe it had. A man, we came to feel again, is not merely an endurance in time but a judgment upon himself. The judgment is implicit in the sum of his acts. At the borders of this judgment, it turned out with increasing frequency that the Law's coherence was not our coherence. To the degree the Law assumed the role of Destiny, there was defiance of the Law. Whatever the constraints of Destiny, we came to behave *as if* we were in control. If that is a grand illusion, it is perhaps our most precious illusion. This brings us back to those demands that have clear and present substance.

If the desire for change is sometimes magnified out of all possibility by the militants, the resistance to change remains a scandal despite all sympathy by embarrassed humanists. I mean the most liberal not the unregenerate. Some of us are severely chastened by student dissent, but we are beguiled by privilege, dissuaded by grants, deflected by Fulbrights, trapped by departments, and—even when conscience is next to overwhelming—returned to sin by scholarly detachment, the academic version of doing your own thing. So the confrontation takes place, with the administrators holding the bag and the trustees retaining the power. Inevitably, the petitions follow after, but that's only the reflex of a static character, returned by habit to a convention. The result is a comedy at our expense. This is invariably the case when scholars in the humanities are defending their disciplines as if they were eternal verities, when in fact a discipline is sustained only by the moving continuity of its dissolutions. Instead of invoking "standards" to preserve what is clearly going under, we might pay attention to what has been recorded all over our literature—that standards are discovered precisely in jeopardy, as a series of abolitions; as William Carlos Williams says in *Paterson,* "knowledge, undispersed, its own undoing."

It is astonishing how much uncatalogued precedent still operates in our procedures, though philosophically we know better. Even what we take to be research at the frontiers of knowledge is still constrained by needless usages from the past. We see that in every discipline that insists on using the word as if there were really defined limits of inquiry rather than a structure of hypotheses about such limits. In the humanities, whose province has customarily included manners and morals and the methodologies of emotion, it may be fair to say that the most genuine research is being done by experimenters outside the system—by activists, mystics, field workers, dope fiends, renegade priests, hippies, occultists, body fetishists, deviants, mutants, and conscientious objectors. All these types have shown that the older uniform society of stable forms was severely limited in its repertoire of behavior and lifestyle choices. As we move inward through invisible space or outward to the galaxies, our values are being challenged by a vaster complex of available roles. Teachers doing analyses of novels that illustrate the destructive element or the demonic shedding of multiple personality or journeys to the heart of darkness or the perverse infractions of the Magic Theater are now facing students some of whom are conscientious practitioners of our most exciting metaphors and formal strategies. Speak of the Double or the Secret Sharer, and he sits there, coolly, wondering whether you have the courage to acknowledge him before your eyes.

Between student and teacher the terms of confrontation are different today, not only because students are gratuitously protesting, but because they are assuming some of these disturbing roles; also because the range of their experience has expanded remarkably in a generation. Certain old pedagogical leverages are gone. Only a decade ago, when I had gone abroad for the first time, I could get a lot of mileage in class by talking of my world travels, confident that the students had never been where I'd been. That automatically boosted the authority I already had. I literally knew more about the world than the student did. That's no longer certain, we know, and the whole issue of experience has been turned upside down. We talk of the great abstractions—Law, Justice, Freedom—but the kids to whom we once despaired of teaching civics in high school have not only been down to the courthouse, but have also been inside the jail. They know political process as we never did.

Literally, increasingly, they have more *experience.* Every day now I encounter students who have seen more of the world than I have seen. Some of them have hitched across the country in the wake of Ginsberg and Kerouac, and others have made their way up and down the coasts of Africa. They have wept beside the Ganges and spent the winter in Khatmandu. "You don't know what it's like in the South," I used to say, having done basic training in Georgia. But we are now talking to students who have knocked on the doors beside the watermelon patches where I trained, and who have scraped the Delta to bring blacks to the polls. Compared to those of us who have garnered our most recent experience from our bibliographies, they simply *know* more.

Our only recourse is to claim wisdom through benefit of years. But which of us, as we study our world, can really presume? We have one sole advantage: all things considered, we are closer to dying, and hence should have thought more seriously about that. But even about dying the young are more inquisitive. There was subliminal fallout in their fingerpainting. When they left Dick and Jane, they went to *The Myth of Sisyphus,* and some have pondered deeply Camus's assertion that the major philosophical question of our time is, why not suicide? They may have thought about it prematurely, but prematurity seems to be the conclusive form of consciousness in a world with its finger on the button. As that modern young woman Antigone says—she who belongs to Death—"There is no guilt in reverence of the dead." The most persuasive thinkers since Descartes have told them that they die into the world, and every authentic rite of passage requires a death. The pain of the future is precisely this requirement of becoming. Their existence is predicated on a void echoing with all the successions of the vanished. It is not only fashion, experiment, and the desire for instant mind-expansion that accounts for the interest in drugs, but also the desire to live sentiently among the successions as if they were simultaneous, not denying but recovering all time.

We are all familiar with the abyss and theories of continuous becoming—at least we are *conceptually* familiar. By such concepts, however, the young have been touched to the quick. Many to whom we have transmitted this legacy of the void have discovered there, in the spectral continuity of absence, the imprints of all previous existence, a memory bank, as if there alone is the reliable living record that survives all credibility gaps. Out of attrition comes creation. It is a creation incessantly recommitted to the test of nothingness. Making and unmaking. At the center of the process is the act choosing the act to come. Philosophy is a dramaturgy of perpetually renewing crisis, or stasis. (Wittgenstein: "The best that I could write would never be more than philosophical remarks: my thoughts were soon crippled if I tried to force them on in any single direction against their natural inclination.") If Authority toppled into the abyss, taking duration with it, a new sort of endurance was born, radical, surreal, post-Oedipal. As Rimbaud defined it, "I am my mother and my child / At each point in the eternal." Pantagruel broke the cradle and now, with the absurd reparation of a dream, we find it endlessly rocking.

If we expect to teach the young, we must study their art, like it or not. Whatever the medium, the stress is ephemerality. The psychedelic posters are the window shades of junk culture. Death being the mother of beauty they celebrate the Grateful Dead. Like the hippies' flowers, the posters are meant to wither, though now that they're mass-produced, replication makes up for perpetuation. There is eternity in the duplicating machine, as in the *Om* made possible by electronic sound. One can think of this negatively as evidence that the young have no staying power and their art-forms no durability. But that's not really the gist of it: the rhythm is tomorrow and tomorrow and tomorrow, to the last syllable etc. *Om*. Magnitude is measured by the willingness to throw away. It takes endurance. There is theory behind it, moreover, and tradition. About the time the Fillmore Auditorium was getting started and the Berkeley rebellion was breaking out, there was an exhibition of Jugendstil and expressionism in German posters at the University Art Gallery. Once again the lesson was learned. The first psychedelic designers were influenced by this exhibit, and one of them had been a student of Albers at Yale. Thus, despite the crudity of the photolithography, there is real sophistication in the color complementaries that contribute to the deliberate interchangeability of figure and ground, and the reversibility of image. True, it's hard to read, which is precisely the strategy you might expect from a disenchanted subculture dramatizing itself a Mystery. The typography is a secret code for the initiates, as in the engravings of Blake, who also knew about acid—and the corrosion of value into value.

There are implications for a curriculum in all this, but it's not a curriculum that needs working out. In fact, the moment these impulses are absorbed into curricular thinking we have a continuance of the academy in the old vein. Let's have a class on it, we say, or a panel discussion; or, since militancy has no lien on wisdom either, let's have a Black Studies program. Teaching the Beatles is not necessarily being relevant. At the deepest level that's not what the students are asking for. That's not what we were asking for in our preliminary search through the ambiguities that sprung loose the power of blackness and the energies of the abyss. What we're all asking for is to reduce the distance between our classes and life, even if it means abandoning our classes. That will require a more radical reformation of our schools than we can reasonably expect. But we must speculate beyond reason if only because, like afterimages in the eye, there comes into the mind what the mind puts off at first encounter, that which is so relevant it can only be seen out of phase.

Antigone was relevant when she confronted Creon. That's still a confrontation to be argued. In our humanities classes we have been conscientious about the *argument,* but we have done very little about Antigone's claims. It may be true, given the enigmatic gods, that nothing can be done, but the students won't concede that—and they will especially have none of that shift in the balance of power which Dürrenmatt alluded to when he said that in the modern world Creon's secretary closes Antigone's case. Actually, it's a case that refuses to be closed. With Creon withdrawn into the obfuscations of power, there are myriads of secretaries around to worry about the curriculum. Like Antigone, however, the students remind us that our profoundest humanistic duty is to the "immortal unrecorded laws" that are "operative forever, beyond man utterly." When Antigone commits civil disobedience, she is not presuming beyond herself. What she realizes is that she is "only mortal" and that with evil all about her, compelled to act, she can hardly "Think Death less than a friend."

Which is not to say she is indifferent about dying. She loves life and abandons it with fear. We know her fate is unalterable, but as we speculate on its meaning we must come back to this question: is there no way of altering the system so the next Antigone won't be put to the test? Since the mechanisms of the state provide for themselves, how can we provide for Antigone? To say that only tragedy can provide is somehow to avoid the case.

We speak of radical alteration of the educational structure, but do we mean it? How much are we, individually, willing to give up? At the end of all our research and analysis, are we ready to act on what we find? How much are we really willing to experiment? Is our literature forever to remain in our literature? When, after a formal analysis of *The Trial,* we come finally to the parable of the door, what do we make of it? Perceiving the radiance in the darkness, do we stand baffled before the Law, teased out of action by our gifts of equivocal thought. ("The commentators note in this connection: 'The right perception of any matter and a misunderstanding of the same matter do not wholly exclude each other.'") Or in some reflex of residual power, do we summon up the courage to walk through? I remember entangling my students in the most appalling paradox of all. Protest as you will, I said, Kafka is unconvinced. As I read it, *you* are the power structure. They were enraged, they refused, they wouldn't see it that way. Academically speaking, they were wrong. Chances are, as it seemed with Joseph K., we may be the victims of a metaphysical hoax and returned, through any door, to the same old structure. But how do we really know until we dare? K., remember, died like a dog—"it was as if the shame of it must outlive him." Whose shame? We hardly need Marcuse to tell us that this society's very rationality is irrational and destructive of the free development of human faculties, whatever security it has achieved based on war and a garrison state.

All around us now, however, there are people daring to set up patterns of radical change—in community experiences, political involvement, and lifestyle. Who can really contend that what is happening in our classrooms has more human significance than all this? The future of the humanities is, at least temporarily, not in our books or our artifacts but in these experiments, which are expanding the repertoire of learning and providing a subtler dialogue between the individual and authority, between person and person. They have brought ideas out of Plato's cave into the realm of action and into the body itself—which is the long-neglected victim of our academic enterprise. Think of all the spiritual disciplines we have talked about, all the sacred texts we have studied, whose proper reading required physical preparation—just as Gargantua had to be prepared physically to be a Renaissance gentleman. We regale our classrooms with the debilities of spectator sports, but nothing in our conception of the humanities makes development of the body an organic condition of development of the mind, nor have we paid much attention to the language of the body as it exists in such disciplines as mime, dance, yoga, or the art of archery in Zen. And music, whose true fundamental is blood rhythm, but which was once part of the medieval curriculum—how is it we have made of it such a specialization that most of our Ph.D.'s are not only musically illiterate, but have no music in their souls? Surely one of the great contributions of the young is to have brought music back into everyday life, and a kind of primitive poetry as well.

Like the rock groups, the experiments I am talking about we are all well aware of. I am speaking of underground worship, with new liturgies and modes of communion; of new communities, like Synanon and Daytop, in which the assumption is that the best therapist is the physician who has healed himself; of ventures in communal design, and even architecture, which involve bringing information and thought off the page and onto the walls; of intellectual task forces and teach-ins, of game techniques, encounters, happenings, T-groups, be-ins, freak-outs, which aim to release lost capacities for play and improvisation; of multimedia scenes like the Fillmore or the Electric Circus; of Operation Bootstrap and sensitivity training—all of which have possibilities for learning environments, as do film, videotape, and the visual and plastic arts if really approached as alternative languages of *inquiry,* as well as alternatives to the term paper. Some of the techniques are already being absorbed—mostly in schools of education or in psychology courses. All of them have been described and exploited in the media and their findings confiscated and adulterated by Madison Avenue, just as the posters that once advertised the Haight-Ashbury are now part of the iconography of the frightened suburbs. Still, none of these developments are discredited by availability or popularity, nor by books on *Education and Ecstasy.* It may, however, be a measure of what's wrong with the humanities that I hesitate to recommend them in a learned journal as a guide to what needs to be done, for there is some lingering tic about academic respectability.

Some of what occurs in all this stuff is boring, naive, and downright silly, but that may be part of its virtue—an immunity to conventional standards of progress, competence, and achievement. It has professional limits, to be sure, but it has released a healthy amateurism. Each of these efforts performs at a more tactile level of awareness than our curricula, exercising the senses—particularly touch, the most unused of all, particularly in the relation of one person to another, particularly directed to the renewal of community. Time enough to declare the limitations and dangers of these processes, the dependence of some of them on pure feeling, the strategic abandonment of the rational, or the emergence of an isonomy, which is a political condition of no-rule. They are vulnerable to hysteria and demagoguery, but Aristotle says that was true of so excellent an art as rhetoric, depending on the intelligence and morality of the user. None of these things is seen, however, in true perspective if not linked to the effort to restore to men what is minimally required for manhood, no less with women making their claims, or crossing genders, if you will—for the materially disadvantaged, an economic base; for the psychically mortgaged, a lifeline to the repressed.

It is no accident that all these developments have occurred simultaneously with the renewal of political and social passion through the disabilities of the cold war. They are all contributing to the struggle to link inwardness to otherness. They involve relinquishment of the ego and intellectual pride to a common humanity, opening channels to the dispossessed. While they may accommodate too easily those who remain paralyzed and distressed, they also attract those resourceful young people whose remarkable talents for social engineering have shown up in the ghettos, in Appalachia, the Peace Corps, and the campaign of Senator McCarthy as well as in the guerrilla tactics of SDS. There may be an ululating mindlessness on the dance floors of some of our stroboscopic emporia, but there are also clues to what moves our students, not only when they've blown their minds but when we want to reach their minds, and to new processes of learning that have been long implied in our critical theory. The appeals are directly to the aural and visual imagination, in the grammar of the body, synesthetically, spatially, in a stream of consciousness, as if the critical theory exploded in the drama of the mind were suddenly released on a stage "autokinatonetically" as *Finnegans Wake,* "anastomosically assimilated and preteridentified paraidiotically, in fact, the sameold gamebold adomic structure . . . , as highly charged with electrons as hophazards can effective it."

If we carry this adomic structure over to education we come, "by a commodius vicus of recirculation," back to the organic environmental learning ideas of Dewey and Rousseau, who have been so long abused for misrepresented theory. As Lévi-Strauss points out, Rousseau, who came nearest of all the philosophes to being an anthropologist, never exalted the Natural Man, nor did he confuse the state of Nature with the State of Society. What he did was to give us a theoretical model of a society that, corresponding to nothing that we actually know and probably nothing that will ever exist, may nevertheless help us disentangle ourselves from the inertia of a system divided against itself because we are divided against ourselves, like Godard's Pierrot, who sees through his eyes and hears through his ears, and feels no unity. Fractured knowledge is unnatural. What was an expedience in methodology became the disease of specialization. We have all been victims of categories, linear sequence, and abstract duration. Certain kinds of investigation require these habits of mind, and no secondhand McLuhanism will abolish them. They are human, but at some limit they are violations of our humanness, and we have sufficient evidence that we've reached that limit. The record is in—from saturation bombing to pollution of the landscape, from political estrangement to psychological disorder, from public indifference to anonymous killing. Jacques Cousteau recently warned that the ocean may be contaminated before we can develop the means to benefit from its natural resources. All of this is a reflection of demographic imbalance in our own nature. We lack identification with the physical universe of a myth-minded age, and we lack identification with the suffering of our own age if we can continue to pillage the earth that might relieve it. Do we believe the old myths that we teach, or the new modern versions—from pollution comes the plague?

In the humanities there is no Final Solution, only the possibility of a change of heart and a return of being to wholeness, or some striving toward it, through any failure of being. About that, it's clear beyond doubt that we have been delinquent. No matter how diligently arrived at, so much of what we teach *feels* useless and inept, disengaged, unnatural, imperious, and, yes, irrelevant. Maybe it is, maybe it isn't. One thing is sure: if we publish it in the bulletin, it is not automatically among the gods. The burden of proof is on us. Only by the intensity of our convictions can we preserve them, and only by incorporating in our style of teaching what we've discovered at the dissolving margins of our disciplines. Far more can be done with the whole environment of learning to incorporate the excluded life that anthropologists, psychologists, and poets have recovered and, now, the students demand. Far more can be done to reorganize the masses of information sprawling behind us in history—indeed, one of the enormities of history. Since *The Waste Land* we've been shoring up fragments against our ruin, without seeing that the poem is not only an object to be studied but also, like the collage or assemblage, a prototype of new configurations of knowledge that can be encompassed in a lifetime and made useful in a life.

There's nothing ignominious or anti-intellectual in yielding to the student or, to negotiate our inadequacies, recognizing him or her as a peer. W. H. Auden said of Freud in a memorial poem: "All he did was to remember / Like the old and be honest like children." The students we teach, born in the atomic age, are the children of darkness. If they become obscene, think of what goes on there in the darkling world of antimatter where foul is fair. Freud, among others, warned that we would have to deal with them differently:

> . . . he would have us remember most of all
> To be enthusiastic over the night
> Not only for the sense of wonder
> It alone has to offer, but also
> Because it needs our love: for with sad eyes
> Its delectable creatures look up and beg
> Us dumbly to ask them to follow;
> They are exiles who long for the future.
> That lies in our power. They too would rejoice
> If allowed to serve enlightenment like him,

Even to bear our cry of "Judas,"
As he did and all must bear who serve it.
Our rational voice is dumb; over a grave
The household of Impulse mourns one dearly loved,
Sad is Eros, builder of cities,
And weeping anarchic Aphrodite.

Look at the students: even the most cataleptic are asking questions, waiting for us. What do we have to answer?—that our institutions must be preserved? I'm not saying they shouldn't be preserved, but why? In their highest idealism the students have taken a cue from Ivan Karamazov, fanatic and cut to the brain with injustice. Our institutions are worthless, they say, if they contribute, despite all wisdom, to the deprivation of powers and to the collective lust to kill. To respond to this does not mean surrendering what we hold to be good, true, and beautiful; only that no mere *argument* for the good, true, and beautiful will prevail. They must be convinced at blood level, or they will not be convinced at all. To them, a conviction is a demonstration. If we are growing tired of the idea of blood consciousness, then we'd better change our reading lists.

If we really mean what we teach, there's no repose ahead for the university. Up to now, the initiative has come from the students, but it grows increasingly hard for us to insist on the disengagement necessary for sober thought. That's disturbing, but it's not too great a price to pay for a revival of faith in our best students to whom no particular subject is, finally, more relevant than any other, though a man in needless pain or a man dying before his time, unjustly, is more relevant than any subject. Can we argue with that? I don't think even Milton would argue with that, who said as good kill a man as kill a good book, for that was prefaced by his refusal to praise a fugitive and cloistered virtue, unexercised and unbreathed. The greatest blessing of our educational system is the refusal of our students to be cloistered, in systems, departments, requirements, or a ratiocinative meditativeness that can destroy. For the time being, we have to be where they are, or we are, for the sake of the future, nowhere at all.

TWO

The Faith-Based Initiative of the Theater of the Absurd

SOME PREFATORY WORDS, or what, in more classical times, might have been called an apology. In the invitation to this symposium,[1] the topic proposed for me was "The Raging Soul of the Absurd." I don't know whether that came out of some tongue-in-cheek take on my temperament derived from the rather reticent things I've written, but as it turns out, though I've used another title, I will be saying something of the soul, not exactly raging, in another context.

There was also a warning with the invitation—and I hope to be forgiven for saying so—that the audience here was not likely to "consist of specialists or academics per se," but rather a group of that "dying breed, the 'educated public,' which means we need to keep vocabulary relatively jargon free and inclusive." As it happens, that gave me the idea for what I have written about, while feeling somewhat like Jack, in *Jack or the Submission,* when he's told he's "chronometrable"—meaning, perhaps, it's time for him to change—after exclaiming, "Oh words, what crimes are committed in your name!" This leads to his agreeing to "abide by the circumstances, . . . the game of the rule," acceding to the familiar, "Oh well, yes, yes, na, I adore hashed brown potatoes."[2] Which, actually, I try to avoid, though that may not keep me, with respect for the game of the rule, from making a hash of words, or to use a word coming up later, an "assemblage."

Chronometrably, I might even wish that Roberta II—Jack's fiancée with three noses—were right and all we'd need "to designate things is one single word: cat," the word *chat,* of course, used as a prefix, sexier in French; though "The cat's got my tongue," able thus to accommodate all propositions. Just before the Roberta with three noses—whose real name, she says, is Liza, with pools in her belly, arms like snakes, soft thighs, and mouth, naked shoulders, hair trickling down—reveals her hand with nine fingers, all the more alluring to Jack, she says, with categorical cattiness: "Cats are called cat, food: cat, insects: cat, chairs: cat, you: cat, me: cat, the roof: cat, the number one: cat, number two: cat," all the numbers and "all the adverbs: cat, all the prepositions: cat. It's easier to talk that way" (109). Maybe so, maybe not, but not, I suppose, for hardened criminals for whom the unspeakable crimes persist, from a sense of unspeakability, germane to the Absurd, as it's been to critical theory—with its nefarious vocabulary, which I may have to invoke, though I shall try in what I'm saying to be nevertheless inclusive.

The focus will be, for the most part, on Ionesco's early plays, the ones we did nearly forty-five years ago, at The Actor's Workshop of San Francisco. As we moved then, with more than a little controversy, from Brecht to the Absurd, at that time very strange, we were with some presumption trying to educate a public, and ourselves, about what turned out to be a sort of preface to or premonition of what critical theory has been worrying about, or worrying, for over a generation. As to what I'll be saying today, it is not by any means a defense of theory, that's boring; so, too, sometimes is the theater of the Absurd—mostly, however, strategically so.

Returning, then, to my title, its initiating theme . . .

Take it on faith. That's usually said, with more or less comic inflection, when faith at some dubious impasse is what we're least likely to have. If that doesn't exactly correspond to the existential condition from which the theater of the Absurd emerged, it does reflect on the absurd condition of American politics that led, through dangling chads in Florida and a Supreme Court decision with no legal substance at all, to the faith-based initiative of our born-again president, who recently put a definitive quietus to any residue of the cold war by looking into the eyes of his Russian counterpart and, yes, seeing into his soul. That any skepticism in the gaze was allayed by a former agent of the KGB is almost too wild a conceit, its disarming suspense of the global melodrama belonging more, perhaps, to a James Bond movie than to the theater of the Absurd. But here it would seem we have no choice: we either take it on faith or laugh out loud, laughter redoubling at the thought that it might be either/or, whereas in the faith-based initiative of the absurdist theater you can, at minimum, have it both ways. I say at minimum because, in the drama of Ionesco particularly, you can in a plenitude of unexpectedness, contradiction, and aleatoric calculation, have it either *and* or, or even otherwise, any which way you wish—although that, too, may be the sort of wishful thinking that sometimes passes as faith, as when Mrs. Smith remarks of Rumanian yogurt in *The Bald Soprano* that it "is excellent for the stomach, the kidneys, the appendicitis, and apotheosis" (10). Which may be what Jean-François Lyotard meant by a "materialist Sublime."

Lyotard was making the case for transcendence flattened by a generation of critical theory which, in the wake of Bertolt Brecht, and revisionist Marx, looked with a jaundiced eye on the "theological space" of theater with its deployment of illusion to put reality in perspective and, determining cause and effect in the appearances on stage—whose psychic economy is essentially bourgeois—something like fate or godhead in the wings. If you've been keeping up with theory, from early deconstruction to the new performativity, you'll have heard a lot of talk about invisible power, legislating meaning and regulating desire, though this, on first appearance, would hardly seem to apply to the capricious imagination or diabolical virtuosity of the theater of the Absurd. Yet if there's no divinity in the dramaturgy shaping our ends, the indeterminacy of the Absurd is not exactly up for grabs, as if in the absence of faith, roots, origin, authenticity, or any grounding for truth, some utterly unaccountable but nonetheless scrupling vigilance presides over the abyss, as over the arbitrariness of the announcement, belabored manically in *The Bald Soprano,* of Bobby Watson's death, which was in the paper and not in the paper, poor Bobby, a "veritable living corpse . . . how cheerful he was!" or was it his wife? his uncle? his aunt? son and daughter? mother? his entire family in fact? all of them commercial travelers, "What a difficult trade!" So much for the moment for the bourgeois family as reality principle in advancing capitalism, but whether or not we think of ourselves as fellow travelers, the dialogue through the sequence, its clamorous orchestration, is more cunningly berserk than "an association of ideas," which is how Mr. Smith says he remembered what he will in a moment confuse again or forget: "Which poor Bobby do you mean?" (11–13).

Anarchic-seeming as it sounded when the Absurd came on the scene, it soon became apparent that there's method in the madness and, given the protocols of explosive disorder in the tradition of the avant-garde, the scandal of form as well, in all the mimicry of chaotic absence laughing up its sleeve, like Mary the maid who confides to the audience that her real name is Sherlock Holmes or the clock striking twenty-nine times (or striking as much as it likes); or for that matter, in the systemic wobble at the play's inconstant heart, the series of baffling recognitions and misidentifications, all of them "true in theory" (23), the gratuitous mystery to which, obviously, everything leads (though, to be perfectly truthful, it was a mistake by an actor that Ionesco let stand, giving the play its title). The critical moment occurs after Mrs. Martin says to the departing Fire Chief—who has confessed in all subjectivity that his dream, his ideal, is that of a world in which everything has caught fire—"Thanks to you, we have passed a truly Cartesian quarter of an hour."

Whereupon, as if reminded to follow through on Descartes's method of doubt, with the requisite objectivity, the Fire Chief stops to say, "Speaking of that—the bald soprano?" Which is, as a philosophical question, the first and last we've heard of her, except—after "*General silence and embarrassment,*" the laughter sneaking in—that "She always wears her hair in the same style" (37). As for the totality of inconsequence in the momentum of non sequitur, abrogating meaning and value, that hardly draws a blank, which is to say there may be nothing to get but we get it nevertheless, like the "Nothing to be done" in *Waiting for Godot,* the nothing that comes of nothing, or the anomaly of a nothingness that not only passes the time but is virtually formulaic.

"How curious it is, how curious it is," as they chant in *The Bald Soprano,* no roots, no origin, no authenticity, no, nothing, only unmeaning, and certainly no higher power—though the Emperor turns up invisibly in *The Chairs,* as from a "marvelous dream . . . , the celestial gaze, the noble face, the crown, the radiance of His Majesty," the Old Man's "last recourse" (149–50), as he says, before he entrusts his message to the Orator and throws himself out the window, leaving us to discover that the Orator is deaf and dumb. Thus the delusion of hierarchy and, spoken or unspoken, the futile vanity or vacuity of speech. But even more curious, "what a coincidence!" (17) is how this empty datum of the Absurd became the litany of deconstruction, which hedges its bets, however, on a devastating nothingness by letting metaphysics in after presumably rubbing it out, that is, putting it "under erasure" (*sous rature*), as Derrida does in his grammatology, conceding what Nietzsche told us, that God is dead, but using the word anyhow, because we can hardly think without it, or other transcendental signifiers, such as beauty or eternity—which are, indeed, the words spoken by the Old Man to the invisible Belle in *The Chairs,* mourning what they didn't dare, a lost love, "Everything . . . lost, lost, lost" (133).

There would appear to be parody here, and one might expect that Ionesco—in a line of descent from Nietzsche to poststructuralist thought—would not only disclaim the older metaphysics but laugh as well at the ridiculousness of any nostalgia for it, as for the originary time of a radiant beauty endowed with Platonic truth. And indeed the Orator who shows up dressed as "a typical painter or poet of the nineteenth century" (154) is, with his histrionic manner and conceited air, surely not Lamartine, who asks "Eternité, néant, passé, sombre abîme" ("Eternity, nothingness, past—dark abyss") to return the sublime raptures they have stolen; nor is he remotely the figure of Keats with his Grecian urn, teasing us out of thought in equating beauty and truth.

What we have instead, in *Amédée or How to Get Rid of It,* is the spellbinding beauty of that which, when they forget to close the lids, emanates from the eyes, which haven't aged—"Great green eyes. Shining like beacons"—of the incurably growing corpse. "We could get along without his kind of beauty," says Madeleine, the sour and bitter wife, "it takes up too much space." But Amédée is fascinated by the transfiguring growth of its ineluctable presence, which might have come from the abyss of what is lost, lost, lost. "He's growing. It's quite natural. He's branching out."[3] But if there's anything beautiful here, it seems to come—if not from the Romantic period or one of the more memorable futurist images, Boccioni's *The Body Ascending* (Amédée's family name is Buccinioni)—from another poetic source: "That corpse you planted last year in your garden, / Has it begun to sprout?" It's as if Ionesco were picking up, literally, T. S. Eliot's question in *The Waste Land:* "Will it bloom this year?"[4] If it not only blooms, or balloons, but flies away, taking Amédée with it, the oracle of Keats's urn—all you know on earth and all you need to know—seems a far cry from the hilarious mordancy of this transcendence, or what in *The Chairs,* even if the Orator had spoken, would have radiated upon posterity, if not from the eyes of a corpse, from the light of the Old Man's mind (157).

Yet the truth is that, for Ionesco, the Absurd is predicated on "the memory of a memory of a memory" of an actual pastoral, beauty and truth in nature, if not quite yet in art. Or so it appears in "Why Do I Write? A Summing Up," where he summons up his childhood at the Mill of the Chapelle-Anthenaise, a farm in St-Jean-sur-Mayenne, "the country, the bar, the hearth."[5] Whatever it was there he didn't understand, like the priest's questions at his first confession, it was there, too, that he was "conscious of being alive. . . . I lived," he says, "in happiness, joy, knowing somehow that each moment was fullness without knowing the word fullness. I lived in a kind of dazzlement." Whatever then happened to impair this radiant time, the dazzle continues in memory, as something other than fool's gold: "the world was beautiful, and I was conscious of it, everything was fresh and pure. I repeat: it is to find this beauty again, intact in the mud"—which, as a site of the Absurd, he shares with Beckett—"that I write literary works. All my books, all my plays are a call, the expression of a nostalgia, a search for a treasure buried in the ocean, lost in the tragedy of history" (6). As for the estrangement, alienation, and the metaphysical anguish that came with that history, they may be, given the politics of cultural studies today, and much theater practice as well, dismissed as disempowering or ideologically redefined, but when push comes to shove in civilization and its discontents, they are for Ionesco, though "unbearable, so empty, and useless" (15), something like the truth of being—though being (*pace* Heidigger) is ideologically suspect, too, as a sin of "essentialism," along with that humanistic entity or mere illusion called "the self."

"I've invited you . . . in order to explain to you," says the Old Man in *The Chairs,* "that the individual"—that avatar of the self spawned by the Enlightenment—"and the person are one and the same." That established, he says a moment later, "I am not myself. I am another. I am the one in the other" (145). About the self, to be sure, there was a certain equivocation on the stage of the Absurd, from Beckett's tramp insisting that the little messenger from Godot not come tomorrow and say that he never saw him to the quarrel about the doorbell in *The Bald Soprano.* "Experience teaches us," says Mrs. Smith in a fit of anger, "that even when one hears the doorbell ring it is because there is never anyone there" (23), as if there were no one to be there, no person or individual, nothing resembling a self. Of course, we don't have to believe her, no more than we believe Derrida or Deleuze or the new orthodoxy of dispersed subjectivity, that the self is no more than the liability of identities elided into language. For in its utter untenability, untenable *as* utterance, the self is also liable to be taken on faith. "This morning when you looked at yourself in the mirror, you didn't see yourself," says Mrs. Martin to Mr. Martin, who is undeterred by that. "That's because I wasn't there yet," he says (36). How curious it is, how curious it is, we somehow think we exist.

As for the existence of a "work of art" in our demystifying period, if art has not been entirely divested of privilege, it has been relegated to the status of another kind of "discourse," while (with the canon in jeopardy too) the aesthetic has been turned into an antiaesthetic. One might think that Ionesco was there in advance with his notion of an *antiplay,* taking to its metonymic limit, not this, *that,* not that, *this,* words slipping, sliding, decaying with imprecision, the empty play of the signifiers: epigrams, puns, platitudes, suppositions, deductions, pleonasms and paradoxes, doggerel, proverbs, fables, the repertoire of prosody, or in a vertigo of nonsense and nonsensical iterations, an eruption of mere vocables, plosives, fricatives, a cataclysm of glottals or, in the screaming choral climax of *The Bald Soprano,* with a staccato of cockatoos, "cascades of cacas" (40) careening over the stage. Or as the Professor demands from the Pupil in *The Lesson,* sounds projected loudly with all the force of her lungs, like that diva of performance art, Diamanda Galas, not sparing the vocal cords, but making a virtual weapon of them. Or the sounds warming in their sensation—"'Butterfly,'

'Eureka,' 'Trafalgar,' 'Papaya'"—above the surrounding air, "so that they can fly without danger of falling on deaf ears, which are," as in the insensible resonance of the bourgeois audience (Brecht's culinary theater), "veritable voids, tombs of sonorities," to be awakened, if at all, by an accelerating merger of words, syllables, sentences, in "purely irrational assemblages of sound," an assault of sound, "denuded of all sense" (62–63).

Manic obsessive, cruel as he becomes, what the Professor appears to be defining, through the crescendo of intimidation, is not only the apotheosis of an antiplay, but a kind of alternative theater or another form of art. Indeed, he might be describing, "from that dizzying and slippery perspective in which every truth is lost," what Artaud tries to reimagine, in relating the Orphic mysteries to the alchemical theater, its "complete, sonorous, streaming realization,"[6] as well as certain experimental events of the sixties, turned on by Artaud's cruelty, *its* faith-based initiative, which came, like the return of the repressed, at the exhilarating crest of the theater of the Absurd. Thus, in the period of the Living Theater and *Dionysus in 69,* or *Orghast* at Persepolis, we saw performers (the word "actor" shunted aside, tainted like "the author" by conventional drama) pitilessly expelling air from the lungs, or caressingly over the vocal cords, which, like Artaud's incantatory murmurs in the air or, in the Balinese drama, the "flights of elytra, [the] rustling of branches,"[7] or, in the brutalizing ecstasy of the Professor's lyric imagining, "like harps or leaves in the wind, will suddenly shake, agitate, vibrate, vibrate, vibrate or ovulate, or fricate or jostle against each other, or sibilate, sibilate, placing everything in movement, the uvula, the tongue, the palate, the teeth," and as you might still see it today (back in an acting class) with exercises in the tradition from Grotowski to Suzuki (tempered by the Linklater method) the polymorphous perversity of it all: "Finally the words come out of the nose, the mouth, the pores, drawing along with them all the organs we have named, torn up by the moth, in a powerful, majestic flight, . . . labials, dentals, palatals, and others, some caressing some bitter and violent" (62–64). And some, too, expressing "all the perverse possibilities of the mind," as Artaud says of the contagious revelation of the Plague[8]—the contagion there, if not the revelation, in Ionesco's *The Chairs,* with "a bad smell from . . . stagnant water" below the window and, with mosquitos coming in (113), the unrelieved stench of the pathos of "all that's gone down the drain" (116).

Whatever's gone down the drain, including the thirty-nine other pupils who gave their bodies, "Aaah!" to the sounding out of *knife,* "my arms, my breast, my hips . . . knife" (*Bald Soprano,* 74), the Professor also seems to be anticipating certain psychophysical effects of vocal behavior that, by way of punk, funk, and heavy metal, are now commonplace on MTV, while on the theoretical level he seems to be outdoing Roland Barthes on "the grain of the voice," through which, when words really speak—that materialization of language by way of the body, its fleshiness or tactility—what you hear is "the tongue, the glottis, the teeth, the mucous membranes, the nose," whose meaning is a seduction from which "*signifiance* explodes," erotically more and other than words, bringing into performance "not the soul but *jouissance*."[9] It's feasible, too, to see the Professor's vocal lesson not only through the perverse possibilities of his mind, but in the terms used by Foucault writing of Deleuze, his theater of phantasms, which functions at the limits of bodies, but *against* bodies, too, sticking to them, but sticking it to them as well, cutting them open and multiplying their surfaces, as a site of metaphysics for the *disillusioning* of phantasms; in short, a space of thought "never hallowed by an idea," a "theatrum philosophicum" as an "epidermic play of perversity."[10] So far as the metaphysics is vocalized in the "phantasmaphysics" of sensations at the skin ("Theatrum" 172), below the eyelids, up the nostrils, or in the dirt below the fingernails, what it is not, as Barthes writes about the membranous voice, is some fetishism of *breathing,* where in the affect(ation) of meditation most techniques begin, bringing into performance, as from a secretly mystical center, some deep emotional truth or facsimile of the soul.

Metaphysics, as Artaud suggests (and Deleuze is indebted to him), may with the sonorous streaming come in through the pores, but only while escaping, in the vibrations, frications, ovulations, sibilations, the repressive simulation or "tyranny of meaning" (Barthes 185). As for the tyranny in *The Lesson,* true, the libidinous soundings of the linguistic theory there—that "all the words of all the languages . . . are always the same" (65)—takes a hallucinatory course to the lethal pedagogy of the knife, which, though the Pupil feels it, voluptuously, in every part of her body, is something else again than Artaud's cruelty or Barthes's conception of voice, whose truth is to be hallucinated ("Grain" 184). Which is not exactly the state of mind of the Smiths and Martins, in the vociferous fury of *The Bald Soprano,* their vain pursuit of meaning, where the concluding lesson is about the runaway signifiers, not this *that,* not that *this,* spreading over the stage: "It's not that way, it's over here, it's not that way, it's over here, it's not that way, it's over here, it's not that way, it's over here!" (42).

But wherever it is or might be, *it,* the indeterminate referent through the anarchy of it all, "a work of art," according to Ionesco—

unembarrassed by the phrase, which he uses frequently, honorifically, without much slippage—"is not a disordered set of associations. It's a structured series of associations around a theme. A work of art is primarily a construction,"[11] though it may be pushed to the point of paroxysm, "where the source of tragedy lies."[12] The tragic, too, has become dubious in our time, as politically disempowering, starting with the critique by Brecht and moving by way of poststructuralism into feminism, the new historicism, queer theory, and the gendered, racial, and ethnic politics of cultural studies. In any case, when Ionesco speaks of art as a construction he doesn't mean by that what, through Foucault and others, we've come to think of as "social construction," as if the work were composed by an aggregation of discursive circumstances or, in the anonymous performance of language, as a sort of accretion of history.

The text may be, as Barthes said in "The Death of the Author," a multiplex space of diverse writings, none of them original, but rather "a tissue of quotations drawn from the innumerable centers of culture" (*Image* 146); but when Ionesco speaks of his work he leaves no doubt that he is—as much as William Faulkner with Yoknapatawpha County—the sole proprietor of the site of multiplicity; and if things need to be deciphered or disentangled by the audience that's because "the mutual relations of dialogue, parody, contestation" focused, as Barthes says, in the reader or the audience (148), has been conceived and perpetrated by the imaginative powers of the artist, who has through those powers the capacity to construct. This is so even when the construction resembles, as at the frenzied end of *The Bald Soprano* or in the equally frenzied arrangement of chairs—when the Old Woman says, "I'm not a machine, you know. Who are all these people?" (*Chairs* 137)—the deterritorialized or nomadic space of *A Thousand Plateaus,* conceived by Deleuze and Guattari as an assemblage, an "*economy of violence*" in which "*speed is added to displacement,*"[13] in what they call the war machine. Which might, indeed, be a description of the accelerating structures of Ionesco's drama, an exacerbation of assemblage, seemingly irrational and denuded of all sense, as the enmity of the characters emerges, as if it were genetic, from the banality of its beginnings.

But if the irrationality is there, in the perversity of the Professor and his harrowing lesson, as in the proliferous invention that, with a teasing hysteria, seems to generate the plays—like the "spontaneous imagination" of the surrealist's creed, to which Ionesco was susceptible—the economy of violence is not without control, nor is the violence of the comic in Ionesco that, brought to paroxysm, circles back to the tragic. Or so it is in conception, whatever it may be in performance. The issue *is* construction, which is not without *affects* that, in "the active discharge of emotion, . . . are projectiles just like weapons" (*Thousand Plateaus* 400), of which the assemblage, with gaps, detours, always decentered, dispersed as it may seem, is the formal cause—so much so in Ionesco that for all the innovative turbulence the form seems merely the warp of something quite conventional. "Assemblages are passional," say Deleuze and Guattari, "they are compositions of desire. Desire has nothing to do with a natural and spontaneous determination; there is no desire but assembling, assembled, desire. The rationality, the efficiency of an assemblage does not exist without the passions the assemblage brings into play, without the desires that constitute it as much as it constitutes them" (399).

For Ionesco, it appears, the order of things is "let the torrent rush in" and then assume "control, grasp, comprehension" (*Notes* 124), but what rushes in, as we can see from play to play, would seem to be a function of the same order of understanding, with a "metaphysical consciousness" that, in a world that is "at once marvelous and atrocious, a miracle and a hell" ("Why Do I Write" 13), determines social awareness, as well as his apparent indifference to the political that made him, through the period of the Absurd, the subject of critique, as, say, Beckett never was—mainly because Ionesco's indifference to the political didn't at all make him indifferent to the critique. The compulsion to respond—from the initial debates with Kenneth Tynan to those with leftist critics when Paris was Brechtianized—was documented by Martin Esslin in his indispensable guidebook to the vicissitudes of the Absurd as it moved into the theater. I won't review the movement, through Ionesco's self-defense, from the judicious to the polemical to the didactic, which could have used now and then, in its more philosophical stuffiness, a little Brechtian alienation. But when he wonders through the didacticism why, in every gesture, if not *gestus,* there is a potential disaster or catastrophe, a killing instinct we can't control, he inevitably returns to the tortuous question of whether or not there is meaning in the world, or whether we were merely born deceived into a reality that is incurable.

He insistently asks the question, but that the natural *is* incurable, like the growing corpse in *Amédée,* is something he refuses to accept. If it's a law, then he denies it, but what to *do* is another matter. If he approaches at times, then avoids, the elegiac estrangement of the Beckettian nothing to be done—whether with Hamm's old stancher or Pozzo's mournful "On!"—he can't quite buy the solutions of those who deny on ideological grounds what he virtually takes on faith, that "a human fraternity based on the metaphysical condition is more secure than one grounded in politics. A question without a metaphysical answer is far more authentic. And in the end [more] useful than all the false and partial answers given by politics" ("Why Do I Write" 14). Unable to imagine the infinite and condemned to know nothing, what we can be conscious of is this: "all is tragedy," universal tragedy, unexplainable by original sin. As for politics, particularly revolutionary politics, that's a delusion. "We make revolutions to institute justice and tyranny. We make injustice and tyranny" ("Why Do I Write" 10). What can be done if at all? Forget ideology, and kill as little as possible. After World War II, what else can you expect? The simple wisdom is this: "Ideologies do nothing but prompt us to murder. Let's demystify" (11).

The irony is, however, as we look back today on the drama of Ionesco, that it's the demystifiers who might still take issue, like the older Brechtian critique, with its circuiting back to tragedy, or the insupportable semblance of it, through the extremities of its comedy. If momentarily eruptive and disarmingly off the wall, the charge might be that it is debilitating in its excess, its elephantiasis of the bizarre merely self-indulgent, a cover-up of paralysis, no more than a copout, in mockery of the reality that absurdly overwhelms it, like the interminable corpse of *Amédée*, "*the long, long body . . . winding out of the room*" (63). No matter that in the absurdity there is a longing for the supernal, or the memory of a memory of a memory of something else, as in the "*sinister room*" with sprouting mushrooms, enormous now with "*silvery glints*" and, as Amédée gazes out the window, all the acacia trees aglow. "How beautiful the night is!" he says. "The full-blown moon is flooding the Heavens with light. The Milky Way is like creamy fire, honeycombs, countless galaxies, comets' tails, celestial ribbons, rivers of molten silver, and brooks, lakes and oceans of palpable light." And the correlative of the corpse in the heavens, its long, long body winding, "space, space, infinite space" (59).

As early as *Amédée,* conscious of the critique that he was jeopardizing human behavior by invalidating objective judgment, Ionesco brought his defense, if whimsically, onto the stage, as when the American soldier, who is helping him with the corpse, asks Amédée if he's really writing a play. "Yes," he says. "A play in which I'm on the side of the living against the dead." And as he says again later, when—though he stands for "immanence" and is "against transcendence" (75)—he's up in the air with the ballooning corpse: "I'm all for taking sides, Monsieur, I believe in progress. It's a problem play attacking nihilism and announcing a new form of humanism, more enlightened than the old" (69). If for Kenneth Tynan—just prior to the emergence of the Angry Young Men, and the renewed vitality of social realism—progress and humanism were still in, with the demystifiers today they are certainly out, as among the illusions of the Enlightenment protecting bourgeois capitalism. If, in any event, there was nothing programmatic to be taken away from the incapacitating ethos of Ionesco's drama, with its fractious view of reality as senseless, purposeless, useless, absurd, there is still in the texts the prospect of performance that is nevertheless enlivening and, if a burlesque of possibility, ebullient in negation, as if the vertigo of nothingness were itself the source of energy that reversed, as in chaos theory today, the direction of the entropic. If entropy was—when I studied thermodynamics, about a decade before our doing Ionesco's plays—a measure of the unavailable energy of the universe, the drama of the Absurd, with its law of increasing disorder and commitment to evanescence, sneaked up in a dizzying anguish on whatever made it available. That too may be an illusion, which is not exactly absurd.

NOTES

1. The symposium was a retrospective, "Fool's Gold: Ionesco and the Theater of the Absurd," held at Stanford University on July 28, 2001.

2. Eugene Ionesco, *Four Plays: The Bald Soprano, The Lesson, Jack or the Submission, The Chairs,* trans. Donald M. Allen (New York: Grove, 1958) 87. References in the text will be to the titles of the plays.

3. Eugene Ionesco, *Amédée, The New Tenant, Victims of Duty,* trans. Donald Watson (New York: Grove, 1958) 15.

4. T. S. Eliot, *Selected Poems* (New York: Harvest/HBJ, 1964) 53.

5. Eugene Ionesco, "Why Do I Write? A Summing Up," in *The Two Faces of Ionesco,* ed. Rosette C. Lamont and Melvin J. Friedman (Troy, NY: Whitston, 1978) 5.

6. Antonin Artaud, "The Alchemical Theater," in *The Theater and Its Double,* trans. Mary Caroline Richards (New York: Grove, 1958) 52.

7. Artaud, "On the Balinese Theater," in *Theater and Its Double* 54.

8. Artaud, "The Theater and the Plague," in *Theater and Its Double* 30.

9. Roland Barthes, "The Grain of the Voice," in *Image-Music-Text,* trans. Stephen Heath (New York: Hill and Wang, 1977) 183.

10. Michel Foucault, "Theatrum Philosophicum," in *Language, Counter-Memory, Practice: Selected Essays and Interviews,* ed. Donald F. Bouchard, trans. Bouchard and Sherry Simon (Ithaca: Cornell University Press, 1977) 168, 171.

11. Damien Pettigrew, from "Interview with Ionesco," *Paris Magazine,* Autumn 1984, 26, quoted by Ruby Cohn, *From Desire to Godot: Pocket Theater of Postwar Paris* (Berkeley: University of California Press, 1987) 93–94.

12. Eugene Ionesco, *Notes and Counter-Notes* (London: John Calder, 1962) 6.

13. Gilles Deleuze and Felix Guattari, *A Thousand Plateaus: Capitalism and Schizophrenia,* trans. Brian Massumi (Minneapolis: University of Minnesota Press, 1987) 398, 396.

THREE

The Soul-Complex of Strindberg

Suffocation, Scopophilia, and the Seer

WHAT I WILL BE SAYING about *A Dream Play* is not necessarily as we've seen it here,[1] but as I've thought about it before, in the mind's eye, with some regret that, though I'd long been tempted to stage it, for one reason or other—perhaps the forbidding prospect—I never came to do it. That it is getting attention now, and not only here, may be telling us something, but as with its Swedenborgian intimations, triplex cosmos, occulted symbols, the "round bored holes and a clover leaf in the door,"[2] the visual warp of the mirrored refractions or, with certain shifts and reversals of vision, recessions of appearance in a sort of camera obscura—the dark picture of a cloud muting the dark picture of a tower—we may not be sure what it is. Or, maybe, appallingly, only too sure, so much so that at some psychic level we might wish we didn't know, like the Quarantine Master at the Dire Straits who wishes he could forget (238). And if, for Strindberg, what there was to be known came in some measure from the vicissitudes of the unconscious, with the libidinal content transformed into phallic aconites and vulvous grottos, or an organ becoming Fingal's Cave, there is also the raw self-evidence, the banality, brutality, inequitably unchangeable, implacable state of things, assailed by his characters with more or less impotency, so that sometimes the dreaming appears to be by default.

"In the old days," says the Captain in *The Dance of Death,* a year before *A Dream Play,* "we fought. Now we just shake our fists!" (163). "Sometimes," says the Student, six years after *A Dream Play,* in *The Ghost Sonata,* "I get a raging desire to say exactly what I think. But I know that if people were really frank and honest, the world would collapse" (306). The horror may be that it wouldn't, and that's the news that Indra's Daughter, with whatever ascending hope, is bringing to the throne above, translated "into language / the Immortal One understands" (*Dream Play* 259). As Clov says in Beckett's *Endgame,* "God be with the days!"[3] But before we count on that, or the faith-based initiative of our dubiously elected president, let's back up somewhat in Strindberg, from "the humiliation and filth" (251) around the mystical dream of redemption—or, with the Poet as seer, "words luminous, pure and airy enough

/ to rise from the [painful] earth" (259)—to the articulation of an aesthetic around "the soul-complex"[4] of an earlier Darwinism.

The soul is there, but less ethereal, in the naturalistic complex of the preface to *Miss Julie.* What we have in the preface—with its particularly estranged and maybe estranging perspective—is also an assault on the state of the theater toward the end of the nineteenth century. It will not be the last time that serious theater has been declared dead or at best a "*Biblia pauperum,* a Bible in pictures" for the petty bourgeois, whom it permits to understand not only complex issues but what Strindberg calls "the basic questions" (50), in rather simplistic, effortless ways. So far as our own period is concerned he might be talking not only of seemingly hip sitcoms passing into commercial theater but even of a play like *Angels in America,* which, with whatever virtues it brought to Broadway, is an updated *Tea and Sympathy* for the theater parties of the baby boomers, sustaining their liberal politics with an easy dose of edification.

For us, today, the more offensive aspect of Strindberg's critique is probably the matter of gender, beginning with his remark that "the theater has always been a public school for the young, the half-educated, and women, who still possess that primitive capacity for deceiving themselves or letting themselves be deceived, that is to say, are receptive to the illusion, to the playwright's power of suggestion" (50). It is, however, precisely this power of suggestion, more than that, the hypnotic effect, which is at the paradoxical center of Strindberg's vision of theater. As for what he says of women (beyond his feeling that feminism was an elitist privilege, for women of the upper classes who had time to read Ibsen, while the lower classes went begging, like the Coal Heavers on the Riviera in his play) his monomania is such that, with some remarkably virulent portraits, he almost exceeds critique; or his misogyny is such that one may say of it what Fredric Jameson said of Wyndham Lewis: "this particular *idée fixe* is so extreme as to be virtually beyond sexism."[5] I'm sure some of you may still want to quarrel about that, to which Strindberg might reply with his words in the preface: "how can people be objective when their innermost beliefs are offended" (51). Which doesn't, for him, validate the beliefs.

Of course, the degree of his own objectivity is radically at stake, though when you think it over his power would seem to come from a ferocious empiricism indistinguishable from excess, and not much diminished, for the skeptics among us, by the Swedenborgian mysticism or the "wise and gentle Buddha" sitting there in *The Ghost Sonata,* "waiting for a heaven to rise up out of the Earth" (309). As for his critique of theater, linked to the emotional capacities or incapacities of the bourgeois audience, it actually resembles that of Nietzsche and, through this Nietzschean disposition and a lethal edge to the Darwinism, anticipates Artaud's theater of Cruelty. "People clamor pretentiously," Strindberg writes in the *Miss Julie* preface, "for 'the joy of life,'" as if anticipating here the age of Martha Stewart, "but I find the joy of life in its cruel and powerful struggles" (52). What is in jeopardy here, along with the sanity of Strindberg—his madness perhaps more cunning than Artaud's, even strategic, since he "advertised his irrationality; even falsified evidence to prove he was mad at times"[6]—is the condition of drama itself. The form has been the classical model of distributed subjectivity. With Strindberg, however, it is dealing with the ego in a state of dispossession, refusing its past and without any future, states of feeling so intense, inward, solipsistic, that—even then with *Miss Julie*—*it* threatens to undo the form.

This is something beyond the relatively conservative dramaturgy of the naturalistic tradition, so far as that appears to focus on the documentable evidence of an external reality, its perceptible facts and undeniable circumstances. What we have in the multiplicity, or multiple motives, of the soul-complex is something like the Freudian notion of "overdetermination," yielding not one meaning but too many meanings, and a subjectivity so estranged that it cannot fit into the inherited conception of character. Thus, the idea of a "characterless" character or, as in *A Dream Play,* the indeterminacy of any perspective from which to appraise, as if in the mise-en-scène of the unconscious, what appears to be happening before it transforms again. Instead of the "ready-made," in which "the bourgeois concept of the immobility of the soul was transferred to the stage," he insists on the richness of the soul-complex (53), which—if derived from his view of Darwinian naturalism—reflects "an age of transition more compulsively hysterical" than the one preceding it, while anticipating the age of postmodernism, with its deconstructed self, so that when we think of identity as "social construction," it occurs as if the construction were a sort of bricolage. "My souls (characters)," Strindberg writes, "are conglomerates of past and present cultural phases, bits from books and newspapers, scraps of humanity, pieces torn from fine clothes and become rags, patched together as is the human soul" (54).

If it seems peculiar to substitute that theological word *soul* for *character* in the materialist economy of naturalistic drama, there are other anomalies as Strindberg works out an aesthetic for the atomized soul of a hysterical age, shortly before Freud and Breuer began their notorious studies of hysteria. For instance, there is a passage in the preface where, observing that people were increasingly interested in "psychological process," Strindberg—whose own essays on psychology had been entitled *Vivisections*—goes on to sound, in the demystifying mode, less like Sigmund Freud and more like Bertolt Brecht. "Our inquisitive souls," he says, "are not satisfied just to see something happen; we want to know how it happened. We want to see the strings, the machinery, examine the double-bottomed box, feel the seam in the magic ring, look at the cards to see how they are marked" (57). But a moment after insisting that theatricality reveal itself, that the apparatus of production be exposed, and presumably illusion with it, Strindberg writes about "the technical aspects of composition," that he has experimented in *Miss Julie* "with eliminating act divisions." Why? To preserve, like Nietzsche, the future of illusion. Or, as Strindberg puts it: "The reason is that I believe our dwindling capacity for accepting illusion is possibly further disturbed by intermissions during which the spectator has time to reflect and thereby escape the suggestive influence of the author-hypnotist" (57).

So much for the Brechtian Strindberg, at least for the moment. For there are other moments, more or less alienating, and so recurrently painful we might wish for the A-effect, even in the hypnotic structure of the more symbolist *A Dream Play,* where the future of illusion comes, as it did at the end in Freud, with civilization and its discontents—if you can call it civilization, "this madhouse, this dungeon, this morgue of a world," which is how the Student sums it up in *The Ghost Sonata* (308) before the invocation of Buddha, the murmuring sound of a harp, the room filled with white light, and then, after the whimpering of a child, Böcklin's painting, *The Island of the Dead,* appearing in the background, with soft, calm music, "gently melancholy" (309). There is in *A Dream Play* compassion for all this, but what sort of creation can it be, the Daughter plaintively asks, in which "the spirit craves other garb / than this of blood and filth," while doomed, moreover, to "endless repetitions. . . . Doing the same things over and over," as the Lawyer says—the compulsions in the repetitiveness by no stretch of obsession what Judith Butler has been writing about, queering the dispossession, the exclusion and abjection, the unliveable and the uninhabitable, by the repetitive and citational practice of subversive bodily acts. Repetition here—as with the pasting of Kristine, who pastes and pastes, "till there's nothing more to paste" (273)—is not "performativity" but a virtual condition of life.

The prologue to *A Dream Play* occurs in a world outside this world, in which most of the play occurs. This world, represented at first by a castle that, phallocratically, "keeps growing up out of the earth," is also differently framed, at least as Strindberg described it: "On the wings, which remain in place for the entire play, are stylized paintings representing a mixture of interiors, exteriors, and landscapes" (213). The world from which Indra' s Daughter descends is *represented* too—there is nothing, after all, outside representation, except the dream of it—in the constellations that can be seen, Leo, Virgo, Libra, and shining brightly between them, the planet Jupiter too, above the "banks of clouds resembling crumbling slate mountains with ruins of castles and fortresses" (210). The world as we know it, or will come to know, is a place into which one *strays* and *falls:* "a circle of vapors called Earth" (211), a place in which it is hard to breathe. Wherever we are on earth, in whatever play, the image of suffocation is ubiquitous in Strindberg.

Yet Indra's Daughter can also see that the earth is, too, "with green forests, blue waters, white mountains, and golden fields" (211), as it might be endowed by Brahma—the natural beauty, however, despoiled, as it might have been in the biblical garden: "something happened . . . , an act of disobedience," crimes which had to be suppressed (212). Why suppressed? There is no way of telling, because the fall has been a fall into language, speech, which is not transparent but has to be deciphered. We live, thus, in an ethos of suspicion, with no reliable hermeneutic and, in the failure of language, the lamentably demeaning rhetoric of no happiness on earth: we hear from Indra's Voice, about those below, that "Complaining / is their mother tongue" (212). If Indra's Daughter refuses to believe that, because she hears shouts of praise and joy, the paternal voice tells her to descend and see, and thus the drama becomes both an ordeal and trial, a disheartening initiation into the blight of being human or what will, blighted at birth—*pace* Heidegger—never come to Being.

As the Daughter falls into life as it appears to be on earth, the scenic image is a fusion of the psychedelic and the fabulous: rising above a forest of giant hollyhocks is the gilded roof of the growing castle, crowned by a flower bud, and then, below the foundation walls, piles of straw that cover manure from the palace stables. If the castle doesn't stink to high heaven, it has "been fertilized," and when the Glazier points out "a wing [that] has sprouted on the sunny side," a flower high up about to bloom, the Daughter is first delighted, then asks: "Tell me, why do flowers grow out of filth" (213). Whether or not "Love has pitched his mansion in / the place of excrement"[7] still remains to be seen, although it seems apparent that Yeats's gendering of Love as male would not be unappealing to Strindberg, captivated as he was by the inexpressible beauty of Harriet Bosse—upon whom the Daughter is apparently modeled—and despite the seductive immanence of the mother of illusion, Maya, a seductive but absent presence in the constellation of symbols.

"And so the world, life and human beings" says the Daughter to the Poet later in the play, "are only illusion, a phantom, a dream image" (270), and if the image seems at first drawn from fable or a fairy tale, it is soon, with psychosexual resonances in the subliminal text, transmuted to an anxiety dream that becomes increasingly nightmarish. While there is really a conventional act-structure to this movement, it appears to depart from the dramaturgy of the West into a parabolic or cyclical quest that is more like the sagas and drama of the East, where illusion dominates as the supreme order of things. Because the reality of the world is illusion, the source of which is secret, when the Officer wants to fetch his bride after seven years of waiting for her at the stage door, he is told by the Doorkeeper, "No one is allowed on stage!" (219). There is a certain resonance in the line that exceeds its status in the dramatic representation, so far as there is in the representation a remnant of "the real." Not only are we not allowed on stage, but "it's the last performance of the season today" (218). If this reminds us, denied access at the last, that the theater at first came with a prohibition, the promise of symbolism persisting in Strindberg is the end of that vitiating principle, representation, transfigured through the imaginary in a purification of theater, alchemical like Artaud's, starting with base matter, the disease of living itself, which at one point in *A Dream Play* is referred to as the plague. Out of an "essential separation," like the sexual division that in the metaphysics of the dream suffuses Strindberg's play, comes an "essential drama" that, as Artaud describes it, passes "by way of all natural resemblances of images and affinities" to its "complete, sonorous, streaming naked realization,"[8] as if by assuming its prodigious energy ridding the world of the plague.

Writing of the viceroy of Sardinia who, at the opening of his essay on "The Theater and the Plague," "had a particularly afflicting dream," Artaud asks: "But is it too late to avert the scourge? Even destroyed, even annihilated, even pulverized and consumed to his very marrow, he knows that we do not die in our dreams, that our will operates even in absurdity, even in the negation of possibility, even in the transmutation of lies from which truth can be remade" (15). If the viceroy "wakes up" on this realization, as if between him and plague there was "a palpable communication" (17)—confirming Artaud in "the notion of symbols and archetypes which act like silent blows, rests, leaps of the heart, summons of the lymph, inflammatory images thrust into our abruptly wakened heads," naming the powers "we hail as symbols" (27)—the problem with symbolist drama (as with expressionism later) is that the thrilling promise of a transfigured reality, to which we come through the dreaming, leaves us with the perpetual irony of something to be desired, not unlike the phantasm of virtual reality in a cyberspatial world. We seem to be promised something *other,* outside, beyond, outdoing to all appearance the system of representation, but if there's an alluring vertigo in the hallucinatory moment, it insists somehow on remaining the same. That in itself may be the substance of the mystery.

Meanwhile, what's really powerful in Strindberg is the recurring desire for transcendence that, when push comes to shove in the vale of repetition, is grasped again by the reality principle, which persists through *A Dream Play* like the force of gravity itself. If we do not die in our dreams—which it appears the Daughter does—sad to say, and Strindberg knows it, we are not necessarily reborn, for other circumstances and history also determine that. Speaking of affinities, and not an accident of history, it has been noticed before that *A Dream Play* appeared just about the same time, at the turn of the century, as *The Interpretation of Dreams,* but the psychopathology of the drama also seems to parallel Freud's *Project for a Scientific Psychology,* which appeared some years before, in 1895. Whether or not Strindberg was aware of either, the affinities are there, and the images, while the mechanisms of displacement, substitution, condensation, even secondary revision (the cover-up for what's too evident in the dream) would by now seem familiar enough as they occur in the polymorphous landscape with a certain perversity: rising castle, towering trees, circumcised candles, spiky or thorny flowers and—with the transpositions of male to female, returning to illusion—cave, grotto, corridor, as well as the alluring secret through the (maybe anal) cloverleaf hole. As for the cathected energy of the gestural language, its ideographic fervor and entropic thrust, there is the autism of the Officer, who strikes the table with his saber in a figure of masturbation and walks up and down before the cloverleaf hole 2,555 times: "Is there someone inside? Does anyone live there?" (220). What he's looking for he'll never find, as the Mother and Father—in a synoptic (if tamer) version of *The Father* and *The Dance of Death*—will never know why they've taunted each other. All they know is what the Mother says when the Father asks forgiveness: "We couldn't do otherwise" (215), which the Daughter as Agnes, wife of the Lawyer, has to endure later in the play, the anguish of it, far from relieved, rather intensified by their having a child: "And so living together is a torment" (233).

If there is a fatality in that, there is also the disposition of symbolist drama to uncover some ultimate secret. Desire is impelled by the promise of a clue to the mystery, the inevitable revelation behind the door with the hole. But the nothing that is not there suggests only the nothing that *is,* and that the answer is elsewhere, not-seen, otherworldly—unless it be, as in the hermeneutics of Freud, that wherever the images lead they disappear at some impasse into the dream's navel, and thence through the mycelium (the term is Freud's, but there are mushroom growths in Strindberg) with its filamenting nerve ends of thought. Which is what makes interpretation, deferred and impelled by multiplicity, as rich, perhaps, as the soul-complex. Before the door is eventually opened, the Officer wants a locksmith, but instead it is the Glazier who turns up, for the system with its symbols is also scopophilic: what is required is not a key but a *seer,* the irony being that vision is consummated—as in the restored mystery of Artaud's alchemical theater—in and through its sonorous substance, the naked streaming realization. What we see and how we see it, with seeing collapsing upon itself, as in a house of mirrors, is actually the substance of that other Strindbergian drama, *The Ghost Sonata,* whose title points to the ear. In that play it's as if reality were a matter of whispers ghosted into appearance.

Do you see? we say, but as in the spectral presence of the audience (with *audition* in the word) there is the listening too. "Is it going to be a musical evening, or what?" Hummel's servant, Johannson asks (289), about the ghost supper, which is in its apparitional orchestration left to our imagining—like the vampire "sucking the marrow out of the house" or the soup stock filled with water—a pitiful feast for the eyes: "they nibble on cookies, all at the same time, so that it sounds like rats nibbling in an attic" (290). Meanwhile, the scenic structure, as in *A Dream Play,* draws conceptually on photographic technique: zooming from exterior to interior, the scenes are at the same time variously mirrored, infinitely receding and, like the space of relativity, turned back upon itself. What we have, then, in the impacted expansion of image is a suffocating enclosure that—with rooms, closets, screens reflecting each other, as the characters also do—contracts and expands again like a Chinese puzzle box, which in the dubious warp of history is, structurally, also a cryptogram.

Which is also reflected in Hummel's view of language, when he says he prefers silence, because you can then "hear thoughts and see into the past," without hiding anything, as you can in words. "The other day," he says, "I read that the reason different languages developed was because primitive tribes tried to keep secrets from each other. And so languages are codes, and whoever finds the key will understand them all." Meanwhile, Nature itself has planted "in human beings an instinct for hiding that which should be hidden," though as we stumble into truths we'd rather not see or know, there is also the impulse "to reveal the deepest of secrets, to tear the mask off the imposter" (298). Thus the Mummy says of the Colonel that everything in his life is a forgery, including his family tree. But what she says of him, as of Hummel—he with the "false name" who also "steals souls" (299)—appears to be the essential reality of the play: life itself is a forgery that might, and this is a long shot, be transcended by the Student and Adele, though the fate of the hyacinth girl is likely to be what we see, a generation later, in T. S. Eliot's *The Waste Land.*

Problem is, as Ibsen understood in his self-assumed rivalry with Strindberg, the past is unlikely to die, except in wish fulfillment. "God, if only we could die! If *only* we could die," says the Mummy. But the human reality seems to be that "crimes and secrets and guilt bind us together!" (294). For Strindberg in *The Ghost Sonata* our lives, like that of the Colonel's, are more or less sustained on a promissory note, *amortized,* the note running its exacting course in an economy of death. Which, as we've come to say in theory, *is* the place of representation.

But back again to *A Dream Play,* and the bafflement at the door: there *must* be a way out, or *in.* How many doors have we seen since, up to and including *The X-Files,* its alien figures, occultism, and obsession with other worlds. "What's behind it? There must be something!" (222)—the ground of all allegory with its broken signs. The Law forbids, of course, the opening of the door, and we have seen that in the mutations from symbolism to modernism, from Maeterlinck's *The Intruder* through Kafka's Castle and *The Trial.* Speaking of trials, and ordeals, the Lawyer in *A Dream Play,* witness and interpreter of the Law and record-keeper of injustice, dreams of nothing but crimes and bears on his face—"chalk-white, lined, and with purple shadows" (225)—the desperate inscription of so much pain and suffering, like the Doorkeeper at the theater, that he thinks of his now as a criminal face.

"Who will pay the final reckoning? Tell me that," he asks the Daughter. How much solace can there be? how much conviction?—she who plays the role today would, I assume, have to deal with that—when she says: "He who feeds the birds" (226). Let me be blunt, secular, immediate, now: I'm tempted to say that's for the birds. If there's a metaphysic in dreams, as both Freud and Strindberg thought, one can't quite count on the spirit, and—for all the orgastic fervor of the fire in the end, uniting the Poet and Daughter—my guess is that Strindberg knew that too. I said earlier that my not staging the play was, perhaps, because it was a forbidding prospect, but what may have been most forbidding about it—through the castle burning and the flower bud bursting into a giant chrysanthemum, the orgastic and spiritual ardor of it—is, still, my own incapacity for a leap of faith, which may be the datum, however, of what I might do with the play. The Lawyer says: "But if He who feeds the birds would come down to the earth He made and see what wretches human beings are, maybe He would have some compassion" (226–27). Maybe. It's an old argument, all this, but in the world as we know it, with its born-again politics in a revival of faith, it would seem to me that compassion is not enough.

When we look in the play, however, for a less mystical or more substantial response, what we encounter are the university faculties: Philosophy, Theology, Medicine, and Law. If the Daughter who passes through the abusive and unsavory rites of being human—vision dimmed, hearing muffled, "bright, airy thoughts trapped in the labyrinth of fatty coils in [the] brain" (272)—is herself treated with compassion, however feeble her responses as an emissary from on high, Strindberg is merciless about what we would call today, after Foucault, the disciplinary regimens of institutionalized knowledge.

> OFFICER: Is there a funeral in town?
> LAWYER: No, it's a commencement exercise.
>
> (227)

There may be a special mordancy today, given the job market, about having to begin all over when "you already have your doctorate" (242), although Strindberg's animus is directed against the epistemological question, which brings us back to the condition of theater—which is now not only institutionalized but among the university faculties.

What happened to this world? the Daughter keeps asking, and then looking into the mirror believes that she sees the world as it really is, "before it got turned around" (228). There is not only, then, transposition, metamorphosis, and abstraction of character in *A Dream Play,* but because of the turn-around—including the sequence of reversed scenes and sites—a question of the status of the mimetic in a world of disbelief, or when, whatever the religious revival, belief is nevertheless shaky.

The Lawyer confirms her sense that the world is a copy, a false copy, which makes representation itself a double deceit, unless you believe it may also be a sort of homeopathic magic. The issue is not so much resolved as intensified by the juxtaposition of the transformation of Fingal's Cave with the manic obsessive pasting of Kristine (229–30). She is a suffocating preface to the marriage of the Lawyer and the Daughter, who learns among other things from the disaster of it, that poverty and filth go together.

The autistic behavior of Kristine may be recalled in another perspective at the Dire Straits, with its open-air gymnasium of machines resembling instruments of torture. Through these scenes—the quarantine beginning, the need to dance before the plague breaks out—we encounter images of history as nightmare or regression, including the ovens for cholera that may recall, today, those Holocaustic images we'd almost rather forget: "How hot does it get in those ovens?" (236).

One may ask: how hot does it get in the play, as the Daughter asks, with permutations, "Hasn't anyone thought that there may be a hidden reason why things are as they are?" (253). If there is—and putting aside the feeling that it's more outrageous then—what about a *cure?* (268). My own temptation is to burst out like Hamm in *Endgame,* "Use your head, can't you, use your head, you're on earth, there's no cure for that!" (53). But in *A Dream Play,* as the Daughter ascends, it's brought back to the Poet, "who understands best how to live / Hovering on . . . wings above the world," plunging "to earth from time to time, / but just to brush against it, not be trapped by it!" (273). As if desperate, however, for the words to guide him, the Poet has snatched a Book of Martyrs from the fire, into which it was thrown by the Dean of Theology, who does rage against "a God who won't defend His own people." When he leaves the stage in disgust, the Poet asks: "Isn't suffering redemption and death deliverance?" (273).

I wonder about that Poet, whether he doesn't need that rage, whether or not he believes, as with Strindberg himself. In any case, if I *were* to stage the play, the rage would certainly be there, pervading the soul-complex, unappeasable rage, in every shadow of the dream.

NOTES

1. The occasion for this essay was the conference "Staging Strindberg," sponsored by the Department of Theater and Dance and the Department of Scandinavian Studies, at the University of Minnesota, on February 17, 2001. The previous

night *A Dream Play* was performed by a (mostly) student cast under the direction of Aleksandra Wolska.

2. August Strindberg, *A Dream Play,* in *Strindberg: Five Plays,* trans. Harry G. Carison (New York: Penguin/Signet, 1983) 220. All subsequent references to Strindberg's plays, from this volume, will be in the text.

3. Samuel Beckett, *Endgame* (New York: Grove Press, 1958) 44.

4. Strindberg, "Author's Preface" to *Miss Julie,* in *Five Plays* 53; subsequent references to the preface will be in the text.

5. Fredric Jameson, *Fables of Aggression: Wyndham Lewis, the Modernist as Fascist* (Berkeley: University of California Press, 1979) 20.

6. Evert Sprinchorn, *Strindberg as Dramatist* (New Haven: Yale University Press, 1982), 2.

7. William Butler Yeats, "Crazy Jane Talks with the Bishop," in *The Collected Poems of W. B. Yeats,* ed. Richard J. Finneran (New York: Macmillan, 1989) 259–60.

8. Antonin Artaud, *The Theater and Its Double,* trans. Mary Caroline Richards (New York: Grove Press, 1958) 50, 52.

FOUR

From the Dreamwork of Secession to Orgies Mysteries Theater

The Enlightenment will come to a bad end. The brain is too heavy and the pelvis much too frivolous.
—OSKAR KOKOSCHKA, *Sphinx and Strawman*

I don't go to the theater
On principle
it is something quite disgusting
the theater
whenever I am in the theater
I am constantly reminded
how disgusting it is
—THOMAS BERNHARD, *The Hunting Party*

I'M NOT SURE whether being a redhead in provincial Austria today would cause you to be laughed at as you walked along a street, or otherwise mocked, despised, or even feared, as an agent of the Devil, but so it was, apparently, when Johann Nestroy wrote *The Talisman* in 1840. Prejudice aside, and its wicked incrimination, the play does something more with his red-haired girl—charged with driving geese from a hayloft before it burned down, obviously caused by her flaming top—it also charges up the drama, a farce with songs, while also baiting the censors, by whom Nestroy himself was often charged, in both senses, making the satire more aggressive, then hardly more restrained, when he was once not only threatened, but sent to jail for several days. As for the censorship, it was itself a dynastic tradition, within the religion of state and law, even as Austria was secularized and modernized, from the more liberated Secessionists to the Viennese Actionists, among whom scandal was sacred in the order of things, with animal slaughter, burnings, and ritualized masochisms, pornography, scatology, self-mutilations, public masturbations, vomiting, shitting, eating shit, near-electrocutions—all forms, as they conceived it, of talismanic disobedience, sometimes so funny you could scream. Thus, it should probably be pronounced, with accent on the obsessiveness, talis-*manic,* or simple manic without the *talis,* that Jewish prayer shawl, which intellectuals in Vienna, many of them Jews, couldn't dream of wearing, even if still willing to be identified as Jews, which many of them refused, some converting to Catholicism, maybe regretting it, maybe not, that equivocal peace with imperial power. As for others who didn't deny it, prospering, entrepreneurial, well-educated Jews, with *Kultur* their true religion, they could be anti-Semitic themselves,[1] while old rigidities persisted, with moral stagnation and ossified institutions, in that presumably opening and liberal world surrounding the Secession.

"To the Age Its Art, to Art Its Freedom." Despite that famous motto—inscribed by the architect on the Secession's modernist temple—when *die Jungen* banded together, in 1897, to release the visual and plastic arts from an imprisoning aesthetic, there was nothing like the performative insolence of Nestroy when, earlier in the century, he assaulted the vapidity and hypocrisies of an often confounded audience, on the edge of shouting him down, yet nervously laughing through it, then dismissing his arrogant wit, as Nestroy knew they would, since they knew no better, ready to go on believing what they already believed. What *he* believed was sometimes baffling, given his wicked tongue, up for grabs in the spiraling nonsense, or with somersaulting puns, buried in the buffoonery, but while he seemed to love performing, there was a time, long before Bernhard, when he found the theater disgusting, the censor in the wings, and the assembled obtuseness, which was all the more reason for staying on the attack. I must confess, having written a book called *The Audience,* after many years in the theater, much of it controversial, that I've often shared those feelings, and done some attacking myself—as in *The Impossible Theater: A Manifesto,* which called for a revolution—though I won't resume that here.

In the attack mode, Nestroy was quite proficient, and, more or less manically later, others like Peter Handke, in his play *Offending the Audience,* devastatingly, it would appear, calling them every name he could think of, scum, worms, monstrosities, sclerotics and syphilitics, foul-mouthed ass-kissers, there, potentially dead, but remarkably unoffended, even by the nonstop, incantatory, merciless verbosity, as word upon word he is soon reversing himself. The play, of course—or what Handke called a *Sprechstücke,* a speak-in where you sit in, the actors told how to listen, the audience taught to be actors, directed from the stage—is really a discourse on theater, the always impossible theater, which accounts for the logorrhea, presumably ending representation, like a Derridean dream, praise be deconstruction! contradicting itself, playing around with play, structure, sign, and play, a spectacle without pictures, pure beleaguered play, only a world of words, abolishing scopophilia in a linguistic and acoustical space, where if you listen to the looking you *hear* it coming back. Handke asserts in a prefatory note that the *Sprechstücke* have nothing to do with representation, but then he admits, with a ready irony, that "they imitate the gestures of all the given devices natural to the theater"—which is why he claims in disclaiming that he's not being revolutionary. The preface ends with the definitive: "Speak-ins are autonomous prologues to the old plays" (ix).

Which brings us back to Nestroy, whose ironies were still directed at, and constrained by, a far from autonomous theater, though in Hapsburg Vienna, with an infection of old plays, even those announced as new, the spectacles could be extravagant, as well as the acoustical space for another world of words—upon which, by the deployment of dialects, jargon, plainspoken speech, funny stuff to make a living, a living he deplored, he was with disgusted fervor also making satiric war. It wasn't quite the war of words declared at the fin de siècle by the much-feared, formidable, incontestable Karl Kraus, who was actually responsible for reviving Nestroy, as a profoundly needed, deep satirical thinker, though not perhaps with the *Geist,* a World-Spirit for Hegel, a mind-spirit for Kraus, an ethical mastery of the Word, which Kraus claimed for himself, not only apostolically, but as its virtual incarnation. Nor, though he'd restored him from oblivion by reading Nestroy's texts in public, he absolutely didn't want to see them in the theater. Opposed to the aestheticizing of instinct, by the *Jung-Wien* and Secession, Kraus also believed that the staging of a text defiled it, and the purity of language as well, thus better to keep it away from the show-off virtuosity, the self-indulgence of actors. Dramatic art could only be preserved, he insisted, by keeping it out of performance. It's hard to say what Nestroy might have made of all this, if it's true that he thought more of himself as an actor than as a playwright. In that regard, whatever the rage of antitheater he might have shared with Kraus, he was still writing roles for himself, and while his own virtuosity was running away with the text—the authority of the author leaving it behind—he had to take the measure of where they could be performed.

The prestigious theater in Vienna was, of course, the Burgtheater, and while it was there in peripheral vision, Nestroy's plays were obviously not compatible with its edifying repertoire of stentorian drama in verse, set at some temporal distance, mainly antiquity, for a pseudocultivated highbrow public. As to what could be shown, what not, even into the next century, with newer stirrings in the drama, certain rules were imposed with an unbreakable rigor by the deputies of the Hapsburgs: no mocking of a monarch, or eyebrow raised in critique; so too with the ecclesiastical, no elements or sites of ritual allowed to be seen on stage: no crypts, altars, funerals, and so, if they dreamed of doing *Hamlet,* the gravedigger was out; incest, adultery, no question, forbidden; nor could a man and woman leave the stage together unless accompanied by a servant. And no lights down—as Schnitzler signaled, with asterisks in the text—while sexuality made the round, that illicit dance of *Reigen* (better known here as *La Ronde*). Thus, anything that was in jeopardy could only show up in the popular theater, or the puppet theater, with its affinities to *commedia* mime. And this, to begin with, was the milieu for Nestroy, whose tall, thin figure often behaved like a puppet, even at the curtain call, when he took a bow, and the audience didn't quite know whether he was mocking their applause. Yet, while he had written for the lower classes who, after crying through the tearjerkers, relished raw comedies, with idiomatic smut and a nativist bumbling slapstick, the audience he was after, when the vitriol soared, were the self-deceiving types of an emerging middle class, who had sold their souls for money; in making this judgment, however, Nestroy played no favorites: common folk would do the same, while the aristocrats he couldn't mention were obviously born without. The newly thriving bourgeois might have sold their souls, too, for admission to the Burgtheater, but not yet eligible there, for seating among the elite, they went instead to the theaters of the *Vorstadt,* those growing suburbs of fashionable Vienna, but outside the city walls, where the censorship was spreading too, becoming metropolitan—though already, under a fine-tuned bureaucracy, the most efficient in all of Europe.

With his antic disposition always under surveillance, there were notorious repercussions to Nestroy's more embittered theatricality, the improvised ridicule and often scurrilous comic assaults, across social classes, on the fraudulent motives and self-deceits, whose manifest content was already spawning latencies, volatile in repression, that the clinician Dr. Freud, delighted by the acuity of Nestroy's clowning, would later come to address—and so did Arthur Schnitzler, whose own manifest content came with a clinical aptitude acquired from training as a physician, though he had learned a little, too, as a man about town. Freud, as the legend goes, thought of Schnitzler as his alter ego, but the latter, unfortunately, was more deeply pessimistic, unable to reconcile sociopolitical realities with the erotic behavior—seen, not seen, often undercover, or with disguised self-loathing—of a hedonist gay Vienna. Combined with his medical background that made for a desolate wit, diagnostic, voyeuristic, he examined the interweaving of Eros and Thanatos in the libidinal economy of the time, or as orchestrated in

Reigen, the sexual trafficking in the social corruption. At a time of neurotic uncertainties, among the artists and intellectuals—mixed marriages, untold affairs, wife swaps, and as with the charismatic Gustav Klimt (whom Schnitzler confessed he dreamed about) a serpentine personal life, with fourteen illegitimate children—the sequential curling of *Reigen* might seem a sardonic enlargement of the decorative arcs and eddies in the brushstrokes of Secession. As a subversive diagram, however, of the trade-off identity politics of Viennese society, where the erotic might even go begging—though much practiced, much maligned—it encircles the liability that the libidinous was libelous, and scandalous up on stage.

And so it certainly was, which kept the play from being produced anywhere in Austria. When it was eventually done in Berlin, there was instant outrage and an obscenity trial, and when finally performed in Vienna, after World War I, the response was even worse, like an emblematic ground zero for anything really new: demonstrations in the streets, the theater assailed, stink bombs thrown, prominent figures implicated, which brought the affair to Parliament; and when the production kept going, under police protection, that didn't protect it from vilification in the press, as pure vulgarity from a brothel, to satisfy the indecent tastes of "Asiatic intruders"—no wonder Hitler dismissed it as nothing but Jewish filth. The virulence was such that Schnitzler forbade the play to be produced in his lifetime. If that wasn't the way with Nestroy, it wasn't because of scandal or the censor that, after *his* lifetime, the work went unproduced, then forgotten, until the intervention of Kraus—who meanwhile, though they agreed about Nestroy, didn't exactly like the Jewishness of Freud. As for his own imperious misgivings about psychoanalysis, Kraus diagnosed it, in a famous remark, as the disease or mental illness for which it purports to be the cure. There was plenty to cure in Vienna, including its anti-Semitism, so it may not have been an apology, but a judgment of Kraus too—who was born a Jew, but changed his religion—that the therapist Freud actually chose to live in a building called the House of Atonement, and was the first to sign up for it, when others were resisting.

And so the dance continues, with its ironic circlings, on what Freud called the "royal road" to understanding the operations of the unconscious. Which may have, that royal road, its own circuitous ironies, in the psyching out of the psyche, dramaturgical and political. *Flectere si nequeo superos, Acheronta movebo*—thus the epigraph to *The Interpretation of Dreams,* which made its first appearance in 1899, as if a fated preface to the century of the modern: "If I cannot bend the Higher Powers, I will move the Infernal Regions."[2] And so they did move, by substitution or condensation, displacement, always dubious representation, and the ready-made fantasies of "secondary revision," which "seem faultlessly logical and reasonable," but are something else again, representation representing, like theater within theater. A sort of "waking thought" (Freud 528), approximating the Real, that subtly fantasized revision is, by whatever infernal power, an ingenious cover-up, thwarting interpretation, so that "we find ourselves helplessly face to face with a meaningless heap of fragmentary material" (529), like the ruins of time spread out before the receding figure of the Angel, in Walter Benjamin's "Theses on the Philosophy of History," or to bring it explicitly, materially, into the theater, like the detritus onstage in Beckett's abbreviated *Breath*.

As disordered as all this seems, in its devious wish fulfillment, the unconscious remains, according to Freud, our oldest mental faculty, and down there in the depths, "at bottom, dreams are nothing other than a particular *form* of thinking" (545). As for Freud's own thinking, *The Interpretation of Dreams* is by no means merely clinical, the foundational treatise of his new science, but a confessional of his own, his dreams their dreams, the analyst analyzed, his own buried self, in a deeply personal counterstatement—and indeed to those higher powers. Theater is theory, I've written, or a shadow of it, and only the shadow knows. So it might be said of the mise-en-scène of the unconscious, with all its shadows in the infernal regions there. What it also represents is the dominance of a reprehensible politics that was, if analyzed, the projection of psychic forces that not only made a mockery of the Secession, but Austrian culture as well, through the defeat of the Central Powers in the Great War, when—returning from theory to theater, with the shadows still there in the dreamscape—Hugo von Hofmannsthal finished his adaptation of *Life Is a Dream,* that prophetic drama by Caldéron.

It was possible to think of Vienna and its avowed culture of grandeur as itself a city of dreams, with both manifest and latent content, and the category of Austria suggesting a glorious past. That, in fact, or fantasy (always hard to distinguish the two), is the legacy which the King in *The Tower*—though the world is "topsy-turvy," threatened by a "raging fire"—is determined to protect, "if need be, with streams of blood" (Hofmannsthal 275). As for post-Secession Vienna, bringing it into modernity, with both past and present conflated, there was an immanent danger there, reality in hiding, but like the bestial figures in the Tower, ready to erupt and pounce. Not unaware of the latent ferocity of it all, there is the character of the famous Doctor, who attempts with Sigismund what we came to know through psychoanalysis as the "talking cure." Behaving like a child, and in a childish voice, Sigismund nevertheless "forgets nothing" (195); haunted by the past, its bewildering and bestial, insecticidal images, he's not sure he is in the world, or where the world *is,* with the boundary blurred "between what's within and what's without" (194). Conceding that the famous Doctor is an astute reader of signs, when Julian, the Governor of the Tower, asks, "What do you see in my face?" (211)—he is given a full-scale diagnosis that moves from the personal to the sociopolitical, preceded by that epigraph from *The Interpretation of Dreams: Flectere si nequeo superos, Acheronta movebo!*

There'll be more to say about the circling in the city of dreams, and while I'm no authority on modern Austria, about reflexes picked up, or so it seems, on the royal road, even among those who initiated the modernizing—like some in the Secession who, later, were either evasive, playing it safe, or turned conservative. Or, like the conservatism of Kraus, harder to read. What does seem apparent is the anxiety and turmoil among those who, conceptually and artistically, were trying to make a difference, even as they were contending with forms of oppression and regression that hardly seemed to have changed since before the time of Nestroy; nor—speaking of atonement, or its absence, from the *Anschluss* to Waldheim and the Freedom Party of Haider—through much of the twentieth century. As for what was really possible in any of the arts, the cynicism was ubiquitous. The reception of Schnitzler's *Reigen* was, perhaps, the worst-case scenario, but the plays of Nestroy might well be seen, retrospectively, as fulfilling what Hermann Bahr asked for in the first issue of *Ver Sacrum,* the organ of the Secession. A sort of manifesto meant for painters, it applied almost more to the theater, as with the plays of the painter Kokoschka, or later with Bernhard, or the theatricalized behavior of the painterly Actionists. To create change where it seemed impossible, Bahr's prescription was this: "One must know how to make oneself hated. The Viennese respects only those people he despises" (qtd. in Selz 149).

However they later went about it, or whatever they targeted, Nestroy's satire was a proleptic summary of what others kept complaining about, writing about, or would assault on stage if they could. It was especially ruthless about the repulsive *Gemütlichkeit* of an ever-futile, static, posturing Austria, in love with its wonderful past, though later described by Friedrich Hebbel as that "little world, in which the big world holds its rehearsals" (qtd. in Steinberg viii). Whatever happened on opening night in that other world, there was in Austria, as Nestroy saw it, no need to wait for that, because for want of a reality principle, especially in Vienna, with its factitious grandeur, like dreamwork on display, there was a more generic investment in the future of illusion, as if no other future, with rehearsal as performance, and performance a way of life. And there was a certain pathos in the unavoidable fact that those who were trying to change it were performing their own illusions. As T. S. Eliot once remarked, in another context, about this double bind, the only alternative is to improve the quality of the illusions, which Robert Musil also suggested in *The Man without Qualities*—with his view, at century's end, that an accelerating instability was itself reality principle, as if in a warp of time. This was beyond measure an embarrassment for Vienna, that enraptured musical city, no way to read the score, whether up or down or sideways, for what things were moving towards. (With twelve tones going, Schoenberg might have told them, or Berg, but they had their troubles too.) It was as if Vienna had entered precipitously into our age of speed,[3] with relativity, sure, across the space of time, but here again with a kind of *Reigen,* as if the curvature of Secession, and all its whirling figures, were there in Einsteinian space, infinitely extended, but curving back upon itself. Which, for Vienna, also felt like stasis.

As for Bahr's invocation, it's one thing to be dissident in the other arts, but there's nothing like being hated when you're up there on stage. Apparently shy offstage, but uncrippled by stage fright (which the best of actors exploit, achieving credibility in the process of covering it up), what Nestroy dared to expose in his own performances—with gestures, songs, pauses, monologues, sidelong glances, obscene asides, and a mastery of taunting dialects—was the posing, the masking, the affectation, of what was something like simulation, or as we've come to say in theory, the mimicry of mimesis in everyday life, thus doubling up on the doubleness of reality in the theater, which is only realized, ontologically, in its (dis)appearance. Ontology, you may recall, recapitulates phylogeny, but if you're wondering why those texts were ignored and untranslated for more than half a century, it's as if the phylogenesis itself were censored in the evolutionary tree of life, that life which is a dream. Nestroy, they used to say, couldn't be played without Nestroy—so much lost without him, no less in another language. Still, there is in the texts themselves, like a cynical stain on the page, more than a residue of bitter critique, usually focused in a surrogate figure, quick on insult and verbal trickery, and disdain for a backward public, in all its squalid smugness, there to be entertained. So with Titus in *The Talisman,* a social pariah, unemployed, also with red hair, whose joking venom is such that he even despises himself, for the climbing of a social ladder that, in repressed rage, he really wants to destroy. It may have been, as he sings, when he enters the play (with now-translated local color and updated dialect), that "coffee with schlag has replaced witch's brew," but even when the era of reason began, with science and technology assuring progress, "Superstition, superstition!" still remained on the scene, with this taboo or that taboo, and for all the mixed feelings, "What [a] convenient condition!" (Nestroy 43).

Indeed, if you reimagine that condition in Nestroy—who played Titus, disguised in various wigs, another device for mocking the audience with what they were laughing at—you could see why they said he was philosophical too, indeed, the only Austrian philosopher then, with a certain practical wisdom. Simply put: it was stupid to be intelligent, as it was intelligent to be stupid, or conveniently superstitious, for the liability of intelligence was coming upon facts and truths, or even the truthful semblance, as in Ibsen's theater of realism, astringent, critical, by which Austria, among the modernizing countries of Europe, was singularly unaffected. As opposed to the conflicted Hedda Gabler, with her father's pistols in a bourgeois parlor, there was, even at the fin de siècle, a self-satisfied dispensation of bourgeois well-being in a society still disposed to the baroque heritage of fantasy, with its cult of beauty, social grace, sensuous charm, and the blissful abandon of an expedient gaiety, still whirling through its illusions in the *Emperor's Waltz*. If there was a demystifying piety to Nestroy's satire, its dialects, rhythms, *G'fallen* signals, the catechism was this: what you don't know won't hurt you, and praise the Lord for those illusions, since—in the corrosive dynamic between the surface seductions of an ornamental culture and the anguished nothingness of alienated being—that's what holds the blemished world together.[4] As for the utopian dream of change, by means of revolution, that was the real delusion of mid-nineteenth-century Europe, and after 1848, that multicultural muddle of a nation in the middle, with its Hungarians, Slovenes, Poles, Czechs, Ruthenians, Romanians, Slovaks, Italians, Spaniards, Croats, Serbs, most of whom had attempted to achieve independence, or dominion over the others, while the empire persisted with its Germanic inclinations and heroic pretense, just right for operetta, the subtext of which was decadence and despair.

For all his satiric prescience, Nestroy never pretended to be a prophet, though even after the fin de siècle, with the Secession settled in, the jaundiced perspective of *The Talisman* still applied: "reliance on science always in season," yet many things believed "without reason," not only with Slavic fatalism or Spanish mysticism or the trickle-down folklore of an amorphous polyglottism, but with dissent still muffled by the hegemony of the church, an always adaptable politics, a convenient conservatism, if not an indifferent or surreptitious hedonism—forgetful pleasures metastasizing guilt—along with the recurrent, almost congenital, nostalgia for the baroque. In any case, sings Titus in an encore, with the inarguable refrain, "People must believe in *some*thing" (Nestroy 44)—when despite all science and reason, and because of the hovering censor, they eventually came round to believing they didn't know what to believe. And this was so not merely out in the provinces, or the *Vorstadt,* but again, among the intellectuals and artists in the Secession, with its emancipated instincts and quest of interior being, where the witches were transfigured by that incursion of Art Nouveau (or the German variant *Jugendstil*), as if eroticizing the waltz into a visual *danse macabre,* vertiginous in its stasis, and exotic too.

Raveled, mosaic, primitive, even Asiatic, with weirdly carnal figures, gold-toned lubricious flesh, Sphinx-like or watersnake women, clawed, phallic, abstracted into castration, with a voluptuous motherliness—thus we see them in Klimt, with fishlike eddies, glistening scales, crowned with laurel, wreathed, tendriled, gowned in mother-of-pearl, and the silken weavings of a peacock's tail. Not unaware of the corruption of art and politics, in a slippery sexuality, he might have borrowed from Schnitzler's *The Green Cockatoo.* But for Klimt, major figure of the Secession, the search for modernity was Orphic and introverted, in the striving toward the mysterious, even Dionysian—behind those veils, lustful desire and torment, with imminent ecstasy. So far as it was performative, however, as painting would increasingly be, there was nothing like the sexual extremity of Artaud's *Spurt of Blood* or, nurtured by the Plague, the naked sonorous streaming of his consummate theater of Cruelty. We'd see something more like that in the expressionist plays of Kokoschka, and when they were still painters, incited by the gestural drips and pourings of Jackson Pollock, but using their bodies instead of canvas, the Viennese Actionists: Mühl, Brus, Schwarzkogler, Nitsch, as they moved, sometimes naked and streaming, their dripping penises painting, from abstract expressionism toward the atavistic Orgies. Yet, even as Klimt mutated from the baroque *theatrum mundi,* with those coiled or admixtured bodies in a pregnant but viscous void, to the Byzantine geometry of more hieratic forms, the eroticism didn't vanish, nor tinseled, tethered, scabbed with silver, Klimt's own obsession with pain, or fear of mental illness, which along with a certain morbidity or mortuary dream—the notion that death purifies—haunted the Secession.

Sumptuous as it could be, with intimations of transcendence, there was an invisible bloodstain in the glamorous fabric of Vienna's ascendency in the art world, its brilliance tarnished not only by that netherworld of patricides, perversions, betrayals, and the death wish engrailed in the sexual fantasies, but something more than fantasy, aspiring to true confession—that process interminable, as Freud himself conceded, with interpretation disappearing into the dream's navel. Not necessarily what Kraus said of it, but so much for the talking cure. Whatever was going on in the dramaturgy of the unconscious, it may have been even more complicated by an actual dire chronicle of empirically verifiable, notable suicides. So with the case of Otto Weininger, the precocious author of *Sex and Character*—an alternative to Freud, praised by Strindberg, studied by Wittgenstein, and in its male/female binary, arguably misogynist, a likely source of Kokoschka's play *Murderer, Hope of Woman.*

Whatever happens in that play, however, or in *Sphinx and Strawman*—with a Sphinx quite other than that in Klimt—there is nothing causal about it, no logic except that of the most pathogenic instincts or degenerative disease. In *Murderer,* the branding of the Woman, the stabbing of the Man, would appear to be reflex and counter-reflex, but the Man's awakening from the lassitude of his imprisonment, to kill the Woman, and everybody else onstage—nothing prepares an audience for that. The gratuitousness of it, the spontaneity or ecstasy, is like that of a nightmare, the dreamwork of atrocity, or the atrocity of dream, as if at the nadir of the navel there were nothing but madness—which, for the spasmic brain of Kokoschka, was somehow exhilarating. What seems palpable about the play, even visceral on the page, is that it requires a staging—if it's anywhere in the vicinity of his epileptic thought—pitched visually at the summit of a scream, not the *Ich* or *Geist,* but a *Schrei,* with every decibel soaked in blood. As for the acting of it, it's not a matter of character, but of elemental urges, simmering, convulsive, or as if brain damaged, passing through nerves, muscles, veins painted by Kokoschka on the performer's bodies when he first mounted the play, the young actors left with bruises. The cultural irony was that he had arranged to do the production, with all its savage intensity, in the charming little theater of the Kundschau pleasure garden, where Kokoschka expected, wanted, outrage and protest, though he may have been disappointed—there are contrary views of what happened—that the furore wasn't there. Which, for him, with an ethic of derangement, would have made the theater disgusting—so much so that, like the futurists, for their performances, he might have incited and staged the riotings.

One might wonder what Weininger would have thought had he actually seen *Murderer, Hope of Woman*—with spiritual male/animal female, but woman immortal, because she gives birth—or about Kokoschka's behavior, not in the theater itself, but when, after a devastating affair with the woman he worshipped, Alma Mahler-Werfel, he went through a psychic crisis to the point of performative madness. Exhausted by an intense possessiveness, Alma went off with the architect Walter Gropius, but confusing husbands or lovers, Kokoschka would show up, with his proto-punk hairdo and bizarre dress, at an artist café each night, carrying a mannequin of Gustav Mahler, which he'd seat at a table, then order drinks, and carry on a conversation. Or he might be seen at the theater, embracing a life-size doll of his loved one, restored in every feature, the two of them seated together. As for Weininger himself, despite the influential *Sex and Character,* which was controversial too, he was not a psychologist, but a philosopher, of extraordinary promise, who might very well have reflected on those oscillations in Viennese thought, particularly among the young, between scientific reason and a liberating, Nietzschean, even sacerdotal instinct, the momentum of which was subject to a stifling intellect, as if madness were being reasoned and reason going mad. That Hamletic impediment may not have been there with Weininger, but in a culture where the Dionysian was just below the surface, yet even Secession stifled, by the desiccated feeling of an impoverished psyche, what explains his committing suicide, at the age of twenty-three? And the additional pathos of it? That would seem in somber perspective, with the gaiety falling away, a Viennese tradition too, if reclusive and not in public, still performative, dramatistic, and with a memorable staging—his having rented a space in the house where Beethoven died. If not guilt, genius by association, and with a great performer.

With madness in mind, the logic of what follows: "What I would really like best would be a completely equipped insane asylum."[5] Thus, another voice of *die Jungen,* and at the level of royalty too: a young Bavarian princess, wife of Franz Josef, acclaimed for her startling beauty everywhere in Europe—an insane asylum, that's what Elizabeth said when the emperor asked what present she would like for her name day. This goes back before the Secession, but as we think about cultural performance in modern Austria, onstage, offstage, where performance might seem, as in Nestroy's red-haired, disenchanted, bread-and-butter vision, a discomfiting way of life, there were also those storied lives with a compelling theatricality. So with that of Elizabeth, which starts out like a melodrama, and might have made an opera, but becomes a virtual model of more radical kinds of performance. The emperor loved her, adored her, but for reasons unknown she didn't or couldn't reciprocate, distancing herself from the court, and from Austria too. She would, of course, have been received royally everywhere, but she preferred, instead, in Munich or London, as she also did in Vienna, to visit institutions for the insane, while also neglecting poor Rudolf, their only son. Heir to the throne, but indifferent to that, his loneliness turned into depression, unrelieved by numerous affairs, and finally to a suicide pact with one of his lovers: he killed her, then killed himself, at a hunting lodge in the heart of the Vienna Woods. About ten years later, in Geneva, escaping Vienna again, Elizabeth too was suddenly dead, assassinated by an anarchist—which, if not poetic justice, seemed an appropriate denouement to the meaninglessness of her drama.

What engages me here, however, is not the drama, where she resembles some of the hysterics that Schnitzler wrote about, but a sense that Elizabeth anticipated, in the undeterred logistics of her imperious derangement, certain extremities of performance or self-punitive body art that we saw after the 1960s, with Marina Abramović in Belgrade or Gina Pane in Paris—and with Valie Export in Vienna, affiliated with the Actionists, but at a feminist distance, who also brought an accusatory pain into what she called "expanded cinema." Or with herself as provocative subject, into "touch cinema," or other body events, where she solicited what might unnerve you, if you touched, and that crossed gender lines. The beauteous Elizabeth was apparently provocative in being inaccessible, maybe untouchable, but there was something painful there. Whether she was making accusations, hard to say, since she wasn't seeing an analyst, probably too early for that, but along with her seeming narcissism, or to exacerbate the hysteria, she was also anorexic. I say exacerbate, because there was a conscious regimen to it, with an aesthetic rigor, as when she'd starve herself for days, with nothing except six glasses of milk, and the requirement, too, that the exact quantity be made known. Or then she'd be calling attention to her long walking tours, often seven to ten hours, at an unusually fast pace, exhausting those in her entourage who tried to keep up with her; or, having traveled with enough trunks to fill several railway cars—so she'd always have available the otherwise unattainable, most stylish clothes—she'd let them languish or discard them for the dress she wore in her walking, over those marathon distances, with her body naked beneath, no undergarments whatever, and to the dismay of her courtly consort, no stockings either, though she'd sometimes wear as many as three pairs of gloves, to protect her exquisite hands. If it appears that the mania here was, in its self-abusive discipline, the insidious inverse of unconscious self-destruction, in an age enamored with death, it was Elizabeth who thought of herself as transcending that, as when she said—and it was she who said it—that "the idea of death purifies," and if reason is going mad, "madness is truer than life" (qtd. in Bettelheim 10).

Or maybe the psychic equivalent. As for the truth about Austria, or Austro-Hungary then, if you could get it from a politician, it was a Hungarian foreign minister who said, after the collective neurosis had moved into a new century, with the death drive, too, being defined by Freud: "We have to kill ourselves before the others do it" (qtd. in Bettleheim 11). He said that in 1912, two years before the war, when it seemed, indeed, that the fixation upon death and self-destruction was not only psychosexual, but with the personal always political, as if the empire were committing suicide. When that Great War was over—no hyphenated Hungary, Austria just itself—the ominous sensation persisted, certainly in the arts, as if that quest to the interior, as for nuclear fission, had always been moving to an apocalyptic end, which Karl Kraus was to prophesy, even foreseeing atomic peril, in that caustically Epic drama, like a memorial in advance, *The Last Days of Mankind.*

As it happens, that monumental play was finished in 1926, the year I was born, unfortunately not as a portent of better things to come, which Kraus couldn't imagine, given Austria's past, its unforgivable present, the debasement of language, along with the flatulent doubleness, since the fin de siècle, of the liberal intelligentsia, predominantly Jewish, whose behavior he contemned more than the ineptitude of conservative Christians. Having renounced what he was born to, and confirmed in another religion, Kraus went on the attack against any sign of a "ghetto-mentality," in manners or behavior, and every ritual remnant of Talmudic belief, no less any shtetl reflex or intonation, synagoguish hat or scarf that might prevent assimilation to the dominant culture—which, with his satiric omnipotence, he was determined to reform. As a "timeless world-disturber," which he said about himself, according to Benjamin, there was in his "incorruptible, piercing, resolute assurance" (*Reflections* 253) nothing compassionate or nobly poetic, which would merely be banal. And as quoted by Benjamin, too, that world-disturbing assurance was also recognized by Brecht, whose own Epic drama was indebted to Kraus: "When the age laid hands upon itself, he was the hands" (253).

Almost eight hundred pages long, with about five hundred characters, from Kaiser Wilhelm to the Grumbler, and the whole of Europe onstage, Kraus's cyclopean play begins with the voice of a newsboy on the Ringstrasse and ends with a pile of unburied, rotting corpses, in a kind of Walpurgisnacht, with the voice of God or his Unborn Son, begging for abortion, lest he enter a "shuddering millennium," where "the air is noxious-foul," so much so, that even Death is crying offstage.[6] There are lengthy arguments—about the press, imagination, language, war, religion, sex, psychoanalysis, acting, the telephone, Goethe, marriage, revolution, the sins of the planet, science, cataclysm: almost anything you could think about, with quotations and other borrowings—between an Optimist and the Grumbler, no doubt representing Kraus, and there's no more time here than there's likely to be in the theater to review what it's all about, either the multifarious debates or the plotless plot, which Kraus himself said were really "intended for a theater on Mars," since "theatergoers in this world would not be able to endure it" (preface, *Last Days* 3). Or as the Grumbler says, with the drama coming to an end (in scene 54 of act 5, condensed edition): "I preserve documents for a time that will no longer comprehend them or will be so far removed from today that it will say I was a forger. But no, the time to say that will not come. For such time will not be. I have written a tragedy, whose perishing hero is mankind, whose tragic conflict, the conflict between the world and nature, has a fatal ending. Alas, because this drama has no actor other than all mankind, it has no audience!" (*Last Days* 195).

As it turned out, Kraus himself was the solution to that, if not the Final Solution, as in the magnitude of his convictions, he was willing to take on the burden of *being* all mankind, becoming that actor in another kind of performance. I mean those public readings, which by all accounts were electrifying, mesmerizing, as he dominated from a lectern, with the visionary fervor of his masterful vocalizations, and what appeared to be a mimetic genius, so superior, he may have felt, to other actors, that he even refused eminent directors like Max Reinhardt and Erwin Piscator, when they requested permission to stage the play. As the setting has been described, with no surrounding lights, only a lamp tightly focused over a green-colored table, Kraus would appear from behind a folding screen, and with seemingly shy, quick steps position himself at the table. And then when he started to read, with accelerating passion, or painful condemnation, his clenched fist might tremble, like the rod of wrath itself, then something melodious, as from a folk song, before a cyclonic eruption, blows cutting the air[7]—and as if he were the one who remembered what Artaud declared actors had forgotten, or what Kokoschka really wanted, the *Schrei,* the scream, inseparable from the Word. As if some madness were really truer than life, there he was in those readings, ready to tear himself apart, that shuddering millennium over, and no wonder Death is crying.

What we may gather from reports about the excitement of those readings is that Kraus, at least in his own imagination, had not only defied the higher powers, but into the capacious polemic of his world-historical mind had annexed the infernal regions. As for the actual, bodily tearing apart, that had to wait for the Viennese Actionists, who did so for other reasons, death-defying too, while aware that the staging of risk, and self-inflicted wounds, has a long history in the arts, and art's consciousness of politics, and often, as in Austria, its subservience to religion. In that reverential context, the Crucifixion was certainly the model for any extremities of performance, especially for Nitsch, a Catholic, who in one early event, not quite ready for being nailed to the cross, had himself impaled on a wall in Otto Mühl's apartment, the act done in front of a white cloth, with the sacrificial figure in a white alb-like shift, and Mühl pouring blood over him. They were, after all, still painters, even if objects were projecting from the frame. As for other risks the Actionists were willing to inflict upon themselves—razored flesh, ripping off a fingernail, or wrapped in cloth, like Schwarzkögler, to the point of suffocation—if the motives were to begin with aesthetic and political, there was, if not a divinity that shaped their ends, surely affinities with the self-flagellation of saints, or using the whip for initiation, as a symbolic means or, with emblematic scars, the sanction of purification, which Nitsch was ready to provide, with ritual slaughter too, in the Orgies Mysteries Theater.

As he saw it, felt it, the bodily sensation of the carcass wet with blood was not only a return to the primordial and mythical, but an epistemological admission of orgiastic impulses in the repressed nature of being. As for the sacrificial Lamb, if the symbolism was religious, the terminal points for Nitsch were related, psychoanalytically, to sublimations and suppressions. Overcoming them was, of course, reason for celebration, and thus the direct experience and sensuosity of sacrifice, the bloodbath of being itself, was orchestrated at the Orgies Mysteries Theater, with what was known in the sixties, with theater spilling into the streets, as a "participatory mystique." But this was Austria, still, and the mystique came from other sources. With the theater becoming a festival, tables were set with food and wine, for eating, drinking, conversation, while Nitsch split open fish, poured fluids on objects and table cloths, eviscerated lambs, performed ritual ablutions, abreactions—in a *Gesamtkunstwerk* extension of that isolated moment, in 1962, when he had himself crucified. The crucifixion, too, was reenacted, and the spillings of blood, but if all of that came later, at no small cost—at his castle in Prinzendorf, a short ride from Vienna—it might be said that the eventual commodification, in the festivities there, has become the fate of art, even at its extremities, as if that were the end of modernism, what it was destined to be.

But in the beginning, the hallowed beginning, and speaking of destiny, as anciently conceived, it's as if the Actionists had taken over Plato's Cave, driven out whoever gazed at the shadow on the wall, or the shadow's shadow, then turned and looked directly into the fire—what they named "Direct Art"—to extinguish it by outdoing it, even burning flesh, and in that defiant regard reauthorizing art, retarded as it was in Vienna, even Art Informel. Insular as it may seem in retrospect, as if still in the Cave, Viennese Actionism was actually quite cosmopolitan, well aware of the art world elsewhere, not only performatively, as in happenings or Fluxus, collapsing the distance between art and life, but at another level of sophistication, in their own painting and sculpture, where they were determined not to be outdone by the avant-garde, in whatever new directions, Arte Povera, Nouveau Realisme, Pop Art, No-Art, Art Brut, or the activism of Joseph Beuys. I've already mentioned Jackson Pollock, and his pouring gestures in an Action field, but there was the more conceptualist, enigmatic Jasper Johns: his beer can, for instance—a painted can? or a painting in the form of a can? That, for the Actionists, with a theoretical disposition, was of epistemological interest.

As they proceeded, then, to deploy similar enigmas in their own Direct Art, there was nevertheless an uncomfortable issue—that is, for the viewer—as to whether that's feces or mud, or something other of brown color, that is being eaten. Or is that fresh blood or some thickened liquid, colored red, that is being spilled on the table cloth, when dinner is being served, and a course coming up, looking succulent, but maybe tasting like shit? Or that artwork on the body, an apparent incision there: is it a wound or a painted line? So, too, their desire for an art destroying art was related to the contradictory practice of Arnulf Rainer, who in 1953 had described his overpaintings as "painting in order to abandon painting" (qtd. in Klocker 101). And if they were going to abandon it, for a sadomasochistic, sacrilegious, performative praxis brutalizing the artist, the purpose was, once more, to reach that infernal region, the recesses of the unconscious, in what they came to think of as an archaeology of the unconscious, or archaeological existentialism—but as if the existential could only exist in an abyss of pure sensation.

Let us not be mistaken, however: the experiments of the Actionists, in all their culture shock and uninhibited disposition, were not exempt from the most venerable of Viennese traditions, which is to say there was splenetic outrage and protest, and on more than one occasion the Actionists sent to prison. It was rather astonishing, then, when in 1988, Franz Vanitzky, chancellor of Austria, attended the opening of "Action Painting Actionism Vienna, 1960–65," in Kassel, Germany. That was quite a turnaround for any government official, since twenty years earlier, in 1968—the year of dissidence in much of Europe—one of the Actionists was sentenced for the desecration of state symbols in the exhibition "Art and Revolution." What Günter Brus did in a performance, after cutting his thigh with a razor blade, was to urinate into a glass, and then drank from it, and while rubbing excrement onto his body, he also masturbated—all rather conventional actions for the Actionists, except that the masturbation was inspired, rhythmically, by his singing of the Austrian national anthem.

What he succeeded in doing was what Hermann Bahr had urged upon the Secessionists; he had made himself despised. Calling himself—after the uproar and calumny that followed the performance—the most hated Austrian, he and his family went to live in Berlin. Even before that, however, as Brus passed from explosive "self-paintings," like bomb bursts, to even more radical psychodramatic actions, he was forced to go underground into a virtual subculture, of which he wrote, about the high fines and prison sentences: "the Austrian believes that what is new and unusual must be prohibited. The Austrian isn't dumb, but . . . [the] incapacity of most Austrians to have their own or new thoughts is the consequence of fearing authority, which is probably due less to Kaiser Franz Josef than to the detrimental influence of the Alps. True is moreover: who in Austria is not criminal is a policeman" (qtd. in Klocker 100). If it was in Brus's nature early on to defy the police, he could also disdain the Junge Generation Gallery, which was equivocating about his work and wondering, if it were shown, whether it could be aesthetically justified. Whereupon Brus conceived *The Vienna Walk,* in which completely painted in white, and with a black line down his face and body, dividing it in half, he walked through the middle of Vienna as a living picture. As for the various actions of self-mutilation, he summed up the radicality thus:

> I lie in white in a white bedroom.
> I lie in white in a white toilet.
> I sit white in a white police office among white policeman. . . .

> I preach in a white church white in white.
>
> I dissever my left hand. Somewhere lies a foot. A suture on my wristjoint bone. I press a drawing-pin into my spinal cord. I nail my large toe to my forefinger. Pubic, underarm and head hairs lie on a white plate. I slit open the aorta with a razor blade (Smart). I slam a wire-tack into my ear. I split my head lengthwise into two halves. I insert barbed wire into my urethra and by turning it slightly try to cut the nerve (autosystoscopy). I bite open my pimple and suck on it. I have everything photographed and viewed. (Qtd. in Klocker 118)

Photographs are fine, and there are those—like some of the Actionists, or the body artist Stelarc, who suspends himself from fishhooks inserted into his flesh—that you can hardly bear to look at. Yet there's always something tempting about sticking your finger into a wound, and I'd like to examine in detail more of the catatonic paroxysms of Brus; or the hermetically shamanistic fastings of Schwarkogler, or the synesthesia of his alchemical isolations (or the rumor of his committing suicide in an event, by methodically cutting off his penis); or the analytical self-extinctions of Mühl; or return again to the festivities at the Orgies Mysteries Theater, as it confiscates ceremonies of the Catholic Church, including the Eucharist, as if for Satanic purposes or a Black Mass. But as with the compendious drama of Kraus, there's hardly time for the harrowing conceptualism and vicissitudes of it, and I'm running over my time. So let me end with an anecdote, which returns us also to the issue of commodification—all the more in a global economy, what appears to be the fate of art:

Some years ago, when I was giving a series of lectures in Vienna, a former student of mine, Hubert Klocker—one of the major curators of Austrian art, and surely the foremost authority on Viennese Actionism—wanted me to meet Hermann Nitsch, and drove me out to Prinzendorf Castle. Nitsch still conducted the festival, but he was also back to painting, and indeed, later in Munich, I saw an exhibition of his work, large impressive canvases, at a major museum there—he was being presented then as Austria's foremost painter. On the way to the castle we were passed in an instant, by a speeding black Lamborghini, no question, a rich man's car. Hubert's car wasn't bad either, and we made our way to Prinzendorf, where Nitsch greeted us, and before lunch, which he'd prepared himself, showed us over the grounds, pointing out where the various rituals took place, including one that couldn't. Nitsch, still a Catholic, intended to marry, in a ceremony he had conceived, and for which he had built a chapel with an altar—not exactly to orthodox specifications. When a priest went out to assess that structure (really a sculpture), the church forbade the marriage, and almost excommunicated him. After he crossed himself at the altar, and closed the chapel door, we went back to the castle, and were about to be served lunch, when there was a knock at the door. Nitsch excused himself, and said there was an Italian there—sure enough, the man in the black Lamborghini, who had lost his way—and somebody had arranged for him to look at the paintings in Nitsch's studio, up above. Hubert and I were reminiscing about the Viennese Actionists, when about twenty minutes later, Nitsch came down, the Lamborghini speeding away, and he said that he'd sold a painting, for enough to pay the annual salary of anybody here in the room. Lunch was served, something roasted. No shit.

NOTES

1. In the preface to a memoir, Marjorie Perloff writes about her Jewish family in Vienna that it "was wholly assimilated," with many of her relatives "having been baptized as Catholics or Protestants early in the century." Anti-Semitism, she adds, "especially for my mother's prominent family, the Schüllers, was something that concerned *other people;* indeed, they were not free of anti-Semitism themselves" (xiv).

2. The epigraph is on the title page.

3. See Virilio.

4. On this issue, see Bennett 103.

5. Qtd. by Bettelheim in his essay "Freud's Vienna" (9), which is focused on the morbid dynamic of sex and destruction, with reference to Weininger and the sad unwilling empress, the beauteous Elizabeth.

6. Kraus, *Last Days* 237. This translation is also a considerably abridged version of the play.

7. I am indebted to, and have improvised upon, the description of Frederick Ungar, in his introduction (*Last Days* x). When he was twenty years old, Ungar attended one of Kraus's readings, and so long as he was in Vienna rarely missed any others.

WORKS CITED

Benjamin, Walter. *Reflections: Essays, Aphorisms, Autobiographical Writings.* Ed. Peter Demetz. Trans. Edmond Jephcott. New York: Harvest / Harcourt Brace, 1978.

Bennett, Benjamin. *The Theater as Problem: Modern Drama and Its Place in Literature.* Ithaca: Cornell University Press, 1990.

Bernhard, Thomas. *The Hunting Party.* Trans. Gitta Honegger. *Performing Arts Journal* 13, 5.1 (1980): 101–31.

Bettelheim, Bruno. *Freud's Vienna and Other Essays.* New York: Knopf, 1990.
Blau, Herbert. *The Audience.* Baltimore: Johns Hopkins University Press, 1990.
Blau, Herbert. *The Impossible Theater: A Manifesto.* New York: Macmillan, 1964.
Freud, Sigmund. *The Interpretation of Dreams.* Trans. and ed. James Strachey. New York: Avon, 1965.
Handke, Peter. "Note on *Offending the Audience* and *Self-Accusation.*" In *Kaspar and Other Plays.* Trans. Michael Roloff. New York: Farrar, Straus and Giroux, 1969. ix.
Hofmannsthal, Hugo von. *Selected Plays and Libretti.* Ed. Michael Hamburger. New York: Pantheon, 1963.
Klocker, Hubert, ed. *Wiener Aktionisme / Viennese Aktionism, Wien/Vienna 1960–71: Der zertrümmerte Spiegel / The Shattered Mirror—Günter Brus, Otto Mühl, Hermann Nitsch, Rudolf Schwarzkögler.* Klagenfurt: Ritter Verlag, 1988. This volume includes essays by Klocker and the Actionists, and was edited in cooperation with Graphische Sammlung Albertina, in Vienna, and the Museum Ludwig, in Cologne.
Kokoschka, Oskar. *Sphinx and Strawman, a Curiosity.* Trans. Victor H. Meisel. In Henry J. Schvey, *Oskar Kokoschka: The Painter as Playwright.* Detroit: Wayne State University Press, 1982. Appendix C, 141–44.
Kraus, Karl. *The Last Days of Mankind: A Tragedy in Five Acts.* Trans. Alexander Gode and Sue Ellen Wright. Ed. Frederick Ungar. New York: Ungar, 1974.
Nestroy, Johann. *The Talisman.* Trans. and adapt. Max Knight and Joseph Fabry. In *An Anthology of Austrian Drama.* Ed. Douglas A. Russell. London: Associated University Press, 1982.
Perloff, Marjorie. *The Vienna Paradox: A Memoir.* New York: New Directions, 2003.
Selz, Peter. *German Expressionist Painting.* Berkeley: University of California Press, 1957.
Steinberg, Michael P. *Austria as Theater and Ideology: The Meaning of the Salzburg Festival.* Ithaca: Cornell University Press, 1990; new preface, 2000.
Virilio, Paul. *Speed and Politics: An Essay on Dromology.* Trans. Mark Polizzotti. New York: Semiotext(e), 1986.

FIVE

Performing in the Chaosmos

Farts, Follicles, Mathematics, and Delirium in Deleuze

LET'S BEGIN WITH THE BASICS: "It breathes, it heats, it eats. It shits and fucks." Sounds like the body, which in a conventional theater may have no trouble breathing or eating, or in various ways heating up, from the weight of a period costume, or angrily, passionately, or more or less imperceptibly, as in a staged embrace. But shitting and fucking, well, except in way-out kinds of performance, or scandalous body art, they're more likely to be *represented,* and where shitting is concerned, even compared to fucking, it's going to be in the wings, and even muted there, that is, the farting and plopping. Back in the theater of ancient Rome, where unsuspecting actors were actually crucified, and sexual intercourse performed without faking it—in festive diversions from the comedies of Terence—it may have been right out there in the open, even elimination, the body or its waste. But now, whether we see it, whether we don't, what we may think of as a natural "function" is not that at all, or so we're told in the *Anti-Oedipus,* by Deleuze and Guattari: wherever we do it, whatever it is, even the eating or shitting is everywhere machines, "real ones, not figurative ones" (and nothing like "*the* id," that egregious mistake of Freud), machines driving machines, however coupled, however connected, or spilling out of the sac, one producing a flow, menstrual, sperm, urine, that the other interrupts, "an organ-machine . . . plugged into an energy-source-machine." There is, to be sure, an uncertainty principle too, as with the anorexic at the mother's breast, whose mouth is wavering between several functions, not knowing "whether it is an eating-machine, an anal-machine, a talking-machine, or a breathing-machine." And if here we're inclined to worry, because of "asthma attacks,"[1] in Deleuze's view of performance that's not at all undesirable, indeed producing desire, whether wheezing, rasping, gasping, spitting up, the bronchial autoerotic, in the nonmimetic effluvium of a delirious scene.

There is in the machinic wavering a prankish perversity (once called "polymorphous") that emerged in an era of fetishized *play.* And even now, about the *Anti-Oedipus,* Foucault's prefatory warning serves: "The book often leads us to believe it is all fun and games, when something else essential is taking place."[2] What's taking place has to do, as Foucault said, with tracking down fascisms, not only those responsible for our genocidal history, but the petty ones that, in the paranoia-machine after 9/11, still constitute the embittering tyranny of everyday life. In a later book, Deleuze separated his own writing into *Essays Critical and Clinical,* but even there, in the space-*between,* where (we're told) the god of theater presides, the vigilant Dionysus, over the "*trajectories and becomings,*"[3] the implications for performance seem what they always were, the autoerotic on automatic in runaway machines, given over to pure expenditure in the libidinal economy—which doesn't seem much concerned, as on Wall Street today, with the prospect of recession, or stagflation. Yet, while "continually producing production,"[4] these amniotic desiring-machines, with their pure naked intensities globalizing delirium, are by no means part of the production apparatus of the bourgeois theater, about which Deleuze was even more jaundiced than Brecht—and so, too, about the dramaturgy of the unconscious, its Freudian mise-en-scène, which Deleuze restaged in his essay "What Children Say" as a "milieu" of subjectivity, a subversive labyrinth confounding the Oedipal structure, with wandering lines, loops, reversals, and unpredictable "singularities."

In this milieu, where "it is not a matter of searching for an origin, but of evaluating *displacements,*" parents find themselves positioned "in a world . . . not derived from them"[5]—mommy and daddy mere walk-ons in a dominant children's theater. With the enlivening performativity of their hand-flapping forgettings and rockabye repetitions, "nothing is more instructive than the paths of autistic children,"[6] the stammering, stuttering, tantrums, and babbling echolalia—as if the primal prototype for the vocal experiments and body language of the clamorous 1960s. As for the multiplicities, disjunctures, flows, inconsequent juxtapositions, subtractions, and amputations—cannibalizing the body, putting its organs up for grabs—they still seem fun and games, while acquiring an ecstatic mission from the messianism of Artaud. It's as if Artaud's Cruelty, with the metastasizing rapture of its miraculated intensities, totalized in the Plague, were absorbed into the Deleuzian *chaosmos* as another universe. If we can put anything of such dimensions into a philosophical perspective, it was the chaosmos that, according to Deleuze, superseded the world, by disrupting the preestablished harmony (defined by Leibniz) of all existing things, thus emancipating the virtual into a kind of spectral history, an atemporal miasma of passing presents and dubious pasts. This in turn produced, in a performative antiaesthetic, what might be thought as a new music of the spheres, all harmony gone, but the replenishing dissonance of unresolved chords. Or descending from the spheres to *A Thousand Plateaus,* "a nonpulsed time for a floating music," in which "forms are replaced by pure modifications of speed." That's how Pierre Boulez described it, but amid the modifications, "movement and rest, speed and slowness, floating affects,"[7] the exemplary figure is John Cage, raising the question of *how* you hear them, when and what, as with the notorious performance of *4′33″* of silence—that suspended music, floating, much admired by Deleuze. We wouldn't expect, of course, that in the void of such a performance, or the performative void, nonpulsed, nonplussed, there'd be any reason for reason, but in the Deleuzian chaosmos you never rule anything out.

Having started, then, with the basics, let's space out to the cosmological: that the universe is rational, or that the idea of rationality is inherent in the cosmos, was held to be true—as we tend to forget—before or without monotheism. Pythagoras saw nature as numbers a century or so before Plato's transcendent realm of Ideal forms, those perfected circles and galaxies of which the material world is merely a flawed reflection. What's nevertheless surprising today is to encounter scientists, whether among subatomic particles or in astrophysics, whose views of an orderly universe appear to be Platonic, as when they speculate, for instance, that mathematics does not describe the universe, but rather that the universe is, by nature or design, mathematical. This would have hardly surprised Artaud, whose hallucinatory states or swarms of images in the brain, its "inexhaustible mental ratiocination,"[8] are there—as through the swirling circles and galaxies of the Balinese theater, its flights of elytra, sudden cries, detours in every direction—with a "mathematical meticulousness,"[9] without which there'd be no pure theater of Ideal forms, yet umbilical, larval, gestures made to last, "*matter as revelation.*"[10] (As for the faith-based folly of the wrong Ideal, it should be apparent that, in the "wholly materialized gravity"[11] of it all, "a new and deeper intellectuality,"[12] Artaud is not talking of Intelligent Design.) Thus, as we may gather from Stephen Hawking, in *A Brief History of Time,* which can no longer be defined by mere succession, nor space by coexistence or simultaneity, there's a mental ratiocination in *equations,* restless, heuristic, an inexhaustible desire, which won't be satisfied without a universe to describe, and with the universe at its service—and a tempting metaphysics, "like indrafts of air around these ideas,"[13]—mathematics is on fire.[14] And so it is with "Creation, Becoming, and Chaos, . . . all of a cosmic order,"[15] what Artaud insisted was the forgotten domain of theater, that temporal form in space, given to disappearance, but oneirically remembered as timeless and rehearsed again by Deleuze.

What comes as no surprise, because for him it's the wrong equation, is his attitude toward mimesis, an impediment to becoming, which is "always incomplete," no mere copy or imitation, in which *this* resembles *that,* but a process, rather, of always being formed, "a passage of Life that traverses both the livable and the lived." If there were an "objective" to becoming, as in the Stanislavski Method, the infinitive phrase would be: *to free Life* from what imprisons it. Or, at another performative level—more abstruse, but with a fastidious grammar—"to find the zone of proximity, indiscernibility, or indifferentiation where one can no longer be distinguished from *a* woman, *an* animal, or *a* molecule"[16]—the indefinite article's power "effected only if the term in becoming is stripped of the formal characteristics that make it say *the* (the animal in front of you . . .)."[17] More could be said (and I've said it) about what's inside that parenthesis, as if a proscenium theater, its unregenerate scopophilia, and what's in front of you there, visibly invisible, dying in front of your eyes. As it happens, and for all the incessant becoming, the spirals, wanderings, reversals, or ambiguous fibrillations, keeping life from being imprisoned, Deleuze has faced it, too, whatever face he put upon it: before his suicide, his own problem in breathing, and the ominous weaknesses of others, Spinoza's frailty, Nietzsche's migraines, the something in becoming that's unbearable in being (for Beckett, *the* Unnamable), whatever it is "that has put on them the quiet mark of death"[18]—the living insignia of theater, seen unseen, its troubling materialization from whatever it is it is *not.*

Are we trapped, then, by mimesis? or is becoming, really, some repetition of being? In the performativity of Deleuze, as in his prose, repetition acquires the value that the word has in French: *répétition,* rehearsal, trying this, trying that, also a form of testing, thus making something new of repetition itself. Or as Deleuze saw it in Nietzsche, each time round extracting something *other,* "the brutal form of the immediate," from the Eternal Return. Kierkegaard, too, felt the immediacy of repetition, but as an infinite power of consciousness; in Nietzsche's case, it becomes a matter of *will,* which is to be liberated "from anything which binds it by making repetition the very object of willing." In that regard, repetition would appear to be a redemptive double bind: "if we die by repetition we are also saved and healed by it."[19] For both Nietzsche and Kierkegaard, repetition is also a double condemnation, of both habit and memory, but as if condemned, then, to be free becomes the thought of the future.[20] Which doesn't quite set the stage for the theater of existentialism, as we saw it in Sartre and Camus, which is still, in dramatic form, a conventional theater of representation. What's imagined, rather, as Deleuze derives his theater of repetition from Nietzsche and Kierkegaard (though the latter's God is not exactly kin to the former's Dionysus) is a "metaphysics in motion, in action," without any mediation, "vibrations, rotations, whirlings, gravitations, dances or leaps which directly touch the mind."[21] And all of this is occurring in an empty space filled by signs, masks, "through which the actor plays a role which plays other roles,"[22] in a Big Bang of pure forces, the dynamics of space itself, spirals of color and sound, a language that speaks before and through words, gestural, spectral, phantasmic, the desiring forces of repetition with an unexpected power, yet necessarily *what it is* in the going beyond itself.

If death has its dominion, which saves and heals, it's also important to observe that Deleuze's notion of becoming as forever incomplete will have undergone a revision through the "dizzying and slippery perspective" of Artaud's alchemical theater, and its reimagining of "the Orphic Mysteries which subjugated Plato" and must have evoked, with its hallucinatory psychology, the density of it, "the passionate and decisive transfusion of matter by mind."[23] Meanwhile, in a shift from the indefinite article to the subatomic becoming, its particle physics, there is the seemingly oppositional nature of quantum mechanics, according to which randomness is all, or at least at the heart of (the) matter, those elementary particles that seem to be everywhere or anywhere, or in a Deleuzian way *nowhere,* until some mathematical measurement arrests promiscuous flux or shapes inscrutable waves, confirming the "hidden variable" theory of the later Einstein, distressed by randomness, about God not playing dice.

It might appear to be chancy still, but with "time *out of joint,*" unhinged, constituted only "*by a vertigo or oscillation,*"[24] Deleuzian performance still has, in its aleatoric vitalism, not only the clinical, but calculating moments, as in his equation for "foreign words," which are to the tower of Babel as "chains of atoms" to the periodic table.[25] If there's some guesswork in that equation, so it is, too, with the conundrums of cosmology, where "law of nature" is either deferential to "truth," mathematically down-to-earth, or for the vertigo up above, a problematic phrase. I don't want to get lost in the cosmos, where the whole world is a stage, or down there in the cellarage, its molecular substructure, but that, indeed, is how Deleuze conceives it, from the "multiplicity of nerve fibers"[26] in all of us performing to the rhizomatics of theatricality on the thousand plateaus, where each of us is several, or more, with nothing like "character" in the becoming of nonidentity, through the proliferous space of the epistemological in-between. Or rather like Genet's Grand Brothel, where life is not only a dream, but with everything betrayed at once, in the becoming of what-it-is-not, an irreverently enacted "nightmare-dream,"[27] which requires in its spatial dynamism "a double theatricality." With image compounding image in the profoundest subjectivity, thus destroying the ego, there is nothing like the extrusion of abstract ideas, which "are not dead things"—certainly not in Genet's theater, as Deleuze perceives it—but part of "a secret cipher marking the unique chance," and here we're back to "a dice throw": if God is not playing, "a Will that throws the dice."[28]

As for the scientific view of the scattering of randomness—or the compacting of it, by intensified gravity, into a black hole—we now hear of a contingency inclination to far-out inquiry, or deep within, that is neither timeless nor absolutist, and if not a secret cipher, virtually Deleuzian in its "law without law." So, too, in string theory, there is the project of "random dynamics" in which physical laws are "derived" as a consequence of "a random fundamental 'world machinery'"[29]—surely the mind-bending matrix of any desiring-machine. And I can say this because of physicists who concede that if, with all the quantum uncertainties, there *are* laws of nature, they might very well have emerged from primordial chaos by fibrils or inchling aeons of cosmological chance, what—like a Deleuzian follicle, the merest "mite" of an energy source —they call "it from bit."[30] All of this is further complicated by the web-spidering of bots in a world of information, where the intrinsic randomness is such that, on any given day, who knows (God knows?) what will turn up online: everything possible, incessant novelty and sameness at once, a fecund universe that in its digitization might be what Foucault meant when he said, "perhaps one day, this century will be known as Deleuzian."[31] Which, unfortunately, can also be profoundly boring. But such is *Life* (his capitalized version of it, revolving *it* from bit—It? [*Pause.*] It all, as Beckett might say) in the vicissitudes of the cosmos, where string theory, the alleged theory of everything under the sun, or in the eternal dark, apparently has 10^{500} solutions. If that's an Einsteinian nightmare, it disarranges, ramifies, aporetically scatters, the world of performance for Deleuze, where, of course, the law of no law *is* a law.

So it is in the theater apotheosized by Deleuze, conceived in "subtraction" by Carmelo Bene, who detested "all principles of consistency or eternity," no less "textual permanency."[32] Charged with narcissism, obscenity, blasphemous kitsch, Bene created a theater with no other purpose than the process of its creation, about which he said: "The spectacle begins and ends at the same moment it occurs."[33] For Bene, as for Deleuze—and the two of them collaborated on a book together—the birth of a possible theater requires divesting it of any complicity with power. If that sounds *echt* Brecht, the "operation" in Bene (he wouldn't use the word "technique") is not to distance by alienation, but "to *amputate* the elements of power"[34] which, even when represented critically, enforce the law, so long as theater is dependent upon the apparatus of representation. Deleuze declares that in Bene's theater representation is cut off "at the same time as the actor ceases to be an actor"; the amputation "gives birth to and multiplies something unexpected, like a prosthesis. . . . It is a theater of surgical precision,"[35] which exceeds that of the A-effect, where the actor calls attention to the fact that s/he is acting. In using the pronoun slash himself—"S/he is an operator"—Deleuze is pointing through Bene to a theater surging forward with a political function in "the strength of a becoming"; instead of magnification, as in traditional stagings of Shakespeare, "a treatment of minoration," as in Bene's subtraction of *Hamlet,* or amputation of Romeo that liberates Mercutio from a textual death into the nondying subject of quite another play. Yet there's measure for measure here, since "to minorate" is a term (Fr., *minorer*) "employed by mathematicians."[36] So, then, let's be precise: if "minority" represents "nothing regionalist, nor anything aristocratic, aesthetic, or mystical," it is not, for Deleuze, ideological either, no mere identity politics, but rather in the presentness of the presenting "a minority consciousness as a universal-becoming."[37]

With his own consciousness of the countercultural aftermath of May '68—brought on by the Living (the French said it without Theater, as if it were Life), when it disrupted the Festival of Avignon, left-wing to begin with, but becoming touristy—Deleuze concludes his defense of Bene's "operation" (he refused to be called a director) by saying, "It is truly a matter of consciousness-raising, even though it bears no relation to a psychoanalytic consciousness, nor to a Marxist political consciousness, nor even to a Brechtian one."[38] Nor does Bene have any patience with the formulas of the avant-garde; thus, the title of Deleuze's essay on the "maker," "controller," "mechanic," undeniable "protagonist," but *not* actor or director, of a minoritarian theater: "One Less Manifesto." That said, let's remember what was posited at the onset of the essay: that in giving birth to the unexpected, with no formula there, just the stammerings and variations, the theater is a "critical theater," with the fabrication of lessness (Bene's, not Beckett's): less "character," less text, no dialogue in performance, but voices superimposed, aphasic, plosive "playback," and with no drawn-out predictable plot, for audience expectations, even a populist audience (like Dario Fo's), a severe reduction of time. Bene's plays are very short, but "this critical theater is constitutive theater. Critique is a constitution."[39] Yet, swear by it as you will, whatever it is that is constituted by the groundlessness of subtraction, the haunting question remains: *why* theater, if what you're after is critique? And despite the disclaimer about the avant-garde, the Deleuzian paradox of his "One Less Manifesto" is that as he superimposes his own voice, there and elsewhere, on the stammerings, stutterings, lapses, parapraxes, aphasia, in what children say, he is not subtracting from but adding to the avant-garde legacy, even the Ubuesque (Bene staged Jarry's play), and when autistic, there is not only futurist noise, but—along with Tzara's manifesto that disavows manifestos—some Dada Dada too.

Think of those "nomadic singularities" of the organless body, its "mad or transitory particles," or the follicles of strata on the thousand plateaus, where "God is a lobster" (like Ubu?), "double pincer, double bind."[40] The double bind is that the pincer seems derived from the futurist Marinetti's "fiscofollia," or "body madness,"[41] while the feverish insomnia of his Variety Theater, with nothing impelling performance but a logic of sensation, sets out the game plan for Deleuze's "phantasmaphysics," the term created by Foucault for precisely that logic, its "fibrils and bifurcation,"[42] which return us through a "reversed Platonism," or converted, subverted, perverted, to an insidious displacement within. In searching out, within the Platonic milieu, ascending to purest Form, then descending to "its smallest details, . . . as far as its crop of hair or the dirt under its fingernails—those things that were never hallowed by an idea,"[43] we come upon those again who wouldn't know it if they had one, and hallowed by Deleuze for that. There, in that impromptu nether region, antidoxological, diapered, undiapered, the milieu of infantility, the reversal occurs at that other orifice, the mouth, "the canal where the child intones the simulacra, the dismembered parts, and bodies without organs, the mouth in which depths and surfaces are articulated." And then moving into the nexus between futurist performance—its *Zang-Tumb-Tumb* (*parole in libertà*) or its machinic "noise"—and the "indescribable vibration"[44] of the alchemy of Artaud, requiring an actor who has not forgotten how to scream: "The mouth where cries are broken into phonemes, morphemes, semantemes: the mouth where the profoundity of an oral body separates itself from incorporeal meaning,"[45] as in "the complete, sonorous, streaming naked realization" of the theater of Cruelty.[46]

Phonemes, semantemes, whatever the realization, this is not quite the Mouth of Beckett's *Not I,* where the orifice, the canal, is a "godforsaken hole," with the "speechless infant" there, "parents unknown . . . unheard of,"[47] and speaking of machines, "the whole machine," asking the mouth to stop, "and the whole brain begging,"[48] maybe to end desire, desire not desiring, "the words . . . the brain . . . flickering away like mad . . . quick grab and on,"[49] which suggests that even delirium has its critical variations, as it does even in Brecht. As regards that canal, or other forsaken hole, Deleuze might have been more responsive to the early Brecht's *Baal,* and the corrosive seriality of its orgiastic hero, who lives deliriously by nature or choice, and with cruelty too, flaunts his nakedness and vice, always ready to "Have some fun or bust! / What you wish, says Baal, is what you must! / And your shit's your own, so sit and have a ball."[50] Here, too, the warped appearance of fun and games, the elephantiasis of it, with Baal outdoing Ubu, bloated in copulation, could be misunderstood, as it apparently was when the play was first produced. The filthy behavior of Baal, unconscionable, even murderous, had, according to Brecht, its political agenda, his worst reflexes mirroring what was worse: again an equation of fascism with the tyranny of everyday life, and what in compliance or self-contempt we imposed upon ourselves. Or, ready to scream, life as a piece of shit, holding it all in.

"Why such a dreary parade of sucked-dry, catatonicized, vitrified, sewn-up bodies," wrote Deleuze with Guattari, having just invoked Artaud's declaration of war against organs—"*To be done with the judgment of God,*" which will not even let you "experiment in peace." In their judgment—like another manifesto, in *A Thousand Plateaus*—all kinds of experimentation, "not only radiophonic, but also biological and political [incurred] censorship and repression," whereas "the BwO is also full of gaiety, ecstasy, and dance." And so it was in the sixties, that paradisal era of the "*hypochondrial body,*" "*the schizoid body,*" "*the drugged body,*" "*the masochist body,*"[51] sodomized too, in the "epidermic play of perversity," or the new dispensation of Sade, where "a dead God and sodomy are the thresholds of a new metaphysical ellipse."[52] The ellipse was a trajectory through the chaosmos, with a celebrative detour through the theater: the Living, the Open, the Ontological-Hysteric, Grotowski's psychophysics, the enraptured stasis and distensions in the stagings of Robert Wilson, *Dionysus in 69* at the Performance Garage, and with "the door off its hinges,"[53] as if Deleuze had loosened a screw, the audience dancing out, taking over performance, in a participatory mystique, drugged out, even fucking, right there on the streets.

What followed in the academy, for over a generation, was a discourse on the body, the all-knowing body, which brought performance to theory, but increasingly ideologized, with deference to sex and gender, race, class, ethnicity. Not all of it was in extremis, like the *Anti-Oedipus,* where the mystique was really contingent upon a derangement of body and thought, as if the asyntactic delirium, its fractures and disjunctures, or schizoid *jouissance,* were what T. S. Eliot never imagined or dared when, with the advent of high modernism, he recovered the metaphysical poetry of the seventeenth century, albeit with mixed feelings about its "dissociation of sensibility." For the emotions they had in mind, Deleuze and Guattari, there was nothing like an "objective correlative," the absence of which, for Eliot, made *Hamlet* an artistic failure. As for Bene's *Hamlet,* its subtraction, his "one less *Hamlet,*"[54] it might have been a prosthesis, claiming nonrepresentation, but whatever there was on stage, or amputated there, it was unlikely to be the correlative of the performative body in the imaginary of Deleuze. Or that banished Oedipal body, not-there in wish fulfillment. "Is it really so sad and dangerous," we were asked in *A Thousand Plateaus,* "to be fed up with seeing with your eyes, breathing with your lungs, swallowing with your mouth, talking with your tongue, thinking with your brain, having an anus and larynx, head and legs?"[55] Sadly perhaps, though up for danger, when this ethos came on the scene, I was sufficiently aligned with Brecht to concur with his Galileo, when he said in defense of reason, though not unsensory, that he believed in the brain. Which with all the fibrillations, ventricles, basal ganglia, within the arachnoid mater—the membrane that covers the cerebral cortex—is hardly disembodied.

So it was in the "ghosting" and "burrowing" of my KRAKEN group,[56] where we were susceptible to, even impassioned, by a synesthesia of organs and body parts, like listening with a kneecap, humming with a thumb, the eyelids avid as taste buds, images there in your gut, or for that shitty matter, no mere fun and games, lifting the elbow to let out a fart. "Why not walk on your head," was the early Deleuzian challenge, "sing with your sinuses, see through your skin, breathe with your belly: the simple thing, the Entity, the full Body, the stationary Voyage, Anorexia, cutaneous vision, Yoga, Krishna, Love, Experimentation."[57] We were not all that countercultural, but indeed, we did it all: instead of Yoga, I taught the Tai Chi Ch'uan, and the actors in the group could perform through contortions or backflips or, with stammerings, stutterings, howls (indeed, I was an "expert witness" at the *Howl* trial), up the nose, down the lungs, corporeal incantations, off-the-wall explosive sounds, with text, without text, but eventually back to words—words

words words—complexly associational, an always elliptical score, while standing on their heads, or speaking of "playback," with ideographic acrobatics and choral precision too, in a surge of disparate voices, high-pitched, guttural, logorrheic machines, or machine-gunned utterance, as fast as words could move, with syllables divided across the length of the playing space, not randomly, by chance, but in the mathematics of ghosting, with exactitude.

Words, body, playback, it was certainly autoerotic, but inquisitional too. And there was method in the madness: at whatever selvage of feeling, in the linguistic abyss or derangement, it was still a matter of *thought*—that thinking with the body, which internalizes delirium or projects hallucination, without indulging fantasy (the vice of psychoanalysis, according to Deleuze) nor the programmatic (his name for experimentation which is antipsychiatric). What we were doing might, in the hysterical passing from one code to another, scramble all the codes, but the burrowing (Kafkesque) or the ghosting (Hamletic) was a rigorous way of knowing, a formation of ideas, with shifts of singularity and multiple affect, but when push came to shove, at the extremity of performance, where there were actual bodily and psychic risks—the actor could really get hurt—the commitment was conceptual, we wanted to *understand,* whatever the psychophysics, with belief in the brain.

Thus, as others have written about it, my difference with Deleuze. But with difference and repetition, it could be a subtle difference. "Give me a body then," wrote Deleuze, with his eye on film, in *Cinema 2*. "This is the formula of philosophical reversal. The body is no longer the obstacle which separates thought from itself, that which it has to overcome to reach thinking. It is on the contrary that which it plunges into or must plunge into, in order to reach the unthought, that is life. Not that the body thinks, but obstinate and stubborn, it forces us to think, and forces us to think what is concealed from thought, life."[58] But here's the difference: what forces us to think even more is that it *remains* concealed, which thus gives life to (the) theater, which wouldn't exist if you could see it; that is, if the absence of transparency weren't, through some ontological fault of becoming, in every fiber, follicle, nerve end of being—where the truth of the matter is, "*matter as revelation,*" we can't tell *it* from *bit.* And that will be no less true, with all those *bytes,* in the age of information.

As for the BwO, that legacy from Artaud—"*No mouth. No tongue. No teeth. No larynx. No esophagus. No belly. No anus*"—it is like Nietzsche's Dionysus, *essentially* imageless, having nothing to do with the body itself, 'nor what remains of a lost totality."[59] And since it's not a projection, resisting being imaged, it can't it be represented, though somewhere there's "a God at work" with the intention of "messing it all up or strangling it by organizing it."[60] Well, let it be blessed by the truer God of Artaud—but despite the ecstatic vanity of his vision of an antitheater, its excruciating mystery, with apparitions from beyond, there is no performance without the always vulnerable, material body; or in its absence, as on an empty stage, the expectation of it, some projection of the body, as in the detritus of its absent being, mournfully there, appalling—what Beckett conveys in *Breath.* If the body without organs is the body without an image, model of "the death instinct," as Deleuze insists, he also insists "that is its name, and death is not without a model. For desire desires death also, . . . just as it desires life, because the organs of life are the *working machine.*"[61] Whatever the model may be, it has been said about death that it can't be represented, but if you think of it in the theater it can only be represented. As for the machine, whatever it may be desiring, it works *as theater* only with the body there—even in its absence, you can smell it in the wings, that smell of mortality, which may come upon us in delirium, as with King Lear on the heath; or surreptitiously, insidiously, as in Strindberg's *Ghost Sonata;* or inexhaustibly in Beckett, giving birth astride of a grave. Double pincer, double bind: God may be a lobster, but "down in the hole, lingeringly, the grave-digger puts on the forceps,"[62] while reminding us that mortality is the unseeable substance of theater, there, not there, which in the consciousness of its vanishing endows it with Life.

NOTES

1. Gilles Deleuze and Félix Guattari, *Anti-Oedipus: Capitalism and Schizophrenia,* trans. Robert Hurley, Mark Seem, and Helen R. Lane (New York: Viking Press, 1977) 1.

2. Michel Foucault, preface to *Anti-Oedipus* xlv.

3. Gilles Deleuze, "What Children Say," in *Essays Critical and Clinical,* trans. Daniel W. Smith and Michael A. Greco (Minneapolis: University of Minnesota Press, 1997) 67.

4. Deleuze and Guattari, *Anti-Oedipus* 7.

5. Deleuze, *Essays Critical and Clinical* 61–62.

6. Ibid. 61.

7. Gilles Deleuze and Félix Guattari, *A Thousand Plateaus: Capitalism and Schizophrenia,* trans. Brian Massumi (Minneapolis: University of Minnesota Press, 1987) 267.

8. Antonin Artaud, "On the Balinese Theater," in *The Theater and Its Double,*

trans. Mary Caroline Richards (New York: Grove Press, 1958) 63. All references to Artaud will be from this text, with titles of essays given.

9. Ibid. 57.

10. Ibid. 59.

11. Ibid. 65.

12. Artaud, "The Theater of Cruelty (First Manifesto)" 91.

13. Ibid. 90.

14. Stephen Hawking, *A Brief History of Time* (New York: Bantam, 1998).

15. Artaud, "Cruelty (First Manifesto)" 91.

16. Deleuze, "Literature and Life," in *Essays Critical and Clinical* 1.

17. Ibid. 2.

18. Deleuze and Guattari, *What Is Philosophy,* trans. Hugh Tomlinson and Graham Burchell (New York: Columbia University Press, 1994) 172.

19. Deleuze, *Difference and Repetition,* trans. Paul Patton (London: Continuum, 2004) 6.

20. Ibid. 8.

21. Ibid.

22. Ibid. 11.

23. Artaud, "The Alchemical Theater" 52.

24. Deleuze, "On Four Poetic Formulas That Might Summarize the Kantian Philosophy," in *Essays Critical and Clinical* 31.

25. Deleuze, "Louis Wolfson; or, The Procedure," in *Essays Critical and Clinical* 17.

26. Deleuze and Guattari, *Thousand Plateaus* 8.

27. Deleuze, "The Shame and the Glory: T. E. Lawrence," in *Essays Critical and Clinical* 117.

28. Ibid. 119–20.

29. Dennis Overbye, "Laws of Nature, Source Unknown," *New York Times,* December 18, 2007, *Science Times,* D4.

30. Ibid.

31. Michel Foucault, "Theatrum Philosophicum," in *Language, Counter-Memory, Practice: Selected Essays and Interviews,* ed. Donald F. Bouchard, trans. Bouchard and Sherry Simon (Ithaca: Cornell University Press, 1977) 165.

32. Gilles Deleuze, "One Less Manifesto," in *Mimesis, Masochism, & Mime: The Politics of Theatricality in Contemporary French Thought,* ed. Timothy Murray, trans. Eliane dal Molin and Murray (Ann Arbor: University of Michigan Press, 1997) 240.

33. Quoted by Deleuze, ibid.

34. Ibid. 241.

35. Ibid. 239.

36. Ibid. 243.

37. Ibid. 255–56.

38. Ibid. 256.

39. Ibid. 239.

40. Deleuze and Guattari, *Thousand Plateaus* 40.

41. Filippo Tommaso Marinetti, "The Variety Theater," in *Futurist Performance,* ed. Michael Kirby, trans. Victoria Nes Kirby (New York: PAJ Publications, 1986) 183.

42. Foucault, "Theatrum Philosophicum" 166.

43. Ibid. 168.

44. Artaud, "Alchemical Theater" 52.

45. Foucault, "Theatrum Philosophicum" 179.

46. Artaud, "Alchemical Theater" 52.

47. Samuel Beckett, "Not I," in *Collected Shorter Plays* (New York, Grove Press, 1984) 216.

48. Ibid. 220.

49. Ibid. 222.

50. Bertolt Brecht, prologue to *Baal,* trans. Eric Bentley and Martin Esslin, in *Baal, A Man's A Man,* and *The Elephant Calf,* ed. Bentley (New York: Grove Press, 1964) 21.

51. Deleuze and Guattari, *Thousand Plateaus* 150.

52. Foucault, "Theatrum Philosophicum" 171.

53. Deleuze, "Four Poetic Formulas" 27.

54. Carmelo Bene, quoted by Deleuze, "One Less Manifesto" 239.

55. Deleuze and Guattari, *Thousand Plateaus* 150–51.

56. See chapters 3–5 of my book *Take Up the Bodies: Theater at the Vanishing Point* (Urbana: University of Illinois Press, 1982).

57. Ibid. 151.

58. Deleuze, *Cinema 2: The Time-Image,* trans. Hugh Tomlinson and Robert Galeta (Minneapolis: University of Minnesota Press, 1989) 189.

59. Artaud, quoted by Deleuze and Guattari, *Anti-Oedipus* 8.

60. Ibid. 9.

61. Ibid. 8.

62. Beckett, *Waiting for Godot* (New York: Grove Press, 1954) 58.

SIX

Seeming, Seeming

The Illusion of Enough

> What was to be done? or, if nothing could be done, was there anything further that I could *assume* in the matter?
> —HERMAN MELVILLE, *Bartleby the Scrivener*

WHEREVER IT COMES FROM, morality or the aesthetic, the antitheatrical prejudice is a conceptual vanity, subject to or victimized by theater, while going through every nerve end to the dubious heart of drama, which has from whatever beginnings always distrusted the theater. I'm not merely referring here, with the author living or dead, to a certain protectionism of the text against the depredations of the stage, a tradition extending, at times with egregious vigilance, from Ben Jonson to Samuel Beckett to, recently and unexpectedly, Sam Shepard—once with-it in the counterculture, and its polymorphous perversions—who refused to allow a production of *True West,* if the combative brothers were misgendered, enacted by women. Propriety aside, and social construction, the liability of the prejudice, whose contingency is theater, is that it's constrained ontologically even before it's thought, for as Heidegger said of language, "Language itself is—language and nothing else besides. Language itself is language."[1] And though it's been institutionalized, so it appears with theater, theater itself is, tautological maybe, but in the immanence of appearance, theater itself is theater, *before* anything else, or—in a spectrum of apprehension from Plato to Genet (sainted by Sartre for sanctifying appearance)—with a duplicitous presence suffusing everything else. That may very well prompt, in the deepest sense, a desire for antitheater, which may paradoxically, in a strategic, desperate, or imperious theatricality, increase the quotient of theater, while never resolving the question of whether, in being theatrical as antitheater, it ought to be more or less.

Either way, in a superfluity of it or on a minimalist stage, theatricality *isn't,* in its containment or presumption of theater, even a shadow of it, only the merest facsimile, and even then we can't be sure; for if theater is not entropic, a sort of leak in the Real, it seems brought into being by thought—though maybe the thing itself, disappearing in the perceiving, is precisely the leak in the Real. It seems no accident that the greatest drama is obsessed with that. As it happens, the most elusively theatrical figure in the canonical drama would seem, in escaping interpretation, to have reflected on this, and if we ask the simple question, what makes theater? the answer might be Hamletic: *thinking makes it so.* What's then to be kept in mind is the theater's incipience as appearance, because we have it in mind, from whatever it is it is *not* (reality? experience? life?), as it must have been, *if it was,* before there was any theater, or precipitous semblance of it, no less anything like the notion that all the world's a stage or society of the spectacle or, making a non sequitur of antitheater, a precession of simulacra. If we're not quite at the end of the real—bereft in an imaged world, with its superfetation of signs, no referentials, no metaphysics, only the vanity of a redundancy without any substance at all, not even the imaginary substance once thought of as illusion—the undeniable truth is that we're not quite sure where we are. And so far as the theater reflects that, we're back through whatever demystifications to its ineliminable *seeming,* or in its doubling over of life, the "Seeming, seeming," distressingly seminal, as if precisely *Measure for Measure* (2.4.151), now you see it now you don't.

Insidious it may be, or a reprise of illusion, but it's not to be done away with by an alienating detachment or preemptive imitation. Nor will it be carried away or contained by a kind of Brechtian narcissism, the "ontological-hysteric" or wired-up objectification, in the theater of Richard Foreman, who's still there pulling the strings, but—even before the dominion of exacerbated digitality—with the video game momentum of somewhat robotic bodies, a little sexier now, but no way "bodies that matter."[2] If the Brechtian paradigm has receded, or is now so familiar it needs some A-effect itself, it was the theatricalization of theory that—with the materiality of the body linked to the performativity of gender—appeared to take over the *gestus,* with a parodic amplification, as in the films of John Waters and the outrageous drag of Divine. In deconstructing Austin's notion of performativity built around the marriage vow, and imitating an origin that really never was, the "corporeal style" of queer performativity—truly queer, celebrating a stigma—derides the notion of a stable or coherent, self-identical body, with a preemptive strike at specularity in a reversal of the gaze. Making a virtue of gender trouble, the bodily inscriptions of the performative are a nuance away from performance and, in its repetitive acts ("truly troubling,"[3] or so it is claimed, in the hegemony of subversion), disdainful of theater—bourgeois theater, of course, which has always distrusted itself.

As with modernist art and thought, which in the era of cultural studies has had a bad rap (masculine dominance, elitism, a depoliticizing formalism, and the emptying out of history), that apparently commodified theater seems at various levels to have anticipated its critique, as if the theater itself were proposing something like antitheater. As for the queer reversed gaze, and its subversive look at the myth of interiority, and the inside/outside binary of what became, in the Method, the actor's psychic space, it may be that its seeming seeing is something other than that. For as queer becomes method, it discovers again—as they did in painting, since Cézanne pushed his big mountain up to the picture plane—that there is no surface that doesn't recede; and if the activity of perception changes what it sees, it's in the seeing itself that interiority persists, as it always has in the theater, subvert it as you will. And so it may be, with all its sophistication, in a "discursive performativity" that, in "arguing with the real" (Butler, *Bodies* 189), confronts an impasse in the parody turning back upon itself—or, as Shakespeare says in a sonnet, with a stylish riff on delusion, "Seems seeing, but effectually is out" (Sonnet 113).

What's in, what's out is itself a dismaying problem—beyond specularity, or even the simulacra—in a dromoscopic, techno-scientific, biochemical, geneticist, informational world, with everything seeming to move, in the wake of the Enlightenment, with the speed of light or, as Paul Virilio thinks it, with "the *light of speed*."[4] Channels, screens, PCs, cell phones, satellite dishes, CDs, webs and weblogs, samplers, Ethernets: in the proliferous sensation of the multitudinous moment, the sheer repetitive promiscuity of the instantly mediated, what happens to temporality, or for that matter, materiality? Lady Macbeth wanted the future in the instant, but with so many futures in the infinity of instants, what passeth show would, if it wanted to show, already be far in the past—though a past is problematic, with the wavelengths and frequencies picking up speed. So it is, if we pick up on the velocity and go with the implications, that theater/antitheater wouldn't even be an issue, though that wouldn't necessarily relieve Michael Fried, who worried about the degeneration of art "as it approaches the condition of theater."[5] Defending an art-as-object wholly manifest in the instant, "a continual and perpetual *present*" (146) insusceptible to the attritions of time, Fried insisted on defeating theater, because it is given over to "a sense of temporality, of time both passing and to come, *simultaneously approaching and receding,* as if apprehended in an infinite perspective" (145). What is past, and passing, and to come might have been thus apprehended, when minimal art, and then conceptual art, first appeared on the scene, but if we're now amidst the megabytes, minimizing the instant and swifter than any thought, what perspective can be expected when what's coming has already passed and the simultaneity, if imaginable, is always already surpassed? So with theater/antitheater: the binary would seem to depend on a *here and now,* but we're living acceleratingly, anaphylactically, in a *then and there,* with nothing like the memory of a Bergsonian *durée,* since, in the immediacy of the remote, light-years faster than the channel changer, "speed is the old age of the world," where if you hadn't seen it all in an epiphanic flash there was hardly even an instant for now you see it now you don't.

Is this not something more than fantasy? Or if still not unfantastic, merely the virtual truth of a prospective virtual world? Maybe yes maybe no. But if Virilio is (as he would have to be, if what he's seeing is so) retrospectively prescient, then with reality "*foreclosed,*" retracted by acceleration, "out of time in the strictest sense" (Virilio 16), any apparency of the real in the form of theater would hardly be worth our attention, no more than a sheet of newspaper in a Florida hurricane. Or for that matter, the end of modernism, which like the end of history is always beginning again—not modernism, remember, but the beginning of its end.

But slowing down for a moment, *taking time* (or the restored illusion of it), in the recidivist way of rehearsal: a brief connection was made before, between modernism and the bourgeois theater, about which—as if in a matrix of anachronism and history (with the universe of the Matrix looming)—I want to say more. So far as that theater is an expressive function of modernism, it was from the beginning a good deal more conflicted, aphasic, destabilizing than, with the advent of critical theory, we've made it out to be—its gravity such, if thought, that its accretions of realism, density impacted, as if becoming a black hole, were an inside out eruption into a more far-reaching amplitude than those apparently predictable plots and box sets would seem to suggest. The atmosphere can be oppressive, but with the constraints of space and time there is, metonymically, a kind of impacted remembrance, too, opening up as in the unconscious, or as in the modernist visual arts, to the spatialization of time. If in Cubism, however, all of history appears to be there, geometrically severed, but (in the wake of Cézanne) up on the picture plane, and with an autonomy there, that would seem to be the reverse of what we have in the theater, with its proscenium arch, teasers and tormentors, surreptitious wings, and legacy of perspective. Yet I've seen productions in open spaces, indoors, outdoors, or sprawling all over somewhere, the legacy there regardless, with text, without text, even through improvisation, old outguessable reflexes, much of it banal, irredeemably locked in the brain, as if a proscenium there—though maybe a false proscenium with no perspective at all.

But "Fie upon't, foh! About my brains," putting it into the plural, as Hamlet does, as if with brain damage arrested, the gaze itself is reversed, as he turns to the "guilty creatures sitting at a play" (2.2.573–75). In a space created, it would seem, by a high-tech Mousetrap—where the watchers are watching the watchers watch—we're talking not only of *graduated* perception, but also, in reflecting that (no less reflecting upon it), unaccountable *degrees* of theater. As for the watchers in the audience, what brought them there to begin with, or—while digesting dinner, as in Brecht's jaundiced view—compels inert attention, tuning in and screening out? Well, we all know that from the plotline, which has an ancient history: appearance, disguise, concealment, the lies, deceits, the overheard, the disclosed, the mortifying confession, guilt again, the cover-up, and (what else to be expected?) the anxious relief of exposure—that suspect heritage in the bourgeois drama of the phallic Oedipal theater, all of which the new historicism or cultural materialism, or gendered or racial versions of the going revisionist Marxism, and with it antitheater, has been determined to expose. And then we go through a cycle where we want to expose the exposure. As the debates continue in theory—and now beyond theory, whose future is dubious too—no doubt about it, there is a cloud of unknowing in our now conventional theater, as if "the scene upon the stage," which Freud might have been describing in *Totem and Taboo,* "was derived from the historical scene through a process of systematic distortion—one might even say, as the product of a refined hypocrisy."[6] Or maybe, after all, not so refined. Anything can be cheapened by performance, but what's not there, and should be, preys upon the brain, all the more as you look with what, "imagination dead imagine," Beckett called "the eye of prey."[7] Is it a case of antitheater when you want to stand up and shout, "Use your brains!"

We've all heard the platitudes (and may even recite them), in courses of dramatic literature, about not knowing a play until we see it staged. But much of the time, up there, we don't see it at all, not to mention the liability—even with a fine performance, and sometimes especially so, as that gets in the way (transposed now to film/video, and frequently shown in class)—of not seeing it in multiple ways, incessantly reimagined or, as by some inquest in the cortex, otherwise rehearsed. It might be thought of as closeting the drama, or resisting theater, but I've been telling students for years (even while staging plays, and this important to the stagings) that they may engage with a play far more profoundly if they *don't* go to a production, and then, grasping my head to define it, I'd insist that the brain is the best stage of all, the most expansive, versatile, dynamic, and volatile in containment. Think of it, I'd say, that englobed space behind the eyeballs (a site of immense "confabulation," with never a repetition, "unstructured immensities," and according to "neural Darwinism," with a "value system")[8]—now that's what a theater should be! inexhaustibly ideational, with a repletion of image, as if the singular brain were fractured, dialectically plural, of untold and variable magnitude, and maybe as antitheater, where (with all the neurons working) you can see it again and again, through every (mis)apprehension, in some other heuristic form, *but not with absent vision.* (There is, as with Charles Lamb and Goethe on Shakespeare, and particularly *King Lear,* an antitheatrical precedent for keeping a play in the text and staging it in the mind, as with Gertrude Stein on reading, but that's not what I'm talking about.) Vision may be, as they say, a "transcendental signifier," but then, so be it: *for* theater, *against* theater, *it always remains to be seen,* and so it is in reimagining what we think of as bourgeois theater, which was once, however impaired, also a matter of vision—and with a materialist disposition, a vision haunted by history, and its visionary gleam.

Arising from the Enlightenment with a thwarted dialectic, it's as if it were inhabited at the outset by some ghosting imminence of Ibsen's *Ghosts,* its remorseless analytic brought to unspeakable terror, with glaciers and peaks in the background bathed in the morning light. Where Peer Gynt once was, the dead may awaken, in a kind of supertheater, site of the world beyond, but unsayable, Wagnerian, at the limit of wish fulfillment upping the ante on theatricality, but as if the subtext of Osvald's final line, "The sun—The sun,"[9] were through the syphilitic blindness a sonorous delirium. How, really, should it be staged, and in the rush of repressed memory, what kinesthetic evocations? And would they be enough? For one can imagine that at the very dawn of the Enlightenment, embodied at dawn in the Festival of Dionysus, the first primeval murmurs were heard—the proleptic soundings of a still-unending cultural hysteria—from those subhuman figures in the caves below the mountain on which, in the Aeschylean drama, the fire-giving god of forethought, Prometheus, was bound, persisting there in a "mad harmony"[10] with the punishing forces of nature, slashing winds, pitted clouds, lightning bolts, earthquakes, serving a higher power.

It may be that Shelley released him, or some revisionist production, but I wouldn't count on that. What is more likely, however, whatever we do in the theater, is that at some subliminal level all of it is remembered, all the more if resisted, and if not quite of the same dimensions, the delirium surely persists. With an ongoing animus against bourgeois theater, but nothing like Wagner's resources for hypertrophic theatricality, something like it was aroused again, in the visceral "grain of the voice," from way down in the throat, lips, tongue, glottis, teeth, the mucilaginous membranes, and scabbily out the nose,[11] by the sound/movement exercises of the 1960s, and the participatory mystique of their psychophysical clamor. As with *Dionysus in 69,* this was one of the ways in which performance, disavowing the conventional actor, mere menial of the authorized text, would "escape the tyranny of meaning" (Barthes 185), dismantling bourgeois value and—with bodies that matter naked, and more or less *jouissance*—thus transcending its theater, the mere "sensuous expression of estranged human life."[12] (Which is actually how Marx described, not irrelevantly, it would seem, the movement of production and consumption.) As for the political apotheosis of that vociferous period, there was, with bodies spelling out its title and then naked all over the stage, the Living Theater's *Paradise Now,* which also passed for the temporal instant as a sort of anarchically mesmeric, unmimetic materialism, with its libidinal economy flowing out to the streets.

In the *Economic and Philosophic Manuscripts of 1844,* Marx spoke of the senses as direct theoreticians, each of them formed by the labor of the entire history of the world (87, 89); but he had in mind another materialism, which had to bring itself first to consciousness, in a "fully-developed naturalism [that] equals humanism, and as fully-developed humanism [that] equals naturalism," only thence "*coming-to-be*" (84), through the long riddling burden of that estranging history, with paradise having to wait. And so it had been in the theater, which is in the play of appearance the form of coming-to-be, as it is—in more than etymology, and not merely with the specular gaze—also the shadow of theory, suffused with all the senses and with a sensory life. (As I used to tell my KRAKEN group, taking that as a datum, what we're doing here is *thinking,* though some might think, in a knee jerk, that's *really* antitheater.) As for performance itself, the sensuous expression of estranged life may occur with a certain dispassion, or as in the antitheater of Brecht, by estranging the estrangement; but so with Ibsen too, in a dramaturgy that was radically other, a good long way from the boulevards and the assembly-line scriptures of Scribe. And if we now think we can predict Ibsen's moves, the degrees of estrangement and passion were once, as contingencies of the perceptual, what aroused critique in the drama, while this degree or that degree, like any gesture on stage, or even an instant of held breath (not to mention Beckett's play), may at a particular moment in history determine the force of critique, which sustains itself in estrangement because, so far in history, there is no other life. As he evolved a utopian vision, Marx was very conscious of that. As for Ibsen, it adhered like a guilty thought to the most ethereal theatricality of his most symbolic plays, as it did through the grain of the voice in the organless bodies of Artaud, and—in the consummate delirium of antitheater—those immemorial incantations, prodigal in the air, also betrayed by the Real.

So, down to earth again, where the cruelties are sufficient. In a remarkable early letter, meant to deflect the Young Hegelians from "dogmatic abstraction," Marx had called for "*a ruthless critique of everything existing,*"[13] but in this regard—if they didn't quite share a politics—it was Ibsen who virtually outdid him in conducting such a critique, which is why (historicize! to be sure, but speaking of truly troubling) one of his plays was attacked as if it were Artaud's plague, as a running sore, a wound, an open drain, a cesspool. As for the dramaturgy of his realism, or the later departures from it, the paradox was that it constituted in performance, the truth of illusion there, a devastating critique of theater, along with the apparatus of representation we've been belaboring since, where the reality of appearance is confounded by the appearance of reality—though we're still not entirely sure which of those phrases ought to go first, or (though I can see everything disappearing into the velocity of the virtual) whether there's any reality at all without the duplicity of appearance. About the future of (an) illusion, it was Freud who acceded to that, after moving, in the antitheater of psychoanalysis, from the mise-en-scène of the unconscious through *Civilization and Its Discontents,* virtually admitting there, with a kind of tragic vision, that demystification had failed. Meanwhile, theater persists through antitheater like the generic ghosting in *Hamlet* through the factitiousness of the Ghost, or, with Hegel turned on his head, through the ruthless critique like "phantoms formed in the human brain" (Marx, *German Ideology,* in *Marx-Engels* 154).

It was during the period, approximately, from Freud's *Project for a Scientific Psychology* to the inconsolable prospect of unpurgeable discontents that, in a sort of Möbius warp, theater and antitheater merged in the vicissitudes of critique: from the early naturalism of Strindberg—whose preface to *Miss Julie* has a surprising Brechtian strain—to Pirandello's bewildered characters and Gertrude Stein's bewildering plays that, with elisions or traces of character, were really antiplays, where "each one is that one and that there are a number of them each one being that one"[14]—which one is only one (and, until recently, a neglected one at that) among the avatars of antitheater in the modernist avant-garde. And there were various ironies there, as in futurism's assault not only on the vacuities of boulevard theater, but also on the naturalism equaling humanism in the fully developed realism. In refusing not only the mere mimicry, but even the accomplished mimicry that—as theory sees it today—reproduced what it critiqued, Marinetti and his cohorts actually went, with all the ferocity of his manifestos, through an exponentially manic reality theater (with its own *Survivor* shows) after the manifest sublimity of a more immediate truth. It's as if he were anticipating—though, for all the ferocity, in a tamer version of less dimension—what Slavoj Žižek wrote about (with another performative put-on of his gleeful dialectic) after 9/11: the fundamentalist terror latent but secreted in the twentieth century's "passion for the Real,"[15] with martyrdom not only impassioned, but real, immediate and, guaranteed houris in heaven, sublime.

There were, to be sure, Boccioni and Carrà paintings, but the theatricalized spirit of futurism was not confined to the flat walls of museums or stage sets, but went instead (as with Tzara and Dada too), to where the real action was, in cafés and cabarets, political parlors, sporting events, the offices of hostile newspapers, or out there on the streets, where in the notorious spectacles, with no playacting, they even beat people up. And while the surrealists were enamored of dreams and the unconscious, they also broke out of the frame of painting and plinth-based art into collage, photomontage, installations, assemblage, noise and body art, environments, and, with multiple sites in the real world, not only performance art but the performance of everyday life. (As for beating people up, the only person I ever heard Beckett talk about with contempt was André Breton, because if you disagreed with him too much, he had you beaten up.) All of these, of course, are the going things today in a performative art world that—as with the blood spatterings of Istvan Kantor, or his Machine Sex Action Group, or the costumes, prosthetics, and role-playing in Matthew Barney's *Viral Infection: The Body and Its Discontents*—couldn't care less about theater. As for the traditional avant-garde, and its incursion on everyday life, they may have deranged it in the process, but what then seemed weird or strange is—on stage, off stage, even in fashion, or blockbuster shows in museums—second nature now.

Or so it is until you think about it, when it may become threatening again, like the very substance of theater, which, not unlike a viral infection, keeps itself out of sight. As for the instrumental theatricality of whatever forms of theater—the entire repertoire of representation, its originary sources or pretensions to sacred rites—that was later exposed by exploitation demonically in Genet, who, as if nurtured by infections, sustains in the theater's seeming what is indelibly there in life. (If that seems to be mocking deconstruction, Derrida tried to make the Genetic best of it in his mirroring *Glas.* This occurred after he already had to acknowledge, in an essay on Artaud, that to abolish representation is a tragic impossibility, that even to think its closure "is to think the tragic: not as the representation of fate, but as the fate of representation. Its gratuitous and baseless necessity.")[16] So it is at the end of *The Balcony,* when Madame Irma says to the audience, while closing up the brothel, before extinguishing the last light, "You must go home, where everything—you can be quite sure—will be even falser than here. . . . You must go home."[17] It may very well be, in our heart of hearts, that we really don't want to go home, which is why I've often felt that at the sticking point of the most powerful plays—say, *Oedipus* or *King Lear* or *Endgame* (among those I've directed over the years)—we tend to be most evasive, as if analysis were closing in, or in the process of absorption also blanking out, or acknowledging a profundity that really we'd rather forget—and in order to get on with it, however estranged the life, that's just about what we do. So, too, with antitheater, as a scourge of falsehood and lies; relying as we do on appearances, it would be hard to live with that. At the extremities of exposure, we may actually incline to comedy, so we can laugh it off, though the comedy that really gets us is when we don't know when to laugh. Is that theater or antitheater, or the seeming between? If there's autonomy there, it's the autonomy of indeterminacy, though I won't say it's antiaesthetic.

It was Freud who said we must learn to live in doubt, but the antitheatrical prejudice, for one reason or another, has had its doubts about that—most of all, perhaps, at the intolerable limits of theater, where we sense ourselves seeing what we maybe shouldn't see. Or through all the seeming, the indiscernible, the insidious, what we really can't. Yet what would theater be if it didn't move toward the unbearable, unless we're prepared to abandon the greatest of all plays, especially tragedy, already much critiqued, or stage revisionist versions that arrest, expose, or otherwise set it right? But that, too, is a vanity of antitheater, for would they really go away—that is, the rage, shame, remorse, immeasurable pain that, prior to any drama, brought them into being, insisting they be represented—if we should rewrite or abolish or parody Lear's howls or his never never never never nevers, or even, in some mind-blowing enraptured form of belated epic redemption, substitute for them Molly Bloom's yes I said yes I will Yes? In all this we might remember that it's not only antitheater or a strategic theatricality that deters what's so overpowering in performance that you almost can't think about it, but simpler things, like bad acting or directing or—again light-years from what charges the theater, its grievous mortality and invisible wounds—lightweight production concepts, antitheater by default.

Having said that, I may now retract it, or at least qualify the apparent fault. For while I think I know bad acting when I see it, or an overcharged or slovenly or empty production, the issue that determined my own rethinking of what I was doing in the theater—after more than twenty years of doing it, radically changing what I did—is this: what do we mean by acting*? where? why? how? for whom? and to what ideological end?*[18] Answering any one of those questions may mean that you're for or against theater, at least *that* theater; and indeed, there is a sense in which the antitheatrical prejudice, or the deployment of theatricality, becomes an issue of this form of theater against that form of theater. From the outset, however, I have not been thinking so much of theater forms as about the troubling question, undispelled by the correlative notion, in the becoming of theater, that theater *is* itself, of the materialization of theater—unless it's *all* theater, reality, appearance, whatever—from whatever it is it is not. Where theater happens in its emergence, as itself or not, it's *something else again,* or at least would appear to be, which—like the "Nothing that is not there and the nothing that is,"[19] or the activated nothing in the "Nothing to be done"[20]—baffles perception itself, and again demystification, or the distantiation of that Brechtian A-effect.

This is theater at ground zero, or like the concept of zero itself, about which it has been said, "If you look at zero you see nothing; but look through it and you will see the world."[21] And beyond mathematics, you may see more than that, or rather, see it and not see it, as in *Hamlet*'s closet scene, where Gertrude says all that is she sees, which, even if he's hallucinating, and nothing there to be seen, is existentially something more—what he sees, what she doesn't—than mere coinage of the brain. And so it is with what's palpably there that none of us can see, neither the characters, nor the actors, nor those of us in the audience, in looking directly at it, or eyes with gazing fed, and no form of antitheater can do anything about that, though it might break the gaze or intensify it, cutting to the brain. And that's no coinage either, or the accursed commodification. Thus, when I've written before that the entire institution of theater, with all its apparatus, is a historical cover-up for the ontological fact that the one performing there, that one, is dying in front of your eyes, I was not, as with queer performativity, talking of corporeal style, but rather—in the bodies that matter, the matter that makes the body—the theater's generic substance, inarguably there but imperceptible, compelling the specularity that it will never satisfy. Yet, if I can believe what I read in the newspaper, what passeth show may be, and sooner than we think, another passing phase.

In his apocalyptic imaginings, which he would insist is the virtual truth (quite literally so), Virilio had already foreseen a superdigitized world whose high frequencies would invalidate the body as an encumbrance, requiring, perhaps, the semblance of a biological body with a body art that mirrors its inexistence (72), with dying then irrelevant. Now we actually hear from (maybe way-out) geneticists—as from molecular artists like Joe Davis, who has made art of DNA by inserting coded messages into bacterial genes—that defeating death may be in the offing, or that, shy of total victory, a life expectancy of 4,000–5,000 years is now a prospect, and in the sights of the avant-garde. When, moreover, we hear from Whitfield Diffie, chief of security of Sun Microsystems, that "we live, largely speaking, in the last generation of human beings," and that there are people alive today who will have unlimited life spans,[22] well, that's really likely to change our thinking about theater, as anything but a residual seeming, since the apparatus of representation on which the institution is predicated, even as antitheater, becomes itself obsolete, as representation itself, reproducing what otherwise disappears, would itself more or less disappear into the *interminable*—which was in that other life the fate of psychoanalysis, in the vanity of interpretation of the dramaturgy of the unconscious.

Meanwhile, as if to augment these prospects there was a production called *The Hanging Man*—brought over recently from England to BAM—in which dying becomes impossible through a series of events that are eccentrically, obsessively, and decidedly theatrical, no question of it. The production was developed by The Improbable Theater, which would seem to be a more sanguine mutation of my own *The Impossible Theater*. Subtitled *A Manifesto,* that book was written with an unyielding reality principle, that the theater itself is a form of impossibility, though impossibly so, or despicably, in the American theater, at the time I was writing the book, after the emergence of the cold war. At one point, merging a phrase from the cold war with terms from the New Criticism,

I made this observation: "The ritual balance of power, the maintenance of ambiguity in perilous tension, has also been one of the major preoccupations of art in the twentieth century."[23] And now in the twenty-first, what we're calling an age of terror, it would seem for the time being, which is the time of theater, that the perilous tension is worse, even more ambiguous, with innumerable bodies dying, whether they matter or whether they don't. Whatever the reasons for it, mea culpa as we wish, Orientalism, Occidentalism, the paranoia is growing, what with tunneled networks, stateless, like dreadnaughts spreading dread, with conspiracy theories and secrecies, homeland security dubious and everything out of sight. If you really think it over, how does any theater, by whatever theatrical means, really match up with that, or the pervasiveness of seeming that, in the material world, not virtual at all, appears *in actuality*—now a perversion of seeming?—to make it nothing but theater.

In this regard, mirrored (paranoia in abeyance), there is a level of behavior in theater that, like a subatomic particle, a muon or charmed quark, would—if there were an electronic microscope powerful enough to bring it into focus—disappear in the energy required for you to see it. (Which we can only hope won't happen with the indeterminate jihad, Al Qaeda, or the suicide bombers.) Materializing as disappearance, theater escapes us in being theater, though we might think of it then as antitheater, or, corporeal as it is, a correlative of antimatter. Which, among scientists, seems to have its own aesthetic. As for actual theater practice, to the degree that it persists through the self-reflexive impasse of an ethos of suspicion, it may acquire a certain energy from what will never be resolved, which is how to determine though all the seeming whether at any historical moment there is an insufficiency or overdose of what we think of as theater. That we can do without it is absurd, since—if we're to engage the issues at the level at which Socrates introduced the prejudice, and Plato pursued it through Socrates' voice—we have no choice in the matter; and we've had a form of theater that, in the perverse excess of its apparent undoings, or nothings to be done, was predicated on the absurdity, though some of the cruder theatricality, and its repetitive acts, appeared to overstate a case that can't be overstated. Still, if we think we have it right, there's nothing more certain in the seeming than the future of illusion, the insubstantial pageant fading, leaving not a wrack behind—except the empty space that, for Peter Brook, is (again) the beginning of theater, if an actor enters the space. My own view has always been that it needs no more than a look.

More theater, less theater. Actors have always proceeded on that wobbling pivot, which also defines historical periods, either acting too much or acting too little, though who in the world can say—actor? director? audience?—what is really enough? Every aspect of theater can be thought of the same way, from scenery, lighting, costumes, sound, to the timing of a play, its two-hour traffic or the aestheticized soporific of Robert Wilson's earlier stagings, attenuated, aphasic, repetitive as a raga, with imperceptible permutations, seen unthinkingly as afterthought. Or, as the theater expands to operatic dimensions, there may very well be, even there in its grandeur, too much to be seen, which was actually an issue in the news the other day—the case of Deborah Voigt, resounding voice, oversized body—the right weight of a soprano to be singing Ariadne, no less (*auf Naxos*) in a cocktail dress. What this suggests, even in the reduced proportions of other forms of theater, is that aside from too much acting there can also be too much actor, literally so, psychically so, which we've heard in a tradition from Gordon Craig to Roland Barthes.

When I said a moment ago that the empty theater space only requires a look, it was not from a desire to create an impersonal art, like Mallarmé and others since, who, in attempting by diverse means to void representation, have wanted the actor out of it, in a vanity of poesis opposed to mimesis. For even when the acting is reduced to the gestural or the ideographic, even when in fact the actor is not there, but replaced by a puppet or other nonhuman figure, the mimetic is not extinguished, representation prevails, and if the human figure seems erased, it is there as on Freud's mystic writing pad, if only as a trace. Theater remains to be seen because it is *as remainder,* and it wouldn't be thus at all if it didn't smell of mortality, something to be seen *feelingly* (as the blind Gloucester sees in *King Lear*) in or out of *the* theater. As for Barthes's essay on the Bunraku, it is also in the tradition of critique that finds nothing more discreditable in the theater, no mode of theatricality, than that associated with mimesis and—with a repertoire of hapless gestures and self-indulgent mannerisms, even when focused in character—the corporeal presence of the actor. For all his exhortation of the grain of the voice (sidelined with the musicians in the Bunraku), Barthes prefers on stage the black-robed anonymous figures manipulating the puppets to the psychologized human body, which is no more than an execration in its posturing mindlessness. In the crossing of theory by practice, I must admit at times, as I've watched or worked with certain actors, sharing this view, though the preference for puppets is sometimes there when certain authoritarian directors push the actors around.

Where the actors are presumably liberated by sense and emotional memory, they would be doubly anathema to Barthes, not only because of their physical presence, and with it the smell of mortality, but maybe even worse, the inside risk of narcissism. As for the Actors Studio actor, with a technique disguising mimesis, or any appearance of theater, the liability in performance is—beyond that in the play—still another illusion, when the refusal of theatricality becomes, as iconically with Marlon Brando, a conspicuous symptom of it. If, meanwhile, there's a certain jeopardy in casting, aesthetically or conceptually it may also be judicious, as a means of augmenting or minimizing theater, and thus, whether or not by intention, an incursion of antitheater. As for what happens in a rehearsal, the degrees of appearance there: Do it again! the director says. What "it," and how much? "It all. [*Pause.*] It all,"[24] or some intangibly furtive part of it? which, as in the Beckettian scene, can nearly drive you up the wall. What wall? Hollow. Like the one Hamm insisted on going to, before being returned to the center—"Bang in the center!"[25]—in the bottoming out of illusion. And how many times does one hear in rehearsal, No! that's not it at all, you're merely repeating yourself. Or, you're merely acting. Which is, one would think, what you're supposed to do in the theater.

What I'm essentially saying here—in a period of jaundiced value, where the familiar is distrusted, as "natural," taken for granted, and essence disqualified—is that the theater is *essentially,* in every nuance, the site of antitheater, and would hardly exist without it, no more than those subatomic particles without their antiparticles. But then, at a last psychic extremity of the antitheatrical prejudice, another nuance of seeming, there's something we tend to forget: another doubleness in the actor, not that of character, but of wanting to act and not. And I'm not speaking of the desire, out of technique into performance, for a consummate realism, but once again of the Real, the datum of any acting, ineliminable in the theater, the reality of stage fright. Shakespeare had it exactly when he spoke (in the best manual of acting I know) of "the imperfect actor on the stage, / Who with his fear is put besides his part" (Sonnet 23)—the implication being that there is no other actor. If that appears to confirm again that the theater is inseparable from some instinct of antitheater, it leaves us with the question out of which—through whatever imperfection, in the actor, in reality, in theater itself—the most powerful theater is made: *why theater at all?*

NOTES

1. Martin Heidegger, "Language," in *Poetry, Language, Thought,* trans. Albert Hofstadter (New York: Harper Colophon, 1971) 190.

2. Judith Butler, *Bodies That Matter: On the Discursive Limits of "Sex"* (New York: Routledge, 1993).

3. Judith Butler, *Gender Trouble: Feminism and the Subversion of Identity* (New York: Routledge, 1990) 139.

4. Paul Virilio, *Ground Zero,* trans. Chris Turner (London: Verso, 2002) 15.

5. Michael Fried, "Art and Objecthood," in *Minimal Art: A Critical Anthology,* ed. Gregory Battcock (New York: Dutton, 1968) 141.

6. Quoted by René Girard, *Violence and the Sacred* (Baltimore: Johns Hopkins University Press, 1979) 202.

7. "Imagination Dead Imagine," in *Samuel Beckett: The Complete Short Prose, 1929–89,* ed. S. E. Gontarski (New York: Grove, 1995) 185.

8. "The Brain? It's a Jungle in There," *New York Times,* March 27, 2004, Arts & Ideas, national ed., A17, A19.

9. Henrik Ibsen, *Ghosts,* in *Six Plays by Henrik Ibsen,* trans. Eva Le Gallienne (New York: Modern Library, 1957) 153.

10. Aeschylus, *Prometheus Bound,* trans. David Grene, in *Greek Tragedies,* vol. 1, ed. Grene and Richmond Lattimore (Chicago: University of Chicago Press, 1968) 104.

11. Roland Barthes, "The Grain of the Voice," in *Image-Music-Text,* trans. Stephen Heath (New York: Hill & Wang, 1977) 183.

12. Karl Marx, *The Marx-Engels Reader,* ed. Robert C. Tucker (New York: Norton, 1978) 85.

13. Letter to Arnold Ruge, *The Marx-Engels Reader* 13.

14. Gertrude Stein, "Plays," in *Look at Me Now and Here I Am: Writings and Lectures 1909–45,* ed. Patricia Meyerowitz (London: Penguin, 1967) 75.

15. Slovoj Žižek, *Welcome to the Desert of the Real* (London: Verso, 2002) 9.

16. Jacques Derrida, "The Theater of Cruelty and the Closure of Representation," in *Writing and Difference,* trans. Alan Bass (Chicago: University of Chicago Press, 1978) 250.

17. Jean Genet, *The Balcony,* trans. Bernard Frechtman (New York: Grove, 1960) 115.

18. See the chapter "Ghosting" in the book written—in that uncertain period when I thought it might start again—around the work of my KRAKEN group, *Take Up the Bodies: Theater at the Vanishing Point* (Urbana: University of Illinois Press, 1982) 78–144.

19. See Wallace Stevens, "The Snow Man," in *The Palm at the End of the Mind,* ed. Holly Stevens (New York: Vintage, 1972) 54.

20. Samuel Beckett, *Waiting for Godot* (New York: Grove, 1954) 7.

21. Robert Kaplan, *The Nothing That Is: A Natural History of Zero* (New York: Oxford University Press, 2000) 1.

22. *New York Times,* November 1, 2004, national ed., A15.

23. Herbert Blau, *The Impossible Theater: A Manifesto* (New York: Macmillan, 1964) 21.

24. Samuel Beckett, *Footfalls,* in *Collected Shorter Plays* (New York: Grove, 1984) 240.

25. Samuel Beckett, *Endgame* (New York: Grove, 1958) 27.

SEVEN

Who's There?—Community of the Question

Is it right to be watching strangers in a play in this
strangest of theaters?
—ELIZABETH BISHOP, "Questions of Travel"

IT USED TO BE, in the clamorous sixties, when with all the enchantments of dissidence we were shattering language, abandoning texts, and going for broke with the body, or extolling *body* language, that dance was preferred to theater, or at least the bourgeois theater, burdened as it was with words—or the words, words, words that are, in their Hamletic disposition, an impediment to action. But if dance and theater were sometimes merged or conflated, as in the tradition of Martha Graham, we have now seen a generation of choreographers, like Alain Platel in Belgium or Jérôme Bel in France, who merge them too, but with street arts or social action, or with a high-tech guerrilla strategy, on rooftops with satellite disks, as if in some radicalized extension of that other tradition, from the Judson Memorial Church, with its offbeat antiaesthetic, during the years of the counterculture. The Judson was not especially political, and there were trained dancers there, like Yvonne Rainer or Trisha Brown, but in renouncing virtuosity, *mere* dance, in favor of "found" movement or task-directed events, there was another kind of activism, which might change the site of performance or the spectator's relation to it—and sometimes in public spaces, where if there was anything like a public, they'd have sure been surprised to see it. Thus, if in the church itself they might have performers upside down on a ceiling or, in autistic slow motion, crawling on a floor, they might elsewhere in the city have them in a spidery web (with rather tenuous ropes) coming down from the top of a building. In their affinities, meanwhile, with new music, Cage's silence, Rauschenberg's collage, and the interplay of performance with all the visual arts, the Judson choreographers initiated still other ideas: exploring everyday movement, the gestures of eating or dressing, with barely a humming sound; and in the relation of movement and time, testing the viewer's endurance, as in a matrix of no-time, monotonic at long duration, with the boredom as conceptual; or, breathtaking, breath-catching, the sonic propelling motion, as if danced on the vocal tract. Such ideas were taken up by or inseparable from alternative modes of theater that, with rock music and blue jeans, soon came over to Europe—along with the Living's rabid politics, which disrupted the vacationing public at the Festival of Avignon.

But here there was a difference, with a certain resonance still. While Judson dance had, inarguably, a major formative impact on companies abroad, especially in France, there was a minimalist/conceptualist side to it, about which—whenever a politics surfaced, long after May '68—there were unavoidably mixed feelings, and then renunciation, to the degree it remained abstract. So it was in Great Britain, with Lloyd Newson's choreography for the DV8 Physical Theater, which (in its deviations) abjures abstract movement in favor of the narrativizing body, because of its presumed necessity for the engagement of social issues, as well as those on the margin ignored by established culture. Meanwhile, if there's been a return to narrative, there is still, with degrees of vocalization, the dubious status of words. And taking that on as an issue—as we've seen recently at the Brooklyn Academy of Music, by way of the National Theater in London—there is the choreography of that latecomer to dance, given to storytelling, the outspoken Matthew Bourne. Or perhaps I should say bespoken, for his *Play without Words*—a retelling of Harold Pinter's script for Joseph Losey's movie *The Servant*—is not only an East End cockney's view of oppressive class distinctions, but impelled by the notion that dance is what the politics of deconstruction used to say of the theater, with its dramaturgical dialogue or familiar garrulous plots, that it is elitist and hierarchical, reproducing bourgeois value and its system of representation.

If that has become something of a litany in theory, the fact is that theater, certainly in the United States, is of little concern to the young, the poor, the otherwise dispossessed, that potentially larger audience, deprived of being a public because, for all the flux of words, or the logorrhea of capitalism in the Society of the Spectacle, they remain without a voice. Or if we think of a subculture with an assertive voice, like the hip-hop or rap of American blacks, also impelled by the body, it's hard to assess what it's really saying today, since what was out is in, and the question is *how* to say it—and boo-yaa, Sucka Free, who ya sayn it to. Briefly confined to the ghettos, it was quickly on DVDs and—in the hegemony of speed that is, with digitality, becoming the way of the world—commodified on the Internet, while in the musicated ironies of consumer culture some rappers made it big, like P. Diddy / Sean Combs, who is not only in the fashion business but, with no experience as an actor, recently on Broadway, in that African American classic (whatever the color line, a long way from rap) *Raisin in the Sun.* Of course they loved him, whoever "they" were, those who could afford a ticket, at nearly $100, which is in that aesthetic economy what still determines the public. Meanwhile, as with British punk rock or Seattle grunge, which took over dress and hairstyles in the Shinjuko ward of Tokyo, and by way of Japanized fashion in Malaysia too, you can see hip-hop now, its break-dance, and all the risky moves, not only among privileged white kids in the suburbs of New York, but on an international scale, from *la génération Beur* in the *banlieues* of Paris, with rap in the service of rage, to the back alleys of Bombay or, with pirated CDs on the streets, like the fallout of corporatization, the breakout scene of Beijing.

But this is far from the dance world that I started talking about, with something like the status of our institutional theaters, though those theaters in America (what we used to call regional theaters, but are now called resident professional) are still nothing like those, however they vary from Hamburg to Warsaw to Zurich, in the European theater tradition. Still, the new claim, from DV8 or Matthew Bourne, is also international, and however paradoxical, it amounts to this: that in *theatricalizing* dance, providing it with a narrative—whose liabilities have been exposed from Barthes's early semiology through Foucault's cycles of power to Deleuze's thousand plateaus—those who have been marginalized could, nevertheless, become an audience, larger than what exists, thus acquiring power, and thereby becoming a public, to which politics would have to respond. Praise be to wishful thinking, but having known a lot of audiences, from many years as a theater director (institutional, activist, and avant-garde), and having written about them too, and the public in absentia, I continue to have my doubts.

Putting them in abeyance, it might seem for the fantasied moment that the DV8 Physical Theater is the generic model or inspiration for those youthful dissident groups, like Pora in the Ukraine or Zubr in Belarus, which in the attempt to overthrow tyranny deployed graffiti, improvisation, and the surreptitious tactics of guerrilla theater. With a subtlety of subversion, somehow diffusing the risk, that's what the Zvakwana group appears to be doing in Zimbabwe, in a performative circulation of the message of "Enough!"—with slivers from bars of soap or matchboxes with songs of resistance or putdowns of Robert Mugabe in festive packets of seeds, while emerging from the underground into a public space. There may be, when the tyrant falls, dancing in the streets, with puppet shows, mime, and such, but here the analogy falters, and aside from the retrograde question, unseemly because aesthetic, of the *quality* of the dancing, there is (overlooking the looting) an unpredictable future in the kinaesthetics of power. And that, with chastening or corrosive or tortuous views of power, is the recurring message of the major dramas of revolution, from Büchner's *Danton's Death* or Przbyszewska's *The Danton Case* to Genet's *The Screens* or Müller's *The Task* to the rather forlorn, post-Brechtian view of it (never mind *The Measures Taken,* which even made Brecht uneasy) in Howard Brenton's *Magnificence* or Edward Bond's *The Worlds.*

Today we hear about Kyrgyzstan and, despite an article in *The New York Times,* with the headline, "Democracy Falls on Barren Ground" (Burkett), here too one hopes for the best. Yet, where democracy is taken for granted, and a mostly uncensored, self-determining culture, I still wince at the platitudes of community that, out of the myths of the ancient world, or the mythicizing of that world, continue to haunt the theater. And the vanity of it would seem to be compounded in the virtual reality of globalization, or the age of information, in which nothing is more virtual—if not evangelically virtuous—than the "moral values" of the public so belabored on American television during our last election, and which have since been taken up, along with the "faith-based initiatives" of George W. Bush, by the communion of "compassionate conservatism" and the religious Right. Let me say that whatever, in the paranoid reality after 9/11, moral values may be, on the right or wavering left, they have little to do with the testing of moral perception that still accrues to the tragic as we have inherited it from the classical drama, whether from Prometheus there on the rock or from the bleeding eyeballs of Oedipus, or even, in a seeming epiphany, when he disappears at Colonus. For it's the *seeming* that suffuses the drama, and still does in the contemporary theater, if the drama is worth our attention. As for the activity of moral perception, that occurs—in a matrix of contradiction, cross-purposes, mixed motives, and loose, but variously possible, mostly unexamined premises—at some limit of indeterminacy where you're not quite sure what you're seeing. Or, as in Pinter's *No Man's Land*—what seems to be Eliot's waste land as voyeuristic scene—even where to look. Or, at the limit of representation, where specularity fails, and with it subjectivity, and identity, and the long-imperiled self (now theoretically banished), you're not even sure who's looking. And where's the audience then? or semblance of a public?

As for the Habermasian notion of a public sphere, where ideas could be debated in a civil way, that seems to have disappeared into technocracy, the media, and as Habermas thought himself, into *publicity,* with the theater a function of it, and of course the spectator too, though with a sort of perverse discretion, there and not there. And I'm not even talking yet of those who may be appear to be in an audience, but with their minds elsewhere or simply bored, or asleep, in that culinary state described by Brecht, in any case not there. Nor has the Alienation-effect alleviated yet the temptations to be at the movies, or staying at home with television, or now with all you can download or the hyper-theatricality, the "liveness" of video games. As for the theater's complicity with publicity, if that started when—ironically through the Enlightenment, with the privileged perspective of a proscenium stage—the audience went into the dark, it can now preserve its anonymity by ordering seats there, even now in state or national theaters, with American Express or a Visa or a Master Charge. But what we still can't take on credit is what remains to be seen.

"Who's there?" As I've written before, those opening words of *Hamlet* (1.1.1)—the wrong character making the challenge, not the one on guard, but the one approaching the ramparts—might very well be addressed to those sitting there in the dark. True, it was afternoon, and many were not then sitting, but even with light at the Globe, it was a proleptic question, with manic obsessive permutations through the entire history of modernism, and not exhausted yet: not only *who*? but *where*? and *why*? and so long as you're doing theater, in a proscenium, on a thrust, even out on the streets, in what *space of thought?* superstructure? cellarage? or in the mind's eye, how are you supposed to *see* it? and then, what *it*? *what it?*—in the disabled spaces of Beckett, *Not I, That Time* ("clearly faintly perceptible" [Ashbery 227]), asked over and over, enlivened by disability. These are the swarming questions of the play within the play, and by that I mean the play which, historically, ontologically, if the audience is never wrong, as they say in the commercialized theater, disqualifies it as a public. For when we think of that today, it is not only a matter of the numbers in attendance, but an attentiveness to an absence, the much belabored otherness in a theater of specularity. Even when a director or a method tries to make the theater participatory, the actors circulating amid the spectators or inviting them on stage, that never quite stops the looking, nor that sense of *being watched,* and with it estrangement and distance. And when we think precisely upon it, even when the spectator is seated close to the stage, eye to eye with the actor, close enough to touch, that doesn't reduce the degree to which *division,* separation, with a ghosting sense of *aloneness*—that impermeable substance of theater, mirrored in the event, *demanding* we think precisely—has since become its subject. What's more, or worse, but what becomes its deepening substance (and this is certainly so when the theater, without mere playing around, thinks through the greatest drama, as if we were thought by it), is an inversion of the voyeuristic fear in the most haunted pages of Kafka: a solipsistic anxiety that *nobody may be looking,* which may be a profounder source of stage fright, that paranoid constituent of the performing self, than the fear that everybody is.

"Is everybody looking at me?" says Pozzo, in *Waiting for Godot* (20), the grandiose foolishness of it going to heart of the problem. For when that play first came on the scene, so far as the public was concerned it had nothing to do with theater, the making of a performance from the "Nothing to be done" (7). But if nothing comes of nothing, it may come with a Nobel Prize, and then, to be sure, the public that's never wrong certainly pays attention, though Beckett continued to say that he was writing into a void. Speaking of void, or into it, that is not unlike the mode of consciousness in that opening question of *Hamlet,* and the equally challenging response: "Nay, answer me! Stand, and unfold yourself" (1.1.2). That may be upping the ante on what's demanded of us all, onstage, offstage, but in the ceaseless hermeneutic within and beyond *Hamlet,* the answer is still unfolding, as at the extremities of subjectivity, identity politics, and with the vanished self, what we now call "subject positions"—and so, too, with the public that, if it materializes at all, is a *community of the question,* whose unity consists of an essential separation.

And so it has been through the history of drama, which has always distrusted theater, that site of mere appearance, from the awakening of the Watchman (that character perfectly named), as if from barbaric darkness, in Aeschylus's *Oresteia,* through the "seeming, seeming" of Shakespeare's *Measure for Measure* (2.4.150) to the mirror stage of the brothel in *The Balcony* of Genet—an apparatus of surveillance that is, as the Madame says, always being watched. When, at the end of that cunningly derisive play, Madame Irma tells the audience to go home, not to worry, things will be no different, even more false, than they were in the Grand Brothel, with its expertise in appearance, all scenarios ending in death, he was not exactly laying the moral grounds for anything like a public. And indeed, the idea of the spectator, *who* is seeing *what,* was—as I've been saying—also in a dubious state, as it was most explicitly in Hamlet's setup or direction of the play within the play, where the watchers are watching the watchers watch. They are also referred to, as you may remember, as (potentially) "guilty creatures sitting at a play" (2.2.588–89), and if in that wider scene, the accusative site of seeing, the play is to be taken seriously—as it mostly isn't, nor is the appalling reality of two thousand years of Western drama—I'm trying to imagine a public emerging from anything like that.

On quite another wavelength, but referring to that tradition, the director Peter Sellars, who has worked extensively in the opera houses and theaters of Europe, has been imagining a theater, on the Greek model, which would have "a seat for every citizen," including those who, in Athenian democracy, women and foreigners, "couldn't vote and had no citizenship." It was with this in mind that he recently did a production of Euripides' *Children of Herakles,* which attempts to open up discourse to everybody in the audience, and to bring into the orbit of performance, wherever it is performed, all those usually excluded. So it was in the city of Bottrop, in the heart of industrial Germany, where Kurdish refugees are being resettled, and were brought together with others who normally don't go to the theater. In reflecting on that production, Sellars remarked about the potential of a democratic public space: "What is public space?—I think [that] is the biggest question of the 21st century" (37). Admirable as that work is, and without denying at all whatever edification there is in implicating those who've never been to the theater, letting them perform, participate, or question, or even tell their stories, it would still seem to me that the discrepancy between thinking a public space and actually achieving it—or how to achieve it, with powerlessness in the presence of the sources of power, somehow able to change it—*that* remains the biggest question of any century.

As for what a public would be if it could be, that is what, with all the talk of community, persists with a certain poignancy at the selvage of perception, with subjectivity slipping but empathically there, at some residual level—which is what, with unexpected poignancy, John Ashbery suggests, through all his ironic worldliness, as if in the mirror stage of his poem, "Self-Portrait in a Convex Mirror":

> . . . a vague
> Sense of something that can never be known
> Even though it seems likely that each of us
> Knows what it is and is capable of
> Communicating it to the other.
>
> (198)

Yet if the likelihood is chancy, it may remind us that whatever the necessities and probabilities of the Aristotelian idea of theater, or the most rigorous staging of any play, as in the productions of Robert Wilson, the fastidious seriality of the most aestheticized detail, the performance always defies it, because temporally and otherwise, in the very breathing of the actor, it is always subject to chance. We may try in ingenious ways to cover that up or, by means of improvisation, to double it up as a virtue. Or to accept it existentially as the condition of any performance. And indeed, according to Alain Badiou in his *Handbook of Inaesthetics,* "Theatrical production, or mise en scène, is often a reasoned trial of chances." And whatever we think of the public, as Badiou goes on to say, it is also on trial:

> In chance, the public must be counted. The public is part of what completes the [theater-] idea. Who can ignore the fact that, depending on which public one is playing to, the theatrical act does or does not deliver the theater-idea, does or does not complement it? But if the public is part of the chance that is at work in the theater, it must itself be as prey to chance as possible. We must protest against any conception of the public that would depict it as a community, a substance, or a constant set. (74)

When Badiou says, however, that "only a *generic* public, a chance public, is worth anything at all" (74), history and social reality are conspiring against that, as it does against the idea of community, since—as I've written in my book *The Audience*—"when there is the semblance of a gathered public, . . . [it] seems like the merest facsimile of remembered community paying its respects not so much to the still-echoing signals of a common set of values but to the better-forgotten remains of the most exhausted illusions" (1).

And we live in a time, it seems, when illusions exhaust themselves more quickly than ever before. As for the appearance of reality in the age of simulacra, dominated by the media—where there appears to be no reality except appearance—it's hard to think of how in that psychic environment there is anything approximating a public. But then again illusion helps, as Freud seemed to understand after *Civilization and Its Discontents,* when, as if there were no other future, he felt constrained to write about the future of (an) illusion. He might very well, in that regard, have been writing about the theater, and what through its discontents seems to bring us together. So we may have enclaves of concurrence for the participatory moment, whether politicized or aestheticized, in everything from stand-up comedy to the current revival on Broadway of *Who's Afraid of Virginia Woolf?* (whose audience will largely be theater parties from Long Island, who can afford the price of a ticket) to Sellars's more idealistic circuit of dispossession with his questioning adaptation of *Children of Herakles,* the premises of which, actually, also need to be questioned.

For the audience in a postindustrial culture is either a scattering of incompatible sodalities, if not competing factions, many of them unstable or a function of the mass, what Jean Baudrillard once called "that spongy referent" (*Silent Majorities* 1), which is enveloped, even mesmerized, by the outlying radiance of the apparency of the social: State, History, Culture, Meaning. In what became over the years an increasingly jaundiced view of the prospect of community, Baudrillard wrote of the mass, it is "an opaque nebula" of atomistic individuals, "whose growing density" will collapse in a "blaze of signifiers" into "a black hole which engulfs the social" (3–4), the end of which he eventually declared. Before it came to that, however, he said the social is not a concept, but "a soft, sticky, lumpenanalytical notion" (4), out of which an audience materializes *as* a concept, like the concepts of class, power, status, or social relations with which it is conjoined or on which it reflects. An acritical notion itself increasingly like the mass, "without attribute, predicate, quality, reference" (5), the determinacy of the social—like television ratings or the viewers at museums, clicked off by an attendant with a gadget at the entrance—is statistical, radically wanting definition. If the mass has nothing to do with a real population, the audience is, even by social class, only amorphously bound, yet predictable too.

Some years ago, on a panel together in Brussels, Baudrillard and I disagreed openly before a large symposium, and then one-on-one at breakfast, about his Disneyland view of the United States, in his book *Amerique*. But his mordancy notwithstanding, he can't quite be ignored, and meanwhile, when I hear the usual banalities about an audience or the theater as a public form, with more or less hypocritical deference to the spectator, I have to resist temptations to jaundice in my own view of it all. Whatever one thinks, and wherever performance occurs—on the streets, in the ghettos, in factories, prisons, churches, or on Indian reservations, in whatever peripatetic or participatory modes—theaters continue to operate, too, with their conventional partition of scenic and spectatorial space, the (seemingly) public and (darkling) private, onstage and backstage, the seen and unseen, or (ob)scene, thus to be kept invisible. This is the old or familiar site of specular alienation, preserving at least a minimal difference between actor and audience, object and observer, and that difference occurs, sometimes not so minimal, even in the alternative, unexpected sites of performance. If this form of theater, however, seems to be gradually yielding, it is not to the Rousseauian ethos that resurfaced in the participatory mystique of the sixties, but in something like a sci-fi, hyperreal simulacrum of it, from the *House/Lights* video trips of the synthetically voice-layered and multi-monitored Wooster Group to the imagistic technoscape of Quebec City's Ex Machina, which its director, the usually cerebral Robert Lepage, brought to Las Vegas in a hydraulic extravaganza, a 200 million dollar collaboration with the airborne acrobatics of the Cirque du Soleil. Not quite on that exorbitant scale, but not impoverished either, the videocast enterprise and megabytes of it all have made their way, with various degrees of synthesized sensation, into the established theaters and proliferating festivals on the European scene, as with the cross-mediated, cross-cultural (Franco-Japanese) production of *Iris* that Philippe Decouflé brought to the new Catalan culture palace, the Teatre Nacional (Marranca 27).

As the mediascape expands into the theatrical scene, it might seem like a redundancy or rather a queer reversal in the age of *informatique,* where much of life, it seems, has already been theatricalized—which is what was dismaying not only to Baudrillard, as he moved with increasing alarm and asperity from a critique of the political economy of the sign through the mirror of production and the shadow of the silent majorities to the precession of simulacra, "whose operation," he came to believe, "is nuclear and genetic, and no longer specular and discursive" (*Simulations* 3); in short, a fact of life. One might not go so far as Baudrillard—or through the sites of an always theatricalized chronopolitics with the supersonic speed of Paul Virilio—but surely there is in our digitized universe, with its cell phones and iPods, and webblogged screens with chatterbots, a certain substance in the sensation of a certain absent substance. If, indeed, there's been a displacement of the real into a shadow of it, more vaporous than appearance—or the appearance of that reality which is the reality of appearance—that would seem to make a vanity of the Aristotelian inheritance of a mimetic theater, with its remedial catharsis in a fiction of the public.

Vanity of vanities, and for all the pixelated truth of being, mimesis still persists, and will probably survive any attempt, theoretical or performative, to make it go away, like the apparently abandoned figure in the era of Jackson Pollock and abstract expressionism, which came back on canvas in neoexpressionism, like the return of the repressed, though a somewhat different figure, due to the effect on painting of body and performance art. Various experiments in modern drama, from Strindberg to Witkiewicz through the Absurd to Sarah Kane, have struggled to overcome the idealist notion of the independent subject / self-identical agent, but, like the figure in painting, it seems to reappear in every blur of abstraction. So, too, through the entire history of the avant-garde—and all the strategies of ruptured form, fragmentation, dispersion of the subject—it is realism and mimesis that have been the measure of the manifestation, whatever it is that shows in the seemingly randomized structures of the discontinuous forms. That is the irony which is *not* romantic, attached as it appears to be to the irrepressible real, mortality itself, that visible invisibility, no more than mere appearance, though—against the grain of going critique—it's no mere social construction, while in the recyclings of power, the threat of reproduction that reproduces itself . . . well, even genetic cloning is being imagined in mimetic terms. As for death, whatever it is, as we've come to say in theory, it can't be represented, yet can only be represented. This is something that Beckett, whose shorter plays in particular would appear to be models of fragmentation in dispersion of the subject, really understood, the haunting tenacity of the mimetic, even when, as in *Breath,* there is no performer at all, or in *Not I,* nothing but a Mouth, and torrentially, unstoppable, those words, words, words—what the nonmimetic theater, or the illusion of such a conception, has also tried to do without.

None of this invalidates, however, our sense of a seemingly irreversible tendency (and you'll notice the iteration of *seeming* in all that I've been saying) toward the end of mimesis by default, or as if in the new reality on the computer, mimesis is not the default. With the displacement of bodily gesture and desire into electronic commands, and the miniaturization of an exhaustive memory that is not, like the Freudian unconscious, a scene of representation, the scene of the world is increasingly dematerialized, and in another kind of culinary theater, divested by swift bytes of all that used to fill it. This includes the body and the real, actors and their fantasies. If in that empty space (not quite Peter Brook's) there is anything like a spectator, s/he is at the nexus of a system of nuclear matrices keeping track of an emptied body of meaning in a vast encoded absence or, in the microsystems of exchange, no more than a succession of instants, which is a far historical cry from the "chips of Messianic time," the redeemable "'time of the now,'" in Walter Benjamin's "Theses on the Philosophy of History" (*Illuminations* 265).

In our emailing universe of spontaneous communication, with nothing quite material to constitute a scene, and with all the advantages of the Internet, our credit cards threatened, and our Social Security numbers, there is a diminution or conflation of public and private spaces, as they were previously understood. In this disembodied context, culture no longer operates through discrete works or, with spectatorial proximity, the sense of a shared event, but through operationalism itself, mass movement or flux, Googled or Yahooed, a sort of Pop

Art version of Bergsonian *durée.* If there were an architectural correlative in the material world—the sort of thing from which Rem Koolhaas has been rethinking urban spaces—it might be Beaubourg, the Centre Pompidou in Paris, with jugglers, mimes, acrobats, and sword swallowers on the plaza, and a steady flux of exposed but anonymous tourists ascending in escalators, in a sort of embodied parody of transcendental signifiers. If that's not so much architecture but a performative space, it's one in which, however, the old dream of symbolic exchange, beyond use value, is not realized, for that implies, as Baudrillard remarked in an early essay, "a sacrificial logic of consumption" ("Ecstasy" 126).

The impersonality of it all, in this spaced-out network, with its nevertheless narcissistic and protean feedback, is not something, obviously, in which there's equal participation, since some of us are keeping our distance, or somehow attempting to, as we proceed with old illusions in a universe that still seems to be functioning under Newtonian laws. But at the same time, as even President Bush has envisaged moving forward in the universe, to new worlds beyond our own, with politicians and schoolteachers in orbit, quotidian space gradually acquires—with anything from Atari games to computer consoles and the dispensation of silicon chips—the features of a terrestrial satellite, in which a weightless body, no longer actor or director or spectator, lives by simulation and not symbol in a denatured, demetaphorized, metonymic sphere, which cancels the public sphere and the private as well, for it "is no longer a scene where the dramatic interiority of the subject, engaged with its objects as with its image, is played out" (Baudrillard, "Ecstasy" 128). Even if this were some sci-fi fantasy of Baudrillard's own, one feels it is like many things of that genre, an accelerated anticipation, but not so long a galactic leap, toward things to come, which certainly will redetermine how we think about the theater, as the dramatic literature—sometimes in apocalyptic ways—has already started to do, as with the plays of Heiner Müller, especially *Hamletmachine,* or a neglected late play by Tennessee Williams, *The Red Devil Battery Sign.*

All of this causes us, moreover, to reflect on what *were* the virtues of the separated public and private spaces of the old scene of representation, which has been, since the anti-Oedipal theory of poststructuralism, so much under assault, as a deceit, lie, fraud, of the logocentric system, with its repressive ideology, purveyor of the mere appearances emanating from the self-serving seat of invisible or secret power. While it is this ideological cover-up or obfuscation that has been subjected to a devastating deconstruction, through the history of the modern theater as well as critical theory, what was hidden in this scene is the existence of that Otherness whose presumable disappearance we may very well regret. If we distrusted the implications of its originary absence, it was that which nevertheless gave us, with whatever grievances, "the symbolic benefits of alienation," in which the Other can fool you, but—and here I am in accord with Baudrillard—"can fool you for the better or the worse" ("Ecstasy" 130). And the final score on that is not yet, if ever, in.

What we think of as theater—action, spectacle, scene—requires the minimal separation that is the beginning of alienation, which does have a tendency to widen its scope, like the reification of representation itself. But to the degree that the alienating risk dwindles into the software of screen and network rather than mirror and scene, the psychological dimension having vanished into the microprocess, we are in the vicinity of obscenity (no-scene) "when all becomes transparence and immediate visibility, when everything is exposed to the harsh and inexorable light of information and communication" (Baudrillard, "Ecstasy" 130), whose post-*jouisssance* or ecstasy *is* obscene. In a kind of perverse utopianism, at some extremity of deluded desire, it's the obscene that does away with the apparatus of representation, every mirror, every image, and presumably every look, and here we are back in the brothel of Genet, when Roger the revolutionary appears, the rebellion having started, as rebellions tend to do, in a pledge of redeeming truth, by "despising make-believe" (55), which like it or not in the theater, if not reality principle, is not to be disbelieved.

Who's there? That, in the indiscernible space between to be and not to be, is the question—and so long as there's anyone looking, it's the unanswerable question, generic, ontological, whenever theater materializes from whatever it is it is *not.* And for a community of scholars that would be, I should think—if all the world's a stage or life is a dream or an insubstantial pageant fading, what's *not* theater?—a still provocative question.

WORKS CITED

Ashbery, John. *Selected Poems.* New York: Penguin, 1985.

Badiou, Alain. *Handbook of Inaesthetics.* Trans. Alberto Toscano. Stanford, CA: Stanford University Press, 2005.

Baudrillard, Jean. "The Ecstasy of Communication." In *The Anti-Aesthetic: Essays on Postmodern Culture.* Ed. Hal Foster. Port Townsend, WA: Bay Press, 1983. 126–34.

Baudrillard, Jean. *In the Shadow of the Silent Majorities . . . or The End of the Social, and Other Essays.* Trans. Paul Foss, Paul Patton, and John Johnston. New York: Semiotext(e), 1983.

Baudrillard, Jean. *Simulations.* Trans. Paul Foss, Paul Patton, and Philip Beitchman. New York: Semiotext(e), 1983.

Beckett, Samuel. *Collected Shorter Plays.* New York: Grove, 1984.

Beckett, Samuel. *Waiting for Godot.* New York: Grove, 1954.

Benjamin, Walter. *Illuminations.* Ed. Hannah Arendt. Trans. Harry Zohn. New York: Schocken, 1968.

Bishop, Elizabeth. *The Complete Poems 1927–1979.* New York: Farrar, Straus & Giroux, 1999.

Blau, Herbert. *The Audience.* Baltimore: Johns Hopkins University Press, 1990.

Burkett, Elinor. "Democracy Falls on Barren Ground." *New York Times,* March 29, 2005, A21.

Genet, Jean. *The Balcony.* Trans. Bernard Frechtman. New York: Grove, 1960.

Marranca, Bonnie. "Barcelona Contemporary." *PAJ: A Journal of Performance and Art* 79, 27.1 (2005): 22–31.

Sellars, Peter. "Performance and Ethics: Questions for the 21st Century." Interview by Bonnie Marranca. *PAJ: A Journal of Performance and Art* 79, 27.1 (2005): 36–54.

Shakespeare, William. *The Riverside Shakespeare: The Complete Works.* 2nd ed. Boston: Houghton Mifflin, 1997.

Virilio, Paul. *Speed and Politics: An Essay on Dromology.* Trans. Mark Polizzotti. New York: Semiotext(e), 1986.

EIGHT

The Emotional Memory of Directing

LET ME BEGIN WITH something like a confession, brought on through a late visa by delayed awareness of where I am, not merely in St. Petersburg, but at a conference of the International Federation of Theater Research. I'm pleased to be here, of course, but I trust that those who invited me to give this keynote were also aware that I've never been a theater scholar, and that whatever research I did before a turn to theory was done *in* the theater, where I worked for nearly forty years, always questioning, in some respect, what I was doing there and why I did it, and at certain critical moments why it shouldn't be otherwise. And so, too, questioning the nature of theater, about which—after a generation of new historicism, cultural materialism and, with essentialism undone and the aesthetic demystified, everything social construction—I find myself unregenerate, by no means indifferent to history, but still thinking ontologically, having asked such tenuous questions as what is it *now, as it occurs,* as it *is,* before the eye? even *here,* what is it, *then,* in the mind's eye? in the confusions of eye, ear and the other senses? in the synesthesia of its perceiving and the being perceived, and though we overlook it, in the embodied theater, as *here, now,* breathing and being breathed? Or: to what does a performance refer except to itself, and what is the ontological status of *that other thing,* if what is there, whatever it is that escapes you, now you see it now you don't, is not the thing itself?

Those were questions I began to think about *in* the theater, which is why I've been given to say, even while working in it, that theater *is* theory, or a shadow of it. And while I'll not be pursuing such questions here, one or another may be implied in passing, as I reflect upon directing in a more or less personal way, as the title is meant to suggest—and so, too, the following three epigraphs, as they're absorbed into what I've been thinking, as if thought before, as a virtual habit of mind, which may be (habitually) a little circuitous as it proceeds:

> When thought has become each thing in the way in which a man who actually knows is said to do so . . . , its condition of possibility is still one of potentiality . . . and thought is then able to think itself.
>
> —ARISTOTLE, *On the Soul*

Only if I am not always already and solely enacted, but rather delivered to a possibility and a power, only if living and intending and apprehending themselves are at stake each time in what I live and intend and apprehend—only if, in other words, there is thought—only then can a form of life become, in its own factness and thingness, *form-of-life,* in which it is never possible to isolate something like naked life.

—GEORGIO AGAMBEN, *Means without End*

But, ah, thought kills me that I am not thought.

—SHAKESPEARE, Sonnet 44

If my title speaks of emotion and the epigraphs then of thought, it's by no means a lapse of memory, about which I've been thinking much these days, having started an autobiography, full of emotional memory—and emotions *about* memory too—including my first encounter with Stanislavski's *An Actor Prepares.* I was not at all preparing to be an actor when I first read that book, but rather desperately catching up with what might help me to be a director, since I'd come to the theater belatedly, by way of a series of accidents that, since I've written about them elsewhere, I won't rehearse here. But since we're here, I might say that, whatever my own naïveté at the time, or insecurities, without a defining voice, the voices I really heard—with a conceptual disposition that I didn't know I had, and an experimental inclination that would sooner than later emerge—were, if not classical, mostly Russian. With the Russians—not only Stanislavski, Meyerhold, Vakhtangov, but first of all, Dostoyevsky, who didn't write for the theater, but seemed to me, with his feverish metaphysics, the greatest dramatist of the nineteenth century; then Tolstoy, who, in presuming to master history, eventually abhorred the theater; and in the theater itself, the suggestiveness of Chekhov, the wayward hints or non sequiturs, even the mysterious cord that, according to old Ferapont, stretches under all of Moscow, or in the sound of a snapped string mournfully dying away—there was a certain magnitude of mind, and with everything beginning at the level of soul, a reform of being, ethics, purpose, no small-mindedness. And what I remember from Stanislavski as much as anything else, as if, morally, a condition of technique, was this injunction: *Don't come into the theater with mud on your feet!* You want to be a director, learn to make a life in art—though like Meyerhold, comes the Revolution, you may also lose it for art.

I haven't quite lost it, but when in the first book I wrote, *The Impossible Theater: A Manifesto,* I called for a revolution, saying in the opening paragraph that when I looked at the state of the American theater, and the despicable behavior of the people in it, I felt like the lunatic Lear on the heath, wanting to kill, kill, kill, kill, kill, kill, there were those out there only too ready to kill me. Forgive this replaying of history (and it *is* history), but that was more than a dozen years after I started working in the theater, and at the time, as we went into the 1960s, other things may have been stirring, but there still wasn't much talk about art. And if I was outraged then about that, it was almost more because, in its uncertain beginnings, at the turn of the 1950s, that was also true of my own theater, The Actor's Workshop of San Francisco, which developed eventually as I wished, or in the vicinity of it, by sheer stubborn will—depending on where and when, a prime requisite for the director—past all resistance. And I don't want to minimize that, coming mostly from people whose greatest impediment was that they had, unfortunately, a good deal more experience in theater than I could claim at the time. In this regard, my innocence, or ignorance, may have been a saving grace. And I don't want to minimize either—though I was reading everything about theater, one play after another, volumes of theater history, and everything else in the arts that might conceivably bear upon it—what it is I didn't know, and particularly about acting. And it's acting that still seems to me, whatever there is on stage, or off stage, there above the teasers or concealed behind the tormentors, out there in the wings, and even with a provocatively self-conscious, conceptually empty stage, whether Peter Brook's or Beckett's—nothing there but a breath, or a faint brief cry, "an instant of recorded vagitus"[1]—it's acting that remains the sine qua non of theater.

And I was all the more convinced of that as I began to realize, through those early years, that even as the actor acquires (in that voyeuristic perversion without which there'd be no theater) the look of being looked at, stage fright is something like an existential condition. Those mandates of Stanislavski for the process of building a character—concentration, focus, circle of attention, units and objectives, public solitude—are also, in becoming something like second nature, ways of dealing with stage fright, while much of what we do in directing is an equivocal cover-up, because the credibility of performance draws upon that fright, hiding it and exploiting it, all the more as we approach the limits of performance. Speaking of limits, however, it's not so much the theater but rather performance and body art that have really explored this issue, and I could examine it in excruciating detail in the now-legendary aesthetic and ritual perils of the Viennese Action group; or Chris Burden, being crucified on the back of Volkswagen or crawling on broken glass; or the cosmetic surgeries of Orlan (actually theorized in the process, by texts she reads aloud), or, Abramović and Ulay, breathing and being breathed, to the point of asphyxiation; or, though you'd certainly wince if you were there (or even looking at the pictures), the exquisite suspensions of Stelarc—over the water in Japan or over a street in New York—by large fishhooks he'd insert, with a studied impeccability, through his own flesh. But lest we think this is merely raw extremity or some gratuitous public display of indulgent self-abuse, we should recognize that there were models and incitations in the classical avant-garde, as well as a reciprocal linkage between the performative body (not yet "queer") and conceptual art, where thought has, indeed, become each thing as a condition of possibility, whether through the mythic incisions of Orlan's facial text, itself a map of myth, or Stelarc's theorization of "the obsolete body."[2]

What I might say here, however, is that as I began to direct, I soon became aware—through a period of happenings and Action Events, and before the insurgence of the body in theater and in theory—that there was more to be learned about what might be done in the theater from the other arts (the visual, the sonic, the plastic, multimedia now and multiple installations) than from the theater itself, or mostly what's happening there, which with few exceptions is usually far behind—and if exceptions, usually because they're aware of what's happening in the other arts. As for what happens in the theater (and here referring in passing to a few plays I've done), do we not want some bodily affect, the wound, the cut, the tear, if not exactly literal, something more than emblematic, at the sticking point of *Oedipus,* that blinded and blinding vision, as if it were thought in the flesh? Or, in another plaintive dimension, the grotesquely blinded Gloucester, after Cornwall does it (and how exactly *does* he do it? spurs, knife, sword? or just fingers? wrist up the channel—which is how, it appeared, we did it), again the sensation of it, seeing it feelingly, as if an act of mind, its factness, its thingness, on the edge of naked life. And then that other extremity, as if it were pure thought, yet somehow felt in the flesh, there on the cliff at Dover, seen in the vast beyond, the impalpable magnitudes of it, from "yond tall anchoring bark, / Diminished to her cock; her cock a buoy / Almost too small for sight," to the indiscernible currents, down there, dizzily, in the depths below—brain turning on the waters with "deficient sight"—where "the murmuring surge," like all of history in the gathered tides, "on the unnumb'red idle pebble chafes" (*King Lear* 4.6.18–22). I've often said to actors that we want that surge, and the chafing of history too, in the most inconspicuous action performed upon the stage.

But then there are times when, it seems, the surge is being monitored, at another psychophysical level, for its libidinal flow. So it is when the house is being watched in the fantasy scenes of Genet's brothel, where all the scenarios end in death. What do we do when we realize that each of the scenarios has its own perversion, like a rite of history—masturbation, sadism, buggery, and with the Envoy there and the Executioner dead—necrophilia too? And how is all that to be acted? Act more, act less? If sometimes less is more, sometimes it's nothing at all; or, while we've learned from Beckett that nothing can be *done,* there's also a sense of not *doing* it when all you're doing is merely acting. As through the years I upped the ante on what I was asking of the actor, I've found myself at some extremity—way *out* there where you're not really sure you should go, or way *in* there where it's almost illicit to be—being next to immoral, and not only being aware of it, the actual jeopardy there, but knowing if we can do it the doing would be superb. Not only is the actor severely threatened, but wanting it, not wanting it, induced to take risks that, psychically, physically, could very well be injurious, but as if homeopathic too, overcoming stage fright by being frightened all the more. And now and again in directing that seemed to apply to myself.

"Every morning since rehearsals started I wake anxious." That expression of anxiety, however, is not quite mine. I'm not doing theater anymore, but adventitiously, as I was writing this talk, it came from a distance as a sort of directorial challenge, with the kind of emotional turmoil that may be, at the same time, an impediment to performance and the impelling substance of it. It came in an overflowing email from a former student of mine, not in acting, but rather a course, as I recall, in the cultural politics of modern drama. She's a beautiful young woman, with glowing eyes and passion, and I'm told she was one of the most impressive actors in the School of Drama. I can't confirm that, because I never saw her on stage, but what I can say is that—with a desperate desire to know, and to know more, whatever there was to know—she was perhaps the most acutely intelligent student in my class. And she has been writing me constantly since she asked for some advice and then went off to New York, where she was almost immediately noticed, and is now in one of the resident professional theaters doing the major role for which, as she describes it, she seems ideal. I hope she won't mind my quoting some fragments of what, if in a play, would seem a long compulsive monologue—the scene familiar, a conventional form of theater, bringing us back into the orbit of Stanislavski.

The character moves, she writes, "from being the beautiful girl, the loved by all, . . . to this ravaged shell of a woman. It is . . ." She breaks off, and then her normally self-reflective, lyrically fluent prose, now repetitive, urgent, regressive, aphasic, seems to be in character:

> I'm scared. I feel scared. I feel like it's this enormous play and . . . I feel like a little girl . . . I worry about what everyone . . . do they think I'm up to it? (which I know is so much about me being like Oh my God I hope I can do this!). . . . And then, and then there are times when I feel like, God, my choices . . . all my characters seem . . . riddled with self-doubt because I am riddled with self-doubt . . . and then just feel like a big fucking sham . . . and the people around me seem so Fearless and I feel like, well god, that's what an actor is supposed to be! Fearless! . . . And I don't feel that way right now. I feel pent up and terrified. And always it's this fear, deep down, that I'm just no good. And that somebody's gonna pull back the curtain and figure it out. Is it just . . . how do you control the doubt? . . . Maybe there aren't answers to these questions. . . . I'm just so rabidly hard on myself. . . . I don't want to do that and I don't know how to not.

Here's the murmuring surge that—sometimes even with the maturest of actors (read Laurence Olivier's autobiography, if you want to check on that)—may very well be the subtext of the subtext in any given rehearsal. If you've directed for any time, you've certainly had to deal with some version of it, and since there are never reliable answers, often guessing what's best to do, or doing nothing at all, or, as I wrote her, "so be it, riddled with doubt, bring the character into the orbit of the riddle, and thence into the ravaged shell of a woman. You should be hard on yourself, that's what it appears to be about."

This was no more, of course, than a variation on affective memory. I was telling her not only to remember it, but to use it then and there, making a virtue of it—as if, indeed, as I thought myself, we must learn to live in doubt. If that was in some respect, too, derived from Stanislavski (maybe by way of Freud), when I first read *An Actor Prepares* there seemed more certitude there. As for the Stanislavski method, it was during those years being taken over by the Actors Studio, which capitalized the Method and also commodified it, with such iconic figures as Marlon Brando and Marilyn Monroe, and even more up-to-date, Puff Daddy or P. Diddy, in a quick recent tutorial for the Broadway revival of *A Raisin in the Sun*. This is not to discount the seriousness that the Studio brought to acting, nor could I avoid the Method as I made my way into the theater.

Actually, my first wife, Beatrice Manley—already an actor of resourceful grace and power, who had been on Broadway before I ever saw a play—had studied with Michael Chekhov and, instead of joining the Studio, preferred to work with a group guided, before he went to Hollywood, by Sidney Lumet. But even so, the emphasis was upon an internalizing technique. Bea and I worked together for over twenty years, and as she taught me much about acting I directed her in performances ranging from Alma in *Summer and Smoke* and Madame Ranevsky in *The Cherry Orchard* to Mother Courage and Madame Irma in the brothel of *The Balcony*. But even after the experience of various destabilizing styles and, as we went on, the quite radical eccentricities of a strategically conscious, avant-garde, often antitheatrical theater, she wrote in one of the two books on acting she published before she died: "Acting is convincing when the emotions are so deep inside the body that they seem to be essential and personal to that particular performer; when it is as though there were no outside world. This is subjective, visceral, inner, private acting."[3]

If there was for her a long circuitous subtext to that visceral inner life, that was not necessarily so for the actors on the scene when I first started directing, though if they had any technique at all, it was some version or other of the Method, the psychological acting still the currency of the American stage. While I did my best to engage it, psyching the actors out, as they were turning in, through the rites of interiority—and becoming adept myself at creating the conditions for that—I was soon, in an inchoate way, conflicted about it too, though I knew nothing whatever then about Brechtian alienation, no less anything as instrumentally hieroglyphic as Meyerhold's biomechanics. Actually, I did learn about the *Verfremdungseffekt* when, in 1957, I directed the first production of *Mother Courage* in the United States. And while I'd have no compunctions now about performing Brecht against the authority of the text, I was very scrupulous then, not only about that, but also the various controls on emotion (like "he said," "she said") in the Brechtian method. I attempted to do it like a model student of the model book, if that had been available. If that wasn't quite true later on—as in a subsequent production of *Galileo*—that was because Brechtian theory and example provided the ideational grounds for turning against the authority of the text, as he did himself with *Galileo* after the bomb fell on Hiroshima. If, as he said in the recorded discussion of *Coriolanus,* we're entitled to amend Shakespeare where Shakespeare needs amending, I would assume the same is also true of Brecht, as I later did about Beckett.

What should be apparent is that Beckett's texts, more than any, have really given us theoretical grounds for revisionist staging, despite his own unbecoming vigilance, the unquestioning devotion of Billy Whitelaw, the dutifulness of certain directors, from Alan Schneider to Walter Asmus, and continued surveillance now by his heirs and reverent scholars, with a deep emotional commitment to something like Beckettian method. If I were to start directing again, however, as I once told Beckett—who always wondered why I stopped, and each time I saw him urged me to start again—I could never do one of his plays, especially when he was alive, because I couldn't promise at all that I'd do it as he prescribed, or as if the text were gospel. And I say that, too, believing that I'd get at some truth in the plays that a more obedient director would miss, and—presumptuous as it may seem—maybe Beckett himself. If there is any psychoanalytical basis to that—and Beckett was once in analysis—the directors I most admire tend to think like that, out of another sense of duty, and maybe, aesthetically, another kind of commitment, with its own emotional truth.

Actually, it should be said of Stanislavski that he seems to have done that with Chekhov, who apparently dismissed the method's public solitude as a pretext for excess, the maudlin self-indulgence or artificial pathos that, in the actor, is the nether side of narcissism. We know that he expected *The Cherry Orchard* to be funnier, and if he'd had his way with Andrei in the fourth act of *The Three Sisters,* where the pain was bad enough without the actor focused inward, commiserating with himself, he'd have had him instead aiming his denunciations of the tedious complacency of provincial life right at the spectators in Moscow, letting them know what they really knew, that their own lives were no less boring, miserable, empty, soporific, and without imagination, next to dead. I don't know that Stanislavski was nearby when Chekhov said it, but outdoing anything we've heard from Brecht, he apparently told the actor playing the role, "He must be just about ready to threaten the audience with his fists."[4] If that resembles Franz Wedekind who, when he acted in his own plays, would break up a scene and leap to the edge of the stage, gesticulating wildly, exhorting the audience to wake up and understand, it would certainly disrupt any "culinary theater," in its own excessive seizure of the Alienation-effect. There have been times when I've wanted to leap on stage and do something like that myself, but as for Stanislavski's suppression of the comedy in Chekhov's plays, when we see nowadays certain productions that, deferring to the author, are farcically overdoing it, we might very well prefer the forgoing of a few laughs in the interests of the empathic, and instead of trivializing the drama, a naturalistic method that gives it credibility.

Whatever the method, however, or stylization in performance, there seems no way of avoiding what Stanislavski required, some *grounds* for emotional truth, which—as I began to perceive through the years—may come through cultural distance or difference or any form of distantiation: not only the Brechtian *gestus,* but a Chinese mask, a shadow puppet, or a Kathakali headdress, or down the *hashigakara* in the Japanese Noh drama, as one of the National Treasures, or honorific performers, takes what seems an eternity to make his way to the stage—but then, mesmerically, stunningly, in a swirl of voluminous robes, as if he brought the space with him, projecting an inner life. Or for that matter, in the early work of Robert Wilson, from *Deafman's Glance* to *Einstein on the Beach,* the seemingly imperturbable absence/presence of an equal amount of time, with not a word spoken, the actor then without training, and unequipped to speak it, no less develop a character out of a causal narrative—not so much an actor then, with a psychological life, but an aural or visual instance, or a passing figuration, maybe sinking into the stage or, weightlessly, emblematically, disappearing from it. There may be in such performance unexpected incursions of feeling, or in its dispersive vision the Sufi whirling semblance of it, but where it comes from, or *why? what for?* we'd find that hard to say, as if the ground of emotion there—in the temporal archeology of the spatial attenuations—were, in Foucauldian terms, from another episteme.

But then, the same might be said, indeed, of my earliest readings of Stanislavski, which took place actually more than half a century ago. What particularly struck me then, in the notorious chapter on "Emotion Memory," was (as I remember) the stress on emotional *truth,* with some indeterminacy remaining to this day on how, in directing, you really determine that, that is, what constitutes truth? truth in what regard? and if not ideologically, on what conceptual grounds? Such questions occurred to me soon beyond the issue of acting, about every aspect of theater, from the most imperceptible breath through every cadenced sensation, in light, sound, fabrics, objects, space, to the performative bodies in the tactile rhythm of thought. That rhythm will surely be altered somehow, in the age of information, by electronic and digital extensions into cyberspace, which in theory, at least, has raised the issue of "liveness," and if I were directing now that would be something to think about. What impressed me then, however—given what's still the unregenerate mortality of the form, with all its human failings, and a complex emotional life—was the reminder to the young actors, by Stanislavski's surrogate, the all-knowing director Tortsov, that while there may be now and then "spontaneous eruptions" of feeling, the truth of emotion cannot depend on that. To be sure, spontaneity in acting is still a desideratum, but if I were to say let's stop and think about it a little, what forms it might take, there'd be some who'd say, that's the trouble, too much thinking.

Yet if, in the American theater today, it's still a pretty standard view that a liability for the actor is thinking too much, the premium placed on spontaneity may have—especially for the actor who hardly thinks at all, in the sort of theater with not much to think about—the dubious virtue of sustaining certain illusions, to which a director, at least, would have to give some thought. So it is when, presumably, the instinctual life takes over during the course of improvisation, and—with the libidinal body coded, an agglomerate of familiar reflexes—we find ourselves dealing with a plethora of banalities, which if not perceived, challenged, rehearsed away, merely serve as verification of what Freud tipped us off about, that the instincts, if spontaneous, are essentially conservative. And quite frankly, those instincts are likely to be no different, despite all claims of subversion, dispersion, multiplicity, in the multiplex of theaters defining themselves by difference, whether gendered, racial, ethnic, queer, or in a body without organs on one of the anti-Oedipal sites of the Deleuzeian thousand plateaus.

As for access to the unconscious—however you think of it, as a linguistic, metaphorical, or dramaturgical structure—difference isn't privileged; so the question is how to get there. Tortsov was actually addressing that when he said of technique that the "cardinal principle" is this: "through conscious means we reach the unconscious," and these conscious means seem to require the deployment "of *repeated feelings* drawn from emotion memory. . . ." When one of the young actors, Grisha, surprised at the notion of repetition, asks whether "in every kind of role, from Hamlet to Sugar in *The Blue Bird,* we have to use our own, same, old feelings?" Tortsov replies: "What else can you do? . . . Do you expect an actor to invent all sorts of new sensations, or even a new soul, for every part he plays? . . . You can borrow clothing, a watch, *things* of all sorts but you cannot take feelings away from another person. My feelings are inalienably mine."[5] No quarrel with that whatever, putting aside the question of soul. But when it's asked on the ramparts in *Hamlet,* "What, has this thing appeared again to-night?" (1.1.21), it's quite another thing, with its vast ghostly repository of feeling, as Coleridge understood, and conceivably Tortsov too, but because of the very elusiveness of the thing, there are still feelings and feelings, and in the actual making of theater feelings in estranged, unsettling, doubtful, delirious, maybe even deranged, or even if pedestrian, always particular contexts, and sometimes an actor's sense, equally inalienable, of not feeling right at all, or not doing this or that because s/he doesn't feel it, though s/he may not feel it if s/he doesn't do it, or even know what it is, as it materializes somehow from whatever it is it is *not* or, at the quick of thought, its factness, its thingness, might conceivably be.

And so it was in my KRAKEN group (and this an emotional memory) when during the course of a long inquiry (I don't say rehearsal, since we were still seeking, in the heuristic methodology of that group, what there would be *to* rehearse), one of the actors stopped and said—as Method actors frequently do, and that was not our method—"Damn! I don't feel this, I'm not feeling it at all." Whereupon I burst forth in no uncertain terms, "I couldn't care less what you feel, or don't, feelings are cheap! *I only care what you think!* What we're doing here is thinking, trying to understand." Which by no means made me insensitive to what the actors felt, for as there are feelings and feelings, there is thinking and thinking, and other forms of spontaneity in their fastidious interaction. And I think over the years we worked together they surely understood that, as they did when I said that what we were attempting to do, with all the resources at our disposal—bodies, minds, psyche, senses, every form of intelligence, neurally analytical, and intuitive too—whatever we were working on, with text, without text (when the text evolved, maybe elliptical, associative, dense as it could be), was *to bring it into thought.* And since the means were psychophysical—the actors so adept with their bodies, breath blood nerves brains, that they could literally perform standing on their heads—I called it "blooded thought."

And that pertains to emotions, too, about which we have to think, because we know very little about them. As it happens, too, while I was writing this, a friend of mine, the poet C. K. Williams, came to Seattle to give the Theodore Roethke Memorial Reading, and I was asked to introduce him. In working up what to say, it occurred to me that he had actually written about the uncertain and troubling way in which we think about emotions. So I looked again, not only at the poems, but at his essays on *Poetry and Consciousness,* in which he admits to having "been puzzled for a long time by what exactly an emotion is." Thinking about that, he wrote:

> Presumably . . . we might say that at least I myself know my emotion. But do I? If I were to describe the feeling itself to myself, what do I say? Much the same sort of thing. I am depressed about . . . death, say, separation, isolation. But these, again, are *conditions* of the

> emotion, frames, even causes; the emotion itself will often remain vague, uncertain, and transitory. Often it seems that by the time we are into the investigation of an emotion, that emotion has been frustratingly replaced by the one attached to the investigation.[6]

Of which, in the work with KRAKEN, I tried to make the central issue, with the investigation itself as the potentiality or prospect of an alternative form of theater. This made the task of directing, too, something else again than what I had been doing, even with the experimental tendencies of radically conceived productions, with scenic ideas coming, say, not only from theater designers but a wide range of visual artists, and with electronic music and sound that, to this day, would be considered way out, hard to take, and—as they used to say, too, about our productions of now-canonical dramatists when they were hardly known—self-indulgently avant-garde. What may have been even more troubling in what I came to do was the movement of thought through a self-reflexively conscious process of indeterminate feeling, or through *a methodical indeterminacy,* the layering of performance in such a way that it's impossible to say, for all its obsessive precision, what exactly is being enacted, or *how much acted,* with what *degree* of representation or, in the semblance of naked life, its seeming actuality, where seeming is seminal, or in the reality of its vanishings, at the selvage of perception, the imminence of meaning or some precipitous truth.

I have no illusions, by the way, that what I'm saying about directing is likely to be possible in every kind of theater, since what led me to think this way, after those many years of staging an extraordinary range of plays (nothing in the country like it), was a desire, for various reasons, to start all over again, as if from ground zero. That required, as you'll see, asking certain questions, which I wrote about in *Take Up the Bodies: Theater at the Vanishing Point,* most specifically at the beginning of a chapter called "Origin of the Species." That, too, starts with an epigraph, and then a reference to the Nordic kraken, which we capitalized and Americanized in the name KRAKEN. Though Tennyson wrote a poem about it, what I remembered, rather, was a letter from Melville to Hawthorne, who had asked, after the publication of *Moby-Dick,* what Melville might be doing next. He said he was after bigger fish, the kraken, which lives in its immensity many fathoms deep, but never rises to the surface, where, if it does, it dies.

That directing, too, has its affective memories I have been suggesting through this talk, and though I vaguely alluded to it a moment ago, I should say that if there's an informing emotion to the epigraph, that came from our failure at Lincoln Center, which I had written about in the previous chapter, no excuses, and the concluding question, taken from *Danton's Death,* with which I had opened the Beaumont Theater there: "What is it in me that denies me?" And the feeling afterward that, if the denial was inarguable, with a sort of emptying out, there were still resources to be drawn upon. But, about that, the epigraph poses a question:

> "Sir, thou hast nothing to draw with, and the well is deep: from whence then hast thou that living water?" (John 4:11):
>
> (. . . in the kraken's wake:) *What we want to show is not only the structure we have come to but the conceiving process in the structure, what led to it and what leads back to its sources, in the world, in us, in the friction between us, the work, each other, the rage, the work, each playing upon the other, receding, the world, our gravity; a memory trace in a spoor of association,* the thinking through. *There is always the haunted and critical moment when what we're after is almost not-there, the moment of Appropriation, the stepping back:* Act? how? why? where? what for? for whom? and to what End? *Why am I doing this in the first place? and can we? and since there is always the likelihood that nobody is listening or, if listening, cares what it means, what difference does it make? It may be that we are all listening to different voices, this candle, that flame; not for love or money the same light.*[7]

Out of this view of things, at that restively self-questioning, transitional period of my life, came another method, taking up those questions, while intensifying the question, for me, of what it means to be a director—or how one can be a director *without* being asked for the answers, because the actors are the answers as the substance of the work. I mean the living and intending and apprehending, an inalienable function of it, what is done and how it's done, its conditions of possibility passing into thought, until through the very facticity of thinking, it becomes the thing itself. As for the friction between us, that's almost inevitable among those who work together long hours daily, with a revealing intimacy or intolerable silence, over a considerable period of time. Whatever the loyalty, love, and affections, there were—and if in any way deflected, deflected into the work—anxieties, distrust, antagonism, resentment, and even in the most responsive accord, *the rage, the work,* the work itself raging, different voices and different value, with both the license and the stricture of competing instincts, the metonymical impetus—and the work was highly verbal, sometimes in the process logorrheically so, suffusive, complex, cerebral—of an always aberrant desire. And not, once fashionable, the post-Lacanian kind, desire desiring desire, but as in metaphysical poetry, thou blind man's mark, thou fool's self-chosen snare. Or as it was in *Crooked Eclipses,* the title of a work we did, derived from Shakespeare's sonnets:

> Look what thy memory cannot contain,
> Commit to these waste blanks, and thou shalt find
> Those children nursed, delivered from thy brain,
> To take a new acquaintance of thy mind.
>
> (Sonnet 77)

As for the entire repertoire of confused and troubling emotions that, as they arise, nobody quite understands, they indeed became frames or even causes, subjects of critique. As the investigation continued, it sometimes seemed, indeed, as if we were hallucinating, or in the shape of dream, as in the stagings of the unconscious, which is not only the deepest form of memory, but where we do our deepest thinking, in a superfetation of image, at the filamenting nerve ends of thought, "A quest of thoughts, all tenants to the heart" (Sonnet 46). Nor was anything censored in the process, even the tendencies of the actors to criticize each other, or me for that matter, all of it caught up in the inquiry and, however sublimated, displaced, projected, suffusing what was done in performance, and so, too, what haunts the theater, ghosting its greatest drama, the ineliminable riddle, the riddle of self-doubt. I wish I had time to explore it, as it informed the work we did, as frame, as cause, as motive, the curious thing being that one can feel enlivened by that. About one thing, however, I have no doubt: though there was a kind of brain fever to it all, at the most haunted and critical moments, the thing *not-there,* whatever it is that escaped us, is also what kept us thinking, what we would never have thought without it, and that more than anything, in its factness, its thingness, as an emotional memory is, to this day, an inspiriting *form-of-life.*

NOTES

1. Samuel Beckett, *Breath,* in *Collected Shorter Plays* (New York: Grove, 1984) 209.
2. *Obsolete Body / Suspensions / Stelarc,* ed. James D. Paffrath, with Stelarc (Davis, CA: JP Publications, 1984).
3. Beatrice Manley, *My Breath in Art: Acting from Within* (New York: Applause, 1998) 16.

4. Quoted in Timothy J. Wiles, *The Theater Event: Modern Theories of Performance* (Chicago: University of Chicago Press, 1980) 49.

5. Constantin Stanislavski, *An Actor Prepares,* trans. Elizabeth Reynolds Hapgood (New York: Theater Arts, 1936) 165–66.

6. C. K. Williams, *Poetry and Consciousness* (Ann Arbor: University of Michigan Press, 1998) 1–2.

7. Herbert Blau, *Take Up the Bodies: Theater at the Vanishing Point* (Urbana: University of Illinois Press, 1982), 77–78.

NINE

The Commodius Vicus of Beckett

Vicissitudes of the Arts in the Science of Affliction

To think perhaps it won't all have been for nothing!
—HAMM, in *Endgame*

WHEN THE THEATER BECOMES CONSCIOUS of itself as theater, it is not so much studying itself as an object but realizing that theatricality, if too elusive for objectification, materializes in thought, like representation for the human sciences, as a condition of possibility, which as always remains to be *seen.* Once that is realized, there is no alternative but for the theater to become more and more self-conscious, even beyond Brecht, reflexively critical, with the dispelling of illusion, however, as another order of illusion in which there will inevitably be a succession of demystifications and unveilings, but as if the teasers and tormentors that frame the stage (even in a thrust, or presumably open stage) were revealing nothing so much as the future of illusion. This might be thought of, too, in its materialization, and especially in Beckett, as the nothing that comes of nothing or, in despite of nothing—as he says of sounds, in "Variations on a 'Still' Point"—"mostly not for nothing never quite for nothing,"[1] the inexhaustible stirrings still, at "the very heart of which no limit of any kind was to be discovered but always in some quarter or another some end in sight such as a fence or some manner of bourne from which to return" ("Stirrings Still" 263). Even if the return were guaranteed by the "preordained cyclicism" that Beckett perceived in Vico,[2] this could, of course, "all eyes"—in the more scopophilic Beckett—proceed "from bad to worse till in the end he ceased if not to see to look (about him or more closely) and set out to take thought," where what goes up must come down, transcendentally deflated, "So on unknowing and no end in sight" ("Stirrings Still" 263).

It is to this no-end that Beckett points when at the quasi beginning of *Endgame*—in the gray light, there at the outset, the depleted limit of the scopic field—the room is exposed, the forms are differentiated, and in a series of unveilings, with the parents in the ashbins, still stirring, the memory of the Oedipal pattern is played out. It's as if consciousness itself is referred back to its real conditions: its contents litter the scene, both as dissociated objects and fragments of desire and longing, the old words, the old questions, the return of the Same as an old compulsion, with something taking its course that, whatever's happening now, may or may not have happened before, and in any case we wouldn't know it as it somehow passes us by, as it does in the prose of "The Calmative," sometimes with "shrill laughter" or "cries of joy toward the comic vast," the something that has to happen, "to my body as in myth and metamorphosis, the old body to which nothing ever happened, or so little, which never met with anything, loved anything, wished for anything, in its tarnished universe, except for the mirrors to shatter, the plane, the curved, the magnifying, the minifying, and to vanish in the havoc of images" (63). As we try, amid the havoc, to put the untellable story together, it becomes quite possible that the myriad of indeterminacies in the virtually nonconscious, receding with every stirring into the problematic of the unconscious, becomes thus coextensive with the drama, all that the drama is left to be.

It is with this in mind that I must confess to feeling about the notion of "after Beckett" as I've always felt when I hear talk—for all that's warranted in critique—of "after Freud," as if there were a sequel, not only to civilization and its discontents, but to the existential datum of the reality principle itself, what I come back to invariably through ground zero in Beckett: "Use your head, can't you, use your head, you're on earth, there's no cure for that!" If there's no cure for it, alas, we still have to use our heads—"he having been dreamt away [letting] himself be dreamt away" ("Still Point" 267)—as in the "talking cure"of Freud, which he tells us is interminable, or in the mise-en-scène of the unconscious, our oldest mental faculty, active in sleep, deeply there, "But deep in what sleep, deep in what sleep already?" (*Endgame* 53), as Hamm asks insidiously, in his scornful rehearsal of undying desire around the unfinishable story of the dubious child. As for the future of illusion, it would seem, for all the demystifications still going on in theory, to be through the stirrings the only foreseeable future, unless in "the poisonous ingenuity of Time,"[3] which the young Beckett discerned in Proust, as in the toneless "fixed gaze" of Clov's grievous wish fulfillment, "it's finished, nearly finished" (1). If grain upon grain, it's nevertheless not quite, whatever it is—"It all. (*Pause.*) It all."[4]—taking its measure is another matter, since if there's any reality there, it "can only be apprehended as a retrospective hypothesis," which is what Beckett says of the Proustian subject in the depredations of Time, its "constant process of decantation" (*Proust* 4), with the hypothetical retrospection like the interpretation of a dream.

Thus, what I think of as Beckettian is that which, whatever there was before, in the "commodius vicus of recirculation"[5] of the something taking its course, imperceptibly *is,* as at the "dream's navel" (Freud's term), unnamably there, where in a collapse of temporality it passes out of sight—*it*? no? nothing?—the deciphering of the dream, which Beckett might insist was not a dream at all, but in the disremembered remnants of what was or may be, the materiality of an absence forever becoming itself. So, before we come to after, let me turn to before, "Another trait its repetitiousness. Repeatedly with only minor variants the same bygone. As if," as Beckett wrote in *Company,* "willingly by this dint to make it his."[6] Which is perhaps to think of after—though there will be other variants—as a habit of apprehension, mainly a state of mind, "Saying," as in "Faux Départs," "Now where is he, no," even with nothing there, "Now he is here" (272).

To be sure, there was considerable talk about nothing before Beckett came on the scene, with his nothing to be done, which became the anomalous grounds of a political activism that—around our first attempt to *do* it, there in San Francisco nearly half a century ago—I've written about before: the apparently purposeless waiting that, before the Days of Rage, became the model of passive resistance. "Because I do not hope to turn again / Because I do not hope / Because I do not hope to turn"[7]—here the voice, as you may know, is neither mine nor Beckett's, but T. S. Eliot's, not quite at the still point, but just before he entered the church, declaring himself a classicist in literature and a royalist in politics. If the variants of the repetitiveness in their equivocating momentum are not exactly a form of activism, what we tend to forget is that Eliot had been much admired by those on the political left, even the radicals of *The New Masses,* when he gave us a devastating critique of modernity, as in *The Waste Land,* which they read as bourgeois reality. If he was, even then, seeking the peace that passeth understanding, "Shantih shantih shantih" (67), a transcendental form of nothingness, he came to that by way of the nothing that with hysteria in the bygone keeps repeating itself:

> Nothing again nothing.
>   "Do
> "You know nothing? Do you see nothing? Do you remember
> "Nothing?"

The autistic intensity of that obsessional nothing, its self-punishing iteration, would seem to be the exacerbated condition of what Beckett later called, in his essay on Proust, "the science of affliction" (*Proust* 4), about which you could also say—whether "in rats' alley / Where the dead men lost their bones" (Eliot 55) or in the "thousand small deliberations" protracting "the profit of their chilled delirium" (Eliot 33)—that nothing came of nothing *in* the nothing to be done.

As for the efficacy of art in that delirium, as in the non sequiturs of the tramps in *Godot,* the thousand small deliberations in the vicissitudes of waiting, where "Thinking is not the worst" or even "to *have* thought," if you could somehow remember, having forgotten the very beginning, "The very beginning of WHAT?,"[8] what you were saying when, Wittgenstein remarked—with reservations about the causal when the problem is conceptual—"In art it is hard to say anything as good as: saying nothing."[9] But if that raises the question of whether saying is doing—as in the "Closed place" of Beckett's "Fizzle 5," where "There is nothing but what is said. Beyond what is said there is nothing," while, with its alienated millions,"What goes on in the arena is not said"[10]—it was W. H. Auden who might have been speaking for Beckett when he said, backing away from the arena, or the early politics in his poetics, that art changes nothing, but it at least changes that.

He might have added, however, that, in the changing of nothing there might also be changes in art, as there certainly were after the incursion of Beckett, not only upon the theater, as in Peter Brook's *King Lear* or, about the same time, my own—but on other modes of performance and performance sites, as well as the emergence of hybrids in the visual arts and music, and now in digitality, where the absences and the nothingness may be of another order. So it is with *That Brainwave Chick,* Paras Kaul, sitting in a chair, like Hamm, something dripping in her head, not from the veins, or arteries, but from digital-system electrodes for neural audio imaging of what's not there when it is, that is, another virtual world. Or there's the cyborgian dystopia of *Remote Host,* a recent computer animation by Katya Davar, with its giddy balloon over a Beckettian landscape which, impeccably rendered by the intuitive graphic interface that inspired Microsoft's Windows, needs only Didi and Gogo to attend to the whisper, the rustle, the voices all speaking at once, in the bleakly alluring nowhere with its woefully leafless tree.

As for the emergence of conceptual art, back in the 1960s, that too was of another order, where everything seemed to be absent, no figures, no tree, no nothing, except the deliberations, what it is to have thought, about what it is to be art, which turned out to be not object or image but context, as if thinking made it so. If art only exists conceptually, it was given definition by Joseph Kosuth's *Art as Idea as Idea,* which, in white print on a black field, consists of the dictionary definitions of "Idea," beginning with the Greek *"idein . . . ,* to see" and ending with "the Phil n *ideatum,* a thing that, in fact, answers to the idea of it, whence 'to ideate', to form in, or as an, idea," and during the course of ideation through permutations in other languages: ideal, idealism, *idée fixe.* Or as if the *fixe* were seeking a site, as with another "work" by Kosuth, *Matter in General,* it turns up with block-lettered words on a billboard (in a gamut of abstraction from RESINS to UNIVERSE) out in an open field, translating from the conceptual or placing it, thus, as site-specific art.[11] In the closed places or arenas of such art—"Place consisting [maybe] of an arena and a ditch," as Beckett says in the fifth Fizzle, with an ominous impassivity: "No interest. Not for imagining," the millions there, "six times smaller than life" (236)—it's as if the idea doesn't materialize until it determines *where* it is, putting in abeyance for the moment the dimensions of the site, which might be considerably larger than the mound of *Happy Days* in which Winnie is up to her diddies; or even than the flattened cylinder of "The Lost Ones," if not its "omnipresence as though every separate square centimeter were agleam of the some twelve million of total surface" (207). Which is what—that prospect of "agleam"—keeps the auratic alive, as if from the lower depths, in the age of deconstruction. "For in the cylinder alone are certitudes to be found and without nothing but mystery" (216). As for deconstruction, it might also be remembered that it also came after Beckett, but as if he had predicated the Derridean writing before the letter that, somehow *avant la lettre,* would surely reverse itself, while the critique of representation with its scourge of the scopophilic—and thus what we think of as theater—would not deter the "unceasing eyes" (212) or "questing eyes" (220) that "without nothing but mystery" approached in the bed of the cylinder "clear-cut mental or imaginary frontiers invisible to the eye of flesh" (216).

Whatever those ubiquitous eyes, all eyes, find there, in the dire vast of the cylinder, the charting of location here, entangled as there with language, is a matter of reading signs, which is to say—as if repeating another bygone, the structuralism of Saussure—situating the signifier within the semiotic system. Manifold, tautological, interminable, it is a system of multiple discourses, from the political to the aesthetic, all informing "what 'it' can be said to *be,*"[12] as one critic wrote about what, like the zones of the cylinder, "if this notion is maintained" (223), is presumably site-specific. Say what you will about it, in Beckett that "it," caught up as it is in discourse, seems not merely conceptual but also ontological, and for the metonymic moment can almost drive you out of your mind: not that, *this,* not this, *that,* or in block letters call it IT, WHAT it? (damn all pronouns!) before it disappears, like—though it seems on another scale entirely, far beyond the scope of a fizzle—Robert Smithson's *Spiral Jetty,* with its commodious Viconian shape, a major site (or is it arena?), which in the Great Salt Lake of Utah is underwater now. And for those who have been there, having seen the photographs, looking for it, it's as if space itself extended through the long solemnity of time, "All sides endlessness earth sky as one no sound no stir." If the vanishing occurred, shockingly, before Smithson had anticipated, there was also—as he thought in archaeological rather than historical time—the expectation of attrition over aeons, as if Beckett had written the scenario at the very beginning of "Lessness": "Ruins true refuge long last towards which so many false time out of mind" (197).

It's no accident, then, that in the "ultramundane margins" around the "four blocks of print" in the visual layout of Smithson's essay, "Quasi-Infinities and the Waning of Space," he quotes the passage from Beckett's essay on Proust about the constant process of decantation, after speaking of "actuality" as a sort of Beckettian *pause* when, as a void between events, nothing is happening. "In art," he says in one of the blocks, "action is always becoming inertia, but this inertia has no ground to settle on except the mind, which is as empty as actual time."[13] There is a quotation from Cage's *Silence* on one side and images of de Kooning and Pollock paintings on the other, but in what Smithson says of action becoming inertia in its movement through empty time, it's as if he were describing (with one omission I will come to) the dramaturgy of Beckett, which, whatever the drama was left to be, seemed inclined to make it less, and at its most reductive nothing more than (a) *Breath.*

Again, this is far from the magnitudes associated with Smithson, who eventually thought of the monumental and, even through the ineluctability of entropic waste, was always imagining more. He started smaller, of course, but elsewhere he refers to his early *Cryosphere,* in which mirrors were built into a hexagonal lattice containing ice crystals, magnifying, minifying, moving through multiplication in an "ambiguous flux," like a version of *Endgame* I saw the inmates rehearsing at Tegel Prison in Berlin, with seven Hamms and seven Clovs reflected through reflections around a wading pool. The *Cryosphere* was a sort of prototype of the expanded site or "self-canceling" system that Smithson calls "a *surd area,*" which, though it seems to fold tautologically back upon itself, is nevertheless, he says, "beyond tautology . . . not really beyond, there's no beyond," and with logic suspended too, the surd defeats "any idea of any kind of system"[14]—the idea for which, however, we later learn in a footnote, was mainly derived from *The Unnamable.*

Putting aside playwrights, from Pinter and Mamet to Sarah Kane or the Egyptian Tawfik al-Hakim, whose *Fate of a Cockroach* is a dialogue of inconsequence with metaphysical intimations, about the struggle of a cockroach to get out of a bathtub, to Chinese Nobel Prize winner Gao Xingjian, whose plays bring to the politics of exile, through a version of lessness, the scruple of Zen, Smithson was hardly the only artist to have specifically picked up on Beckett. This was apparent in my own experience with artists in San Francisco, who almost never went to the theater, or pretty much disdained it as a form that was retarded, all the more because of the drama, which even if subject to the Brechtian A-effect, was still predictably mimetic and not sufficiently surd, never mind *ab*surd, "quaquaquaqua," where "for reasons unknown no matter what matter the facts are there and considering what is more much more grave," there seems no system to cancel, and if also no beyond, the matter still "unfinished," as at the end of Lucky's speech (*Godot* 29). We were already doing work that was considered avant-garde, but it wasn't really until *Waiting for Godot* and *Endgame* that an array of visual artists became engaged with other productions, quite explicitly then because they began to design for our theater. As for myself, paradoxically, it was during this period that I was thinking of leaving the theater, because—through inclinations partially nurtured by directing Beckett, and images, objects, aspects of the work: the silences, pauses, the meticulous mathematics of an antiaesthetic, the timings down to the second or "(*Smooth grey rectangle 0.70m. × 2m.*)," and then, as if painted by Brice Marden or inflected by Robert Ryman, "No shadow. Colour: none. All grey. Shades of grey"; in short, "Forgive my stating the obvious" (*Ghost Trio* 248), with correlatives in the other arts—I was far more interested in what was happening there, and in alternative modes of performance.

If what was emerging in the art world, particularly visual culture, but in the newer music too—from the "noise" in Cage's silence to the longing in Feldman's durations to the sustained repetitiveness of Terry Riley's middle C, its preordained cyclicism—corresponded in strategies to what we see on stage in Beckett, it included the "energy-drain" in the action of inertia, which caused Smithson to write elsewhere of "the flat surface, the banal, the empty, the cool, blank after blank," in short, the blank planes of an art "going nowhere,"[15] and which, in its "lugubrious complexity," is enlivened by "a new consciousness of the vapid and the dull" (13). These were qualities, of course, invoked by those who were puzzled or even outraged by the earliest productions of Beckett. What may have been missing, however, in the conceptual substance of the artists referred to by Smithson in "Entropy and the New Monuments" (Flavin, Judd, Lichtenstein, LeWitt, Morris, Thek) was, along with the poignancy of an unpurgeable nostalgia, the residual metaphysics in the diminuendo of being, the mourning in the entropic, so endemic to Beckett, or what even in the dominion of nothing always inclined toward lessness—"Blank planes touch close sheer white all gone from mind" ("Lessness" 197)—but was somehow quite enough, whatever it may have been. And so it is, even silence: "Too much silence is too much. Or it's my voice too weak at times. The one that comes out of me. So much for the art and craft" ("Enough" 186).

But what we have in the art and craft, suffused as it is with nostalgia—"More and more. All was," as at the end of "Enough" (192)—is what might be considered, through the facet-planes of the impasse that, oxymoronically, makes Beckett postmodern, the last of the modernists, for whom what can never be anymore, maybe, when remembered, really couldn't have been. In the visual arts, modernism was in the 1950s—when at The Actor's Workshop of San Francisco we turned to Beckett's plays—still the historical and critical matrix of the major forms of art, as with the abstract expressionists, whose erasure of the figure, or nonobjectivity, took place in "an arena," as Harold Rosenberg called it, where "action painting," was in its performativity "not a picture but an event,"[16] yet still an assertion of valued identity rather than a testament to nothing. Things were moving in that direction, however, when the painters and sculptors sponsored by Clement Greenberg, and later by Michael Fried—whose "Art and Objecthood" was an obdurate resistance to the theatricality taking over painting and sculpture[17]—were challenged by artists as diverse as Jasper Johns, Richard Hamilton, and Joseph Beuys, as well as the Pop Art that, in restoring the figure, enlivened emptiness, or brought the notion of nothing, as in exchange value, into the image of commodification. If there was a certain equivocation in such art about being commodified itself, the equivocation disappeared into the phenomenon of Andy Warhol, who seemed to be painting next to nothing when he did his Campbell Soups, as if willingly by this dint the repetitiveness was no longer a bygone, but the marketable immediacy of the evacuated thing itself.

Meanwhile, the sophistication of advertising is such today that it can even deploy with ambiguity a sort of Beckettian nostalgia, as designers manage to bring, through fantasized images of duration and loss, a sense of dispossession to fashion models on the runway, while endowing certain objects with a patina of cryptic time, even now in the tearing of jeans, making a sales pitch out of the memory of what never really was, or was it? in a maybe guarded recall of the dubiously recoverable, the loss of which is a question better not to ask. (Especially at those prices.) Or there may be with a certain jaundice, confessing that "all is false," as if drawing on *Texts for Nothing,* a sense of "no way out," and in a reality that's factitious with plaintiveness aside, letting ourselves "be dupes," as Beckett wrote of the nothing to understand, except no more denial, "dupes of every tone and tense, until it's done, all past and done, and the voices cease," superficial or profound, "it's only voices, only lies" (*Texts* 3:109). As for the market or the shopping mall, if they hardly exist in Beckett—unless in the "tattered syntaxes of Jolly and Draeger Praeger Draeger" of "All Strange Away" (169)—when we encounter objects, their melancholy might be ascribed to their never being so desirable as to achieve, shabby or makeshift as they are, the ignominy of commodification.

This was not a problem, however, to artists who, in 1986, were part of an exhibition on reference and simulation in painting and sculpture, the title of which was "Endgame," the reference there, no question, precisely to Beckett. For Peter Halley, Sherrie Levine, and Philip Taaffe, the commodified world is not only the context but the ceaselessly reproductive source of their art, abstraction itself or simulation a thriving commodity, which is the absence of longing, even as they iconicize emptiness, for anything like an existential void. As can also be seen in the installations of Haim Steinbach and Jeff Koons—his vacuum cleaners, for instance, encased in plexiglass boxes—emptiness can be glamorized and even the void sold.[18]

It wasn't so much the void, but the recursiveness of the language and the extremes of human behavior that excited the video artist Bruce Nauman in the work of Beckett. What attracted him first of all, like others to this day, were the clownish types or gestures, from the Chaplinesque of the tramps to Buster Keaton in *Film,* along with the incapacity in the ashcans or the urns or up to its neck in the sand. Thus, in *Clown Torture* (1987), there's a figure stressed out on one leg, and then—as if with the carafe and cubes in *Act without Words*—forced to balance two fish bowls and a bucket of water, while shouting "No, no, no" and "I'm sorry" to the nobody listening there. Even before that, in *Slow Angle Walk* (1968), which was subtitled *Beckett Walk,* Nauman himself performed a series of impaired or spastic Clov-like movements, including a stiff leg up in the air, with his body swivelling around to get the leg back on the floor. Nauman has also done environmental videos in which the spectator is made wary of what's not (yet) there or otherwise demoralized by a babble of disjunct words, as in the *Deep Sleep* of John Jesurun (1985), where a sea of associations ("deep in what sleep already?") going on incessantly suggests the elliptical stream of words from Beckett's disembodied Mouth.

But to go back to when happenings and installation art were first making the scene, in the work of Allan Kaprow, Jim Dine, and Claes Oldenburg: their influence was such, eventually, that there seemed to be a virtual moratorium on painting. Or you might see the virtual equivalent of the picture in Beckett's *Endgame* that—though looked at bitterly, sardonically, by Clov, without letting us see it—is otherwise turned to the wall, as it might very well be in the send-up gallery of Ben Vauthier or the rubbish-strewn cellar of Terry Fox, which might have been swept up by Beuys and, in an impeccably minimalist glass-enclosed case, which might have been done by Koons, exhibited with the broom. This was the period when Yoko Ono did her *Painting to Be Stepped On* (which, with loose fabric on the surface, is actually an assemblage) and Robert Rauschenberg exhibited, in *Trophy III (for Jean Tingueley)* a see-through picture frame in which the picture was replaced by a miniature piece of bedspring, a swag of knotted cloth, and up one side of the chipped and abraded frame, with small objects protruding in, a thin ladder that if larger might have been used in the cylinder by the lost ones struggling to climb—the art object rather elegant, like some stagings of Beckett, in its impoverishment. Nor was Beckett alone in denying us a look at what, perhaps, was not really there to see, though if it was, its visual status was like that of the mechanically drawn lines of Piero Manzoni, rolled up in a tube, stored, and for those all eyes, unavailable to be seen.

At the same time, in Italy, there was the *arte povera* of Jannis Kounellis, Mario Merz, and Michelangelo Pistoletto. Their constructions from any material whatever (animal, vegetable, mineral) conveyed, like Gogo's boots, the pathetic tree, the three-legged toy dog in *Endgame,* Krapp's spool or banana, a tailor's scissors out of the flies or the littered stage of *Breath,* the dull and vapid absurdity of a reality that—whether dissolving in five seconds, two seconds, two seconds, five seconds, or in . . . *but the clouds* . . . was replenished or augmented by "something else, more . . . rewarding, such as . . . such as . . . cube roots, for example"—seemed increasingly, nonetheless, to amount to nothing, "that MINE," undermined, yet issuing forth again (261), a view that sustained itself even as prices went up on this impoverished art, as Beckett's stock rose into canonization with his Nobel Prize.

If there are artists, like Steinbach and Koons, who've created a quite consciously superficial aesthetic of commodity culture, there are those like Christian Boltanski who have with layers of impacted history aestheticized waste and impoverishment, even as Beckett has done with decrepitude, but with affects exceeding any aesthetic, or perhaps compounded by it. In *Reserve* (1989), Boltanski littered half a ton of ragged and smelly clothes on a gallery floor. The mute shamble of a presence created by the cheap material, showing signs of long use, was due to its having been worn by now-anonymous poor children. What was conveyed by the massive heap—this, too, an "impossible heap" (*Endgame* 1), the muteness only disturbed when gallery viewers shuffled through—was a certain eeriness, a deadliness, like that of a mass grave, which, through the evasive (now commonplace) laughter, might be in the wings of *Godot.* Or never mind the wings, but as if it were reeking somehow from their own smelly clothes, Didi and Gogo sense it, right there on the stage—"Where are all these corpses from?"—or maybe out in the audience, the maw of absence there: "A charnel-house! A charnel-house!" At which you don't have to look, but "You can't help looking" (*Godot* 41).

If there is voyeurism in Boltanski, compulsively solicited, as with the tearings at caecal walls, the slow killings in the skull, "the fornications with corpses" ("Calmative" 61), all eyed in Beckett's prose, it is with the remembrance of what at some unseeable limit makes those questing eyes go still, as after a rare erection in the cylinder, "the spectacle . . . remembered of frenzies prolonged in pain," which, when "desisting and deathly still," verges on the obscene. Whereupon, "Stranger still at such times, [the eyes] fix their stare on the void or on some old abomination as for instance other eyes and then the looks exchanged by those fain to look away" (220). As for the logorrheic rehearsal of the egregious comedy of the plays—like the scene where, if the tree is up for a hanging, the tramp might get an erection—the void is there still to be stared at, and the abomination, prolonged as it was in pain, the unspeakably obscene. So it is when, sitting there in the dark, staring at the stage, no looks exchanged in the audience, there is the whisper, the murmur, the rustle, and those voices all speaking at once.

Meanwhile, if you didn't look away, there was surely an affinity between the flea-market compositions of certain artists, or wasteland installations, and the bleak, forlorn, or found-object landscapes of Beckett: aside from the boots and radishes, or Lucky's empty bag, the mound, the mouth, the urns, the nine-step passage of *Footfalls,* the standard lamp with its skull-sized globe, zero out the window or behind the hollow wall, or "facing other windows," the old rocker, mother rocker, "other only windows" (*Rockaby* 277, 280) looking out on an empty quad. "Area: square. Length of side: 6 paces"—that might have been the space in which Marina Abramović and her former partner Ulay, when they were still together, paced (a duo instead of four), "On the basis of one pace per second and allowing for time lost at angles and centre approximately 25 minutes," at first crossing paths "without rupture of rhythm, [but] if rupture accepted" (Beckett asks in stage directions: "how best exploit?"), they'd exploit by increasing the pace, two bodies repeatedly passing (but without the gowns and cowls, naked as not in *Quad*), gradually touching each other, then colliding at high speed, perhaps at quad's E, "supposed a danger zone," and then they'd pace, collide, pace, collide—no instruments necessary, "All possible percussion combinations given," until they "complete their courses" (*Quad* 291–93), as they did in utter exhaustion, in 1976 at the Venice Biennale, "Time 58 minutes."[19] In their work, as in Beckett, duration was also an issue, and when Abramović and Ulay stared at each across a table for 16 hours—with "Thoughts, no, not thoughts. Profounds of mind" or in that commodius vicus, as desideratum, "mindlessness"—not only the table ("say 8′ × 4′") might have been borrowed, but the profounds too, from *Ohio Impromptu* (285, 288).

Yet these performance events, transmuted as they were into rituals of high risk, were also meant to give access to otherwise forbidden consciousness or, without self-jeopardy, consciousness unattainable. But for Abramović particularly, there is also in the danger zone, as if she were listening to Hamm when he insisted we use our heads, a residuum of the reality principle: thus, on this earth, there might be a sense of the sacred, but *without* transformative powers. With a despair almost beyond Beckett's, who didn't bother much with the sacred, except at the furious thought of it, with the most disdainful humor, Abramović said mournfully, "It is too late, the destruction is already such that the world can no longer be 'cured'. . . . Its destruction will continue, inevitably. I only want to prepare people for the fact that we are all on a dying planet and that we will all be destroyed. I see a chance or a possibility of at least dying in union with the earth, at last grasping reality one single time."[20] Grasping the possibility if not the reality, there was, in her *Relation Works* with Ulay, an impetus toward the dissolution of boundaries, psychic and sexual, with such intensity as to exhaust or exceed the body, its capacity to withstand the ceaselessness of a singularity entailed by two, as in the seeming binary of the tramps in *Waiting for Godot,* one of whom would seem to exist only in the pulse of the other, the waiting itself an endurance. Thus, in *Breathing In / Breathing*

Out (1977) Abramović and Ulay relinquished autonomy, as they'd done of course before, but this time by sharing a single breath. Nostrils blocked, they pressed mouths together and synchronized their breathing, she inhaling air exhaled by him, he breathing the air exhaled by her. With ever-increasing concentrations of carbon dioxide, they breathed to the point of asphyxiation. Time: 19 minutes.

If there is in its sadomasochism an intimate theater of Cruelty, the same might be said of Beckett's. For all the compassion there, or, in the inconsolably deep structure of ungrounded dispossession, the pain of unnoticeability—like the tramp with the Boy, or the figure in the urn: "Am I as much as . . . being seen?" (*Play* 157)—there is with fastidious understatement, or aphasic compulsion, a Nietzschean side of Beckett, drawn like Artaud to cruelty, and the discomfiting pleasures of pain. Sometimes the unnoticeability can give that pleasure too, as in the unpublicized disappearances performed by Jochem Gerz and—having announced he would disappear, which he proceeded to do with no one seeing—Chris Burden, whose body art was otherwise known, like Gina Pane, Stuart Brisley, or Rudolf Schwarzkogler, for self-inflicted cruelties, sometimes excruciating. As Nietzsche remarked, in *The Genealogy of Morals,* "pleasure in cruelty is not really extinct today; only, given our greater delicacy, that pleasure has had to undergo a certain sublimation and subtlization, to be translated into imaginative and psychological terms in order to pass muster before even the tenderest hypocritical conscience."[21]

If the sublimation, translated, is nowhere more imaginative than in the plays and prose of Beckett, with subtleties unforeseen, in Schwarzkogler's case the subtlization was, in the extremity of its cruelty, next to suicidal—which turned out to be a preface to what he actually did, after the long rumor that he'd done it before, actually in performance, by methodically slicing his penis. Here the implacability is what, about certain mutilations, we may also remember in Beckett, both in physical images and as damage to the psyche, in the crisis of identity going back to *Molloy.*[22]

"And to tell the truth," says the Molloy who speaks at the end of the novel, "I not only knew who I was, but I had a sharper and clearer sense of my identity than ever before, in spite of its deep lesions and the wounds with which it was covered. And from this point of view I was less fortunate than my other acquaintances. I am sorry if this last phrase is not so happy as it might be. It deserved, who knows, to be without ambiguity" (233). As it turns out, though they were not acquaintances of Beckett, there were certain artists in the period following on what we call the sixties (which was mostly the 1970s) who were only too ready to do without the ambiguity. In that regard, with not even wounded vanity, they appropriated or canceled the iconic figures of high modernism by outright replication, thus undoing, presumably, the claims of the modern to posing serious ontological and epistemological questions. In this, they were taking a bypath from the practice of Beckett, where self-reflexivity and a relentless self-canceling was a way out, by going compulsively *in,* of the mortifying trap of identity—no less complicity with hierarchy, power, and the ideology of essence. In the act of replication, as in the painting of Peter Halley, who negated the factitious content of geometric abstraction, there was something like a secular conversion, a purgation of the modernist sin of a valorized self-indulgence, the vainglory of an identity celebrated in art, as the prerogative of genius: *a* Pollock, *a* Rothko, *a* Reinhardt, and—particularly unnerving, if haunting to Halley—the auratic zip in a Barnett Newman.

If formalists could argue that abstraction and nonobjectivity, the absence of narrative image, focused in the visual arts what is intrinsic, the sort of replicated abstraction practiced by Halley turned the modernist argument on its head: "art survives now," wrote Thomas Crow in 1986, "*by virtue of being weak,*"[23] a conviction linked in its way to the dismissal of authorial presence by Roland Barthes and Michel Foucault. It is that art which was featured in the exhibition "Endgame," though Beckett's weakness and the manic obsession of its reflexivity, is something else again, and again, and again, aphasically so, restoring essence despite him, no mistaking identity, even when he says, especially when he says, as he did in "First Love," "it is painful to be no longer oneself, even more painful if possible than when one is" (31). No doubt, the weakness is weakened even more by "the saturated, unending longing"[24] that Morton Feldman admired and, with the vanity of remembrance, like the failing memory of a self, tried to bring to his music. As he remarked in a book of his own, "we do not hear what we hear . . . , only what we remember,"[25] the question being—as Clark Lunberry, a student of mine wrote, in a just-completed dissertation—"how we might hear *that,* as if, once-removed, the remembered sounds, decayed," as in *The Unnamable,* "might somehow be made to return (in some ghostly manner) to sound, perhaps inaudibly, in their own resounding absence."[26] Which is what Feldman tried to achieve in his String Quartet II, through what seemed in performance the bodily fatigue of the musicians, as if it were, indeed, the orchestration of the unending, or as Beckett said of "the way out" in *Texts for Nothing 9,* "isn't it like a duo, or a trio, yes," not quite a quartet, true, but what variety, what monotony, "what vicissitudes within what changelessness" (137). And given the nature of the vicissitudes, while there are plenty of analogues to Beckett, and imitators too, as well as revisionist productions that—unbecomingly to his modesty, he also tried to stop—who can mistake *a* Beckett, even when deconstructed.

There is much more one could say about art after Beckett, its genres and speciation, or that which is more or less explicitly in its image. But about the unmistakable endurance of that which, in the before or after, remains inarguably his, one may say, as the narrator does of himself in the early story "Assumption" (published in 1929), that for all of Beckett's recurrent talk of dying—not even a slow death, but no sooner one is born, the (actual) death of the author, that "timeless parenthesis," there is in everything he wrote "the unreasonable tenacity with which he shrank from dissolution" (6). And if we were (as is customary in cultural studies today) to historicize this predilection, it might be said that what Beckett pushes to its extreme—or with the body, no body, to its extremities, "of so exquisite a quality as to exclude all thought of succour," as in the story "The End" (97)—is not exactly the end, but the beginning of the end which is our history, which is another way of defining modernism, among its vicissitudes being recurring announcements of its death.

Thus, the primary emotion of the modern, even when making it new and always subject to change, is *mourning,* which would seem to have reached its nadir or apotheosis in the lamentations of Beckett, though one hears much about it now in theory, as one does still in the arts, if mixed with degrees of indifference, or even exultation, about modern being the name for what's not possible anymore. When appropriation art appeared on the scene, as in the "Endgame" exhibition, there were those, like Yves Alain-Bois, who took to task the "manic mourning," or "pathological mourning," of such art, reminding us in a Freudian way that mourning has to be *worked through;* and so the end, endlessly so, without, however, elaborate mechanisms of defense, so that—in what seems like a paradox of endlessness—there would be a final "settling [of] our historical task: the difficult task of mourning" ("Endgame" catalogue 47). Difficult, no doubt, even absurd or appalling, but the notion of a nonpathological mourning might be incomprehensible to Beckett, who was for a time in psychoanalysis, but as if, in his obsessional case, to alleviate the working through. No sooner does he say, as in "Faux Départs," "Never ask another question," then imagination dead imagines "a place, then someone in it, that again," and the talking cure seems to consist of his "talking to himself the last person" (272). As for mourning as pathology, if he couldn't quite absorb that, "never see, never find, no end, no matter" (273), that's because it's not only a matter of modernity but closer to the human condition, so long as one is sufficiently moved by the immitigable impasse of the human itself, which can neither be painted, sculptured, installed, caught on a videodisc, nor, in or out of the theater—no less with "performativity," the going thing in theory, the solace of "bodies that matter" (it used to be "bodies without organs")—somehow performed away. "No future in this. Alas, yes."[27] Which, if the annulment of every no, leaves us with nothing yet.

NOTES

1. Samuel Beckett, "Appendix I: Variations on a 'Still' Point," in *The Complete Short Prose, 1929–1989,* ed. S. E. Gontarski (New York: Grove, 1995) 267; unless otherwise specified, all references in the text to Beckett's prose will be from this volume.

2. Samuel Beckett, "Dante . . . Bruno . Vico . . Joyce," in *Disjecta: Miscellaneous Writings and a Dramatic Fragment,* ed. Ruby Cohn (London: Calder, 1883) 21.

3. Samuel Beckett, *Proust* (New York: Grove, n.d.) 4.

4. Samuel Beckett, *Footfalls,* in *Collected Shorter Plays* (New York: Grove, 1984) 240; all references to Beckett's shorter plays are from this volume.

5. James Joyce, *Finnegans Wake* (New York: Viking, 1955) 3.

6. Samuel Beckett, *Company,* in *Nohow On: Three Novels* (New York: Grove, 1992) 10.

7. T. S. Eliot, *Ash Wednesday,* in *Selected Poems* (New York: Harvest/HAJ, 1964) 83; all references to Eliot are to this volume.

8. Samuel Beckett, *Waiting for Godot* (New York: Grove, 1954) 41–42.

9. Ludwig Wittgenstein, *Culture and Value,* trans. Peter Winch (Chicago: University of Chicago Press, 1980) 3.

10. "Fizzle 5," in *Complete Short Prose* 236.

11. These examples of Joseph Kosuth's conceptualism are in Ursula Meyer, *Conceptual Art* (New York: Dutton, 1972) 153–54.

12. Nick Kaye, *Site-Specific Art: Performance, Place and Documentation* (London: Routledge, 2000) 1.

13. Robert Smithson, "Quasi-Infinities and the Waning of Space," in *The Collected Writings,* ed. Jack Flam (Berkeley: University of California Press, 1996) 35.

14. "Four Conversations between Dennis Wheeler and Robert Smithson" (1969–70), in Smithson, *The Collected Writings* 198–99.

15. Robert Smithson, "Entropy and the New Monuments" (1966), in *The Collected Writings* 11.

16. Harold Rosenberg, "The American Action Painters," in *Tradition of the New* (New York: Horizon, 1959) 25.

17. Michael Fried, "Art and Objecthood," in *Minimal Art: A Critical Anthology,* comp. Gregory Battcock (New York: Dutton, 1968) 116–47.

18. See David Joselit, "Modern Leisure," in *Endgame: Reference and Simulation in Recent Painting and Sculpture* (Cambridge: MIT Press, 1986) 71–89. The exhibition was at the Institute of Contemporary Art in Boston.

19. Paul Schimmel, "Leap into the Void: Performance and the Object," in *Out of Actions: Between Performance and the Object, 1949–79* (London: Thames and Hudson, 1998) 101.

20. Marina Abramović, quoted by Linda Weintraub, *Art on the Edge and Over: Searching for Art's Meaning in Contemporary Society 1970s–1990s,* with essays by Arthur Danto and Thomas McEvilley (Litchfield, CT: Art Insights, 1996) 64.

21. Friedrich Nietzsche, *The Birth of Tragedy and The Genealogy of Morals,* trans. Francis Golffing (New York: Anchor/Doubleday, 1956) 200.

22. Samuel Beckett, *Molloy: A Novel,* trans. Patrick Bowles, in collaboration with Beckett (New York: Grove, 1955) 233.

23. Thomas Crow, "The Return of Hank Herron," in *Endgame: Reference and Simulation* 16; italics mine.

24. Morton Feldman, quoted by Everett C. Frost, "The Note Man and the Word Man," in *Samuel Beckett and Music,* ed. Mary Bryden (London: Oxford University Press, 1998) 51.

25. Morton Feldman, *Give My Regards to Eighth Street: Collected Writings of Morton Feldman,* ed. B. H. Friedman (Cambridge, MA: Exact Change, 2000) 209.

26. Clark Lunberry, "Situating Silence, Articulating Absence: Sites of Time and the Object (Lessons) of Art," Ph.D. diss., University of Wisconsin–Milwaukee, 2002, chap. 4, n.p.

27. Samuel Beckett, *Worstward Ho,* in *Nohow On* 91.

TEN

Among the Deepening Shades

The Beckettian Moment(um) and the Brechtian Arrest

IT MAY NOT BE, as Nietzsche said in *The Birth of Tragedy,* that illusion as the "reflection of eternal contradiction, begetter of all things," will lead to "a radiant vision of pure delight, a rapt seeing through wide-open eyes."[1] But if, as Freud thought, illusion has a future, with civilization and its discontents, it must surely include certain illusions about illusion and the means by which it is produced—what Brecht called the "apparatus," through which society absorbs "whatever it needs to reproduce itself," and which imposes its "views as it were incognito."[2] If one may speak not only of the illusion of reality but the reality of illusion, what shadows Brecht's critique is the question that prompted Nietzsche and has always haunted the theater—synoptically there in Beckett's Breath, or in the "Mere eye. No mind" of the "[*Repeat play*]" of *Play*[3]—as to whether the illusion produced is a doubled over redundancy, now you see it now you don't, mere eye insufficient, whether dazzled or baffled, distracted by the gaze, in a world made out of illusion.

The canonical drama dwells on that, and despite the deconstruction that was—after the Berliner Ensemble came to Paris in 1954, shortly after the appearance of *Waiting for Godot*—a partial outgrowth of Brechtian alienation, there is a residue in our thought of the resonance of illusion: all the world's a stage, life is a dream, the insubstantial pageant fading . . . into the "precession of simulacra," as Jean Baudrillard would say, when he announced the end of the real,[4] or into the Society of the Spectacle, which, as Guy Debord had said in the wake of the sixties, "is *capital* to such a degree of accumulation that it becomes an image."[5] Nor is that any the less illusory for being thought of as commodification in a factitious economy of invisible power. In a notorious passage of his *Short Organum* Brecht wrote scathingly of the capitulation to such power in tragic drama: to the gods who, beyond criticism, punished Oedipus, and of "Shakespeare's great solitary figures bearing on their breast the star of their fate," life becoming obscene as they collapse, "those dreamlike figures up on the stage," while the representation of their fate remains, through the "irresistible force of their futile and deadly outbursts" (*BT* 189), also beyond criticism. Despite the force of Brecht's remarks, irresistibly absorbed into an almost relentless critique of tragedy in poststructuralism, feminism, the new historicism, those dreamlike figures persist in thought, sometimes so vividly if distressingly that what we took to be illusion seems more like reality principle, with demystification itself drawn into its service.

So it was with Derrida, at the end of an essay in which he virtually identified with the ideas of Artaud, whose theater of cruelty, as the beginning of the essay insisted, "is not a *representation.* It is life itself, in the extent to which life is unrepresentable."[6] Whatever life may be or, if all the world is not a stage, however theater emerges from whatever it is it is *not*—reality? what's left of the real? what is presumably *not* theater—Derrida had to concede that "to think the closure of representation is to think the tragic: not as the representation of fate, but as the fate of representation. Its gratuitous and baseless necessity" (250). As for thinking the tragic in Beckett, or its leftover symptoms there, his solitary figures may not be great, in their futile and deadly outbursts, whether Pozzo, Hamm, or the Mouth, or without any figures at all the "recorded vagitus" of *Breath,* the two identical cries (211), but he would certainly understand the gratuitousness and the baselessness, with the declension of necessity into "Something is taking its course,"[7] instead of a star on the breast, inside the breast "a big sore" (*Endgame* 32), or something dripping in the head—"A heart, a heart in my head" (18)—or, even more alarmingly, a vagrant flea in the crotch.

If such, with painful laughter, is the Beckettian fate of representation, let us go back for a moment to commodification: while the markets are described by distinguished economists as being in an essentially unstable state of "dynamic disequilibrium," controlled if at all by an "invisible hand," the spectacle is still being rehearsed in critical theory, along with the apparatus of representation, as an "economy of death," as if, Hamletically, it were ghosting itself. Preempting the ghost was, of course, the initiating prospect of Brechtian method, by strategic repetition or quotation refiguring representation, breaking down the apparatus by turning it against itself, thus producing a dynamic disequilibrium for subversive purposes, supplanting the invisible hand with a signifying body or an acutely visible sign, the *gestus,* or what Frederic Jameson calls "a properly Brechtian materialism."[8] In a curious turn of his own, Jameson sees the source of that materialism now in the Taoism of the Chinese Brecht, and he seems to be invoking another kind of ghostliness when he says of the secular and skeptical, disruptively cynical Brecht that a "hermeneutics of suspicion" is suspended "for the metaphysics that have become impossible" (12)—by which Jameson means, in his own disappointment with the future of an illusion, the metaphysics in the teleology of Marxist utopianism. It is, to be sure, the metaphysics that have become impossible which, with a dynamic of attrition in the disequilibrium, accounts for the repetitiveness in Beckett, like a pulse of dispossession or momentum of deferral that, in the permutations of absence, seems not at all strategic, or if so, vain, ill seen ill said, which is itself a kind of ghosting, of what, not sure: "No longer anywhere to be seen. Nor by the eye of flesh nor by the other. Then as suddenly there again. Long after. So on"[9]—approaching in the warped teleology of its compulsive vanity, aphasic, unutterable, nohow on, the asymptotic mirage of whatever it is, or was, "that time you went back that last time to look,"[10] even if it wasn't, "no better than shades, no worse if it wasn't" (*That Time* 231), the impossible thing itself.

As to what you went back to look for, Brecht would agree with his friend Walter Benjamin that "nothing that has ever happened should be regarded as lost for history," but Benjamin would seem to encompass Beckett as well as Brecht when he says, in his "Theses on the Philosophy of History," that "the past can be seized only as an image which flashes up at the instant when it can be recognized and is never seen again." This is not a matter of recognizing, as in an older misguided historicism, "the way it really was," but rather of taking hold of "a memory as it flashes up at a moment of danger."[11] But the danger for Beckett is that whatever flashes up is in "no time gone in no time," which recurs again and again in *That Time* (235), "from the first and last that time curled up worm in slime when they lugged you out and wiped you off" (230), without anything like the "temporal index by which," as Benjamin says in the "Theses," the past "is referred to redemption" (256). As for history, if it is not there in the "old style," as Winnie might say of the Portrait Gallery, "when was that," in *That Time,* "there before your eyes when they opened a vast oil black with age and dirt someone famous in his time," or "there in whatever thoughts you might be having whatever scenes perhaps way back in childhood or the womb worst of all or that old Chinaman long before Christ born with long white hair," then it is "just one of those things you kept making up to keep the void out just another of those old tales to keep the void from pouring in on top of you the shroud" (*That Time* 229–30). It may be that the tales, the old tales, belong to "the whore called 'Once upon a time' in historicism's bordello," as Benjamin says ("Theses" 264), but the relay of voices in *That Time,* "without solution of continuity" (227), the void pouring in, the shroud, would seem to do what he wants, and what Jameson quoting Benjamin attributes to Brecht, that is, "to blast open the continuum of history" (264). As it turns out, in a peculiar twist upon the void, nobody does that better than the shrouded Hamm—making metaphysics impossible too—when the shroud is taken off: "But what in God's name do you imagine? That the earth will awake in spring? That the rivers and seas will run with fish again? That there's manna in heaven still for imbeciles like you?" (*Endgame* 53).

We are endowed, Benjamin says, with "a *weak* Messianic power," in a "secret agreement" with the past ("Theses" 256), through which we come to the present "as the 'time of the now' . . . shot through with chips of Messianic time" (265). If there is the dying fall in Beckett that suffuses the time of the now, the vehemence, when it erupts, seems something more than weak, as when Hamm assures Clov, "*with prophetic relish,*" that he will one day go blind too: "Infinite emptiness will be all around you, all the resurrected dead of all the ages wouldn't fill it, and there you'll be like a little bit of grit in the middle of the steppe" (*Endgame* 36), which may lack the luster of a Messianic chip but has its history too. And if memory flashes up, it is out of the bottomless pit of an incapacity to forget, if not history, the illusory promise of myth, and so it is in the gray chamber when Clov stares at the wall. "The wall!" rages Hamm, as if he had conflated the Book of Daniel with the Platonic Cave, the archetypal site of illusion: "And what do you see on your wall? Mene, mene? Naked bodies." Clov: "I see my light dying" (12).

But speaking of danger and redemption in the light of that dying light, as if the secret agreement were being made, and made again, by those dreamlike figures on stage with what, recurrently, is a ghost of the past: "What, has this thing appeared again tonight?" What was asked on the ramparts of *Hamlet* (1.1.21)—and what I've written about before, the illusive substance of theater, which does not exist if it does not appear—became in the hollow of *Endgame,* "This . . . this . . . thing" (45), while the nothing that came of nothing in pursuit of the thing itself became the Beckettian premise: "Nothing to be done."[12] As for this too, too solid flesh—for all the talk of the body as discourse, words, words, words, the words flying up, the body remaining below, naked body, libidinal body, all the bodies that matter or, with *its* repetitive acts, the body of "performativity"[13]—if it resolves into a dew, adieu, adieu, it is born astride of a grave, the light gleaming an instant, then gone, with maybe a forlorn sense, as always in Beckett, that it might have been once or never—even when parodied, all the more poignant for that—a visionary gleam: "Look! There! All that rising corn! And there! Look! The sails of the herring fleet! All that loveliness!" (*Endgame* 44). Or so it was in Yeats, recalled in . . . *but the clouds* . . . , "when the horizon fades

. . . or a bird's sleepy cry . . . among the deepening shades." Even in the measured countdown, there on the video screen—"*5 seconds. Dissolve to* M. *5 seconds. Fade out on* M. *Dark.* 5 *seconds*" (*SP* 262)—we are still the stuff of dreams, rounded to a sleep, though if dreams are wish fulfillment they may not feel as we wish, no more than the begged appearance, "a begging of the mind, to her, to appear, to me," by the voice in the "little sanctum" of the figure with "robe and skull," and the sleep may be dubious too, begging there in vain, "deep down into the dead of night," alienated in being, whether awake or asleep, and—even with "break of day, to issue forth again" (260–61), voiding the little sanctum—can we be sure of that?

Meanwhile, the question of vision persists through the eternal contradiction that, even with eyes wide open in the dispensation of the gaze, is more like a failure of the begetting in some perversion of sight. Thus it is with the woman in *Rockaby,* "famished eyes / like hers / to see / be seen" (*SP* 279), among the "successive fades" that have replaced the deepening shades—"Jet sequins to glitter when rocking" and pale wood "polished to gleam" (273)—saying to herself when being rocked, or in that othered, recorded voice, "time she stopped / *time she stopped*" (277) till "the day came / in the end came" (278) and "dead one night / in the rocker" and the rocker "rocking away" (280)—like O rocks in *Film,* cringing "away from perceivedness" (*SP* 168) but not immune to the gaze—"fuck life / stop her eyes / rock her off / rock her off," but even through the ending echo "coming to rest of rock" (*Rockaby* 282), something is stirring still, what, or what where, not sure, since it seems to escape perceivedness—and in all the texts for nothing, by whatever number or name, it may only be an illusion but there appears no end to that.

Nor to the various ways we think about it. If illusion commingles with faith and, to all appearances, may be thought of as fantasy too, it may also be, as in Brecht's *Galileo,* with history taking its time, "consciousness impatient for truth," as Althusser said in an essay on the Piccolo Teatro and Brecht. Or it may be "the image of a consciousness of a self living the totality of its world in the transparency of its own myths."[14] As a function or necessity of the political, illusion may be social construction or what, without knowing it, in the ether of ideology, we have somehow come to believe. And while it is this, of course, that would seem most germane to Brecht—whose "principal aim," as stated by Althusser, "is to produce a critique of the spontaneous ideology in which men live" (144)—it is not quite where we will see certain affinities with Beckett. That is more likely to occur with various degrees of subjectivity in the act of perception itself, despite the dramaturgical gap between a critical arrest in the service of *Verfremdung* and somatic immersion in the "science of affliction," where—as Beckett said in his essay on Proust, a proleptic definition of what infected his own thought—"the poisonous ingenuity of Time" subjects the individual to a "constant process of decantation," which leaves it "innocuous, amorphous, without character."[15]

Yet, while Brecht moved from the deobjectified characters of his early plays to those in a more gestic solid state, we have to deal in his work, as we do more egregiously in Beckett, with the perceptual status or analytics of the performative body, from Galy Gay as a human fighting machine to Dumb Kattrin's blinded eye, eye of flesh, eye of prey, to the predatory presence of the Inquisitor, alone, silent, stately, incising an empty stage, bringing to Galileo the liabilities of perceivedness, as with the swiveling light on the bodiless heads in the funeral urns of *Play.*

There are characters in Brecht who, like Anna Fierling, never miss a trick but fail to see, though we are likely to find little in Brecht that, like Beckett's body parts or absent bodies, severely abstracting or disfiguring space, not only direct but demoralize, even stigmatize perception, in the stigma directing it even more: Winnie, up to her diddies in the mound; a back, a bare foot, an arm, or even the "trace of a face";[16] or, with "head bowed, grey hair," the dreamer of *Nacht und Träume* and, with the dreamt self, dreamt hands, palm upward, joined, gentle, those dreamt commiserable hands, not like those in *Catastrophe,* with "fibrous degeneration" (298), crippled to begin with and, speaking of a Brechtian *gestus,* made to look like claws. If that suggests, affect aside, or because of it, that there's a chastening semiology in Beckett, it is not quite, even in *Catastrophe* (dedicated to the imprisoned Havel), like Brecht's pointing toward the action not-done through the action that *is,* deciphering and exposing social cause. Yet it is possible to see in *Catastrophe*—its exposure of the production apparatus, the director's tyranny and the assistant's servility, what is pernicious and vitiating in the constructed mise-en-scène—a more virulent critique of the theater itself than almost anything staged in Brecht.

Meanwhile, if there is the "agony of perceivedness" (*Film* 165) there is the wanting to be seen, or in the inquisitional light of *Play* something equivocal about that: "Am I as much as . . . being seen?" With a slightest shift of accent (being *seen, being* seen) the issue of recognition passes into the notion that, however unnerving it may be, "mere eye," just the gaze, to be looked at—"Just looking. At my face. On and off" (157)—there is no being at all, nothing like identity, without being seen. Which is what Didi conveys when he advances on the Boy from Godot and says, "(*With sudden violence.*) You're sure you saw me, you won't come and tell me tomorrow that you never saw me!" (59). Here, through the stasis of the waiting, dispossession, desperate, is speaking for itself, as P in *Catastrophe* does at the end, however minimally, when he raises his head and confronts the audience with more than a trace of a face. Which is something else again than the willing anonymity of the agitators in Brecht's *The Measures Taken,* who "must not be seen," blotting out their faces on behalf of the oppressed workers of Mukden, "To win the victory / But conceal the victor."[17] This is the problematic context in which the Young Comrade, who puts "his feelings above his understanding" (87) and, taking the revolution upon himself, tears off his mask, revealing his "naked face, human, open, guileless" (102), before capitulating to the will of the Party, accepting the measures to be taken, extreme as they are, letting himself be shot and thrown into the lime pit.

The play has been attacked as an anticipatory defense of Stalin's purge trials and, despite the animus of Brecht's critique, defended as tragic drama, and its dialectic is such that, were it to be rethought today in rehearsal, as the *Lehrstücke* were in theory meant to be, we might theorize alternatives to the Young Comrade's chilling sacrifice. This is, of course, an extremity to which Brecht himself was never quite submitted, in his more agile and cryptic dissidence in East Berlin, nor in his cautious debates with Lukács about the proprieties of socialist realism. Yet he considered the play absolutely central to what he was attempting in the theater, and it remains a temporal index of a question persisting through his work, as to how much subjectivity not only the revolution can allow, but also the Epic theater, as it sublimated, say, the unappeasable appetites and narcissism of Baal, the utterly carnal version of the Canaanite fertility god, seen in cosmic scale in the opening Grand Chorale, as if he were the eroticized avatar of illusion itself. Grown in "his mother's womb so white"—and so primal, ecstatic, synesthetic, he seemed like the sky itself, "Naked, young and hugely marvelous"—Baal comes into being as something more than a subject, or less, with the voracious innocence and assurance of the modernist criminal/saint: "Baal will drag his whole sky down below,"[18] as if, incestuously, the Great Mother imaged there, he would seduce the universe itself.

When he does seduce a young woman, who drowns herself in shame, he sings a song—with another sort of detachment, not yet of the A-effect—about her slow descent: "The opal sky shone most magnificent," but as the song continues we get the nether side of Baal, who could be embraced by beauty itself, all that loveliness! and, as if longing for desecration, never leave it at that. As she floats downstream like Ophelia, there are no transfiguring garlands, no willows askant the brook, only "wrack and seaweed" clinging, with creatures and other growths, to the forlorn body that rots—as Baal's does eventually too—and he seems to relish that: "I see the world in a gentle light; it's the good Lord's excrement" (*CP* 1:46). If that, for Yeats, is where love has pitched his mansion, it is also not far from Beckett, nor is Gougou far from Gogo, but with "a cold in the lungs," in the scene at the abysmal bar, the mordancy takes over in a tone resembling Hamm's. "A slight inflammation. Nothing serious." And when Baal says of the past that it seems a strange word, Gougou ignores the notion of any secret agreement, of which, according to Benjamin, the historical materialist is aware. "Best of all is nothingness. . . . Yes, that's paradise. No more unfulfilled desires. All gone. You get over all your habits. Even the habits of desire." And when the beggar woman Maja—with a child in a crate, about as promising as the boy out the window in *Endgame*—asks, "And what happens at the end?" Gougou says, grinning, "Nothing. Nothing at all. The end never comes. Nothing lasts forever." It is here, momentarily, that Baal seems to take a position like that of the later Brecht, or a parody of him, as he rises in drunken indignation, or a mockery of it: "The worms are swelling. Crawling decomposition. The worms are glorifying themselves. . . . Bag-of-Worms, that's your name," he says to Gougou (43–44).

As it happens, "crawling decomposition"—like the disjunct narrative of the man crawling on his belly in *Endgame,* and not only him, but "the place was crawling with them!" (68)—would seem to be a fair description of the momentum of Beckett's aesthetic, though the crawling accelerates from the muck in the waiting or the mud of *How It Is* to the "lifelong mess" of *That Time* (230), with its curled up worm in slime, or the vertiginous "out" of *Not I,* not merely decomposition, "but the brain—. . . what?" (217) and the body with it, never mind desire, "whole body like gone . . . just the mouth . . . lips . . . cheeks . . . jaws . . . never— . . . what? . . . tongue?" (*SP* 220), torn between screaming and silence, "crawl back in," and then through all the buzzing, "godforsaken hole . . . no love . . . spared that" (222), until the wished-for end, "God is love . . . tender mercies," bag of worms aside, "back in the field . . . April morning . . . face in the grass . . . nothing but the larks . . . pick it up" (222–23). If the larks are not exactly, though "God is love," singing hymns at heaven's gate, the entreaty to pick it up may suggest the final scene of *The Good Person of Szechwan* when Shui Ta / Shen Te, who has been washed in gutter water and also known the muck, entreats the

Enlightened Ones to stay, though the gods—having had enough of how it is, which is how it is going to be—fly homeward to their own nothingness, leaving the tender mercies to the audience, to whom the epilogue is addressed: "That you yourselves should ponder till you find / The ways and means and measures tending / To help good people to a happy ending" (*CP* 6:104). Which—lips, cheeks, jaw . . . never—. . . what?—sounds like tongue in cheek.

It would certainly make Gougou laugh, or Garga of *In the Jungle of Cities,* who says, "We thought the planet would change course on our account. But what happened? Three times it rained, and one night the wind blew."[19] As for Baal, who is at the end the stinking image of crawling decomposition, Brecht apparently did not entirely realize that almost everything about him, when the play was first done, would be seen as politically incorrect. But some years later, reviewing his early work, he took note of the criticism: "*Baal* is a play which could present all kinds of difficulties to those who have not learned to think dialectically. No doubt they will see it as a glorification of unrelieved egotism and nothing more."[20] If the dialectic seems a little devious, given the antisocial nature of Baal, he remains through Brecht's reassessment a virtual prototype of the lifestyle social protest, not unideological but at the extremity of it all, that we encountered in the sixties, when the apparently apolitical waiting for Godot could be taken as a model of passive resistance—as it was in San Francisco when I first directed the play, in 1957, the same year I staged the first American production of Brecht's *Mother Courage.* As I have pointed out before, it was *Waiting for Godot* that turned out to be, against the grain of the political Left, or—to use Benjamin's phrase from the "Theses"—"brush[ing] history against the grain" (259), the most influential play, politically, of that period,[21] taken up then by the Left, which was ready to dismiss it as avant-garde indulgence. We did not do *Baal,* but we should have, because—despite its apparent misogyny—it opened up ideas of sexuality that, as Sue-Ellen Case pointed out in the eighties,[22] we are still coming to terms with now. If the Young Comrade is his dialectical opposite, Baal remains a model of a polymorphous perverse spirit taking the pleasure principle to the threshold of exhaustion, where reality kicks in like the woodcutters going out, suggesting as they go a little *Verfremdung:* "Try to look at things more objectively. Tell yourself that a rat is dying. See? Just don't make a fuss. You have no teeth left." And then, as one man leans down to spit in Baal's face, another gives an additional piece of advice: "Try to schedule your stinking tomorrow" (*CP* 1:55–56).

Yet, if Baal is omnivorous about his living he is about dying as well.

And if the anarchic nature of his corporeally indulgent body had to be curbed to the ideological policy of the later plays, it is not entirely extruded, for as even one of the woodcutters had to concede: "He drank like a sponge, but there's something about that pale lump of fat that makes a man think" (56). Which is about as good as you're going to get in defining the materiality of the A-effect, its arresting substance (which is what Joseph Beuys understood when he picked up the fat and used it, conceptually, in his estranging installations). One may ask: where does Baal, however surreptitiously, make his appearance in this or that play, as with the priapic figure in the garden in Galileo's meeting with the Little Monk, and when does he disappear, as Azdak does (rather like Falstaff in *Henry IV, Part II)* when a more rational order needs stabilizing toward the end of *The Caucasian Chalk Circle*? To the degree that his science is self-indulgence, an appetite, insatiable, Galileo is eventually excoriated. It is as if Baal represents, too, at another level the murky intuitive process that, as Brecht says in his essay on Chinese acting, commenting on Stanislavski, "takes place in the subconscious." This may be where it should be in what we call Method acting, but the subconscious, Brecht adds, "is not at all responsive to guidance; it has as it were a bad memory" (*BT* 94).

In a sense, then, Brecht struggled throughout his career with techniques for managing or disposing of Baal, though killing him off was itself a dangerous project: "Sometimes Baal plays dead. The vultures swoop. / Baal, without a word, will dine on vulture soup" (*CP* 1:4). If there is nothing so cunningly lethal in Beckett, his plays and short prose, as if with a failure of memory, appear to be taking place at some level of the psyche below the subconscious, though we may have to remember that the forgetting as it turns up in the unconscious is, as Freud remarked, the deepest form of memory. As for Brecht in the period of *Baal,* and *In the Jungle of Cities,* it may be the wrong word, but a sort of faith accompanied his cynicism, or to use President George W. Bush's phrase, a "faith-based initiative," as when Shlink urges Garga not to quit because, speaking of things below, "the forests have been cut down, the vultures are glutted, and the golden answer will be buried deep in the ground" (*Jungle* 160). But then he may be speaking, too, in the Chicago setting of that play, of environmental depredations, corporate profits, and like President Bush today, reserves of oil in the ground.

In what would seem another definition of the Brechtian *gestus,* "a configuration pregnant with tensions" (or what Roland Barthes, writing of Brecht, calls "the pregnant moment"), Benjamin remarks that "thinking involves not only the flow of thoughts, but their arrest as well," giving the "configuration a shock, by which it crystallizes into a monad" ("Theses" 264–65). That figure is, however, in the allure of its crystallization, better suited, perhaps, to the Imagism of H. D. and Ezra Pound or, epiphanically, certain ideographic moments in the poems of T. S. Eliot. But if, as Eliot once said, as a virtual preface to the writing of Beckett (who was not at all indifferent to Eliot), words slip, slide, decay with imprecision, will not hold still, the monad is always threatened, which Brecht (whose early work, we forget, emerged into modernism with Eliot's) certainly understood. The trouble with thinking, always—to cite that dreamlike figure again, who is if anything pregnant with tensions—is that there is nothing either good or bad but thinking makes it so. If, then, the complex pedagogy of *The Measures Taken,* its painful dialectic or unbearable lesson, is characterized by the oxymoron of an ambiguous didacticism, the apparent nihilism of *Baal,* its sheer perversity, is eventually relinquished in the desire for a supportable pedagogy, which is not so much what Brecht wants us to think but rather the method by which he causes us to think.

Speaking of a certain calculated unreality, like a dead man singing, in the manifestation of a *gestus,* Brecht remarks in a footnote what we have come to expect, that this does not preclude an element of instruction, though the irrationality or even seeming lack of seriousness contributes to the gestic content that registers and defines the theatrical moment as meaning, though with the metaphysics at bay the meaning may be provisional. In Beckett, of course, with a seeming lack of seriousness the impossible and the provisional are maneuvered into a laugh: "We're not beginning to . . . to . . . mean something?" But before Hamm says "(Vehemently.) To think perhaps it won't all have been for nothing!" he pauses to wonder, "Imagine if a rational being came back to earth, wouldn't he be liable to get ideas into his head if he observed us long enough" (*Endgame* 32–33). And whatever he says to mock it, if you did not get ideas, a myriad of ideas—as in the circuitous, self-canceling, tortuous thinking of thought that Beckett calls the *pensum*—you must be out of your head. And the ideas, moreover, if you observed them long enough, that is, as they occur in performance, whatever the nothing done, arise from a certain ordering of perception that corresponds to an issue further defined by Brecht, still resisting illusion in the apparatus of representation. Yet, though he might put it another way, it is as if he agreed with Eliot's remark that, confronted as we are by the indeterminacies of the modern and a culture of disbelief, what we need to do is improve the quality of our illusions. Among which is the possibility entertained by Beckett, despite and by means of the derision of

Clov, that we do "Mean something! You and I, mean something!" (33). As for the theater, what makes it mean something is, if by nothing more than intelligence (which was at a premium in the American theater when they first came on the scene), shared by Beckett and Brecht.

If in the culinary theater, as Brecht describes it in the *Short Organum,* the eyes wide open may signify a trance, as with the sleepers of the house who stare but do not see, the eye which observes long enough, "which looks for the *gest* in everything is the moral sense."[23] Yet, if what Brecht is seeking is a moral tableau, as Diderot might have defined it (what Barthes later admired), it is not without an element of subjectivity, as when, suspended in the gaze, Galileo studies the moons of Jupiter or when, with voracious appetite and inarguable passion, he says he believes in the brain. If Beckett had any affectation it was the habit of denying its importance, but he also had quite a brain, and considerable erudition. Yet if in the elemental substance of his obsessive subjectivity—the subject seeking its subject in the regressive desperation of a never-ending quest—there is the *risus purus,* the laugh laughing at the laugh at anything like a moral sense, he is by no means without that either. And while there would seem to be a world of difference, though the actions in each instance are similarly unmomentous, between Mother Courage closing her pocketbook on the life of her son and Gogo pulling at his boot or Didi's buttoning his fly or Gogo later leaving his boots neatly at the edge of the stage, for another who may come, "just as . . . as . . . as me, but with smaller feet," he gives to that *gestus* or tableau the perhaps pathetic irony of a not unmoral sense, even through what may seem to be the burlesqued jaundice of the following exchange, about the boots being left behind:

> VLADIMIR: But you can't go barefoot.
> ESTRAGON: Christ did.
> VLADIMIR: Christ! What has Christ got to do with it? You're not going to compare yourself to Christ!
> ESTRAGON: All my life I've compared myself to him.
> VLADIMIR: But where he lived it was warm, it was dry!
> ESTRAGON: Yes. And they crucified quick.

Didi, after a silence, says there's nothing more to do there of the nothing already done, and Gogo quickly replies, "Nor anywhere else" (*Godot* 34), which is not exactly promising for social change. But what could be seen in the whole sequence about the boots is the sort of sly paradox or cunning reversal you can also find in the capricious jurisprudence of Azdak in *The Caucasian Chalk Circle* or in the water-seller Wang's opening remarks, while waiting to welcome the gods, in *The Good Person of Szechwan.* As he sizes up passersby, he says of two gentlemen, they "don't strike me as gods, they have a brutal look, as if they were in the habit of beating people, and gods have no need of that."[24] One might make the case that the moral sense, in subtle and nuanced ways, suffuses the plays of Beckett, as it does through all the apparent caprice, hyperbole, and gratuitous cruelty of Hamm when he says, at one point in his narrative about the man who crawled toward him on his belly and wanted bread for his brat, "In the end he asked me would I consent to take in the child as well—if he were still alive. (*Pause.*) It was the moment I was waiting for. (*Pause.*) Would I consent to take in the child . . ." (*Endgame* 53). And the moment is suspended, with the moral issue, as Hamm breaks off the narrative, until the end of the play, before he puts on the stancher, when he comes back to the child, if, whoever he is, "he could have his child with him":

> It was the moment I was waiting for.
> (*Pause.*)
> You don't want to abandon him? You want him to bloom while you are withering? Be there to solace your last million last moments?
> (*Pause.*)
> He doesn't realize, all he knows is hunger, and cold, and death to crown it all. But you! You ought to know what the earth is like, nowadays. Oh I put him before his responsibilities!

If that is not a moral distinction, at the sticking point of thought, I do not know what is, though it is a disturbing moral. And there is nothing here like what we might see elsewhere in the almost demonic eloquence of Hamm, there at the nerve ends, going to the quick, an extraordinary passion deflated by irony. As for the moral sense in Epic theater, it may be hard to work out the proportions of detachment and subjectivity, through an always strategic irony, but in any case, as with the three cases distinguished by the voice of . . . *but the clouds* . . . , or the "fourth case, or case nought" (*SP* 261), Brecht might have been making a case for Beckett when he said, "out of mistrust of the theater" which, whatever the case, "theaters it all down, . . . [s]ome exercise in complex seeing is needed." When he adds, however, that "it is perhaps more important to be able to think above the stream than to think in the stream,"[25] it might be hard for Beckett to imagine anything like that, for imagination dead imagine the stream is all there is. And if you cannot step into the same river twice, as Heraclitus said, that is because you are always in it, even in *Come and Go*. "May we not speak of the old days? [*Silence.*] Of what came after?" But the after is more of the same and—"Holding hands . . . that way. / Dreaming of . . . love" (*SP* 195)—you can somehow never get out.

If the complex seeing occurs in other ways, Brecht nevertheless also shares with Beckett, despite the rap about *Verfremdung* subduing emotion by detachment, a "sensitivity to subjective differences," while there is a similar compulsion to differentiation that, as Adorno remarks about Beckett, "glides into ideology" too. Which does not, as Adorno also says, in countering Lukács's charge that Beckett reduces humans to animality, qualify Beckett to "testify as a key political witness . . . in the struggle against atomic death."[26] For in Beckett's writing the terror of such death seems to be as it always was—the dreadful thing has already happened, "a heap, a little heap, the impossible heap" (*Endgame* 1)—inseparable from the ordeal of being human. If Beckett is not guilty, as Lukács also charged, of "an abstract, subjectivist ontology" (Adorno 15), his view of the subject—or at least the subject of modernity—might have been defined by Brecht when, in his earliest definition of Epic theater, he said in no uncertain terms, "The continuity of the ego is a myth. A man is an atom that perpetually breaks up and forms anew. We have to show things as they are."[27] The new purpose, for Brecht, in the era of "the petroleum complex" may have been "paedagogics," as he says in the essay "Form and Subject-Matter," but the fact of the matter for the subject, in things being shown as they are, is that it can no longer appear in the drama with the old features of character, nor with the sort of motives imputed by Hebbel, Ibsen, or even Chekhov. In a world where "fate is no longer a single coherent power," but dispersed into "fields of force" radiating in all directions, actions must be shown as "pure phenomena" (*BT* 29–30), as they are with a motiveless specificity in *Baal* and in *In the Jungle of Cities,* more devastatingly so there than in the more rationalized epic of *Galileo* or in *Mother Courage.*

Yet, Courage pulling her wagon, after the death of Dumb Kattrin, aimlessly at the end—"infinite emptiness" all around her, as Hamm says apocalyptically in his warning to Clov, and imagination dead imagine the resurrected dead of all the ages combining with those of the ceaseless war—is an even bleaker image of a pure phenomenon than the dying Shlink asking for a cloth over his face, like Hamm, because "he doesn't want anyone to look at him" (*Jungle, CP* 7:161), or Garga in the office of the late Shlink, saying in the final lines, "It's a good thing to be alone. The chaos is used up" (163). Or even the dying Baal, that pale lump of fat, with no teeth left, crawling on all fours like an animal to the door, for one last look at the stars. With the used-up chaos as the datum of thought, or the fields of force more entropic, this is all the more so in Beckett as he encapsulates the gratuitous and baseless necessity of the utterly negated subject, with its excruciating consciousness, or disjuncture of it, from the hollow in the wall of *Endgame* or the seeds that will never sprout to the diminishing returns or spastic brevity of the aphasic later plays.

Moreover, what we appear to encounter in Beckett—even in the plays with a more explicit political content, such as *Catastrophe,* and the clownish cycle of torture ("give him the works until he confesses") that followed in *What Where* (*SP* 315)—is not merely "the nausea of satiation" or "the tedium of spirit with itself," which Adorno invoked in his essay on *Endgame* (11), out of his own aversion to the politics of Lukács. Never mind the abstract, subjectivist ontology that Lukács charged Beckett with and Adorno rejected. Lukács may even be right, and there may be something like that there, though abstractions live in Beckett, like the pauses and silences extruded from Chekhovian realism, in the lymph nodes and bloodstream of thought, where alienation is a reflex with illimitable affect that elides in the pure phenomena certain figures and gestures resembling the A-effect, as if the Brechtian arrest were in the Beckettian moment(um) the subject of thought itself. As for the subjectivist ontology, what may be most compelling or unnerving in Beckett is his response to a certain harrowing stillness in the barest rumor of being that is, all told, and told again, till the telling is intolerable, thus further dispersed in thought, as with the ceaseless stirrings of the equivocal word *still* (is it motion? or time? as endurance? or all of it under duress?), the ontological ground, if ground there be, of the subtlest, most seductive, imperceptible form of illusion, what in the living end dying can never be seen, or seen as being, and therefore never told.

Still: "Something is taking its course." Estrange it as we will, it still seems passing strange, only the passing certain, as in the stasis of the momentum and the plaintively quizzical moment of the waiting for Godot, when Didi wonders, with Gogo falling asleep, and he not sure he is awake, whether in the nothing that happened twice anything happened at all, "That Pozzo passed, with his carrier, and that he spoke with us? Probably. But in all that what truth will there be?" (58). It was precisely that, the apparently impotent subjectivity of a ubiquitous indeterminacy, all the more alluring for its teasing out of illusion—"They make a noise like wings. / Like leaves. / Like sand. / Like leaves"

(40)—which Brecht thought he might change when he considered revising the play, linking its oddities and incapacities to material interests and the past that is disremembered ("a million years ago, in the nineties" [7]), or not remembered at all ("What were you saying when?"), surely not the beginning ("The very beginning of WHAT?" [42]), bringing it in line with a more progressive sense of history. Yet, for all the ideological pressure of recent years to historicize! historicize! one is occasionally tempted to say with Gogo—who either forgets immediately or never forgets, who knows only that "Everything oozes" and that "It's never the same pus from one second to the next" (39)—"I'm not a historian" (42). And for the moment arrested, still in the time of the now: the boots, the carrot, the tree, from one second to the next, no time that time, and the waiting consigned to illusion.

NOTES

1. Friedrich Nietzsche, *The Birth of Tragedy* (and *The Genealogy of Morals*), trans. Francis Golffing (New York: Anchor/Doubleday, 1956) 33.

2. Bertolt Brecht, "The Modern Theater Is the Epic Theater," in *Brecht on Theater: The Development of an Aesthetic,* ed. and trans. John Willett (New York: Hill and Wang, 1964) 34; this volume will be abbreviated as *BT.*

3. Samuel Beckett, *Play,* in *Collected Shorter Plays* (New York: Grove, 1984) 157, 160; this volume will be abbreviated as *SP.*

4. Jean Baudrillard, *Simulations,* trans. Paul Foss, Paul Patton, and Philip Betichman (New York: Semiotext(e), 1983) 1–79.

5. Guy Debord, "Separation Perfected," in *Society of the Spectacle* (Detroit: Red and Black, 1983), item 34, n.p.

6. Jacques Derrida, "The Theater of Cruelty and the Closure of Representation," in *Writing and Difference,* trans. Alan Bass (Chicago: University of Chicago Press, 1978) 234.

7. Beckett, *Endgame* (New York: Grove, 1958) 13.

8. Frederic Jameson, *Brecht and Method* (London: Verso, 1998) 8.

9. Beckett, *Ill Seen Ill Said,* in *Nohow On: Three Novels* (New York: Grove, 1996) 56.

10. Beckett, *That Time,* in *SP* 229.

11. Walter Benjamin, "Theses on the Philosophy of History," in *Illuminations,* ed. Hannah Arendt, trans. Harry Zohn (New York: Harcourt, Brace and World, 1955) 256–57.

12. Beckett, *Waiting for Godot* (New York: Grove, 1954) 7.

13. See Judith Butler, *Bodies That Matter: On the Discursive Limits of "Sex"* (New York: Routledge, 1993) 9, 12.

14. Louis Althusser, *For Marx,* trans. Ben Brewster (London: Verso/NLB, 1982) 144.

15. Beckett, *Proust* (New York: Grove, n.d.) 4–5.

16. Beckett, *Catastrophe,* in *SP* 299.

17. Brecht, *The Measures Taken,* in *The Jewish Wife and Other Short Plays,* trans. Eric Bentley (New York: Grove, 1965) 81, 83.

18. Brecht, *Baal,* trans. William E. Smith and Ralph Manheim, in *Collected Plays,* ed. Manheim and John Willett (New York: Vintage, 1971–) 1:3; these editions will be abbreviated as *CP,* with volume number.

19. Brecht, *In the Jungle of Cities,* trans. Gerhard Nellhaus, in *CP* 1:158.

20. Brecht, "On Looking Through My First Plays [ii]," in *CP* 1:345.

21. See, for instance, the preface to my *Sails of the Herring Fleet: Essays on Beckett* (Ann Arbor: University of Michigan Press, 2000) 4–5.

22. Sue-Ellen Case, "Brecht and Women: Homosexuality and the Mother," *The Brecht Yearbook* 12 (1983): 65–74.

23. Brecht, "The Modern Theater is Epic Theater," *BT* 36n.

24. Brecht, *The Good Person of Szechwan: A Parable Play,* trans. Ralph Manheim, in *CP* 6:3–4.

25. Brecht, "The Literarization of Theater (Notes to *The Threepenny Opera*)," *BT* 43–44.

26. Theodor W. Adorno, "Trying to Understand *Endgame,*" *New German Critique* 26 (1982): 15.

27. Brecht, in an interview, "Conversation with Bert Brecht," *BT* 15.

ELEVEN

Apnea and True Illusion

Breath(less) in Beckett

> Astride of a grave and a difficult birth. Down in the hole, lingeringly, the grave-digger puts on the forceps. We have time to grow old. The air is full of our cries.
>
> —BECKETT, *Waiting for Godot*

AND, EVEN NOW, UNRELIEVED by his winning a Nobel Prize, some of us still hear them—although sometimes we're not sure whose cries they are.

Some years ago, that time, I was having a late lunch with my son Dick and his partner Jane, fair food, good conversation, when I had a vague sense of their staring at me, and looking puzzled at each other, as I kept on talking, of I know not what, just talking and talking, with no sense of what I was talking about, or for that matter, who I was, at what turned out to be some logorrheia of incoherence, or a regressively aging "dehiscence," a word used by Beckett for coherence gone to pieces, but otherwise made familiar through the Oedipal fractures in the mirror stage of Lacan, with its drama of a specular ego, and the mirage of identity, still haunting the personal pronoun, I, not I, as we'll certainly see in Beckett, brought on by some primal discord, and subsequent paranoia, at "a real *specific prematurity of birth*."[1] When they took me to the emergency room, babbling into a murmur, "infant languors in the end sheets," as in one of the *Texts for Nothing,*[2] as if falling out of a dream, it was diagnosed as a transient ischemic attack, or momentary stroke; yet since I was not unable to talk, speech not blurred or impeded, but rather accelerated, as from the Mouth of *Not I,* "but the brain still . . . still . . . in a way,"[3] it was more like a kind of psychogenic amnesia, what they call a "fugue state," or dissociative identity disorder. If there was anything polyphonic in what I was saying, or somehow contrapuntal—"From the word go. The word begone"[4]—I have no idea, but from what I later heard from Dick and Jane, relieved when I came to myself, not I, my self, whatever that may be, "Thought of nothing? . . . Forgotten nothing? . . . You're all right now, eh?"[5] I was indeed saying things over and over, to some indeterminate other, by way of anxious others, who could hardly decipher anything in the disjointed repetitions.

"We have time to grow old." But as you get older, and memory fails you, forgetting a name or a face—or, as with me, more frequently now in a class, you suddenly lose the lines of a poem long known by heart—it's hard not to think of Alzheimer's, from the complications of which my brother recently died, the last time I saw him not knowing who I was. The fugue state, however, was apparently nothing like that, and for all the repeats within it, they say it happens only once. But if I somehow came to myself, it must be "painful to be no longer oneself, even more painful if possible," as Beckett wrote in *First Love,* "than when one is. For when one is one knows what to do to be less so, whereas when one is not one is any old one irredeemably" (*Prose* 31). Still, depend upon age to keep you guessing at the edge of consciousness, or for that matter, deep down, in the identity disorder of the unconsciousness of sleep—"But deep in what sleep, deep in what sleep already?" as Hamm says in *Endgame*[6]—where even dream isn't, at least for me, what it used to be. And here Hamm elides with Hamlet, when he says, "O God, I could be bounded in a nutshell and count myself a king of infinite space, were it not that I have bad dreams" (*Hamlet* 2.2.251–52)—in which, if our little lives are rounded with a sleep, it's far from infinite space, or even as he waits to be whistled, staring at the wall, the "Nice dimensions, nice proportions" of Clov's sequestered kitchen, "ten feet by ten feet by ten feet" (*Endgame* 2); indeed, in a nutshell, or, as from the Book of Revelations, the length and breadth and height of it, Clov's occluded cube, or the root of it in the pyche, my dreaming's claustrophobic. For in rather distressing, anamorphic, eye-opening ways, I'm crawling through a tunnel, a shaft, or drainpipe, or in a cramped elevator, or with a pounding heart in a windowless room, or smothered under a blanket, legs drawn under, as if curled up still in a womb, that "god-forsaken hole" (*Not I* 216), or "some old grave I can't tear myself away from,"[7] then suddenly I'm awake, panicked, wanting to speak but unable, or ready to wawl and cry, as if I'd just been born, if not birth the death of me, as now and again in Beckett, terribly short of breath.

Which turns out to be the title of his shortest play, *Breath,* about thirty-seven seconds on stage: inspiration, expiration, with those "instant[s] of recorded vagitus," a wail or cry of distress, birthright, death rite, out of this world, or in, with the stage directions insisting that the "two cries be identical, switching on and off strictly synchronized light and breath" (*Plays* 211), all timed exactly, all time, no time, through the final silence, no light, no cry, no breath, an eternity, that time, no more than five seconds. Over the asphyxiating sensation, however, I had no such control, nor did Beckett, actually, in the panic of similar seizures, for him lifelong, and as he has described it—once in a conversation, suddenly stuttering, when he was writing *Comment c'est*—even more severe. They call it sleep apnea, a blockage of air in the windpipe, which at its worst seems to be caused by the nervous system's not getting an expected signal from the brain, which otherwise never stops, what leaves you breathless in Beckett. It's as if he'd transposed the nocturnal attacks, the fear, the blood pressure rising until it was about to burst, or the terror of expectation, the waiting, for the imminent suffocation, heart racing, audible thumping, to the debraining volatility of his most compulsive texts. Or to see it another way, it's as if the specific prematurity could only become a subject, as through the mirror stage, by finding itself in words, but in the insurgency there (in the Imaginary, not the Symbolic, but headlong toward the Real), spastic, aphasic, the rush of words or "sudden flashes," the elliptical "vain reasonings" (*Not I* 217), with "the whole brain begging . . . something begging in the brain . . . begging the mouth to stop," but no stopping, the buzzing, "the brain . . . flickering away on its own," like mine in the ischemic attack, "now this . . . this . . . quicker and quicker . . . the words . . . the brain," as if brainless, "flickering away like mad"—and even when it wasn't happening "this other awful thought" (219–22), some whisper in your head, "Isn't that what you said? . . . the whisper . . . the odd word" (*Eh Joe* 204), that it might be happening again, with "the words . . . everywhere, inside me, outside me, . . . impossible to stop, I'm in words, made of words, others' words, what others," as with Dick and Jane that day, "the place too, the air, the walls, the floor, the ceiling, all words, the whole world is here with me,"[8] and then again the breathing stops.

Is it mere coincidence that these sensations of apnea appear to have increased, with the memory of amnesia, as I was thinking of Beckett again, as if his own history of tormented sleep, palpitations, spasms, suffocations, and memories of forgetting, or the always egregious aggregate of those he'd rather forget—not only sebaceous cysts on the anus, eczema, or herpes on the face, but a life before birth, which he always claimed to remember, his own stifling fetal existence, "curled up worm in slime,"[9] the intrauterine position, trapped there, imprisoned, crying out to escape, nobody hearing, nobody listening—were responsible for my symptoms? As for his symptoms, they appeared to be, as in *The Unnamable,* the identity disorder of a nonidentity, or equivocal dubious being, referred to as I, that most pernicious pronoun in the semiosis of Beckett, *I,* not me, "it is not about me" (*Unnamable* 3), as it appears to be in *Endgame,* when Hamm removes the handkerchief from his face, and announces, "Me—(*he yawns*)—to play" (2), in the objective case. But in the preamble to *The Unnamable* that never comes to an end, perhaps because it never begins, the "affirmations and negations invalidated as uttered, or sooner or later" (3), always return to the "I, of whom I know nothing. I know my eyes are open because of the tears that pour from them unceasingly. I know I am seated, my hands on my knees, because of the pressure against my rump, against the soles of my feet, against the palms of my hands, against my knees." But what is this pressure, that retrograde pressure, in which the hypertensive body may not, with tears flowing, really be sure which end is up? "I don't know. My spine is not supported. I mention these details to make sure I am not lying on my back, my legs raised and bent, my eyes closed" (22)—darkling there, forgotten, as if abandoned before birth.

If there's long been, not only in the theater, but in my writings on Beckett too, that virtual habit of thinking *through* him, his words my words, or by means of the aporias in his own afflicted thought, ephectic, solipsistic, and even masochistic, that occurs by something more than the self-commiserating solace of sympathetic identification. What drew me to Beckett to begin with, from the "Nothing to be done," the line that launches the waiting for the absence known as Godot, to the traumatizing mathematics in his shorter plays and prose, was an activating *exactitude* about an encrypted void, what otherwise seemed hopeless, or what if you really engaged it, through the temptations to laugh it off, what Beckett himself provoked (but mostly overdone now in stagings of his plays), was really unnerving too. That is, it was still disoriented, even desperate, for all the going "On!" as when Pozzo takes off with Lucky,[10] to those late *Variations on a "Still" Point,* "he having been dreamt away [letting] himself be dreamt away,"[11] over the abyssal depths, "Whence when back no knowing where no telling where been how long how it was."[12] There is always that impasse in Beckett, whether waiting, going or coming, the hopeless detour of an incessant impasse, where you try to go on and you can't go on, and the talking seems to continue, call it the babble or drivel, "that's what hell will be like," says Henry, in the long opening monologue of the radio play *Embers,* which also begins with "On. . . . On!" (93), which "always went on for ever" (94), like the stories he told himself, "Stories, stories, years and years of stories, till the need came on me, for someone, to be with me, anyone" (95), but Ada? hellish, a conversation with Ada, "that was something, . . . small chat to the babbling of Lethe about the good old days when we wished we were dead" (96).

One might say, not only with Pozzo's coming and going, or the stories, stories, that Beckett gets a lot of mileage out of the vicissitudes of despair, and when the measures are taken, the astringent mathematics, with the abyss more or less at a parodistic distance. So with *Rough for Theater I,* when B in his wheelchair asks the blind fiddler A, "why don't you let yourself die?" and A says he's thought of it, whereupon B says in irritation, "But you don't do it!" To which A replies, and with some violence when B pursues it, "I am not unhappy enough!" (*Plays* 69). Now I grant you that "Nothing is funnier than unhappiness. . . . Yes, yes, it's the most comical thing in the world," as Nell says in her ashbin, before she's pushed down with no pulse, and the lid closed again, "we laugh, we laugh," but then, "like the funny story we have heard too often, we still find it funny, but we don't laugh anymore" (*Endgame* 19).

And so it must have been for Beckett, at the extremities of despair, in letting you see what you wouldn't, sometimes manic obsessively, if the exactitude weren't *exacting,* like the nothing to be done that had to be *done,* to become the nothing that *is,* which would be the merest nothing, without a psychic cost, inscribed on the body as well. And it could be, like the "fibrous degeneration" in his play *Catastrophe* (*Plays* 298), felt at considerable cost. One of the tumescent or edemic conditions from which Beckett himself suffered—a thickening of deep tissue that passes from palm to fingers, causing the hands to claw—it was inflicted on the character P, the barefoot protagonist up on a plinth who seems nothing more than a prop—fists clenched, face down, black wide-brimmed hat, black gown, not hooded or veiled, but like the now-notorious figure at Abu Ghraib, up on a pedestal too, with electric wires attached to his hands. With D, the director as chief sadist, the torture is a performance, or the performance tortuous, prepared by precise instructions to A, the more than willing female assistant, with a "craze for explicitation! Every i dotted to death!" (299), every element carefully staged, but as if for a Broadway audience, or the French boulevards, in the composition of pain.

Elsewhere it might be diagrammed or timed down to the second, or as in the play *Play,* with "faces lost to age" (*Plays* 147), up to their necks in the urns, not "just . . . play" (153), but "all out, all the pain" (148), with a direction to "REPEAT" (160), the repetition for confirmation like an experiment in a lab. For there is in Beckett, with his own explicitation, a microphysics of misery or, as he once said about Proust, a "science of affliction,"[13] in which at some self-punitive molecular extremity, or ineluctable non sequitur rage, there's a desire for atomization, as with Mrs. Rooney in *All That Fall,* "never tranquil," laughing wildly, "oh to be in atoms, in atoms! (*Frenziedly.*) ATOMS!" (*Plays* 17)—in the annihilating wish of despair, subtextually, subatomically, an apotheosis of dehiscence. Now, there's not only a science here, with those words behaving like quarks, a Beckettian string theory, but also an aesthetic: in the birth that is the death of him, as it happens again, "no difficulty there," there happens to be an exception, "imagination not dead yet, yes, dead, good, imagination dead imagine"[14]—which, imagine, puts the burden on you, and yes, dead, good, if you ever had imagination, the question is whether you can, including, from "a thousand little signs too long to imagine, . . . the infinitesimal shudder instantaneously suppressed" (*Imagination* 185).

Meanwhile, with a philosophical disposition that Beckett often denied (or was disturbed by in others when applied to his work) there is an epistemology, too, in the tormented susurrus or superfetation of words, that "sudden urge . . . to tell," get it all out, if not a confessional, "nearest lavatory . . . start pouring it out . . . steady stream . . . mad stuff . . . half the vowels wrong . . . no one could follow" (*Not I* 222). I mean the whole heart-breaking excremental glut, "That's right, wordshit, bury me, avalanche" (*Text 9* 137), if not then silence, words unspoken, errors acknowledged, knowledge unknowing, "Thoughts, no, not thoughts," rather "profounds of mind. Buried in who knows what profounds of mind. Or mindlessness"[15]—which, with no relief, deep in what sleep already, brain still going, dream-thought, you have to bring to mind. There is, of course, the minimalist side of Beckett, the parsimonious aesthetic, the "mere-most minimum,"[16] of those claustral plays and prose, where "Words are few. Dying too" (*Monologue* 265). But when it comes to thinking the worst, ill seen ill said, who was saying it better, what where, and who would have thought that in the "accusative [of] inexistence," along with a rush of amnesia, "no notion who it was saying what you were saying," there is also a "Grand Apnea" (*Text 8* 134), taking your breath away—what signal from the brain, what particle physics, *apnea with a grandeur?* "whose skull you were clapped up in" (*That Time* 231), where else would you find that but Beckett?

"Can there be misery," says Hamm, yawning, "loftier than mine? No doubt? Formerly. But now?" (*Endgame* 2). "What remains of all that misery?" says Krapp (*Plays* 58), playing and replaying his tapes, as if it were desired. "Be again, be again. (*Pause.*) All that old misery. (*Pause.*) Once wasn't enough for you" (63). Better if only remembered, since more than enough of it now, including the telling and retelling of what forever escapes you because you can never forget, "those things you kept making up to keep the void out just another of those old tales to keep the void from pouring in on you the shroud" (*That Time* 230). Nothing personal, of course, or merely personal, never mind the shrouding, the mess is universal, or as with Krapp, every new retrospect, moving between the two, the mess and those other "Moments. Her moments, my moments," even "The dog's moments. (*Pause.*) . . . he took it in his mouth, gently, gently. A small, old, black, hard, solid rubber ball" (*Krapp* 60), what he might have kept, something solid in his life, but he gave it to the dog. As for the mess, "Everything there, everything on this old muckball, all the light and dark and famine and feasting of . . . (*hesitates*) . . . the ages! (*In a shout.*) Yes! (*Pause*)," even the drifting pleasure, "among the flags and stuck" (62–63), gently up and down with her, be again, be again, some old chance of happiness, what all told, rewound on spools, he "revelled in the word. . . . Spooool!" (62), you'd still rather forget. And what is it there in *Breath,* that mimicry of a play, with its two vagital cries, what is it being remembered, except remembered being, being bygone, if it ever was, always nostalgia for it, or something more than being, with nothing there on stage, except a litter of rubbish, as if some token of the ruins of history, which gives another dimension to the birth astride of a grave.

"Know minimum," wrote Beckett, in *Worstward Ho* (91), but at meremost minimum that pitiful rubbish was proleptic about what, ideologically, we've since encountered in critical theory, most specifically through Walter Benjamin in his "Theses on the Philosophy of History." For it suggests the wreckage of time accumulating before the "Angelus Novus," as described by Benjamin in a painting by Paul Klee. Wings outspread, caught up in a violent storm from Paradise, the Angel is being blown backward into the future, facing the catastrophe of the past, the debris growing skyward before him,[17] from which Beckett might have gathered the litter, as a kind of bricolage, scraps and tatters from those ruins of time, "no verticals, all scattered and lying" (*Breath* 211), not flat-out, but at minima, if not Benjamin's "chips of Messianic time" ("Theses" 265), an ideographic suggestion of the Beckettian view of history. Thus it is that the rubbish on stage might also be a corrective to what Theodor Adorno wrote, in an essay on *Endgame,* with profounds of mind (and the philosophical disposition, to which, when they met, Beckett more than objected),[18] about the play not meaning anything becoming the only meaning, and with that certain certitudes about Beckett's indifference to history.

As if he were giving another contour to his well-known assertion that there could be no poetry after Auschwitz, Adorno insisted that

Beckett actually excluded history, because "it itself has dehydrated the power of consciousness to think history," desiccating as well "the power of remembrance."[19] For the most part rigorous in its focus on Beckett, there is in the essay a passing vengeance on "totalitarians like Lukács," still serving their Stalinist bosses, while despising the decadence that, from Baudelairean disgust to existential nausea, the "nausea of satiation," won't follow the party line ("Trying to Understand" 11). Yet, in countering Lukács's judgment of Beckett as irresponsibly nihilistic and politically irrelevant, with a "subjectivist ontology" that becomes "the excavated index of degenerate art because of its worldlessness and infantility" (15), Adorno is nevertheless still selling him short, because he doesn't think that Beckett has much to say about politics either. Overtly, to be sure, no politics on stage, in any usual way, nor even as it turned up in the theater of the Absurd—with which, misleadingly, in Martin Esslin's eponymous book, Beckett was identified. But in the past I've made the case that when his plays first appeared on the scene, particularly in San Francisco, where various events ignited the dissidence of the sixties, they had more political immediacy than the plays of Bertolt Brecht, which I had also directed—and this despite Beckett's denial, though he served in the French Resistance, of bearing "political witness," to use Adorno's term (15).

"Yes, no more denials, all is false," but the fact is—and "dupes" we may be, "dupes of every time and tense, until it's done, all past and done" (*Text 4* 109)—that Beckett, like some of his characters, or not quite characters, for all the lapsing remembrance, fact, I say, and not factitiously, never seems to forget, like the voices of *That Time* or the Mother in *Footfalls* or, back in the time of the waiting, in the frenzy of Lucky's speech, from the existence as uttered forth of a personal God through the death of Bishop Berkeley to the skulls in Connemara, never mind all the tennis or the quaquaquaqua, or paying attention to it, the skulls the skulls, as to some cacophonic sounding of the calamity of Western culture, echoed by Clov in *Endgame,* but anally, acidically, parsing the horrors out, the inexplicable punishment, zero out the window, the hollow in the wall, since he remembers everything, so appalling he wants it finished, "it must be nearly finished," even his walk impeded, that "*stiff, staggering walk,*" with a sort of raging measure, six steps, three steps, one step, brief laughs (1), why should he move at all? *how* can he move at all? as if he had to will it, in a vertigo of stasis, thus the stiffness, movement spastic, so much history on the brain. As for the subjectivity in Beckett, sure it's ontological, and no mere "subject position" (defined by race, class, gender, ethnicity), as in cultural studies today;

and so far as there is, with imagination dead imagine, anything like the vision that came from imagination, maybe only "The semblance. Faint, though by no means invisible in a certain light,"[20] it is no mere social construction. It may resemble, however, the semblance, more than faintly in a certain light, those sublimates of material life-process, what Marx speaks of as phantoms of the brain—or be haunted there, as with Marx himself, for all he tried to dispel it, by the future of illusion in the catastrophe of the past, about which one may say (and I've said it, taking a cue from the later Freud, what accounts for his tragic view in *Civilization and Its Discontents*) there is no other future.

So much, for the illusory moment, of what Beckett saw of the semblance. There was a time, there was a time, in his earliest story *Assumption,* where he sublimated, in the anguish of a young man struggling to be an artist, his own pretentious doubts and grievances "with the vulgar, uncultivated, terribly clear and personal ideas of the unread intelligenzia" (*Prose* 3), who'd never understand his desire, inherited from German romanticism, for "a wild rebellious surge" that, aspiring "violently towards realization in sound," would restore the "inexplicable bombshell perfection" that came with Promethean fire. What he wanted—perhaps to offset that other anguish, the palpitating terror, the rush of blood in the body that kept him breathless at night—was another pain, "the pain of Beauty" (4), which has been dismissed since deconstruction, along with Vision and Imagination, especially when the words are capitalized, as transcendental signifiers. Back in the 1950s, before that critique occurred, Beckett asked in a text for nothing, with nothing like Promethean fire (and the usual absence of the question mark), "And beauty, strength, intelligence"—of which he wrote in the same light as the semblance, or "a kind of light, sufficient to see by"—simply more of the same? "the latest, daily, action, poetry, all one price for one and all"? Now the words embarrass him, they always did, but even more, the mind slow, the words slow, the subject there dying in an unpredicated clutter. "If only it could be wiped from knowledge. To have suffered under that miserable light, what a blunder" (*Text 2* 106).

Still, with Beckett you never know, for in all "times and tenses," he's surely blundered worse, like giving himself up "for dead all over the place," only to find that there's "nothing like breathing your last to put new life in you"—with, of course, the mutterings undiminished, "the same old stories, the same old questions and answers" (*Text 1* 102–3), but the same plus one, and therefore not the Same—as Nietzsche declared, speaking of beauty, strength, intelligence, about the Eternal Return. Be eternity what it may, "now here, what now here, one enormous second, as in Paradise" (*Text 2* 106), within a page or so of the shorter prose it's possible to move, with nuances of disdain for each nuance, from desolation to nostalgia to transcendental longing, for the outside prospect of some otherness there, or maybe there on the inside, "other others, invisible" (106), or from whatever it was in the semblance to thoughts in a dry season, not quite like T. S. Eliot's (whom Beckett early admired), not quite the waste land either, but on a Sunday morning, with no paradise to be lost.

"Dry, it's possible, or wet, or slime, as before matter took ill." And then the familiar sensation, with slime, if that, the originary trace, as when he was still unborn, some continuity with the womb. "Is this stuff air that permits you to suffocate still, almost audibly at times, it's possible, a kind of air," says the voice of a text for nothing, turning to "one more memory, one last memory, it may help, to abort again." But will memory never cease, for that aborting again suggests what Beckett apparently said about himself to the psychoanalyst Wilfred Bion, about an inadequate parturition, still unborn when he was born, and out of breath, repeatedly. As for the dry season, however, there were signs of renewal there, and if not Eternal, "it was none the less the return, to what no matter, the return, unscathed, always a matter for wonder. What happened? Is that the question? An encounter? Bang! No." No Big Bang either, nor creation myth that day, yet if something more than a semblance, nothing more than "a glow, red, afar, at night, in winter, that's worth having, that must have been worth having" (107–8).

Sometimes you can maybe see it, sometimes you have to listen, and keep what you hear in mind. "A voice comes to one in the dark. Imagine." After that opening line, from *Company,* triple space, section break, aporetic silence. For the sake of imagining. "To one on his back in the dark. This he can tell by the pressure on his hind parts," the pronoun *This* confounding, *what* can he tell? *that* he is in the dark? or that the voice comes? and how do the hind parts certify that? or, if it is the voice, by virtue of this or that, what exactly can he tell of it, or being in the dark itself, "by how the dark changes when he shuts his eyes and again when he opens them again"? Whatever we imagine, he, whoever he is, "must acknowledge the truth of what is said. But by far the greater part of what is said cannot be verified."[21] Which is, of course, the way with Beckett. "For why or? Why in another dark or in the same? And whose voice is asking this? Who asks, Whose voice is asking this?" (*Company* 16). Of course, we'll never know, but whatever is there to know or, as here, "a certain mental activity" (7), high order, low order, or crawling "the mute count. Grain by grain in the mind," as at the beginning of *Endgame,* with the fugual desire to be finished, Clov's "impossible heap," but the mute count not so punishing, nor those grains so metaphysical, the futile desire to be finished, though of that we can't be sure, in the arithmetical introspection. "One two three four one. Knee hand knee hand two. One foot. Till say after five he falls. Then sooner or later on from nought anew. One two three four one" (36). I could go on, but I won't go on. I'll keep him company.

Whatever it is that, "with no dead end for his pains," might set his mind in motion, his mind, mine, the mind needs company, "what if not sound, . . . Sight? The temptation is strong to decree there is nothing to see. But too late for the moment. For he sees a change of dark when he opens or shuts his eyes." And let there be light, the faintest light, should they happen to be open, "no longer perceived than the time it takes the lid to fall," the seeing unseeing, and so with taste or touch, "The thrust of the ground against his bones. All the way from calcaneum to philoprogenitiveness," ever failing, failing better, a consensus of the senses, "Smell? His own?" or "a rat long dead. Or some other carrion. Yet to be imagined" (37). Or maybe a sixth sense, or as if evolution were reversed, crawling, eyelids stirring, "till the last thump" (29), stirring still, if not "pure reason," an awakening dehiscence, *le déreglement du sens* (Beckett had lectured on Rimbaud), and it will be, you can be sure, as Artaud said of the naked, sonorous realization of the essential theater, "as localized and as precise as the circulation of the blood in the arteries or," in the impeccably ordered disorder that is a compulsion in Beckett, "the apparently chaotic development of dream images in the brain"—what in his manifesto for the theater of Cruelty, Artaud called "true illusion."[22] And while there's a far cry between them—not only Artaud's actor signaling through the flames, whom Beckett would never direct—there is in both a rigorous intellectuality and, as Artaud saw it in the Balinese theater, a "mathematical meticulousness" to the "inexhaustible mental ratiocination, like a mind ceaselessly taking its bearings in the maze of its unconscious."[23] As for what they take to be "the truthful precipitates of dreams" (Artaud, "Manifesto" 92), for the ratiocinative Beckett the precipitations are endless, "what vicissitudes within what changelessness" (*Text 9* 137), yet if "Never but in passing dream the passing hour long short,"[24] there remains for him the semblance, shrouded perhaps, and obscured by history—returning to which, as to the dreamscape of a nightmare, there was surely much to remember, word unspoken, but Auschwitz there, and a century of rational slaughter, or promiscuous devastation, the Holocaust, Dresden, Hiroshima, and beyond the Gulag, genocides yet to come; in short, a real theater of Cruelty.

In this regard, speak as we wish, through the fetishism of writing in theory, of the text as body in the body of the text—and Beckett's writing may be the exemplary model of that—I'm speaking now of his undeluded awareness of those corporeal bodies out there, or once there, but incinerated, or buried too, some of them, not where death came with birth, but where, dead, yes dead, imagine, they've never yet been found, or in a mass grave, among the multitudinous dead. "Dying on. No more no less. No. Less. Less to die. Ever less" (*Monologue* 266), because so many wantonly dead, though in the dialectic of Beckett, if less is not more, *Lessness* (the title of one of his stories) is no less than never(the)less. Which, for all the syncopated changes, ever more, ever less, are no mere contradictions, though sometimes too they come, as in sundry stage directions, with the rage I mentioned before, if not an eruptive virulence, then caustically ironic, seething, barely contained. Thus, when Hamm moves from his taunting scorn for Clov's stinking to "The whole place stinks of corpses," and Clov deflates it or maybe trumps it with "The whole universe" (46), that may seem a Beckettian joke, as it may with the tramps in *Godot,* when to somehow reduce the misery, they think they are maybe thinking, and suddenly realize, even "in no danger of ever thinking any more," that "What is terrible is to *have* thought," which leads to the question that, however we screen it out, is always subliminally there: "Where are all these corpses from?" And then, though they may be putting on the audience, as from the edge of the stage, caught up in specularity, looking at those looking, at a presumably safe distance, the spectators in their dark: "A charnel house! A charnel house!" (41).

If not writing for the dead, as Heiner Müller claimed to be doing—with his usual mordancy, because the dead are in the majority, and it's properly democratic to write for the majority—Beckett did say, even as his plays were being canonized, that he was writing into a void. And that goes, in its incriminating alienation, far beyond the Brechtian judgment of the bourgeois audience, not to mention the universe, or with atrocities unending on a global scale, the world as we know it today: not only the spectacle of televised terrorism and the war against it, with the actualities unseen, suicide bombings, death squads, beheadings, as well as the fallout killings and scandals that, with the "doctrine of distinction" and collateral damage, are the coefficient of invasive democracy, but also the widespread torture of massive poverty, tribal murders, sectarian cleansing, ears cut off, toes cut off, janjaweed rapes, then *zina* (women punished for fornication), forced migration, labor camps, smuggling of the unnamable, not only drugs and teenage girls, but an international trade of prostituted children, and then those other diseases, yard-long Guinea worms in slime, AIDS, blinding trachoma, and other abysmal plagues. Now, it would seem that this is not the kind of thing, for all his laughable lists at which you couldn't quite laugh, that Beckett would catalogue. And there is certainly substance to the view that "the focus of injustice in Beckett is almost never local, civil, or social, but cosmic, the injustice of having been born."[25] But if his work didn't seem to draw upon what, page by miserable page, shows up every morning in my reading of *The New York Times,* beside larger and larger ads for Tourneau watches, Gucci bags, or Ferragamo shoes, he was very well aware, too, of what—as he read of it in *Le Monde* or *Libération* (which he *did* read, a French newspaper, though rumor was that he didn't)—you can hardly bear to read. When Clov said "The whole universe," that was not merely cosmic, and Beckett knew very well, as Clov said at the wall, through the subjective ontology of that claustrophobic space, "Beyond is the . . . other hell" (26), and if that still sounds cosmic, "Outside of here it's death" (70)—which is something other than the death of him, something more brutally lethal, the untold numbers dead, not in a text, no text for nothing, but in the brutal material world.

"There's something dripping in my head. (*Pause.*) A heart, a heart in my head," says Hamm, in what would seem the introjected extremity of his solipsistic mode (*Endgame* 18), but as Clov has his telescope, the magnifier, to liven up the deadliness, there is in Hamm's heart and head, "*With prophetic relish,*" another magnitude, where "there'll be no wall anymore," and if not infinite space, Hamletic, "Infinite emptiness," which "all the resurrected dead of all the ages wouldn't fill," and if that, in Hamm, still sounds magniloquent, what he goes on to say would be merely vapid if there wasn't in Beckett himself some unapocalyptic sense of the unresurrected dead or the universe of suffering, the unconsoled reality of it, that Hamm takes upon himself: "Yes, one day you'll know what it is, you'll be like me, except that you won't have anyone with you, because you won't have pity on anyone and because there won't be anyone left to have pity on" (36). No doubt, as formerly, the outburst will be deflated and, what a pity, it seems walled in again, the pity, "But you," and this comes at the end of the play, "you ought to know what the earth is like, nowadays" (83). No more no less.

And I knew him well enough to know that no more no less was, in his "poor mind,"[26] with all the brilliance of it, the equilibration of human misery with something like infinite pain, which he could also parody, mixing the personal with the abstract, as in *Rough for Theater II,* when A and B are summing up the reasons to let the suicidal figure jump: "Work, family, third fatherland, cunt, finances, art and nature, heart and conscience, health, housing conditions, God and man, so many disasters" (*Plays* 78). If there seems no measure here, of what comes together in pain, from the personal to the political, from the aesthetic to social disasters, there is in the story *Enough,* where the focus is personal and the voice is that of a woman, whose mental calculations or "flight into arithmetic" are not unlike Beckett's, who could be more than uneasy about it: "The art of combining," she says, "is not my fault. It's a curse from above. For the rest I would suggest not guilty" (*Prose* 187–88).

Which, peace to Sam Beckett, is at best a guilty plea, or like one of his "Faux Départs" (from a novel called *Fancy Dying*), maybe a false start, or pretext for starting again, "talking to himself the last person. / Saying, Now where is he, no, Now he is here,"[27] and in the Grand Apnea, the elision of texts as I think them, "what . . . who? . . . no! . . . she!" who, as the words pour out of the Mouth, that sliver of body on stage, with a silent Auditor there, whose sex is undeterminable, comes "out . . . into this world . . . this world," out "before her time," but is it out of, or into, that "godforsaken hole," where she "found herself in the dark . . . and if not exactly . . . insentient . . . insentient," remembers the fetal position, as Beckett remembered it, or something much like it—what it was "she did not know . . . what position she was in . . . imagine!"—maybe because that's the place, if it was, where you take on the suffering, for what you can't forget. And it starts all over again, "but the brain—what?" the words coming on like mad, from the first awful thought to another, each "dismissed as foolish," like being punished for her sins, "as she suddenly realized . . . gradually realized . . . she was not suffering . . . imagine! . . . not suffering!" but with no steady state in Beckett, or on the Möbius strip of misery, or just short on a Sigmoid curve, "unless of course she was . . . *meant* to be suffering . . . ha! . . . *thought* to be suffering" (*Not I* 216–17), as if thinking itself were the sin, nothing more terrible than to *have* thought, that for the anxious moment, and then again a "sudden flash . . . very foolish really but— . . . what?" we'll take a Beckettian (*Pause*), as from the causal of the fugual or, there again (*Pause*), for all the truthful precipitates, the substance of a bad dream, but good or bad, "revolving it all?" and "Where it began. (*Pause.*) It all began," the absurdity of it, that *It,* "It all. (*Pause.*) It all" (*Footfalls* 243, 240), never it all but the semblance, the shadow of true illusion, or maybe a *faux départ,* another false start, taking thought, last thought, perhaps the thought that's lasting, damn that sin! another way of thinking—and even when breathless, the pity of it, the pity, the revolving never stops.

But wait, wait! in all the despair, is there anything like hope, even if true, something more to that illusion? You can be sure there's a text for that. "A pity hope is dead. No." Yet, now and again, with the same old cries, or moans and groans, from the cradle to the grave, even down there when the grave-digger put on the forceps, "How one hoped above, on and off. With what diversity" (*Text 2* 108). Diversity? Well, it's not exactly affirmative action, but speaking of moans and groans, even short of breath, the cost of inspiration, why is it that the work of Beckett, woeful, mournful, impossibly painful, or simply ready, as in *Rockaby,* to say, "fuck life" (*Plays* 282), is more enlivening than other things we encounter with a more sanguine, less grievous, funny not funny, funereal view of it all? One two three four one. "Better hope deferred than none. Up to a point. Till the heart starts to sicken. Company too up to a point. Better a sick heart than none. Till it starts to break." Now, take a breath. "For the time being leave it at that" (*Company* 18).

NOTES

1. Jacques Lacan, *Écrits: A Selection,* trans. Alan Sheridan (New York : Norton, 1977) 4.

2. *Texts for Nothing 13,* in *The Complete Shorter Prose, 1929–1989,* ed. S. E. Gontarski (New York: Grove, 1995) 154; abbreviated as *Prose.* After first citation here, selections from this volume will be referred to only by their titles, sometimes abbreviated, as with *Text* (and number) for *Texts for Nothing.*

3. *Not I,* in *Collected Shorter Plays* (New York: Grove, 1984) 217; abbreviated as *Plays.* After first reference to a play here, or in the text, only its title will be given, sometimes abbreviated.

4. *A Piece of Monologue,* in *Plays* 269.

5. *Eh Joe,* in *Plays* 202.

6. *Endgame* (New York: Grove, 1958) 53.

7. *Embers,* in *Plays* 98.

8. *The Unnamable* (New York: Grove, 1958) 130.

9. *That Time,* in *Plays* 230.

10. According to Beckett, the last word of his father on his deathbed, passed on to Pozzo, as he leaves the stage with Lucky, in *Waiting for Godot* (57).

11. *Sounds,* appendix I: *Variations on a "Still" Point,* in *Prose* 267.

12. *Still 3,* appendix I, in *Prose* 269.

13. *Proust* (New York: Grove, n.d.) 4.

14. *Imagination Dead Imagine,* in *Prose* 182.

15. *Ohio Impromptu,* in *Plays* 288.

16. *Worstward Ho,* in *Nohow On: Three Novels by Samuel Beckett* (New York: Grove, 1996) 91; the other two novels are *Company* and *Ill Seen Ill Said.*

17. Walter Benjamin, "Theses on the Philosophy of History," in *Illuminations,* ed. Hannah Arendt, trans. Harry Zohn (New York: Harcourt, Brace & World, 1968) 259.

18. About Beckett's disdain for Adorno, see James Knowlson, *Damned to Fame: The Life of Samuel Beckett* (New York: Simon & Schuster, 1996) 428.

19. Theodor W. Adorno, "Trying to Understand *Endgame,*" in *Samuel Beckett's "Endgame,"* ed. Harold Bloom (New York: Chelsea House, 1988).

20. *Footfalls,* in *Plays* 242.

21. *Company,* in *Nohow On* 3.

22. Antonin Artaud, "The Theater of Cruelty (First Manifesto)," in *The Theater and Its Double,* trans. Mary Caroline Richards (New York: Grove, 1958) 92.

23. Artaud, "On Balinese Theater," in *Theater and Its Double* 57, 63.

24. *Lessness,* in *Prose* 200.

25. S. E. Gontarski, in his introduction to *Prose* xxiii.

26. *Footfalls* 240.

27. Appendix II: "Faux Départs," in *Prose* 272.

TWELVE

Art and Crisis

Homeland Security and the Noble Savage

RECENTLY I WAS ASKED PERMISSION to reprint an essay that I was first asked to write, over forty years ago, by the novelist Saul Bellow, long before he became a Nobel laureate. It was for a periodical he once coedited called *The Noble Savage*—with that other spelling of the word, not the name of the munitions maker, who created a peace prize, too, from the invention of dynamite. As for *The Noble Savage,* there was a romantic irony in the appropriation of that romantic figure, whose mythic purity—according to Rousseau—was an innocence upheld by natural law, while its possible resurrection, during the period of the cold war, was little more than a Bellowish joke of a knowing wish fulfillment. Speaking of savagery, if not purity, I should say that the essay I wrote was eventually absorbed into my first book, *The Impossible Theater: A Manifesto,* which was described at the time as a savage indictment of the American theater, with chapter titles drawn from the language of the cold war: Fallout, The Iron Curtain, The Balance of Terror. The title of the essay was "The Public Art of Crisis in the Suburbs of Hell," which was not exactly what John F. Kennedy had in mind when, at his inauguration, he spoke of New Frontiers.

Actually, the provocation for the essay's title came from a somewhat remoter source, John Webster's *The Duchess of Malfi,* one of the splendidly corrosive tragedies of the Jacobean age, in which, outdoing *Hamlet,* there was not only reason in madness but, with madness being reasoned, reason was going mad. And with a certain cacophony in the music of the spheres—God in the expanding heavens already in jeopardy—it was an age that, despite the colonizing reach of imperial power, felt as we've come to do, in the new imperium of capitalism, that it was losing control of a world going increasingly global; in our case, with the return on investments abroad including a venomous hatred and, with martyrdom in the madness, a fanatic will to destroy us. If the fall of the Iron Curtain seemed for some years to open things up, Homeland Security—for understandable reasons, beyond John Ashcroft's vigilance or Susan Sontag's outrage—is closing things down. If we thought when the Soviet Union was breaking up that the threat of nuclear holocaust was over, what we're hearing about now is the remarkable versatility of "weapons of mass destruction" (the phrase a sort of litany), some of them insidious, not merely the Big Bang or familiar mushroom cloud, but anthrax, sarin, smallpox, and menaces unforeseen, like snipers in the suburbs, or—in the imagining of the inevitable: is it merely paranoia? or something more than fantasy?—bombs in a baby carriage going off in a shopping mall.

"Security some men call the suburbs of hell, / Only a dead wall between."[1] When I quoted that from *The Duchess of Malfi* those many years ago, it was in a context where, with the Berlin Wall still standing, the stalemate of détente seemed like the human condition, while the soporific passivity of our theater made it seem marginal or irrelevant to everything that was urgent in our culture. Given our vulnerabilities now—the circulation of terror in a limitless war, or the foreboding infinity of the undeclared—the following passage from the essay may seem like a melodrama of overstatement, though it was written when, having thumped his shoe on a table at the UN, Khrushchev was still in power, and with Kennedy concealing his osteoporosis, shot full of cortico-steroids, up on amphetamines, during the year of the Cuban missile crisis: "In public life a condition of insupportable tension . . . may be made liveable by the illusions of greater production, more conspicuous consumption, the strategy of controlled depression, and the whole Disneyland of shelter programs and stockpiled weapons." But in art, "real art"—what most of our theater wasn't—"the same condition of insupportable tension, felt in privacy and cutting to the brain, is brought to even greater tension in the interest of *truth,* however unsayable, indefensible, or unbearable" (89). If the theater's status in our culture, with the media and the Internet taking over performance, hasn't changed all that much, I still tend to think of it (when it is as it should be) as the public art of crisis in a virtual state of crisis—all the more so in "a world of *Realpolitik,* sneak attacks, and holy wars" (100), though I wasn't thinking then, through the disappearance of bin Laden and the dispersal of Al Qaeda, of the wider, more virulent network of a mostly invisible jihad financed by charities, drug smuggling, bank robberies, laundered money, and mandated in the madrassas—for a growing population of otherwise futureless young people—by the hallowed verses of the Koran.

As we put that in some impossible perspective, along with the faith-based initiatives of our born-again president against the "axis of evil," it isn't a question of cost accounting, even if we had an Arthur Anderson for some of my liberal friends (whose politics I otherwise share). I mean those who say—as in the first email message I received the morning of 9/11—that "the chickens are coming home to roost," and point to years of exploitation by corporate America, from pumping oil to agribusiness, and the brutalizing of dissidence by various dictators and paramilitaries sponsored by the CIA. Add it all up as you will—including our support of Saddam Hussein, who was an ally before he became a monster—there's no such thing as balancing terror, no more than knowing in advance how, with Iraq, a policy of preemption would work, either as a bluff to insure inspections, upping the ante on the UN, or, expecting deceit from Saddam, the Predators in place, with smarter bombs and Special Forces, going for broke on a change of regime. What there's no discounting, however, is the new reality principle, immediate and, for any foreseeable future—with all the data-based resources of asymmetrical might: from weather precision-guided munition (WX-PGMs) in a global positioning system (GPS) to new microwave E-bombs that fry the computer circuits of any threatening missiles—just about irreversible.

And how art assesses that is pretty indeterminable, and so, too, its capacity to keep up with the impermeable stream of events around, behind, or inaccessible to the instant mediatization that—with its superfetation of commentary, the balanced equations of talk shows or the bully pulpit of *Hardball*—anesthetizes attention. Nor is it always a penchant of art, even the avant-garde, to keep itself up-to-date by being dutiful to the headlines. Between Ezra Pound's conviction that poetry is the news that stays news and William Carlos Williams's sense that "It is difficult / To get the news from poems," there is the long-nurtured suspicion—and sometimes conviction too—that while the news may prompt a poem, neither poetry nor any of the other arts, including theater, is particularly concerned with that, as anything more than a pretext, where the art most deeply exists. As for the use of the arts in a time of crisis, one comes back to the paradox—despite Picasso's *Guernica* (1937) or Goya's *3rd of May* (1814), rare exceptions to the rule—that their use or proleptic power is in their uselessness. And though that ethos has been much debated, along with issues of art and politics, it would seem inarguable in one respect: that while art may characterize with harrowing accuracy a certain kind of terrorist, like the insidious Verkhovensky in Dostoyevsky's *The Possessed,* it hasn't much to tell us, at this baffling historical moment, about how to turn the others off, averting among the martyrs, or the anonymous cadre of the envenomed, the rites of (dis)possession, or the long-smoldering animus of "the wretched of the earth."

As we try to absorb that, we might turn back—though it may seem anomalous now, if not unpatriotic—to Karl Marx, who gave us an appropriate warning in the middle of the nineteenth century: "our difficulties begin," he wrote in *The German Ideology,* "only when we set about the observation and the arrangement—the real depiction—of our historical material, whether of the past epoch or of the present."[2] But for those who've been engaged, through the revisionist Marxism of the last generation, in a ceaseless assault on "the ideology of the aesthetic," that is, the legacy of high modernism, with its disposition to form and its ethos of "difficulty," this should be (though it won't) a chastening moment. For it should be apparent, too, that various terms once associated with modernism in the arts, out of a critical warp of the humanistic tradition, seem to have returned, after demystification, to undeniable *relevance.* Here I'm using a term from the 1960s, that contentious period which initiated deconstruction to begin with, and the politicizing of the arts, along with the ideological matrix of cultural studies, with its quadrivium of gender, race, class, and ethnicity. And while these categories are by no means to be dismissed or minimized, all the issues filtered by a modified Marxism through feminism, psychoanalysis, the new historicism, and queer theory, are out in a wider transnational scene a sort of ironic double trouble, arising as they do *from* the humanistic tradition, born of the Enlightenment, which, if excoriated here by the ideological Left, and for other reasons by the fundamentalist Right, is detested elsewhere, in the fanatic fundamentalism of the Islamic world, for its liberal attitudes toward behavior, dress, sexuality, the status of women, freedom of speech, faith or nonfaith, and an array of dubious practices at the extremities of what, before the 1960s, was not yet called "lifestyle." What we see now, through the immanence of globalization and the nervous cosmos of colliding cultures, is "the shock of recognition" (a talismanic phrase from the old New Criticism) that "tension," "paradox," and the "seven types of ambiguity" are back—and maybe a few that we never knew existed, while all the talk of "hybridity" and a radical "decentering" is a theoretical indulgence, certainly in other parts of the world, where nationhood is still a necessity, and identity up for grabs, or virtually nonexistent, when not fiercely imposed by religious doctrine that despises—as if in accordance with the theory now coming home to roost—"the hegemony of the West."

About that, and its relation to impending disaster, if the arts have been delinquent, now and again in the media we're likely to hear more, if not in the editorials, in letters to the editor or on the Internet. "We will not make progress toward peace," says a letter in *TIME,* "until we treat the causes of terrorism, not just the symptoms, as we are doing now."[3] Thus the voice of reason, and who can argue with that, though even in its idealism, at some impasse of the real, there's a certain jaundice in art—no less, when the idealism isn't there, a remorseless objectivity that may at its most exacting, as in Beckett or Genet, refuse its own desires, or, as in Brecht's *The Measures Taken,* commit itself ideologically to what seems almost inhumane. Meanwhile, we can find versions of that letter in other journals, from *Newsweek* or *The Nation* to *The New York Review of Books,* or in newspapers all over the country, as well as on CNN, not to mention countless classrooms in our universities. But still the symptoms accumulate beyond the ameliorative pace of any imaginable progress, and would, even if we altered our foreign policies tomorrow, or Ralph Nader were to replace Paul Wolfowitz as brain trust in the Pentagon or Jesse Jackson took over from Condi Rice as national security advisor. The fact is that no immediate change of heart will diminish the perilous threat of multitudinous others who look upon us as a menace to what they believe (benighted as some of it seems), or as a domineering power without the capacity—in the worldwide dominion of suffering, for which 9/11 was only partial recompense—to feel their pain or to remember the atrocities perpetrated, for strategic or corporate or ethnocentric purposes, by the moral blindness of the West. Nor will there be a change of heart in the bilious back streets of the Muslim world, so long as the West is inseparable from the spread of modernity, technology, electronically delivered imagery, and even the tourist trade, and—as in Bali or Thailand—the morals that go with it, some of them brought there through the Vietnam War or, by "the greatest generation," back in World War II.

Moral blindness, spiritual blindness: these are traditional concerns of art, particularly tragic drama, where the crisis, if irreparable, is so painfully explored as to bring wisdom from suffering, or so, in their woeful lamentations, the ancient choruses say. But that implied a cultural unity that—even if we wanted it, in this age of border crossings, romanticized in the academy, but abysmal for many who cross—is only to be remembered, and even then as something questionable or unobtainable, or, as Euripides saw the civilizing claims of the Athenian Empire when it was about to go under, a worn-out fiction, delusional too. It may be that ground zero is where our sense of the tragic revives, as when references were made, during the memorials, to Bobby Kennedy's quoting, after his brother's death, the Aeschylean chorus about the pain that drips upon the heart. But drip as it may, wherever, beyond the warp of the messianic, if there's anything that unites us, East and West, it's a common demoralization, though there's now and then a kind of blindness, morally obtuse, that has unexpected perceptual benefits. Thus, for the imperturbably conservative Dinesh D'Souza (best known, perhaps, for his debates with Stanley Fish), the West can't conceivably be ethnocentric because it had come up—wouldn't you know?—with the concept of the noble savage, as a preface to the social contract in which natural liberty led to civil liberty in a morally edifying outcome. (With the approval of Jerry Falwall, who has his doubts about Islam, God bless all Native Americans!) Yet it would also seem, in one of the consummate mordancies of the dialectic of the Enlightenment, that the concept of the noble savage bears rather, in its exalted image, on Osama bin Laden (whose apparent innocence was enhanced by wealth before he became a mastermind) and the new legions of suicide bombers, who claim a certain nobility in the savagery that will be rewarded—at least for the males among them—by forty houris in heaven. It's not yet clear what's in it for the women.

Or is that remark, insensitive to cultural difference, another form of Orientalism, also morally obtuse? If so, tell that to Salman Rushdie, who recently—not wholly forgiving yet of the fatwa issued against him—wrote with unstifled vituperation about the sharia court's sentence, in Nigeria, ordering that a woman be stoned to death for adultery, as well as about other ominous or grisly punishments to be inflicted on dissident Muslim females, and the "killing, looting and burning" that occurred in Kaduna when it was said that the prophet Mohammad might, if he were at the Miss World contest that has since moved to London, want to marry one of the beauties competing. "Where, after all," Rushdie asked, with the intemperance of the artist impelled by his own experience, "is the Muslim outrage at these events? As their ancient, deeply civilized culture of love, art and philosophical reflection is hijacked by paranoiacs, racists, liars, male supremacists, tyrants, fanatics and violence junkies, why are they not screaming?" For Rushdie, this is not a matter of the hegemony of the West, but rather that "the moderate voices of Islam cannot or will not insist on the modernization of their culture—and of their faith as well."[4] His faith is such that his recent fiction and essays are caustic about all this, the satire thicker (or maybe thinner) but not as impressive as his earlier fiction, which is not to say that outrage can't be the substance of art.

So far as our common outrage is concerned, not to mention our views of Islam relative to 9/11, very little of that has found its way into art, by no means to the extent that we've heard it in media politics, if muted, however, into a sort of subtext, though Donald Rumsfeld at his sardonic best (like him, not like him) sounds like Rushdie, and I'm talking here of performance, against the grain of my own politics. As it turns out, next to Rushdie's article, in an op-ed column of the *Times,* the liberal journalist Thomas Friedman, taking on the role of George W. Bush, writing to the leaders of the Muslim world, repeats in a more temperate voice just about what Rushdie had said, quoting at one point, however, from the very conservative *National Review,* what both Rushdie and Rumsfeld would have read with approval: "No faith will make rote memorization of ancient texts, suppression of critical inquiry and dissent, subjugation of women, and a servile deference to authority the recipe for anything other than civilizational decline" (*Times* A23). Whatever the politics woven through these voices, if they were orchestrated in a play, I'd prefer it to the pretense of moderation about what's out there in the Muslim world, not to mention the political correctness telling us what we know, that not all Arabs are alike.

Nor, for that matter, are we, including the Arabs among us, as if to those who want to kill us that makes any difference. It was a conviction about that, by the way, that caused a judge—just last week on the TV series *The Practice*—to rule with disgust, because it seemed to violate the Constitution (and he hoped his ruling would be overthrown in a higher court), that an airline could nevertheless refuse to fly Arab passengers. Was it art? Not to be expected from television, though it was much more strenuous around the moral issue than plays like *Copenhagen* or *Proof,* which presumably brought into the theater what has been praised there as higher intelligence. With the arguments made by the lawyers and the reasoning of the judge, the episode was a piece of old-fashioned realism redeemed through rather familiar emotions by unexpectedly incisive reflections on what—dismayed as they were by the prospect of racial profiling—was nevertheless, too, a justifiable paranoia.

Up to 9/11, for most Americans, ground zero was middle ground, and if at this still-destabilized moment—the devastation mainly psychic with the debris cleared away—it has shifted more to the right, by way of patriotism to militarism as the major response to terrorism, there's not altogether something senseless or insensitive in that, even if the long-term planners of the now-globalized Manifest Destiny need to do a lot of rethinking of how, empathically and ethically, we engage with the rest of the world. And in this regard, I don't mean the moral clarity that an all-knowing pious blowhard like William Bennett wants, or Dick Cheney's wife when, as head of the National Endowment for the Humanities, she resisted every major form of research in what we now call cultural studies, repudiating all political correctness except her own, while deriding multiculturalism, and wanting not only to teach more American history but as if, somehow, that were the end of history. Which is not to say that cultural studies, which now dominates the curriculum in our graduate schools, doesn't have, as I've suggested, its own ideological disposition with predictable readings of history, and dubious attitudes toward what Bush and Cheney and Rumsfeld and the seemingly dissenting Powell ought to be doing, what not, at this conflicted and dangerous fadeout of history when—even as I was writing this—the audiotape with what is purportedly Osama bin Laden's voice was broadcast by satellite on Al-Jazeera, praising the bombings in Bali and the Chechen hostage-taking in Moscow, and once again threatening we know not what.

It's precisely that, *we know not what,* that is the particular jurisdiction of art, with a reflexive indisposition to any claims or semblance of certitude, especially one's own, in the myriad indeterminacies of the moral morass of crisis. What one expects from art then—again, if it's really art, and I may be speaking only for myself—is a perceptual resilience that is something more than a reductive view of it all, no less (though for the harrowing moment they kept the advertisements off TV) the eventual commodification, after 9/11, of the images of disaster, and the memorials too. Whatever the unappeasable loss that some have suffered, as with the atomized bodies in the toppling towers, there were through the inevitable repetitions the persisting banalities, though there *were* heroism and grief and mourning, *about* the heroism and grief and mourning, and the "need for closure," even among those far away from any site of disaster, and "getting on with our lives," which most of us were doing in any case. Which is not to say that there weren't real feelings at a distance, including confused feelings about what we were feeling or what we should feel or why, somehow, some of us couldn't feel anything at all—not even sure, if we felt it, about a surreptitious feeling of dread.

Art arises from such sensations, in a web of inchoate emotions, while somewhere in its emergence might be the possibility, out of self-critical severity, that anything felt might be factitious, and the less said about it the better, which—if inconceivable in our mediatized reality today—is what Theodor Adorno apparently felt when he said that after Auschwitz there could be no more poetry. Of course, that wasn't so: "The rest is silence"—but as with Shakespeare, who said it, or after the Holocaust, Paul Celan, only poetry knows it, compelling attention to what, in all perceptual vanity, is at the exhausted limit of words:

Do not read any more—look!
Do not look any more—go! . . .

The place where they lay, it has
a name—it has
none. They did not lie there. Something
lay between them. . . .

Spoke, spoke.

Was, was.[5]

And what now appals us in the age of terror—for all that is spoke, spoke, was, was—is that it's very likely to be, is, is, intolerably in the present tense without any end in sight.

Yet, nevertheless, as if with a sanity out of the past, judicious voices, like George McGovern's, in a moving article in *Harper's,* warn us about an excessive pessimism that, pervading the Bush administration's obsession with evil powers, infects as well our sense of the future. "There has been evil in the world," McGovern reminds us, "at least since Cain and Abel, and there will be evil after all of us are gone from the earth. God might be able to change that, but not us mere humans. I look into the future with far less fear and therefore far less cynicism."[6] Yet it wasn't the downturn of an apocalyptic disposition that led his old liberal colleague Gary Hart to say, when he and Warren Rudman issued their report on domestic security, "The world is divided between those who believe the worst is over and those who believe the worst is yet to come."[7] If Hart is misleading in any way, in keeping the alarm going, it's in the implication of an even division, since there are very few, indeed, even among the more sanguine, who are likely to feel that the worst is over, or that our vulnerability has been safely diminished since the horror of the fatal day. As I dwell on the worst of it now, wondering why I'm doing it, what seems at times to be diminished is the relevance of art. But then we do what we must, and the way I'm thinking here is, for better or worse, in the orbit of the impossible, turning things over and over, which is what you do in rehearsal, turning them over again, as I've always thought in the theater. If one wants anything at all from art in a time of crisis (and I'm not always sure that we do) it is—at the nerve ends of thought where thought escapes us, causing us to pursue it, thus enlivening thought—the activity of perception that is something like moral rigor, demanding from every brain cell even more thought, acceding to the indisputable when it's there, though it's not very likely to be, and seeing with the utmost compassion, at the limit of endurance, what we'd mostly rather not.

To be sure, art in a time of crisis will attempt to do other things, though there was also likely to be, given the dimensions of 9/11, a sort of moratorium, with a sense that anything art might do would only be anticlimax. The same was true for the media and popular culture, but just as we've recently heard that everything around lower Manhattan's Ground Zero was not exactly heroic—that there were those who searched the names of the missing as a way of locating empty apartments, and that even certain firemen going past an office up in a tower ripped off a thing or two—so there was the episode of TV's *Law and Order,* in which a man who murdered his wife, who worked at the Trade Center, cut off her hand and left it at the site. If this, as a plot complication in the series, was demonically artful, it is not exactly art, though it may have been more so than any of the plays produced one September evening at Town Hall in New York, commemorating 9/11 under the overall title "Brave New World." Well intended as they were, and a few quite moving as testaments to those who died, almost all of them were recognizable variations on the conventional forms of psychological drama—about a troubled marriage or a strained reconciliation between mother and daughter—that might very well have been written, with some other provocation, before the world had changed.

If it was understandable that there might be something cautious about what could be represented or done, the question in any event was exactly how to do it. After initial circumspection about emotions to which they did not feel privileged—whether the emotions of the bereft or, if anything, more grievously, unimaginably, those falling out of windows—it was also to be expected that somebody would, however tentatively, try them on, at least those that, somehow, seemed to be accessible. So it was with Michael Smuin, with the Dance Theater of Harlem, when he choreographed *Stabat Mater,* to music by Dvorak, for the "Evening Stars" series at Battery Park—a year to the day after a scheduled performance that never took place at the World Trade Center. The crucial image in the ballet was prompted by Smuin's seeing a woman faint, falling back into a man's arms at the televised funeral of a fireman. The image was replicated over and over by four female dancers who fell back into the arms of their male partners, while a single woman dashed through the recurrently falling ensemble, with a vitality out of the past, which was represented by a ghostly partner, perhaps the one who would never return. It's hard to speak for what others feel about any image, but however moving this may have been, it would seem to be even more so, if seen as a pathetic gesture, incommensurate with the events, and the complex of emotions, that induced the televised image from which the choreography was derived.

For the composer John Adams it was, as he remarked, a matter of coming to terms with complex feelings when he was called upon by the New York Philharmonic to memorialize 9/11. In his operas, *Nixon in China* and *The Death of Klinghoffer*—on the highjacking by Palestinians, in 1985, of the cruise liner *Achille Lauro*—Adams has focused before, with a certain immediacy, on political and moral issues, but he was especially aware this time that music, with its capacity to bypass rationality and touch the emotions, could edify an audience by exploiting the remembered anguish of that devastating day. He was aware, too, as he expressed a rather conventional faith in the power of art to transcend the moment, of the power of the media to debase it, in the incessant superfluity of their own momentariness. If the woman fainting at the funeral of a fireman was moving, "The first time you see a photograph of a fireman crying," said Adams, "you are shocked. But if you see the picture over and over and then as an advertisement for a politician, it's beginning to be corrupted." And then, if he was quoted correctly, he said, "What I am trying to do is go back to the original emotions to create something out of time, the way great art ought to."[8] What great art ought to only great art knows, and even then, perhaps, when the artist is dead and gone. But putting aside whether his new work qualifies, Adams came up with an orchestral score, featuring a violin ensemble, with electronic reverberations echoing the live sound, over and around the audience, while adult and children's choruses intoned or chanted a spare text drawn from the posted messages around Ground Zero and the "Portraits of Grief" in *The New York Times,* as well as a random collage of victims' names and a phone call from one of the highjacked airplanes. The intention was to create a ruminative space as in a medieval cathedral, more as a sanctuary for the survivors than a testament to those who were lost.

Whatever the affect of this musical event, and the restrained grandeur of its conception, it still has to be measured, it seems, against the conception of the event that, in the cunning imagination of its own heinous aesthetic, was of inarguable magnitude—and so, too, the recording of it, especially there in New York, the sunburst of egregious flame and then the dissolving towers, which will no doubt be canonized among the infamous images. Which is not to overlook the elegant minimalism of a picture in *The New York Times,* of a body from on high, striations of the building behind it, falling upside down; none like it afterward, as if in its awful sublimity it were far too much to bear. It may be fortuitous or utterly germane that, as we reflect on art in a time of crisis, we might very well have begun with the aesthetics of terror itself, particularly as we encountered it in those devastating events, since the aesthetic was apparently there, within a pedagogical framework, in the perpetrator's conception. Or was it, rather, an egregious mockery that the hijackers had code-named the Pentagon "the Faculty of Fine Arts," and the twin towers "the Faculty of Urban Planning."

As to Ground Zero itself—the urban planning of it now—aside from the persistent question as to what will ultimately replace the towers, there is also the running debate as to how, aesthetically, the horror of 9/11 should be memorialized. In this regard, temporal distance is an advantage—as with Daniel Libeskind's Jewish Museum in Berlin, impressive when empty (and wasn't it meant to be so?), the no-exit acuity of its unnerving space—and proximity a liability. This was apparent in the intemperate argument, at the New York Historical Society, between Libeskind and Leon Wieseltier, literary editor of *The New Republic* and author of *Kaddish* (about his father's death) who, with Sherwin Nuland, author of *How We Die,* wanted to protect mourning from the overbearing presence of architecture. For Wieseltier, the burden is spiritual not architectural, which in the vanity of its advanced aesthetic, no less the idiosyncrasies of its antiaesthetics, would convert lower Manhattan, if not into a theme park, into a sophisticated mausoleum. On this site, for him, emptiness is an option: "The void should be there to give a sense of finality and facticity," yet with sufficient impartiality to accommodate both "godfulness and godlessness, certainty and doubt, anger and hope."

If 9/11, as he thought, was also the death of architecture, mourning should be in the Judaic tradition, a matter of words and ritual not buildings, statues, idols. In accord, but less combative, Nuland also shared (with John Adams) a desire for a meditative space, which Ground Zero already seemed to be, with people moving through it or gazing at it, with respect for the "vanished bodies and their dreams," which might be consecrated there, as Nuland conceived it, in a garden conducive to silent thought, a tribute to them and consoling to us. Libeskind, however, would have none of this, no less a view of the Judaic tradition as defined by words alone; the Jews, after all, built synagogues and cemeteries. Nor would he have anything to do with what he saw as the specter of the philosopher Heidegger in "that kind of

Nazi notion that language is the home of man. Language is not the home. We are not at home in language. We are at home at home." And that means building, he said, stone and steel, the materiality of architecture. When Wieseltier accused Libeskind of precisely that, materialism, and said he was offended at the thought that architecture would contaminate a site that should be reserved for spirit, Libeskind went on to say that Wieseltier's idea of architecture was a fascist one, coming "straight from Ayn Rand."[9] If the argument appeared to be, at times, about literature as opposed to architecture, it might also be summed up this way: if Libeskind wanted, as with the Jewish Museum, a building with a void, Wieseltier seemed to want nothing but a void. Whatever or wherever the void, the intensity of the debate suggested, if nothing definitive about memorials, that while some artists, at a moment of maximum disaster, think their art inconsequential, there are others, like Libeskind, who think it unconscionable to abandon their art, since there's nothing else with the power to materialize an adequate response.

In any case, it's not only memorials that art has to respond to in a time of crisis, especially when the crisis is drawn out, its parameters indeterminable, and as potentially demoralizing as a war against terror, a phantom war, if not a fantasy, in which the enemy is not a discernible state with an army, or at times in any way discernible at all, its legions transnational, underground, even disguised in our own cities, leading normal lives, but with toxic substances, homemade explosives, flight training, and multiple credit cards, in maybe Seattle or Lackawanna, deployed in "sleeper cells." If all of this is cunningly seditious, there are also artists among us capable of thinking of it another way, as in perhaps the most notorious incident of art about 9/11, by a figure of some consequence, indeed a poet laureate, not proceeding by image or indirection but taking it head on. Since there are stranger things in heaven and earth than the conspiracy of nations, I won't judge Amiri Baraka's poem, "Somebody Blew Up America," as the Anti-Defamation League did, or Governor James E. McGreevy, who asked for Baraka's resignation as New Jersey's honorific poet. Not only did he refuse to resign, but he wouldn't in any way recant what he wrote of the attack:

> Who knew the World Trade
> Center was gonna get
> Bombed
> Who told 4,000 Israeli workers
> at the Twin Towers

To stay home that day
Why did Sharon stay away?

I'm not entirely sure, though I'm a Jew myself, why Sharon should have been there, but then I'm not part of the Zionist plot. Nor, for that matter, part of George W's inner circle, which was apparently in on it too. "If you dont think President Bush knew, man, you are back," said Baraka, "in the cartoon days."[10] Well, despite my own misgivings about Bush and his close advisors, I'll have to concede that liability, as I ponder how, at times, art passing as art proceeds from outrage to outrageousness, though I suspect, however—returning to Ezra Pound's distinction—this is the news that will not stay news, even if Baraka remains, as I think he should, the poet laureate.

Meanwhile, there are some works that seem, adventitiously, to anticipate the news, as with Bill Viola's recent video installation at the Guggenheim Museum, which in turn seemed to acquire an unforeseen depth from the fatal events of 9/11. In the cinematic fresco of *Going Forth by Day*—actually indebted, despite its high-definition video technology and digital compositing, to Giotto's fourteenth-century Scovegni Chapel in Padua and Signorelli's fifteenth-century fresco cycle in the Orvieto Cathedral, it's as if the images of fire and blood, or those of exhausted rescue workers attending victims of a flash flood, were laminated by emotions arising from the dust of the vanished towers. But if the image of a woman waiting for news of a loved one seems touched by prophecy in view of what did happen in lower New York, the epic spectacle constructed on videotape from the Egyptian Book of the Dead is perhaps, after all, mythicizing too much, thereby separating itself from the grim materiality of what, truckful after truckful, was removed from the pitiless site, not only the shattered concrete, glass, and twisted steel, but bones, limbs, fingers, not only the amputated but atomized or disintegrated remains, and so the dust consigned to dust, as maybe even the biblical prophets never quite imagined. In that regard, Viola's epic, with its images of a wounded humanity marching in endless procession on the path of life, along with a redemptive image of a man, rising from a water hole, seems rather sentimental, even despite or because of certain painterly images of classical restraint. If this quite imaginative work is nevertheless a case where an aestheticizing of apocalypse is merely out of its class, that would seem to be the provisional fate of anything still too close to the dimensions of this catastrophe, with its demoralizing temporal axis, unconscionable causes going back in time, and causes notwithstanding, the mortifying actuality of what, until the ravaged Pentagon and the cataclysmic towers, we'd never seen here, the repercussions of which are already happening there.

"Like you look at their face and you can't make anything out; there's nothing left," said a young vacationer from London, as he described the screaming chaos of the blast in Bali, and the man who appeared to be running toward him at one of the Kieta Beach dance clubs, though he was not sure through the flames whether the man was alive or already dead.[11] We speak of people dealing "with unimaginable horror," as Fiona Shaw did in an interview about her performance in that tragedy of atrocities, *Medea,* directed by Deborah Warner. But then, as McGovern said of evil, we have always lived in a world of unimaginable horror, all the more unimaginable, of course, when it does happen elsewhere in the world, as in Rwanda or Bosnia or Chechnya. And the question is always how far away does the horror have to be so we can then forget it, how close before we say, as Shaw did, when she spoke of rehearsing a scene "where the messenger comes in and describes the deaths of Creon and Glauke. It is like what people lived last year," she said, though she might have added that what tragedy records across all cultural and historical difference is always being lived somewhere.

What she remarked about particularly is "people saying simple things about a state of affairs that seems impossible to comprehend—but we do have to comprehend it." Warner went on to say that *Medea* has an even more immediate relevance, given Tony Blair's support for a U.S. attack on Iraq, and therefore the need for debate when, as she feels, democracy is wobbly, and Greek plays a model of what, by implication from its aesthetic, it might otherwise be. "Greece was a very new democratic nation, and a barbaric world was not very far behind them. They offered their plays as places of real debate. We can't really say the theater is a true place of debate anymore, but these plays remind us of what it could be."[12] Maybe so, maybe not. We need the reminder, but the liability remains what it was when I wrote "The Public Art of Crisis in the Suburbs of Hell," that the debate would be no better than what we already have on TV. Were that to change, it would be a testament, if only for the theatrical moment, to the complexity with which the crisis is seen, and I'm not sure that comes with people saying simple things.

What, for me, accounts for the power of performance is the depth of apprehension, not merely its commitment—no less its ideological disposition, the playing out or enactment of what's pretty well known in advance—but the conundrum of commitment itself, affect and disposition pulling in opposite ways, values intersecting and virtually canceling each other out, unanticipated conflicts between what we thought to be so and what we may have imagined, especially when the imagining, following *its* disposition, is ready to take perception over the deep end, where seeming and being struggle, invention and actuality, faith and skepticism, what you believe to be true foundering in the desperation of belief, as what you may have hoped for is suffused with the unavoidable and palpable evidence of the unforeseeable, or indeed what may never be seen, but only wished for or guessed, or hopefully never seen—but *there it is before you,* undeniable now, too clear, demanding that you think or do what you never dreamed before. If then you're in the presence of what will change the debate, it may be well to remember that it may not change the world. If you want some solace about that, it may be well to remember too, as W. H. Auden once said—as if he were speaking of Beckett, oracular voice of ground zero—that art changes nothing, but it at least changes that.

NOTES

1. *The Duchess of Malfi* (5.3.334–35), in *Drama of the English Renaissance,* vol. 2, *The Stuart Period,* ed. Russell A. Fraser and Norman Rabkin (New York: Macmillan, 1976) 511.

2. Karl Marx, *The German Ideology,* in *The Marx-Engels Reader,* ed. Robert C. Tucker (New York: Norton, 1978) 155.

3. Letters, *Time,* November 18, 2002, n.p.

4. Salman Rushdie, *New York Times,* November 27, 2002, A23. All references to the *Times* are from the West Coast edition.

5. *Poems of Paul Celan,* trans. Michael Hamburger (New York: Persea, 1995) 141, 147.

6. George McGovern, "The Case for Liberalism: A Defense of the Future against the Past," *Harper's,* December 2002, 38.

7. Gary Hart, *New York Times,* October 26, 2002, A1.

8. Quoted by John Rockwell, "Challenge of the Unthinkable," *New York Times,* September 17, 2002, online.

9. Sarah Boxer, "Debating Ground Zero: Architecture and the Value of the Void," *New York Times,* September 30, 2002, B3, 3.

10. Amiri Baraka, *New York Times,* November 18, 2002, A27.

11. *New York Times,* October 14, 2002, A1.

12. *New York Times,* September 29, 2002, Arts, 7.

THIRTEEN

Ground Zero

The Original Vision (May 16, 2008)

My being here today is suffused with multiply raveled memories, going back to a troubled time when, amid my reassessment of a long career in the theater, I was confronted with the prospect of conceiving CalArts, where in crossing the various disciplines all the world might be a stage. If that seemed to begin with an illusory promise, if not the ghost of a chance, so much happened in the performative dissidence of those turbulent years, which I've written about before, that when Steven Lavine asked me to speak, it occurred to me there wouldn't be enough time for it all—and you'd have to put off the graduation. But as with certain kinds of art, if not quite minimalist, I'll try to be restrained, as I reflect on what he asked me to talk about, and that, indeed, was "the original vision" for CalArts.

As I thought it over, through what was happening then, relative to what, who knows where, may be happening now, in the arts and what affects them, something else intervened, with a maybe appalling, if retrospective relevance, which on this otherwise jubilant day you'd probably rather forget. Fact is, however, that in an age of cultural explosion, scientific, political, even psychedelic, the original vision came, or first intimations of it, from a premise of "ground zero." And I even used that phrase, attached now to the fatal morning, after which, in what seemed a weird presumption, one of the world's more innovative composers challenged the powers, the significance, and dimensions of the arts—which, in the conceptual documents, we appeared to be doing ourselves. That Karlheinz Stockhausen (who died last December) had some bearing on those dimensions may be recalled from one of his operas, in which a string quartet performed in helicopters hovering over a concert hall, where the audience listened; or by his image on the Beatles' album, *Sgt. Pepper's Lonely Hearts Club Band;* or by the resonant spectrum of those he influenced, from Frank Zappa and Pink Floyd to the eccentric Björk, and even Miles Davis. But what others, nevertheless, may unforgivably remember is what he said about 9/11, in remarks that became a scandal—that the cataclysm produced, as through a cloud of unknowing or an hallucinatory light, the most majestic work of art there has ever been. Appalling, to be sure, but what he really had in mind was some "cosmic spirit of rebellion, of anarchy," with a high degree of "perverse intelligence," whose only mode of being, not knowing how to live, is to create by destroying creation—and in attempting to do so, as Stockhausen saw it, achieved in one nefarious act what those in music or the other arts, or prophets of a Total Theater, could never or only dream.

That may still, by no means, be a redeeming vision, but that there's been a destructive element in the arts—equivocally there, between the creative and self-defeating—has long been known to artists, and indeed that famous phrase, "In the destructive element, immerse" (from Conrad's *Heart of Darkness*), was very much on the scene with the emergence of modernism, or the extremities of it, wild, mad, insurrectionary, but now canonical, taught in the universities—as in a course I've been giving, called Traditions of the Avant-Garde. Now, that's an oxymoron: futurist noise and riots, Dada as tradition. And when some of those traditions first materialized, provocatively, outrageously, as with Duchamp's urinal or Cage's silence, or, without the unattainable ecstasy of Artaud's Plague, *Waiting for Godot,* with its "Nothing to be done"—only you had to *do* it, that is, do *nothing*—there were always those around to say, that's *not* art. Or as with Pollock's pouring of paint on an Action field, well, anybody can do that.

But putting those unregenerate, ineradicable know-nothings aside, there are times when artists themselves are not entirely sure what they're doing, nor in an age of the antiaesthetic, that they ought to worry about it; or if, for better or worse, what they're doing *is* art. For the poet W. H. Auden, struggling with religion to an awakening politics, the purpose of art was "to tell the truth, to disenchant and deintoxicate," which he was well aware could be done in various enchanting or intoxicating ways, even while certain kinds of art—from the conceptual to cold abstraction, or Brechtian Alienation—were determined to subvert the legacy of illusion. In recent years, moreover, with the advent of deconstruction, Beauty was out, Imagination was out, as "transcendental signifiers," with the notion of artistic genius a merely elitist illusion.

As for the issues implicit here, and others I might rehearse, they were already there at the founding of CalArts, with tendencies, too, for diminishing the distance between art and life. So, too, between teachers and students, who ideally taught each other, though in the secret agenda of art, there are things you can't quite teach, and—call it elitist, call it illusion—an impasse more distressing: there you are, at some extremity of desire or selvedge of perception, way way out where you've never been before, or darkling there within, and what you're after seems impossible—well, who gives a damn what they think, that's all the more reason to do it, you do it *because* it's impossible. Which is what I wrote about in my first book, called *The Impossible Theater: A Manifesto.* As it happens, that also caused a scandal, beginning with its first paragraph, where I said, when I look around and examine the state of the American theater (this from the early 1950s heading toward the 1960s), with "the despicable behavior" of most of the people in it, complaining about what it isn't, but not wanting to venture to make it something other, I felt like the lunatic King Lear on the heath, wanting to "kill, kill, kill, kill, kill kill"—the liability, of course, being that there are those who'll want to kill you. So be it. Art is always in peril, that's its virtue, and reward; that is, if the one who presumes to be an artist is willing to take the risk.

Presumption, assumption, all of that was challenged, including the original vision, what it was, what it wasn't, what it was meant to be. Yet, whatever the challenge, what I will say in all vanity is that when CalArts was conceived there was nothing like it anywhere in this country, and as I told the board when they first interviewed me for the job as provost, who'd be putting the thing together, there were only two precedents elsewhere: the Bauhaus of the Weimar Republic, with the intellectual and theoretical rigor behind its experimentalism; and (though the word didn't exist then) the countercultural Black Mountain, from whence Cage, Cunningham, Olson, Tharpe, Rauschenberg, and others emerged. I remember telling them that if we put the two ideas together—while encouraging nevertheless what was never there before—the visionary structure of CalArts would be unprecedented. And so it was, and so far as I can see is still trying to be, at least from the President's Message, where the idea of *risk* is foregrounded, as it is in a brochure of REDCAT, announcing a new season, as "a celebration of risk."

The risk, of course, when you celebrate it, is that risk may be over with, or taking off in another direction. For risk, too, is a function of history, where you are, when, and the reality principle there, especially when it came, as if genetic at CalArts, to the mixing of art and politics. There were plenty of banalities then, in the uproar of the sixties, surging from the Days of Love toward the Days of Rage, which in the warier age of globalization remains an egregious problem, while assessing the powers of art, and—with everything being commodified and terror in the wings—still trying to ascertain how art can be empowering. While there have always been certain artists whose passion on the outside, in the form of political activism, was already there within, impelling it even more, there are others who, visually, poetically, acutely synesthetically, may seem unpolitical, and yet they cause you to see what, or how, you've never seen before, so that even the strictest formalism may, in politics as in ethics, become a mode of judgment, hearing every nuance, with a moral exactitude. There were debates about it, sure, but the mandate to begin with was not to favor one artistic inclination over another. And in the imagined coalescence of the various schools, assuming to begin with a Tradition of the New, "what we will be after," I wrote, "is a discipline of the New, open to the unpredictable and taking energy from doubt."

As to where the action is today, as you've probably learned at CalArts, it's all over the landscape of vision, from installations to metacreation, and even with transgenetics, still there out on the streets, on-screen, off-screen, in the performative body or now in virtuality. Or there it is in fashion, design, advertising (take a look at *Artforum,* where it dominates the art), new soundscapes, digitality, and crossing the corporate world, what's now "the art of production," with outsourced labor, technocratics, and custom fabrication. So, along with the now iconic, ballooning, polyurethaned Jeff Koons, there's Olafur Eliasson or Takashi Murikami, or the recent curatorial *Truth* of Choi Jeong Hwa, who in his Gaseum Studio was already merging graphic design with industrial, architecture and art. With Carlson and Company, one of the major fabricators, right nearby in the San Fernando Valley, I'd suppose that students at CalArts are familiar with the technological resources, not to mention the funding, that are for the moment, probably, somewhat beyond their means. As for the ballooning technophilia, that could hardly be imagined, even by the fluorescent artist Dan Flavin, when he described, just before the founding of CalArts, "the scented romance in fiberglass or anodized aluminum," or along with his own "neon lights . . . , the very latest advance in Canal Street technology." The neon may seem antiquated, or the romance of fiberglass, but the dialectic continues between the singular work of art and what, if not quite off the assembly line, is by measures algorithmic meant to be reproduced.

Meanwhile, in an online, weblogged, curatorial world, with designers, engineers, and globally teamworked art, there is still some loner in a studio, over the bridge from Canal Street, even beyond Brooklyn, where art never was before, or on the fringes of L.A., with some other obsessive introvert going about her business, which she'll never think of as such, or as if with cracked vision, still on canvas, or coming off the wall. And so, too, there's a composer, with synthesizers abounding, turning out a score, for instruments, mind you, which nevertheless has something of a destabilizing vision, so that if you think it over, listen, *hear* it, you can somehow really see. Which is what, as we put CalArts together, we thought the arts should be, however you did it, with electronics or animation, whatever the apparatus, or intensive introspection, or in those heady days of happenings, with Fluxus there too, out on the meadows, in the canyons, the studios abandoned, and doing it there collectively, with video or vegetation. As for performance art, body art, with Woman House on the scene (and I gave them the money for it), it might even cross genders with the utmost sexual fantasy—polymorphous perverse in a participatory mystique. Or in the method we called "ghosting," perverse but impeccable, developed with actors who, later, were part of my KRAKEN group. And then there was Critical Studies, unprecedented too, and though the source of a lot of trouble, with its ideological activism, in those spaced-out days of the radical thinking body, with plenty of argument and counterargument about where it ought to be, and in the questioning of what to read, reading across disciplines, with competing ideas of history, in its incursion upon the arts.

Whatever the excesses and even absurdities, as I've said of it before, I never expected in my lifetime to encounter a pedagogical situation even remotely like that. All of this was taking place, in earthquake country, like a kind of culture shock, and while I left CalArts in a bitter controversy—not giving up the ghost, but doubling up the shock—it was a time I'll never forget, which has carried over into the work, artistically, theoretically, I've been doing ever since. For those graduating today, whatever the art, however done, if some risk-taking semblance of that original vision persists, it should be the same for you.

FOURTEEN

Blessings to *The Pope and the Witch*

(The controversy over the production of Dario Fo's play was initiated by the Catholic Church, in January 2007, when its spokesman threatened the University of Minnesota with withdrawal of promised funds for construction there, after protests by the Catholic League and the archbishop of Minneapolis–St. Paul. The president of the university and the dean of Liberal Arts held firm, while rehearsals went ahead, and before the production opened there was a sort of town hall meeting, on March 8, 2007, at which I was invited to speak by Michal Kobialka, chair of the Department of Theater. After my talk, I moderated a discussion, among faculty, students, and people from the community. Among those who participated were Catholics on both sides of the issue. The play opened that night to a civil and positive reception.)

Over the years, including nearly forty in the theater, I've given talks, and even done productions, in churches and schools of various denominations, from the Unitarian to the Catholic to the Union Theological Seminary, which published my talk there in *Christianity and Crisis.* And more often than not I was invited by some informed, lively, and not uncritical minister or priest who was quite aware of the avant-garde, often near-scandalous, sometimes explicitly anticlerical plays I had directed.

That was especially so at The Actor's Workshop of San Francisco, where—and this developed over half a century ago—we had an excellent relation with the Jesuits at the University of San Francisco. They not only admired our production of *King Lear,* and its uncompromising devastation of value, Lear's "Never, never, never, never, never," and those grievous lines after the unconscionable, inexplicable, unjustifiable death of Cordelia—"Is this the promised end?" "Or image of that horror?"—about which one might think, in a post-Nietzschean way, that if God is not dead He has a lot to be accountable for. The Jesuits were very moved by that production, mortifyingly so, and in an entirely different mood, they were constrained to laugh against their holier judgment when we did plays by the Irish dramatist Sean O'Casey, no less those by Beckett, Pinter, and Genet—all of whom made it quite difficult to believe at all, no less in a good and just God.

Yet, when we were rehearsing a production of Bertolt Brecht's *Galileo*—and the Marxist Brecht, surely, no lover of the Lord—we needed some help with a scene in which they were dressing the newly elected pope, whom we had seen before as Cardinal Barberini, a fashionable figure, witty and intellectual, and sensuous too, in a setting with resplendent ladies of pleasure, like a Renaissance version of *la dolce vita*. Yet even there, he was by no means a proponent of Galileo's *Discorsi*—useful science, sure, but subservient to Scripture, and soon suppressed under an edict of the Curial that kept Galileo for years under virtual house arrest. As the worldly Barberini takes on the holiness of the pope, of which the dressing was emblematic, I wanted it to be authentic, in meticulous detail, as it might be at the Vatican; so I called my friends, the Jesuits. They researched how it was done, and though they knew they were in antipapist, near-blasphemous territory at The Actor's Workshop, they nevertheless came down to the theater to show us how the dressing should be done: the order of garments, the binding, the whole sartorial transformation a ritual in itself.

The scene was extraordinary, and they had my blessings for it, me with a Jewish background, but utterly faithless as I am—which on one or another occasion we also talked about. So I did one time, too, with Jesuits right here in Minnesota, when I was giving a seminar at the University of St. Thomas, and after being put up first in the president's house, somebody else was scheduled to be there, and they asked if I minded moving over to a housing cluster where the Jesuit faculty lived. In the mornings, we went long-distance running together, my ungodliness no deterrent, even when I described the kind of plays we were doing, which I was alluding to in the seminar, and in lectures I was also giving at the College of St. Catherine.

What those priests understood, I think, is that there are works of art and certain artists—and Dario Fo was certainly one, long before the Nobel Prize—whose most rudimentary honesty, down-to-earth, satiric, ribald, presumptuous as it may seem, is ultimately more pious, more dutiful to what one might think of as God's will, even while exposing in more than fantasy what may be an embarrassment to the church. Each sin feels its own deformity (as a metaphysical poet once wrote), but to work on behalf of justice, the poor, the dispossessed, some fundamental equity of being, may be closer to the originary Mystery upon which the church was built. There are, to be sure, other mysteries, or secrecies, and we have recently seen the papacy's integrity threatened by priestly indecencies that for years it ignored or tried to hide. As now and then a diocese, after paying for desecrations, has to declare itself bankrupt, the church now talks of transparency. Far better, then, to see in the open, as a moral obligation, what in the secrecy of the Vatican it may reprove itself. As for the purported sacrilege or scandal of Dario Fo, if the church doesn't like it, or it has no substance, let the absurdity expose itself. Far better to laugh it off, which itself might be a gesture of divine patience.

Among the priests I have known, as well as Catholic friends and colleagues—some of the most discerning also the most devout, and with a wit enforced by faith—my guess is they would, if they saw *The Pope and the Witch,* be prepared through laughter to have a go at Fo, exercising a spirituality not only through forbearance, but awareness, and by suggesting that even the pope, perhaps, in the avoidance of hypocrisy, may be all the more infallible by laughing at himself. Or at least at the person—a Catholic spokesman here, like Cardinal Pialli in the play—who wrote about this production of *The Pope and the Witches* that it's like some follower of Hitler mocking Jews. I must confess, though Jewish, that I have always been, since I first read St. Thomas Aquinas—whose mode of reasoning I deeply admired: the ability to state the other position even better than it had been stated, before attempting to refute it—far too Thomistic to see anything but a pitiful, execrable, if not laughable analogy there.

As for what Dario Fo represents, his long career attests to that, the abundant selflessness of it, acts of compassion and charity, which really speak for themselves—though when he accepted the Nobel Prize, he suggested the personal cost, to himself, but especially to his wife and collaborator, Franca Rame. "We've had to endure abuse, assaults by the police, insults from the right-thinking, and violence. And it is Franca who has had to suffer the most atrocious aggression. She has had to pay more dearly than any one of us, with her neck and limb in the balance, for the solidarity with the humble and the beaten that has been our premise." What he didn't say exactly is that she had been tortured and raped, if not by Nazis, by fascists, those right-thinking zealots, for the almost saintly things she and her husband did.

Birth control and abortion will be cultural issues, to be sure, for some fundamental, in the course of our next election, as with appointments to the Supreme Court. But not to think of birth control, abortion, and yes, condoms and contraception relative to the Third World's mind-bending poverty is irresponsible, really sacrilegious, and that's what the sometimes over-the-top, mind-blowing farce of *The Pope and the Witch* is about. As for the pontiff's own high-strung traumatic stress disorders in the play, they suggest in judiciously overamplified globalized terms that there is some institutional, epistemological, theological, maybe ontological, even linguistic flaw in any social or religious organism, even the Vatican, that lets such suffering persist.

And who can argue with the final line of the play, which quotes St. Augustine: "Woe to the man of power, who takes the side of those who have no power." So, too, with the artist who does, and not merely in passing, as in the nomadic theater of Fo, but at the recurrent risk of his life. As for banning the play on a college campus—where we may think about whatever at the most disturbing extremities of thought—no moral grounds for that.

FIFTEEN

The Pathos of Dialogue

Unable to Speak a Word

IT'S BEEN QUITE A WHILE that we've been aware, on stage, off stage, that the appearance of dialogue may be misleading, and people talking to each other may be talking past each other, putting each other on, or really going nowhere with words, words, words—or sometimes searching for the one word that will set things right, like that word in the beginning that became, in T. S. Eliot's *Gerontion,* "the word within a word, unable to speak a word, / Swaddled with darkness." And the darkness was, if anything, augmented by deconstruction, and the theoretical obsession over the last generation with the ethos of suspicion about the entire repertoire of slippery signifiers, about which Nietzsche had warned us that since every word we speak is an insidious metaphor, it is, all said and done, nothing but a lie. Such is the fate of dialogue, and we didn't have to wait for those politicians with their specious invitations, "Let's dialogue," with each other, with the public—that spectral vanity of television—to have some sense of the enormity of the lie.

As for the Society of the Spectacle or age of simulacra, where we live through the high velocity of images in a mediated world, time itself becoming speed would, if any remaining impulse, leave dialogue behind. "The spectacle," wrote Guy Debord, back in the Situationist sixties, "is the existing order's uninterrupted discourse about itself, its laudatory monologue." So, what are you talking about, what's this about dialogue? What we're left with, it seems, is nothing but mere talk. Or in the world of instantaneous communication, the dominion of the media, merging with the Internet, the communication is, despite the chatterbots and weblogs, for the most part exchanged in a vacuous economy of blather, where polling is community and, with Letterman, Trump-it, *Hardball,* no less Limbaugh, and the *O'Reilly Factor,* dialogue a laugh.

Nor, if we had paid attention to what had been happening in the theater, would we have been surprised. "What is there to keep me here?" asks Clov in *Endgame.* "The dialogue," says Hamm, well aware of the "blathering," as they call it in *Waiting for Godot,* "about nothing in particular. That's been going on now for half a century." And that was, when I staged the play in San Francisco, almost exactly another half a century ago! But then, as Gogo says, when pestered by Didi to remember what happened a few moments before, "I'm not a historian." Adorno doesn't have it entirely right about Beckett, when he says about *Endgame,* that "history is excluded"—indeed, it's rather impacted, inescapable, mortifyingly so—but as one thinks back through the century before the millennium (and if anything it's worse since), Adorno has reason for saying that history itself "has dehydrated the power of consciousness to think history, the power of remembrance. Drama falls silent and becomes gesture, frozen amid the dialogues." Which is not quite the gestural life, the concrete language of theater, or the "naked, sonorous, streaming realization," that Artaud had in mind when he said that "dialogue—a thing written or spoken—does not belong specifically to the stage, it belongs to books."

As for a perversely fractured play like Heiner Müller's *Hamletmachine,* remembering with a jaundiced mordancy the superfluity of words, there's no pretense of dialogue, for, as he's said, "no substance for dialogue exists anymore because there is no more history." Whether that's so or not, if there's anything like a dialogue, it takes place with the dead, for "the dead are in the overwhelming majority when compared to the living," and "literature, as an instrument of democracy, while not submitting to, should nevertheless be respectful of majorities as well as minorities." There may be, in that view, some tongue in cheek, but it causes you to wonder too, as we ponder the fate of dialogue, whether—given the precarious state of the world, with global warming, nuclear threats, jihads, suicide bombings, a century of rational slaughter displaced by preemptive warfare, Third World genocides, appalling poverty, AIDS—that's now a privilege of the dead, and what, if so, they may be saying about us.

But then, too, let's not sentimentalize the dead. We may grieve for them or forget them, or in imagination speak to them for relief—unless we happen to be among those who, no mere minority now, born-again and awaiting apocalypse, will have a dialogue with them. For the rest of us: Anybody there? Listening? Care to talk?

SIXTEEN

Thinking History, History Thinking

Of course, this complex process is all haunted by real history. But everything cannot be said at once.
—LOUIS ALTHUSSER, *For Marx*

And if you can remember, it may be history but it is not historical.
—GERTRUDE STEIN, *The Gradual Making of the Making of Americans*

IS THERE A REAL WORLD OUT THERE? I'll soon be moving the question to other perceptual sites, but at bedrock, ground zero (now hallowed by 9/11), or when push comes to shove, making their peace with deconstruction, few historians deny it—and come, let's face it, none really can (no Bishop Berkeleys among them), it's real enough for them. With all the signifiers shifting, and some of them under erasure, there may be uncertainties in the referential structure, as out the window, through the rain, across the lake from me now in Seattle, what should be the Cascades is, with a hint of snowcaps above, mainly a minimalist gray vaporous wall of clouds, nothing to be seen on the landscape of what I am sure was there, but then for a moment the trees (from Berkeley's forest, perhaps?), but not as metahistory. And so it may be with the recuperated vagaries of any historical context that, however obscured by the years, somehow inhabited time, or survived the attritions of time, to more than suggest, if not certify, that there was a there there. The important thing, of course—no different in this millennium, but after the collapsing towers suddenly a crazier world, with there all over, dispersed or even secreted—is to determine how to get there, with the swift accrual of history affecting theater history.

This is complicated, too, by a very mixed sense of things as no longer Eurocentric, though the euro increases in value, and cities in East Asia are looking European, or euro-polyglot, with maybe Dutch housing or from the Côte d'Azur, while in the post- of postcolonial some are talking empire (by no means always against it), and with English as lingua franca the more than gradual making of the making *by* Americans—not only with preemptive strikes, but shopping malls and Big Macs, and naturally Disney Worlds. As for the critique of Eurocentricism, from the academic Left, that had to be put in abeyance when France and Germany united against Bush and Cheney on the war in Iraq, with ethnophobic Americanism now the villain of the peace, when now, too, there is none, and inarguable that there are, if not an axis of evil, enemies out there who—whatever we did to deserve it, and could we deserve it enough?—really want to kill us. What's more, it has dawned upon us, there are generations of them, growing up in madrassas with another view of the world, or of another world, this one unreal, the other with houris in heaven, as promised to suicide bombers or those who, with their own faith-based initiative, crashed into the towers.

And do I say all this at the risk of buying into Orientalism? Or is it that the cunning of history is buying into the critique, as digitalized capitalism diversifies the world, a sort of corporate takeover of morphological flux, which (even through the fugitive terrorism, computerizing its caves) might be seen as the apotheosis of multiplicity and hybridization, incessant calls for which we've heard in cultural studies, from all the border crossings to a thousand plateaus. From the Deleuzian to the delusional, there has been a virtual litany about the "fragmenting, dissociating, dislocating, and decentering" that would liberate us from the self-validation endemic to a "universalizing historicism."[1] As for the post-Derridean dissemination of an antiessentialism, it has reified the question with which we started, about the reality of the world, and how in the world we'd know it through the free trade of appearance, no less how it came to be from what we remember of the past, with the seeds of history spilled upon the ground. That's how Walter Benjamin saw them, with a historical materialism both compromised and redeemed by a "*weak* Messianic power"; or, with an imagistic shift in the mythos, "a secret heliotropism" that turns the past "toward that sun which is rising in the sky of history."[2] If that skyey vision seems like William Blake's, there are not many historians who are likely to be blessed with the heliotropism. And lest we forget, "vision" is a transcendental signifier; despite Benjamin's own leanings toward Leibnizian monads and the Kabbalah, one might assume that, over the spectrum of Marxisms on the scene today, history would have been purged of anything theological. It seems, however, that in the essentialism of the materialism (e.g., Jameson's "political unconscious") it's been turned upon its head, like Marx with Hegel, now the other way around, merging in psychic shock with reality and appearance, shadowing each other always, as if material life-processes, too, were phantoms of the brain.

As for theater historians, on the initial question, they are and always have been, in a somewhat anomalous position, for what in the world of theater—the *strangeness* of its emergence (derived from ritual, *really?* ask the anthropologists, and anyhow, *why theater?*), doubling up on appearance, making a fetish of it, or disavowing the fetish—are we to make of the other world? We may think of the theater itself as the reality of appearance that is the appearance of reality, but with insidious mutations in the canonical drama (which probably wouldn't exist if we could really distinguish the two), is it the other way around, this world that world, or some ghosting extension of it, the appearance of reality that is the reality of appearance? "Seeming, seeming," the impelling substance of Shakespeare's plays, suffuses *Measure for Measure,* but is that (by what measure?) less so with reality itself? And having darkened the comedy thus, what do we do with the old beguiling notion that all the world's a stage, and if not, what of "the society of the spectacle" and its "precession of simulacra"—all the men and woman still merely players, but in somewhat lesser roles, and whatever the identity politics with an identity crisis too?

With the insubstantial pageant fading, on stage, off stage, or any stage between (not to mention stage fright in the human condition itself) there was always an identity crisis in the work I did in the theater, exacerbated by the desire, unabating through the years, to know through its genetic vanishings what the theater *is.* This led to a sort of subatomic physics or ontology of the form, arising from an almost manic obsession, passing from theater to theory, with precisely what escapes us, the materialization of theater from whatever it is it is *not:* life? reality? history? you name it. But as we lose our bearings in the questions, it's as if (the absence of) history were being replayed, not through the *Verfremdung* of Brecht, but the reverse English of Slavoj Žižek, always turning things around (a sort of heuristic put-on) in his Lacanian mirror, where what is being staged appears to be, in the dialectic of seemings we've been rehearsing here, one or another of Zeno's paradoxes. "How Real is Reality?" Žižek asks, in the first chapter of *Looking Awry,* but however you look, and the more you look, the more it looks like theater. And whatever the permutations, if it sometimes seems, to all appearances, as if the long-familiar phrases in their baffling orchestration have, among theater historians, screened the reality out, that's because it would—not mere singsong, the reversals taken seriously—surely invalidate what we normally think of as history.

Which is why we have, too, an equally long history of an antitheatrical tradition that is either a way of protecting the other world, by exposing the apparatus of reproduction (thus the A-effect) or, like Mallarmé's occulted theater, forgetting about it entirely, or there in the closet drama at least pretending to. As to the archaeology of knowledge in the order of things—reality of or appearance of, or just more of the Same—like the future of illusion (or the illusion of a future), this is not merely a matter of discourse. Nor is it when, radically widening the episteme, we try to imagine human history not in archaeological but in astronomical terms, in that infinitely expanding universe that, as Einstein saw it, is in the curvature of the cosmos turning back upon itself—thus following, it would seem, the retroflexive pattern of reality and appearance. Or is that, too, the other way around, the pattern there in the relativity, the *gravity* of it being (and the source of tragedy too?) that entropy is in the system with $E = mc^2$? Whatever the thermodynamic, when the Bomb went off—the nuclear historical nightmare that Einstein warned against—we really had to take the measure of the *unavailable* energy of the universe, what entropy used to be before redeemed by chaos theory, bringing the random data into the order of things.

One wonders, indeed, how history deals with that, in an age of information, appallingly supersaturated, but that, we're told, only in its redundancy overcomes the "noise," thereby reducing entropy, which otherwise inclines to the maximum. As we still try to take that in—staying moored in human history, seeds upon the ground, but with a rocketing boost to the heliotropism from President Bush's visionary plan for moving "forward into the universe," preparing thus "for new journeys to the worlds beyond our own"[3]—we also hear that newly perceived old galaxies are undoing long-held theories around the Big Bang, and that the universe was actually growing, moving toward where we are, faster than anyone thought. Nor is it a movement, as verified before, from the slight dumpiness in dark matter that, swollen by hydrogen gas, then collapses into galactic clusters gathered in long strings (in light years, 2,000 billion billion miles long), with gigantic, almost stupefyingly empty voids between. What has been discovered instead, through what is known as the Gemini Deep Deep Survey, is that massive galaxies were forming, not through small clusters, but in quick-time, that is, only a billion and a half years or so after the Big Bang. Now this, to be sure, is still mind-blowing history, but as it reflects on theory, and how we think history, it's germane to where we are (and I don't mean at all in a play by Michael Frayn). Chance and history may conspire, but as it turns out, there is in the cosmic indeterminacies of reality and appearance, another sort of reversal, in that the data concur better with how the astronomers saw it *before* the development of the dark-matter models, when they theorized that the largest galaxies did form first. "If we presented this to astronomers 25 years ago," said one of the principal investigators, "they wouldn't have been surprised."[4]

So we might say, when looking again at the past, not billions of light years away, but only since the chorus appeared at dawn at the theater of Epidaurus, about ways of writing history that have been severely critiqued over the last generation: for residues of the theological or for claiming to be teleological or refusing to concede that its narrative status is not much different from fiction—which, one might guess, is more than likely to confirm the established social and political order. Thus, too, back in space: that the Hubble telescope confirmed, three days before the Deep Deep announcement, what had been discovered, by spotting a galactic cluster located earlier in time than anyone believed possible, well, let us remember that the Hubble itself is a cultural artifact of global, now spatial, capitalism—infinitely expanding, too, and curving back upon itself. What we want to question closely is the invisible writing on the lens, with, no doubt, its hegemonic inclinations. But then (just as I was writing this) NASA took care of the ideological problem. Shifting resources now, as directed by the president, to those journeys to other worlds, the agency stunned the scientists by announcing that there'd be no more shuttle visits to the Hubble, for replacing batteries and gyroscopes, thereby dooming it to death in orbit in a few sad years. Scientists were dismayed, but no matter, historicists can turn their attention to the robotic machine named Spirit (humanoid, cyborgian), and the equally suspect writing of what seems an impending imperialism on the desert sands of Mars.

With the "ethos of suspicion" extending to outer space, what's more than apparent here is a reflex of cultural theory, almost doxological, with fallout into theater studies, not so much of performance events doing the right thing (sexually, racially, multiculturally), but there in the temporal distance, with the mimetic now problematic as a form of affirmative action. If Artaud's theater of Cruelty, as Derrida had to concede, failed to abolish representation, grammatology still persists in determining how the past manifests itself: if it's no longer a dialectical process in the Hegelian sense, a teleology arising from the absence of static essences, history is never present to us in anything but a discursive form. To what degree, however, is that a revelation? If the pressure felt by historians from poststructuralism and "the linguistic turn" pushed one or another to mockery or disdain for "discourse about discourse about discourse,"[5] even the most recidivist empiricist would acknowledge that as the past is experienced, thought through, felt, then reexamined, not even cliometrics or microhistory can keep out subjectivity, or the encroachment of language on how history is conceived. As for what actually happened (*wie es eigenlich gewesen*), there are still historicists, in the Rankean sense, who remain attached to some reasonable facsimile of a scientific hermeneutic, wanting to stay with the facts, but knowing at the same time that the writing of history occurs through the questions asked about it, with unavoidable special interests from contentious points of view, from which—with documents, texts, archives, objects, and objective commitment too—they know they're not exempt.

Axiom: fact is fact, depending on how you look at it, or as mirrored in the mind. If it wasn't so once, or didn't appear to be, that's the history of modernism, and its reality principle too—which doesn't necessarily invalidate the fact, or as Hemingway once put it, "the sequence of motion and fact." Nor does it invalidate, in the accrual of history, the assiduously sought particulars, the "sum / by defective means," which is how William Carlos Williams put the issue in the historical bricolage of *Paterson,* where "rigor of beauty is the quest." True, beauty has not had much status in the hegemony of critical theory, but as it seems to be returning like the repressed, Williams could have been speaking proleptically when he asked, "But how will you find beauty if it is locked in the mind past all remonstrance?" And he might have been asking it, too, of an eminent scholar who recently tried to purge himself of the suspicious excess or paranoia about literary and dramatic "power" that, among the new historicists, his work had previously nurtured.

But before we come to that, there are further complications, as the speeding up of its scattering bewilders our sense of history, what's coming so fast it's already past. If history to begin with has always been self-reflexive, and with the spaced-out fractures of modernity polymorphically so, it is now all the more attenuated, dispersed, digitized, diffused, not only by the media and its epidemic of image, but a globalized network of electronic textualization that, with its circuitry of the immaterial, beyond simulacra, makes Baudrillard's "end of the real" something of a non sequitur. As for Fukuyama's "end of history," that would seem to be a laughable legacy from the theater of the Absurd. With the Enlightenment dimmed, or fuses blown, and progress a worn-out notion—the mournful fallout, it seems, of "tomorrow and tomorrow and tomorrow"—it's as if, paradoxically, there's the "future in the instant," as though Lady Macbeth, surfacing on the Internet, finally had her way. And how can there be an ending, with the future like that, an incessancy of instants, but never the last instant, nothing but history, if maybe a different kind. One can hardly speak of that as a *context,* but given the cybernetic amplitude of symbolic exchange, with thought being encroached upon by virtual reality, the important thing for theater history—at this paranoid impasse of the millennium (with surveillance exceeding the panopticon, but somehow more justifiable through Al Qaeda's secreted presence in the Foucaultian spirals of power)—is how to keep its bearings in the idea of history. And when I speak of the *idea,* I mean as distinguished from metahistory or the otherwise suspect fiction that—given the ideological disposition behind variants of the mandate, "Always historicize!"—history is taken to be.

The movement of truth through history can be, to say the least, peculiar, even with science, no less ideology. To return again to the cosmos, that illimitable context, when it seemed less boundless and could even be aesthetically figured: when Copernicus threw the earth into orbit around the sun, diminishing its stature in the universe, he intended to preserve or rescue circularity in the heavens, without, however, the complications of concentric spheres (was there friction producing the music?) or what the new historicism went after in our time, the Great Chain of Being. Abandoning the Ptolemaic view was a move toward simplicity in the skies. When Tycho Brahe subsequently restored the older order of things, with earth as the center of the system, he was not only mathematically more sophisticated than Copernicus, but even more accurate about the behavior of the stars. Yet, in the long historical perspective, we live in a Copernican universe, that is, if history has it right. That it's hard to get it right might be thought about, however, with the attitude of a more impeccable, but wary science than that which determined the shaping of history in the nineteenth century. So, back to the subatomic: in a recent experiment that tracked as exactingly as could be the subtly wavering dance of particles called muons, alluring evidence was found of a "vast shadow universe of normally unseen matter existing side by side with ours." Unfortunately, if tempting, the evidence is also subject to the liability of mathematical error and the actuality of theoretical disagreements by physicists around the world, all of whom apparently agree that if the Sufi whirl of the muons occurs as it seems, the shadow not illusion, few discoveries in science would be any greater. But as the associate director of nuclear physics at the Brookhaven lab remarked, "The theory situation is still not under control. It's just maddening to me."[6] And so it is to me, with history relative to theory, as we now encounter it in theater studies.

Always historicize! But the question is *how?* in whose sense? Benjamin's, with his monads, shadowed by mysticism? Jameson's, out of the political unconscious, with Marxism there as a virtual transcendental signifier? or the late or early Foucault (and to what degree Nietzschean?), or Deleuze and Guattari, whose pushing the libidinal economy to the extremity of the machinic seems, desiringly, to sneer at history. Actually, in the anti-Oedipal logic of an ecstatic excess, or what Foucault called their *theatrum philosophicum,* they would seem to be the theorists of the electronic wide world dreaming on things to come: cheap and effortless affect, free-floating sexuality, a promiscuous complex of graduated thrills, in a virtual "body without organs" that, in its queer way, consumes (performatively, of course) whatever appears to be marketed on the computer screen. How to decipher through all this what we mean by history should, I'd think, be up front in the curriculum, perhaps its primary question, since whatever it once was, it is now something more or other than the past, or even its pastness, proceeding now as it seems with unstinting (Virilio) speed, "the location and the law, the world's destiny and its destination."[7]

If there's anything in the destiny that is residually teleological, that may not so much mean a faith in progress, or conviction about causation, but rather an admission that, conceive it as you will, history will always be written, through its recurrently seeming ending, with an inexpungeable trace of an intended end, that is, teleologically. And that seems inevitable to the extent that any historical perspective is determined by desire, informed as that may be by what we know and assume, how we came to know it, and even if we are conscious of potential faults in our assumptions—and, to be sure, we should be, before turning as readily as critical theory to the suspect assumptions of others. It's through my work in the theater that I've come to believe this: it's when inquiry is grounded, methodologically, in a kind of conscientious ungrounding that there's a vertiginous sense of history maybe thinking us. But if we're to think historically at all, there remains the recurring question of how much, if ineliminable, teleology is admissible; so it is with theater history in its encounter with the past, however it seems to be moving, and at whatever speed.

If here, *now,* is a dubious moment, already past as I think it, no wonder, *then,* that historical context at a temporal distance is increasingly an issue—and precisely the issue that theater history has insistently to keep in mind, that is, how to think *history* when it appears through all the evidence that, even back then in the slowdown, history is thinking itself, in *the years, the years* (as Virginia Woolf felt them too, when not in the room of her own). If beyond individual will and below the workings of power, and with whatever differential purposiveness coming from who knows where, history occurs by accretions, as if inscribed on time, it is thus historiographic, ambiguous perhaps, elusive, nevertheless graphically so. But in the hegemony of the historicism that, out of the revisionist Marxism, dominates cultural studies, including the theater too, everybody is talking of "social construction." That there is such construction seems self-evident, and it should be recognized that—from the emergence of historical consciousness in the nineteenth century through *la longue durée* of the Annales school to those today resisting deconstruction—most historians take it for granted. Moreover, it would seem apparent that if history is being *written,* the writing is overdetermined, by social structures, economics, progressive intentions or polemical purposes, as now by identity politics, and by way of psychoanalysis, feminism, queer theory, partisan attention to the marginal, in the now ubiquitous categories of race, class, gender, ethnicity, which in the process of correction (not to mention correctness) are indeed historicizing, which often means parsing out history in certain predictable ways.

What's not so surprising is that even the best of the new historicists are becoming wary of that, and particularly in historicizing the theater (mainly Elizabethan and Jacobean) where they were focused to begin with, though not upon the aesthetic where rigor of beauty was the quest. What they were concerned with, anecdotally, but implacably, in the anthropological vein of Clifford Geertz, and as demystified by Terry Eagleton, was "the ideology of the aesthetic." But like Eagleton's own recent shamefaced attitude to the love and longing, sense of evil, death and suffering, morality and metaphysics, the essences, universals, and objectivity mostly discounted or ignored by theory, that's now radically changing, as we can see in the current work of Stephen Greenblatt, as if he were the one who, unlike Hamlet, had made his way through purgatory. Beyond what is intimated in the rather defensive book with Catherine Gallagher, *Practicing the New Historicism,* there is a quite different ethos in *Hamlet in Purgatory,* with a reaestheticized sense of theater history. And here it's as if thinking history is more like history thinking (which is what I felt with my KRAKEN group where we were "ghosting" the text of *Hamlet* in what became a work called *Elsinore*).[8] What we'll get then from theater history, if at all the truth of the past, is what there was in the theater then that made it worth remembering, as something more or other than another document of the past, so far as it is a document that, like a Shakespearean text, gives us access to it, in often uncertain, undecidable, or maybe inscrutable ways—the very inscrutability telling us more than less.

So far, too, as theater history is concerned with something mesmeric in *Hamlet* that, however much socially constructed, seems to exceed it or escape it, then the activity of thinking history by the writing of it, will in some way be charged by what it would seem to be charged with, that is, *responsible for,* as a register in the present of what was happening then. What was happening then, however, couldn't be seen now unless it was, with more or less immediacy, being reimagined. Here the injunction to historicize takes quite another form. When Greenblatt decided to write "a book about Shakespeare as a Renaissance conjurer," with a capacity to summon up through words "those things—voices, faces, bodies, and spirits—that are absent," he found himself drawn again (as we were in our ghosting) to that spirit which haunts the night, "the weird, compelling ghost in *Hamlet,*" whereupon the newer historicist felt his own compulsion to immerse himself "in the tragedy's magical intensity."

There was, indeed, a blushing realization of some betrayal of the sort of theater history to which Greenblatt had been committed, though he had actually equivocated about that before. He nevertheless felt obliged—if he was to write with any acuity at all about what was there, historically *there*—to return to the palpable substance and circumstances of Shakespeare's conception (no death of the author here), which, exciting his own imagination, induced thus "a powerful gravitational pull that [made] it feel almost wrenching to turn back to the thing that was the original focus of interest." As for the notion of a "magical intensity," he wrote: "It seems absurd to bear witness to the intensity of *Hamlet,* but my profession has become too oddly diffident and even phobic about literary power, so suspicious and tense, that it risks losing sight of—or at least failing to articulate—the whole reason anyone bothers with the enterprise. The ghost in *Hamlet* is like none other—not only in Shakespeare but in any literary or historical text that I have ever read. . . . I wanted to let this vividness wash over me, and I wanted to understand how it was achieved."[9]

If this is a historian speaking, it is likely to be better history for that. What needs scrutiny and deciphering then, on the basis of the evidence, from whatever sources, and this time mainly the text, is what persists through history, irrefutably so, in that apprehension of the past, not only what happened then, but as it's happening still, *which is not saying this is that.* But so it goes, the appearance of reality or the reality of appearance, in the temporal form of disappearance, whose aesthetic is a matter of time, where whatever is coming in is always leaking out, the seeming, seeming, all of which causes us to think, as I once wrote, "that theater is the world when it's more like the thought of history. It is, however, a form whose signifying power, like that of language, far exceeds what the world in its opacity offers to be signified."[10] Whatever else it is that s/he does—and even that slash is a problem now, contributing to the opacity, as we think of "other histories"—the historian is responsible to that, especially if it's beautiful, the particulars, the sum, by whatever defective means. If that seems strange, reality or appearance, what we mustn't forget, too, is that we're talking of *theater* history, and if memory serves, the theater was once an art, as was the writing of history.

NOTES

1. Edward Said, "Orientalism Reconsidered," in *Reflections in Exile and Other Essays* (Cambridge: Harvard University Press, 2000) 211.

2. Walter Benjamin, "Theses on the Philosophy of History," in *Illuminations,* ed. Hannah Arendt, trans. Harry Zohn (New York: Harcourt, Brace & World, 1968) 256–57.

3. Quoted in *New York Times,* January 15, 2004, A1; all references to the *Times* are to the national edition.

4. *New York Times,* January 8, 2004, A19.

5. David Hollinger, "Discourse About Discourse About Discourse About Discourse? A Response to Dominick LaCapra," *Intellectual History Newsletter* 13 (1991): 18.

6. *New York Times,* January 9, 2004, A15.

7. Paul Virilio, *Speed and Politics: An Essay on Dromology,* trans. Mark Polizzotti (New York: Semiotext(e), 1986) 151.

8. For a sense of the ghosting and the text of *Elsinore,* see my book *The Dubious Spectacle: Extremities of Theater, 1976–2000* (Minneapolis: University of Minnesota Press, 2002) 70–117.

9. Stephen Greenblatt, *Hamlet in Purgatory* (Princeton, NJ: Princeton University Press, 2001) 3–4.

10. Herbert Blau, *Take Up the Bodies: Theater at the Vanishing Point* (Urbana: University of Illinois Press, 1982) 199.

SEVENTEEN

Why "*WHAT* History?"

History is hysterical: it is constituted only if we consider it, only if we look at it—and in order to look at it, we must be excluded from it. As a living soul, I am the very contrary of History, I am what belies it, destroys it for the sake of my own history.
—ROLAND BARTHES, *Camera Lucida*

What, are thou mad? art thou mad? is not the truth the truth?
—FALSTAFF, in *Henry IV, Part I* (2.4.221–22)

MY PRESIDING OVER THIS CONFERENCE is a sort of presumption, if not of historical dimensions, about the substance of history, since as Gogo says in exasperation in Beckett's *Waiting for Godot,* when Didi keeps pressing him as to where they are and how they got there, "At the very beginning. The very beginning of WHAT?" the boots, the tree, what happened a minute ago, "I'm not a historian"[1]—though I bring some history to the thought of performance, having first staged that play only a few days short of half a century ago, on February 28, 1957. And now, as aging comes, and goes, while I'm writing an autobiography, that line remains with me, memory failing, or maybe retrieving what I'd sometimes rather forget, as a chastening refrain, which might be juxtaposed, however, to the equally chastening view of Marx, that "men make their own history, but they do not make it just as they please."[2]

If Marx's view of the matter came with a certain economic determinism, to which one wants to be attentive, there is something in the movement of time, or so it seems, in the seeming itself—the apparitional substance of theater, like Marx's phantoms of the brain—which escapes all materialist scruple. Those phantoms may indeed be "sublimates of their material life-process," but whether or not "empirically verifiable," as Marx contends, quite another matter, and in the sorting out of the process and its "material premises"[3]—social, political, cultural, over that economic base—you may find yourself scrupling over the varieties of materialist history, even those profoundly historicist, that qualify, ramify, or contest each other, while trying to understand the past *wie es eigentlich gewesen,* as it really was. That phrase and the mandate came in the nineteenth century from Leopold von Ranke, with his focus on nation and state, but as the scale of history changed, big history, small history, by whatever hermeneutic, the phantoms are still there, maybe ineliminable and virtually immeasurable, the appearance of reality that is the reality of appearance—as if the nature of theater, *its* ontological base, were the problematic of history.

If history is what happened, it cannot be made to happen again, but can only be rehearsed, what's there not there, ghosted by (dis)appearance. Or if it does repeat itelf, as Marx amended Hegel, first as tragedy, then as farce, those who endure the second time may not consider it funny at all—which, not at all incidentally, may remind those who work in the theater about what the laughs disguise, what in recent theater history Beckett understood, passing it on to Pinter, funny, no longer funny, what they knew in the ancient world, as if extruded from the tragic, the painful nature of farce. Or so it was in Aristophanes, a conservative but not compassionate, with the Peloponnesian War, its endless absurdity, even Iraq far short of that.

It may be, indeed, that people make their own history, but when you pick up the morning paper, as I compulsively do, and encounter unceasing reports on atrocities in the world, from the familial to the global, the multiplicity of things so irreversibly hideous that—if not pure evil, some teleological hysteria or monstrous farce—history seems deranged. And perhaps to assuage the pain, with a certain wish fulfillment, there's been talk of "the end of history." But, of course, it's always *that* history. As we have seen, too, in a range of theorists, Carl Schorske, Gianni Vattimo, Jean-François Lyotard, we have moved into a world, or "world picture" (Heidegger's phrase) in which, as the "grand narratives" have receded, so has the pastness of the past, a disinclination to history in modernism itself—or existing still, as before the winged creature in Benjamin's "Theses on the Philosophy of History," blown back into the future, the seeds of history spilled upon the ground, postmodernism there in the haunted bricolage.

But as we find ourselves now in the post-post, there are, pitiful and pitiless, the *soundings* of history, too, and as it continues to echo through the "ideological reflexes . . . of living individuals" (the term Marx used,[4] not Barthes's "living soul," though early on he was Marxist) there are the tremors of psychohistory, and another chastening view, with some nostalgia for the soul, in a founding document of modernist poetry:

Think now
History has many cunning passages, contrived corridors
And issues, deceives with whispering ambitions,
Guides us by vanities. Think now
She gives when our attention is distracted
And what she gives. Gives with such supple confusions
That the giving famishes the craving. Gives too late
What's not believed in, or if still believed,
In memory only, reconsidered passion.[5]

Which doesn't preclude at all a continuing passion for the empirical, which you could see not only in microhistory, but even in the magnitudes of the French Annales historians, like Ferdinand Braudel, who viewed history as the sum of all possible histories.

In his two-volume study of the Mediterranean, with its vast geographical scale, Braudel's *Gesamtkunstwerk* or total history purported to go deeper than an economic base, taking into account what Marx disclaimed, "natural conditions in which man finds himself—geological, orohydrographical, climatic,"[6] or global warming today, which would have had to be considered, according to Annales history, over "*la longue durée*."[7] That the long duration, and its demographics, might include the eating habits of peasants in the Languedoc, could be seen in the work of Le Roy Ladurie, who also changed the scale, and in a book on the structural history of climate actually showed—back in the 1960s, long before the current alarm—how global warming affected the lives of human beings.[8] Ladurie expanded the scope of history with reference to tree rings, harvest dates, glaciers, but back in the cunning passages, contrived corridors and issues—what the Annales school might think of as *mentalités*—one may ask whether or not history should be construed in the feminine, as T. S. Eliot does in those extraordinary lines from *Gerontion* (perhaps the best he ever wrote).

I'll put that in abeyance, though in our current historicisms it may now be a matter of subject position or identity politics. And the great liability of writing history today is the immanent question: who are you writing it for? and the corollary question (for those prepared to ask it), is there anything about history that for the definitive moment crosses any divide, thus canceling difference? And I mean something other than the hybridity of Homi Bhabha, that "negotiation" rather than "negation," but with a partisanship of its own—what for all the amorphous prospects is a pretty well fixed position, its own "rationality smoothly developed, its identity as socialist or materialist (as opposed to neoimperialist or humanist) consistently confirmed in each oppositional stage of the argument," as Bhabha writes of others in "The Commitment to Theory."[9]

Committed to theory myself, with whatever whispering ambitions, "I would," as Eliot said, "meet you upon this honestly," confessing "after a thousand small deliberations" in the writing of my own life that it seems to be "a wilderness of mirrors,"[10] all the more with archives, letters, journals, promptbooks, program notes, often confirming remembrance, or so far as memory serves, bringing a nuance to it, or "assured of certain certainties,"[11] then suffused with contradictions. If this has somehow determined how I've been thinking history, or what I've written about recently as "history thinking,"[12] it may also have prompted this conference, its conception or thematic, or maybe guided by vanities the possible bias of it. For even if I *were* a historian, I did nevertheless presume, when inviting our distinguished group of speakers, all informed by historical research, to send on what was not quite a prospectus, but my own view of what was occurring not only in the study of theater and performance, but in the displacement of literary studies by cultural studies in the curriculum of our graduate schools. I was aware that what I wrote to them might be reflecting my own disposition, ideological or otherwise, and that what I was saying might be construed as a critique of what one or another of them has been doing in her/his theoretical or scholarly work.

So be it. Through whatever supple confusions, let me read a slightly edited version of what I wrote to them, explaining the italics in the subtitle of the conference, or that big red-lettered *WHAT?* in the poster for it, that colorful emphasis borrowed from the visual art of Barbara Kruger, with its always verbal/political challenge, while echoing, too, "The very beginning of WHAT?"—capitalized in the text of the non sequitur history of the waiting for Godot. It was gratifying that all those invited responded quickly, and it seemed positively, although they may address the issues, having thought them over, in diverse, elliptical, or maybe contentious ways. Here, then, is what I wrote:

"When it's not being anthropological (or a facsimile of it), there is much talk of history in performance studies today, though most of us still read at a distance and, with a wary eye on the past, for the most part hopelessly so. For the historical fact is that most of us are not historians. And even for those who are—since the incursion of 'metahistory' turned history into fiction, when it's not bourgeois discourse or mere 'social construction'—the history that has always escaped us, at the selvedge of the real, with traces of actuality, seems to escape now into illusions of historicity. Historicize, historicize, 'Always historicize!' we were exhorted by Fredric Jameson, and if, as Foucault remarked, 'History has become the unavoidable element in our thought,'[13] among the ironies of that thought is that it has become increasingly predictable, since the historicizing has been largely done through a revisionist or quasi-Marxism, as if it were in perpetuity the only defensible idea of history.

"This is not to put it down, but even Stephen Greenblatt has, in an apologetic rethinking of *Hamlet,* brought the New Historicism back into Purgatory. Still, that's a subtlety not yet widespread in literary or cultural studies, nor in performance studies, with its anthropological disposition, which keeps it from thinking theater in ontological terms, that is, as an *emergence* in reality—if maybe before ritual, initiating history—with the materialization into performance of whatever it is it is *not.* Is it not precisely that which has always been distrusted in the canonical drama—the appearance of reality in the reality of appearance? Or is it the other way around, the reality of appearance in the appearance of reality, with all the world a stage or life as a dream? Such questions are not high on the agenda of those still historicizing today, and still pretty much dominant on the academic scene, approaching the theater in institutional terms, as an apparatus of reproduction that reproduces itself, thus sustaining established power. Which hardly does justice to the history of the mimetic." No less to what Greenblatt speaks of as "magic," which draws him "again and again to the weird, compelling ghost in *Hamlet.*" But since I'm interjecting here, let me quote further what he said of that in his prologue: "My only goal was to immerse myself in the tragedy's magical intensity. It seems a bit absurd to bear witness to the intensity of *Hamlet,* but my profession has become so oddly diffident and even phobic about literary power, that it risks losing sight of—or at least failing to articulate—the whole reason anyone bothers with the enterprise in the first place."[14]

Which may or may not be true of everybody here. "In any case—with attentiveness to the quadrivium of race, class, gender, ethnicity—we now think 'subject positions,' while the Marxism has been filtered through psychoanalysis, feminism, or more recently, queer theory, with Foucault recycled (on the panopticon and sexuality) like his recyclings of power, and Walter Benjamin still a venerated source (with little attention to his interests in the Kabbalah, Leibnizian monads, and the surrealist avant-garde). What we've seemed to have forgotten in all this, or discredited ideologically, are those alternative views of history of which various historians—having assimilated by now over a generation of deconstruction, as it critiqued their discipline—are once again reminding us, while defending the sort of inquiry that has rarely suffered the hubris of pretending to an absolute capacity for an objective knowledge of the past.

"In recent years, there have been any number of books published by historians (I mean history historians, not those of theater/performance) with new perspectives on historical writing, but informed by reassessments of major historians from the past—and maybe even picking up again, against the grain of literary or social construction, everything being discourse, on J. B. Bury's Regius Professor Lecture (in 1903), in which he declared, 'History is not a branch of literature.' Meanwhile, so insufficiently informed are our programs in the humanities about variant ideas of history that if one course were to be absolutely required at the graduate level it ought to be in historiography." And, as I've said, it is in this context that this conference, "Performance and History: *What* History?" has been conceived.

If I've had any second thoughts about that, I'll keep them in abeyance too. But one thing more, about history not being a branch of literature. Sometimes yes, sometimes no, my own bias here being toward the *quality* of the literature. That there is, if not a fictive, an aesthetic element to history was certainly recognized through the emergence of history as a form of inquiry by the great historians, including von Ranke, who thought of history as a science, but inseparable from art. This appears to be conceded now by Greenblatt, whose historicity always appeared to have had an aesthetic. And we might remember, too, that the second Nobel Prize for literature, awarded in 1902, went to Theodor Mommsen. If there is, as various novelists and playwrights have thought—from Tolstoy, Woolf, and Faulkner to Brecht and Genet—a testamentary quotient to art that exceeds what we find in history, we must remember, too, that what happens on a stage or off a stage, in various kinds of performance art, may provide a quite different kind of testament. In saying that, I'm remembering what Henry James thought when he approached the American scene on his return from Europe, that it was putting out "interrogatory feelers." So far as historicizing it was concerned, he took courage "from the remembrance that history is never, in any rich sense, the immediate crudity of what 'happens,' but the much finer complexity of what we read into it and think of in connection with it."[15] James is speaking, of course, of the writing of history, and one may think of the writing too, as theorists have in our time, as performance. But one last thing to remember: the crudity remains, things happen, sometimes appallingly happen, that brutal burden of history.

Think now. Think *now* . . . And welcome all, whatever your disposition, as history keeps us thinking, over the short *durée* of these two promising days.

NOTES

1. Samuel Beckett, *Waiting for Godot* (New York: Grove Press, 1954) 42.

2. Karl Marx, *The Eighteenth Brumaire of Louis Bonaparte,* in Karl Marx and Frederick Engels, *Selected Works,* trans. unnamed (New York: International Publishers, 1968) 97.

3. Karl Marx, *The German Ideology: Part I,* in *The Marx-Engels Reader,* ed. and trans. Robert C. Tucker (New York: Norton, 1978) 154.

4. Ibid.

5. T. S. Eliot, "Gerontion," in *Selected Poems* (New York: Harvest/HJB, 1964) 32.

6. *Marx-Engels Reader* 149–50.

7. Ferdinand Braudel, *The Mediterranean and the Mediterranean World in the Age of Philip II,* trans. Siân Reynolds, vols. 1 and 2 (New York: Harper & Row, 1972, 1973).

8. Emmanuel Le Roy Ladurie, *The Peasants of Languedoc,* trans. John Day (Urbana: University of Illinois Press, 1981); and *Times of Feast, Times of Famine: A History of Climate since the Year 1000* (New York: Farrar, Straus & Giroux, 1988).

9. Homi Bhaba, "The Commitment to Theory," in *The Norton Anthology of Theory and Criticism* (New York: Norton, 2001) 2385.

10. Eliot, "Gerontion" 33.

11. Eliot, "Preludes: IV," in *Selected Poems* 23.

12. Herbert Blau, "Thinking History, History Thinking," *Theater Survey* 45.2 (2004): 253–62.

13. Michel Foucault, *The Order of Things: An Archaeology of the Human Sciences* (New York: Routledge, 2001) 238.

14. Stephen Greenblatt, *Hamlet in Purgatory* (Princeton, NJ: Princeton University Press, 2001) 4.

15. Henry James, *The American Scene,* ed. John F. Sears (Hammondsworth: Penguin, 1994) 136–37.

EIGHTEEN

The Human Nature of the Bot

THE ISSUE OF LIVENESS—which Philip Auslander, in "Live from Cyberspace," has moved to center stage, where we thought it had always been—has various levels and phases, reimaginable now, indeed, in cyberspatial terms. There was a time, however, when it seemed perfectly understandable to speak of "live" or "living" theater as distinct from acting on film or even, with the closing down of the screen, the immediacy of television. Yet, long before the Internet, it might seem a failing distinction. For there were times within that time when I'd be tempted to say—in disenchantment with what I was seeing in the mainstream of American theater—that the presence of live actors made no real difference: stage or screen, the effect and/or affect was very much the same.

What I meant was that everything was so unenlivening in its predictability, so insusceptible to the unexpected, so invariable once staged, that it seemed (to use an image from another era) like a carbon copy of itself. As for the text, when the play was the thing, it might have done better in a reading without any actors at all. And of course there was the tradition, from Kleist through Gordon Craig to Roland Barthes on the Bunraku, in which puppets were preferred to actors whose impoverished subjectivity only got in the way, except that the acting I am talking about seemed, in its empty sameness, to be without any subjectivity. Whatever the ontological distinction between the one-dimensional figures on the screen and the presumably rounded figures in perspective on a proscenium stage, the felt actuality was such, in various productions I saw, that the quotient of liveness seemed more in the transparency of film. Indeed, it was apparent that the factitious reality of the figures on a screen could have considerably more vitality, as if they were truly alive, than the flesh-and-blood actors up there on the stage, whose behavior was so thoroughly coded and familiar it might as well have been canned.

That has by no means changed entirely in the contemporary theater. But shifting contexts altogether, Auslander writes about the programmed responses in text-based digital environments, in which words and word patterns are picked up so that "it is now possible to be engaged in conversation with a chatterbot without knowing it." When you're on an email list, he adds, or in a chat room on the Internet, "it can be impossible to know whether you are conversing with a human being or a piece of software." But sometimes, too—it may be chastening to remember—you may be conversing with a human being and feel the same way, as if the person were programmed. Which may suggest that liveness is variable in definition, with inflections of value through a spectrum of meaning from being alive to being lively. In shifting the notion of liveness from the ontological to the temporal, "a relationship of simultaneity," an event in real time that can be watched as it occurs, Auslander refers to a passage in *Blooded Thought,* in which I wrote that the ontology of theater may be predicated on the existential fact that the person performing is dying in front of your eyes. This is not to deny, however, that the substance of that insidious truth may be more or less diminished by the dubious presence of the actor in a facsimile of performance that, if occurring in real time, nevertheless feels like a rerun or rather embalmed in advance; without the stink of mortality that, as in the irrefutable testimony on the heath of *King Lear,* is the appalling truth of theater.

If bots are virtual entities that, because they are without biological presence or corporeality, are virtually immortal too, subverting "the centrality of the live, organic presence of human beings to the experience of live performance," they'd hardly have any presence at all, any sense of liveness whatever, were it not for the omnipresent shadow of the apparently vanished being, who, dead or alive, endows the notion of liveness with meaning or substance to begin with. Auslander says that the chatterbot "casts into doubt the existential significance attributed to live performance," but I'm not quite sure what sort of doubt he has in mind. We're obviously engaged with a technology of production capable of making of performance something other than "a specifically human activity," but it is the specifically human activity that—if not reproduced by the bot, which draws its material from databases—remains the inalienable referent around which the data's collected, just as the human conversation is the datum from which, by whatever ambiguous means, the chatterbot proceeds.

It's certainly imaginable to me that a bot may chat not merely with humans but with other bots, or that at some millennial moment of simultaneity there may be in real time a performance without any human participants at all, even to be mistaken about what's real, what's not. But then it would seem that the question of liveness would have been not merely reopened and reframed, as Auslander says it is by the existence of chatterbots, but something of a non sequitur. It may be defined as live, but what can liveness really mean in the absence of a subject for whom what's real, what's not, is of inarguable consequence on existential grounds. As for the performer, one wonders what accrues, or doesn't, to the growing immanence of the bot in the absence of those liabilities—stage fright, lapses of memory, a stomach ache on stage, a coughing fit, unscripted laughter—that give a local habitation, in the body, to the succinct and apposite admission of imperfection that no bot will move us by—"We are all frail"—no less the myriad inflections of a performance that, intended or unintended, really make it live. What we have through the digital technology is the invisible appearance of liveness, but not what—at the sticking point of performance, rarely to be sure—is its inarguable manifestation.

NOTE

These remarks are a response to Philip Auslander, "Live from Cyberspace, or, I Was Sitting at My Computer This Guy Appeared He Thought I Was a Bot," in *PAJ: A Journal of Performance and Art* 70, 24.1 (January 2002): 16–21.

NINETEEN

Virtually Yours

Presence, Liveness, Lessness

THE ACTUAL HUMAN BODY BECOMES OF LESS IMPORTANCE EVERY DAY.
—WYNDHAM LEWIS, "The New Egos," in *BLAST* 1

I began to wonder at about this time what one saw when one looked at anything really looked at anything.
—GERTRUDE STEIN, "Portraits and Repetition"

Little body little block heart beating ash gray only upright.
Little body ash gray locked rigid heart beating face
to endlessness.
—SAMUEL BECKETT, "Lessness"

BEFORE THE OPENING of the Beaumont Theater at Lincoln Center in New York, as we were finishing up the lights for the first preview of *Danton's Death,* what was then (in 1965) the world's most advanced switchboard couldn't quite control the "ghosting" on stage—that is, the trace of lights after dimming, the aura here or halo there, the stubborn residue of illumination that wouldn't, for all the electronics, go entirely dark. Designed by George Izenour, the computerized system was something remarkably new, though the technology still worked at the time not through the mysteries of software but—as with the archetypal Colossus, the vacuum-tubed first electronic computer—by means of a quite hefty pack of punch cards. We shuffled the cards, or read them like Tarot, but when the ghosting persisted, we called Izenour, reputed sage of techno-theater, down from Yale to see what he could do. That didn't quite solve the problem. Each time we'd set up the lights and turn them down, he'd look at the luminous trace that everybody could see and give us a theoretical explanation as to why it couldn't be. Even then, I had no indisposition to theory, "But George," I'd say, "look again!" and again he'd look and explain why it couldn't be, as if we were somehow hallucinating. As it turned out, our technical director José Sevilla managed to operate the switchboard without the computer, running the entire show—the preview not canceled—by taking the dimmers between his fingers and moving them up and down the otherwise hapless console with exquisite precision on cue. The technology was primitive, but the ghosting had disappeared.

Or at least as it was in the lighting. What I'd overlooked then, however, in the urgencies of the moment, is what remains a crucial distinction in the ontology of performance, as we think of it now through the media and the prospects of cyberculture. For once you *look* in the theater, no less *look again!* (as the Furies chant in the *Oresteia,* seeming to initiate specularity as the theater's compulsive tradition) then with or without lighting, the ghosts are already there, and once the lights are up (over the mountaintops from Troy or, lights, lights, lights! as on the play within the play, or in the movement from Plato's Cave to the dialectic of enlightenment, or even with Clov in *Endgame,* who sees his light dying), no matter what's there, or not, it's with *the look of being looked at.* Which is, in performance, the anxious datum of "liveness."

As for liveness in the theater, which seemed to be its distinction, that's been complicated in recent years not merely by the hyperbolic computerization of Broadway scenic effects, escalated at Las Vegas, but by widening magnitudes of performance that seem to be leaving the theater behind. After the carnivals, festivals, pageants, and ritual forms of other cultures, performance seems to be moving beyond the ethnographic, with its residuum of the aesthetic, through technology and corporate management into outer space. I'm not merely referring to media events circling the globe by satellite transmission, but in the ever-increasing panoptic vision of performance studies, to everything from the operations of the Hubble telescope to some nomadic or dysfunctional rocket in the ionosphere, or some years back, the atomization of the *Challenger,* the radiant image of which, played over and over on television, virtually transfigured disaster like, in those brain-draining bursts, before they became a sepulcher, the resplendent aureoles of the collapsing towers. Yet remote from Ground Zero, even spaced out, through the "strange loop" phenomenon of missile guidance systems,[1] if there is anything theatricalized, it requires a *site* of performance; and if the scale is reduced again, down to what's basic in theater, not the old two boards for a passion or, for that matter, what Peter Brook had in mind when he said theater begins with an empty space, luring the actor in.

"There's no such thing as an empty space," said John Cage, "or an empty time."[2] That was the premise of an early essay on experimental music as the becoming of theater, which *"is continually becoming that it is becoming"* (*Silence* 14), which is to say, a space of performance, subject to the look, which for more than a generation has been, as folded into "the gaze," the subject of deconstruction. But with the obduracy of the gaze in mind—and a sense of its *gradations,* as with presence itself—I've written elsewhere that in the apparently empty space you don't even need the actor, the space no longer empty so long as there is someone seeing.[3] As for the semblance of time in space, we may not have been seeing the same, since the same can never be seen, not in a temporal form, but what Cage didn't say, looking through music to theater, is that it's the *seeming* in the becoming that invites and escapes the look, which in the consciousness of looking, as at the substance of seeming itself, suffuses time with thought—which is what theater does, even when troubled by it.

For the liability in the suffusion is a metaphysics of seeming, perpetuating in appearance the future of illusion. Less disturbed by that than the theater tends to be—or at least its canonical drama, in its congenital distrust of theater—the minimalist aesthetic of conceptual art, and the installations that followed, evolved in *theatricality,* which for an unregenerate formalist (specifically, Michael Fried) seemed to be the end of art.[4] The beginning of the end could be said to have occurred in that ur-setting of theatricality, the anechoic chamber at Berkeley, in which, through the absence of other sound, Cage listened to his nerves and heart, then thought of himself listening, out of which came the performance, itself canonical now, of 4′33″ of silence. Some years after, there were repercussions of this silence, inflected visually, in a primitive manifestation of media art: Nam June Paik's prototypical Fluxus film, made in the early 1960s, picking up on Cage's Zen. Paik's later video installations were, with a sometimes monumental array of monitors and his usual visual cunning, extravagant displays, baroque, but back then, if the aesthetic was minimal, it was somewhat out of necessity because of minimal cost: no actors, no expensive effects, optical or otherwise, no film stock to edit either. What Paik projected, inside a TV set, was nothing more than a thousand feet of unprocessed 16-millimeter leader, which ran imagelessly on a screen for thirty minutes, the effect on the viewer being—if not a sense of malfunction or unreflective indifference—a participatory impulse.

That was, in any Fluxus event, the performative prospect at least, presumably canceling the inertia of the passive observer, with consciousness itself emerging as the sine qua non of performance. As if Baudelaire's boredom, recycled, had been activated on the screen, the (seeming) tabula rasa of the illuminated space was, in subsequent viewings, complicated and enlivened, minuscule as they were, by dust and scratches on the leader stock. The liveness there, of course, was in the consciousness solicited by those chance "events," though it's possible to argue that the events themselves were symptoms of liveness, even in the absence of any human image on film, just as the "miscellaneous rubbish," the rising and falling lights, the sounds of inspiration and expiration, and the faint cries, each "instant of recorded vagitus," convey a more poignant absence—the liveness of it, no actors there on stage—in the performance of Beckett's *Breath*.[5]

On a larger scale, the notion of liveness entered the agenda of performance theory through film and (even more) the televisual, and the "remediation" that Philip Auslander has tracked from stage to screen to stage, and through the recording industry: from the lip-synch scandal of Milli Vanilli to CDs, DVDs, and back through rock concerts, where the performance of Madonna, U2, or Eminem, the truth of liveness there, is determined and authenticated by what's been seen on MTV. If this merely updates, according to Auslander, what we should have known all along, "that the live can exist only *within* an economy of reproduction," what's all the more true in the technological versatility of the dominion of reproduction, the fantasy-making apparatus itself, "is that, like liveness itself, the desire for live experiences is a product of mediatization."[6] Meanwhile, as the vacuum tubes were miniaturized, first by transistors, then integrated circuits, and afterwards silicon chips, with fiber-optic bundles enabling globalization, it was to be expected that the question of liveness would extend to virtual reality, as well as to futurological fantasies of a digitized human race that, with whatever forms of intelligence in a dematerialized body, would certainly alter our thinking about the meaning of *presence* in liveness.

Until that millennarian day, however, we'll still be contending with the banalities about "living theater," which attribute to real bodies on a stage more presence than some of those bodies may actually have in performance, no less anything like a charismatic wholeness, which this or that body may *appear* to have, if nothing more than appearance. Yet, if there was no point to stressing liveness before the advent of photography and the phonograph—though even the Festival of Dionysus or a chorus at Epidaurus was part of an economy of reproduction—the notion of living theater also has to be historicized. When we used to speak of living theater, before the insurrection of (what the French call) *the* Living—with "polymorphous perverse" bodies proclaiming *Paradise Now*—what we had in mind, by contrast, was the appearance of theater on film, though the incursion of the Living, in the dissidence of the 1960s, was also a claim to liveness as opposed to the dehumanized. And that was a condition just as possible in the theater as it was on film, or later television, not to mention the prospect that dehumanization will be, in the apotheosis of virtual reality, the (im)material condition of liveness. Relieved or distraught by the absence of presence, relentlessly demystified in theory, some who see liveness alive and well in the media—which mediatize themselves in remediation—are essentially making a defense of another kind of presence, an electronic presence, as we pass to the Internet, where, instead of metaphysics coming in through the pores, as Freud and Artaud thought, it comes in, rather, in bytes.

When we think of the age of information, and digital traffic around the globe, there's a tendency to imagine the networks as a ramification of the "superhighway" of image culture, or as the hypertrophy of image, its proliferous reification, from the age of mechanical reproduction (Benjamin) to the society of the spectacle (Debord), with its investment in, or investiture of, the precession of simulacra (Baudrillard). But the virtual realities of information are something else again. While the photographic, filmic, or televisual image is still attached to the material site of representation in a legacy of realism (however the image is produced, indexically or analogically), the substance of the virtual, digitally produced as it is through the wobble of one and zero, may appear to be three-dimensional, but in the electroluminescence of the apparency of a stage, there is only an "empty display,"[7] nothing to feel, nothing to touch, only the phosphorescent presence of what—unlike the object of the camera, however abstracted—was never there to begin with. In some interactive continuum of the cyberized space itself, the sensation may be that of a body virtually there, but that's it, virtual, maybe quickening apprehension in its shimmering subjunctivity, with a certain charm or enchantment, perhaps, like an alibi of the spectral wishing it could be more, maybe even mortal, but with evacuated gravity, never meant to be.

The space is interactive, and the virtual is a lure, but the real agency is the artificial intelligence, the prior programming, that creates the virtual scene. If, through the resourcefulness of a database, that scene is analogous to the real, one can be immersed in the analogy, which is cyberspace, without the visceral sensation of being there, since there is no there *there*—not even, as things are, the appearance of it, which is with all its impediments, however unaccommodated, the vexing thing itself. With all the promise of digitality, there is also something poignant: *the subtext of the virtual is that it really wants to be real.*[8] And whatever that may be, the index of its truth—as with any manifestation in whatever performative mode, across any stylization or cultural practice, ritualized or mimed, masked or mediated, even performed with puppets—will always be subject to that, the real, as the body of information will be referred to the body itself, that body, the real body, and I don't mean a social construction, no less what they're calling a bot.

Still, somewhere in all this, there seems to be a new reality, as the seemingly manipulable but abstracted world of data, supradiaphanous, immaterial as it is, bears upon life as we've known it, material as it is, and unlikely to go away, unless the genetic codes are somehow added to the data, ending life as we've known it in a life without end. Which, however that may be, may vex us even more—if performance theory survives—by making liveness moot. Be that as it may, this is certainly a view of the future that Bertolt Brecht didn't anticipate when, after the bomb on Hiroshima, he revised his Epic theory in the *Short Organum,* to take cognizance of nuclear power, beyond the "petroleum complex," even before which he had thought, "Some exercise in complex seeing is needed."[9] In the world of feedback loops accelerated by microcomputers, and with cyborgs on the scene about to take over performance (or even, since queerer than queer, what is called "performativity"), Brecht's critique of "culinary theater" would seem to be arrested in history, without any object at all, since the disappearance of an organic body with conventional subjectivity makes the culinary a non sequitur: out in cyberspace, nothing to cook and nothing to eat. But if the audience in the bourgeois theater is there to digest its dinner, so it might all the more in front of a computer. Still, if what's programmed there is in a postculinary world, immersed in virtuality, there's no guarantee whatever that its values are improved by the data with which, in the absence of anything else, we may identify in performance. Meanwhile, for cybernauts and cybernerds, and all us foreseeable cyborgs, there seems to be—except for incompetence on the computer—no digital equivalent of the Alienation-effect. Which is to say, we're no better than ever, through all the information, in the complex seeing we need, when time must have a stop, for a reflective look, wherever we are in the virtual, at the reality passing by, susceptible to illusion, maybe nothing but appearance, all the more in the paranoia of a world besieged by terror, with "weapons of mass destruction," once a refrain on the evening news, now only in abeyance.

There are also certain factors that make seeing at all complex. Thus, when performance occurs at a digital distance, out there in cyberspace, where power is a function of remote control—in a world inconceivable without its image, or in the unstoppable seeming, an obscenity of image—remoteness itself is the sticking point, hardly reducible to a Brechtian *gestus.* As with the smart bombs of the Gulf War or in the Shah-i-Kot Valley after Al Qaeda, in or out of the caves, or even the scandal of Enron with the shreddings at Anderson, for all we see, we don't see it, though we may be watching all the time. As opposed to the theater, or even film, what we have on television is a virtual allegory of the remote. What we see there, as we move from channel to channel, is the liquidity of culture, both in the sense of gathered, processed, edited, and collaged images, screened as they are from the cathode tube, and in the sense of commodification, with the illusion of liquidity there, the images presumably at our disposal, the remote like a magic wand or scepter, giving access to the Imaginary. Yet, for all that imperial remoteness—programs on and off at will—it's an illusion of power out of hand, a lot more feeble than fabulous, more like impotency after all. Nobody forces anybody to watch television, but very few resist, and putting aside what's brainless, or what we know we've seen before, no matter how new it appears, it's hard to watch for any length of time without feeling the saturation of apparent news, the ad nauseam of the commentary, and even if the screen is small, a frustrating diffusion of thought. Not only in surfing channels, but in what we do when we watch, the experience is that of modernity in the Eliotic sense, distracted from distraction by distraction.

In this regard, the mediatizing of culture is not only a matter of how it is represented, or who represents it, but how that is factored into a virtual ontology of distraction, which bears upon what we think and how we see ourselves in time. Or for that matter, out of time, because our sense of temporality is increasingly preempted by the allure of the televisual, and with it telepresence,[10] which may encounter time in its occurrence, but not in any perceptible cycle of duration, stasis, motion, or decay. Time on television—where we rarely see the process of time—is processed, and what just happened will move instantly into the archive, to be reprocessed, even images of the past susceptible, as Margaret Morse points out, to a sort of digital updating or "electronic revision to meet today's expectations," so that the grainier black-and-white documentations of the past are not preserved as access "to flickering shadows in the cave," but are rather shaped up to the "spatiotemporal and psychic relations [of] the realities it constitutes" (110). Which are, as they now impinge on performance, realities of distraction.

At the same time, there is a certain tactility in the mediatizing of culture that has not so much to do, as we tend to think, with the formation of attitudes or the maneuvering of public opinion—the commentary on the polling that inevitably determines the polls—but rather with the activity of perception at the heart of representation; or in reverse, the activity of representation that forms perception, and therefore, indeed, the way things are thought. Thus, in the operations of television graphics, as in the close-ups of a television interview, we may have the sensation of proximity to an object, seeing it closer—in the case of virtual images, as if they were, in extreme nearness, eliciting our sense of touch, as with fabrics on home-shopping channels or the bombshell rapper Eve, or lovely breasts on forensic detectives, or in the magic world of the Law, the receding older Order, sexy legs on *Ally McBeal.* If what is called "blue-screen technology" can create virtual sets that make small-market studios, and their unknown anchor people, look prime-time, so complex motion design, enhanced by the computer, makes it possible not only to define but to move around an object in discursive space, with diverse angles and points of entry, the sort of topology that defies the burdensome laws of gravity in the cinema as we know it, no less on the theater's stage. Sometimes the sense of motion is such, in computerized graphics on the screen, especially in fantasies of outer space (transposed to selling the Lexus), that the ground of representation itself seems to be taken from under us. Yet the fantasies of weightlessness are competing, as they did way back in Ibsen's *Lady from the Sea,* with the deadweight actuality of our actual bodies. It may be that virtual worlds are preparing us psychically for the zero gravity of outer space or some virtual interior life, but for the time being or, irreversibly, the reality of being in time, our bodies inhabit a space (even floating out there in a capsule) that is irreparably down to earth. And I didn't intend a pun on the *Columbia* disaster.

In Datek ads or Hellomoto, Motorola's Datamoto, it might seem it could be reversed, and every now and then we hear that either biogenetics or some high-tech implant is going to bring it about. Actually, there is considerable speculation, and some pontification, more or less idealistic, about the out-of-body promise of digital worlds, and the status of the virtual in the reality that remains, what—according to theorists from Benjamin to Baudrillard—may only be a remainder amid the ruins of time. Given that ruinous context, seeds of history upon the ground, what is virtual reality? The truth is that, psychically and otherwise, no less realistically, we know very little about its cultural substance and prospects, its possibilities for performance, or its eventual effect on what we take to be human. And when we advance through electronic culture to this impasse, we're somewhere beyond the horizon of performance in the media, even those films they're now trying to make, with actors replaced by the ingenious animation of digital tech, leaving us with the question: is the increasing likeness to be thought of as liveness? And by what criteria do we determine that?

To be sure, it was the escalation of mediatization that appeared to bring into the theater itself, and to the live bodies there, reflexes and habits of mind that seemed less natural or organic than mechanically reproduced—not by some postmodern offshoot of Meyerhold's biomechanics (which was actually derived from Taylorism) or by some recidivist sign of passion from the repertoire of Delsarte. If we've long been aware of the stale predictability of Broadway's assembly line, and of actors repeating themselves, that was because, as in digital culture, it was possible to process behavior and homogenize it as code. This is all the more so today in the precession of simulacra, where it's possible to think of liveness as playing roles on screen, precoded parts written for us in advance, so that we're signs of what we appear to be, not even representations but their merest facsimile. And if this is so, then the actor who appears on stage is the redundancy of a redundancy, performing an otherness that only pretends to be, so well known has it been that it can only be rehearsed, the image of an image of something that, coded to begin with, has otherwise never been. That, I suppose, is the worst-case scenario. As for actors repeating themselves, that was in any case to be expected, despite all versatility, from those who achieve stardom on stage or screen. As for any appearance in the flesh, whatever the quotient of liveness, it may of course be augmented, as well as credibilized, by previous celebrity in the media, which function in visual culture by their long-belabored expertise, whatever else they may be doing, in commodifying the look—not quite that of being looked at, in the sense I've been talking about, which seems brought into being by another liveness, the liveness overlooked, that of perception itself, as it makes its way through appearance.

If that's not always what it appears to be (or even if it is), that's also due to perception, which in abrading upon reality also makes it theater. As if he were enunciating Heisenberg's principle of indeterminacy, William Blake said that the eye altering alters all. And any way you look at it, the body on stage is suffused with the vicissitudes of appearance, which complicate the question of liveness, all the more because you look, off stage, on stage, with more or less reciprocity during the course of performance—the irony being here that sometimes less is more. Which is to say that the quality of liveness, the felt sensation of it, may not necessarily diminish as it moves from the interactive or participatory to a more contemplative mode. What mediatizes culture there, beyond any previous accretions, is the activity of perception, however rigorous or involuntary, or intently voyeuristic, "lawful espials" or "seeing unseen" (*Hamlet* 3.1.32–33) or, with one or another mode of alienating distance, the seeing or unseeing in an impersonal or clinical look. "Am I as much as . . . being seen?" says one of the figures in the urns of Beckett's *Play,* which wouldn't be as much of a question—being *seen* or *being* seen? (how should the actor say it? and how much is she being seen? depending on how he says it?)—were you to see the figure on film.

As we reflect on the difference in being, as Heidegger might have seen it, from being as being-seen, it would seem that the affectivity of presence—its liveness, so to speak—might better be thought of, through the undeniable palpability of its metaphysical absence, as gradations of presence escaping itself in a sort of microphysics. About which you can say, as the greatest of dramas do, you can only see so much—even if you put it on film, or with a video monitor, or by storing it as information in a computer's memory bank. If the theater, as I said in *Take Up the Bodies,* "is the body's long initiation in the mystery of its vanishings,"[11] I wouldn't count on computer memory, ready for instant messaging, to keep track of where it went, or even to serve for cultural memory, since in the mysteries of digitization it somehow erases the difference between where we were and where we are, as well as now and then. There are those, to be sure, who are hardly disturbed by that, and some of them, who have grown up with or into cyberspace, are developing modes of performance that have already gone online, like the Creative Outlaw Visionaries or Law and Order Practitioners or, mobilizing micronetworks for an agit-prop agenda, Ricardo Dominguez and the Electronic Disturbance Theater. If Dominguez prefers the Internet to the stage because of the subversive possibilities, on quite another scale, one can imagine computer types who might indeed prefer the protocols of digital exchange, whether anonymously or otherwise, to the regimens of performance as we've known it through the impediments of flesh and blood. One of the capacities of digitality is not only to speed up exchange across unconscionable distances, but, as if it were some new outreach of ritual drama, to occult it once again. It may very well be enticing to a performer who could, in the theater, only imagine shadows, doubles, and the traces of ghostliness, to dematerialize online and resurface in code and image in a new Theater of the World, where liveness came from elsewhere than being born astride of a grave.

If then, coming back to earth, liveness comes as well with a certain paranoia, that's because—mediated or remediated as the theater might be, not only in the recyclings from film or television, but in the infinity of its repetitions (what drove Artaud mad) from whenever the theater began—there is in all the remediation something irremediable, the disease of time in a time-serving form. It can be put in various ways, more or less anodyne or evasive, but there are times when liveness itself is exalted by its most disheartening truth: it stinks of mortality, which may be the ultimate subtext of stage fright—no virtual reality that, but ineliminably there, however disguised, or (as actors may say) made use of in performance, in any case encroaching on or reshaping presence, and even if it doesn't stink, bringing us back to what, as reality principle, ghosts us after all. Even on the cybernetic threshold of a cyborgian age, "we really do die," which is what, in simple truth, Donna Haraway said when she stopped short on the utopian prospects and warned against "denying mortality."[12]

What is, then, the material condition of liveness, its inevitable "lessness," will continue to be so until our nanotechnology produces—as K. Eric Drexler promised when he started manipulating materials that are utterly out of sight—self-replicating subatomic engines that will not only remove diseased DNA from our perishing bodies, but also repair our aging cells, making us (nearly) immortal. Which is not to mention the visions of robotic bodies of a postbiological age into which, as into computer memory, we can download the forms of thought and desire that once went into our drama. As we might have guessed, the media—as in AT&T's *"YOU WILL"* campaign[13]—are encouraging these prospects as something more than fantasy, not dreamt of in our philosophy, maybe, but in the more numinous spinoff from *Blade Runner,* the techno-transcendentalism or epiphanic redemption of entropy (not to mention social justice)[14] that comes with being Wired. Whatever the liveness dreamt of, it's not quite that which the newspapers were conscious of in NBC's prime-time coverage of the Winter Olympics in Utah. The relative reality there was "live live" (designated "Live" in the upper left corner of the screen) or "nearly live" (a skeleton, skateboard, or bobsled event that happened, say, an hour before) or the "live that looks like live, yet is not" (Bob Costas in the studio chatting with Jim McKay) or the "nonlive, which does not mean dead, just taped."[15] Or, as we've seen it in Afghanistan, on tape, maybe alive, maybe dead, and if no "Live" up in the corner, maybe a ticker of news at the bottom, keeping the options alive, or announcing a vote on Osama bin Laden's liveness, as they've done on CNN.com.

If there is, whatever the vote, something simply obtuse or a bad puerile joke in that, the suffusion of our reality by the media, live live, nearly live, nonlive, is such that, even when you turn it off, it seems somehow to be on, as if there were channels in our heads, which at some devastating moment of history we might wish would simply go blank. Or give us a moment's respite. But, as if the media were itself a function of our manic obsession with image that in its stupefying excess is the matrix of the real, that isn't meant to be. Nor can we separate the superfetation of image from the mesmeric redundancy of the noise that passes as information, which is not what Lionel Trilling once meant by "the hum and buzz of implication," to which, judiciously, you might turn an attentive ear. Nor is it even the noise that John Cage talked about, and deployed, as early as 1937, "The sound of a truck at fifty miles an hour. Static between the stations. Rain"—about which he said, "Wherever we are what we hear is mostly noise. When we ignore it, it disturbs us. When we later listen to it, we find it fascinating." And with electronic control of amplitude and frequency, it is possible to take "any one of these sounds and to give it rhythms within or beyond the reach of imagination" (*Silence* 3). This is not the noise we hear on the media every day.

Thus, for all the depth of grief and mourning after the disasters of September 11, the one inconceivable testament to its unspeakability would have been, at ground zero of sensation, darkened TV screens and, for one unmediated day of quiet reflection, no anchors, no talk shows, no Imus in the morning or *O'Reilly Factor* at night, no Leno, no Letterman, no *Crossfire* or *Hardball,* or speaking of liveness, *Larry King Live,* no profusion of replays: *silence.* Which is, perhaps, when history hurts, the only reliable echo of liveness. That the media, however, saturate culture, both inducing and preempting what we feel, is by now, even when on their best behavior—the relief of absent commercials after the towers collapsed—an inarguable fact of life, as it is of the theater, which even before Pirandello could no longer think of art imitating life, for life is no longer the referent, but only life as mediated, as if theatricality were appropriated on its own terms, as the pure Imaginary. If it's long been apparent that anything which goes on in our minds, almost very gesture we make, what passes as love or longing, just about every instinct, has either been determined, foreseen, programmed, or mimicked by the media, so it seems, too, that in an age of information virtually everything to be known is out there on the Net for the asking, and with the savvy of software accessible on the computer. Yet the more we ask the more demoralized we may be.

Meanwhile, the World Wide Web is the global space of performance, where the notion of living theater seems the merest anachronism, if nothing more than because the intensities and energies producible (never mind reproducible) on film, video, CDs, and DVDs exceed in their cumulative affect or outright sensation anything achievable by flesh and blood on a stage, except insofar as the body's vulnerability, the weak flesh itself, becomes in its mortality the literal issue. For all the recycling of liveness, or the remediation (carrying rather insensibly the notion of a remedy), it's hard to imagine any image on the screen, however violent, lustful, demonic, barbaric, no less intimate or lyrical, that could match the close-up effect upon spectators of an actor who, as in the extremities of performance art—Gina Pane up a ladder of razors, Chris Burden having himself shot, Fakir Musaphar's self-impalings, Orlan's cosmetic surgeries, Schwarzkogler's bandaged suffocations, with live wires exposed, on the edge of suicide (which came when he went over the edge, by throwing himself out of a window)—actually cuts his wrist or slits another's throat or (as a friend of mine did) swallows a bottle of pins, or a scene in which the lovemaking or fucking is not merely simulated, but nakedly there, cock into cunt, right there before your eyes, not garrulously so as in *The Vagina Monologues,* making up for lost time and the carnal by merely talking about it, in the vacuity of a voice. I've seen people wince at pictures of Stelarc suspending himself by fishhooks, as they do with some of the more perilous things on *Survivor,* or recently on *Fear Factor,* when certain minor celebrities were crawled over by worms, roaches, and snakes. But suppose that were done close up, live, as in a gallery space or intimate theater, and you were sitting right there. Never mind the factitious violence as it comes with popcorn-boggling credibility from Hollywood's editing rooms—if what they apparently do in "snuff films" were done on a stage there'd be no doubt whatever about the *difference* in liveness, dead or alive, to use our president's words about the evildoer hiding out, no doubt applicable now to those in Kashmir or Pakistan who beheaded Daniel Pearl. As for the videotape not yet on the networks (and quite unlikely to be), that would be difficult to see if they showed it, but imagine it done on a stage, where what's *not* done may be done with a valence that, formed as it is by the media (and reducing the level of sensation), is something else again, like the nothing to be done in *Waiting for Godot* that, in its most elemental liveness, cannot *not* be done. Which is where, if only with the illusion of the unmediated, the most complex performance exists.

The issue remains, however, as performance extends beyond theater or performance art to fashion, politics, pedagogy, corporate management, polymeric composites, rocket boosters or missile defense, whether the narrow circumference of a stage, and *human presence,* can continue to hold attention in ways the other media can't. For the theater, as already suggested, is mediatized too, that is, something other than raw experience, not at all immediate, which in its corporeality we sometimes tend to forget. The mediatizing of culture was surely ramified and accelerated from photography and cinema through television to analog/digital technology, but its effect upon performance was already registered before the end of the nineteenth century, in the preface to Strindberg's *Miss Julie,* which went beyond the relatively conservative dramaturgy of naturalism—purporting to focus on the documentable evidence of an external reality, its facts and material circumstances—to the multiplicity of "the soul-complex," which is something like the Freudian notion of overdetermination, a subjectivity so estranged that it cannot fit into the inherited conception of character.

Thus the notion of a "characterless" character. "Instead of the 'ready-made,' in which the bourgeois concept of the immobility of the soul was transferred to the stage," Strindberg insists on the richness of the soul-complex, which—if derived from his conception of Darwinian naturalism—reflects "an age of transition more compulsively hysterical" than the one preceding it, while anticipating the age of postmodernism, with its utterly mediated and deconstructed self, so that when we think of identity as social construction, it occurs as well as a sort of bricolage: "My souls (characters)," Strindberg writes in that proleptic preface, "are conglomerates of past and present cultural phases, bits from books and newspapers, scraps of humanity, pieces torn from fine clothes and become rags, patched together as is the human soul."[16] And one of the patches is from the theater itself, as it is with the valet Jean, who says, to account for the knowingness beyond his station, that he's been to the theater often. Unfortunately, if that brings a certain mediated presence to his pretensions, of the sort we might acquire today from film or television, it wilts before the voice of the Count coming down the speaking tube. All through the play, actually, the tube itself is a presence, as that other tube is today: the medium is the message, and it's still a message of power.

As we move, however, toward virtual worlds, the claims of the body to presence—or attributing presence to the body, as confirmation or affirmation—may appear to be disrupted by the reformative flow of postlinear devices and systems: fast forward, rewind, stop, eject, play, and the whole array of recorders, tapes, CDs and CD-ROMs, as well as the chat rooms and chatterbots on the Internet. And we have seen performance events with more or less impacted technology that seems to parse the body, with real-time digitized contours that seem to be floating in infraspace, as in the work of Matthew Barney, that is, a performance space of image projectors that may also seem, through computer programming, to be spuming or liquified, itself floating or hyperextended, with its payload of partial bodies, spindrifting to cyberspace. Here, corporeal identity may appear to warp, reform, dissolve, be refigured there online, but however the body is thus deconstituted and/or restored, its image persists through it all, along with—if not there in actuality—the desire to have it so. If cyberspace itself is the consensual hallucination that is the consummation of virtual technologies, the hallucinatory consensus extends to notions of performance disassociated from the mundane gravity of the corporeal body. But just as cyberspace is unthinkable without the alphabetic and mathematical system of representation that supports and sustains the logocentricism presumably displaced, so the dematerialized figures are unthinkable without the bodily presence presumably vanished, nothing occurring in cyberspace that isn't contingent on that which, seemingly, it made obsolete.

Whatever the circularity—the looping of liveness through the space of reproduction—there is no escaping in remediation the reductio ad absurdum, which is to say, bereft, forlorn, alienated, replicated by technology, the nevertheless refractory body to which, unavoidably, we refer anything on a screen, in the ghostliness of three dimensions or in the wraithlike space of the virtual. That live presence has been devalued in mediatized culture, and that the degradation of the live has been compensated for in large-scale live performance, rock concerts or sporting events, by "videation" or Diamondvision and instant replays (Auslander 35), still leaves us the lamentable body in its dispossession, and given the scale of the media, "little body little block heart ash gray only upright," which has been from whatever beginnings the carnal datum of theater. As to what passes through liveness when truly alive, no videation or instant replay can ever get at that, what's there indubitably but invisible, right there before your eyes. Merely the thought of it is sufficient to make theater, in the scenic site of the mind, what beats there, as in the incipient madness of King Lear. Which is not to say that it's realized in the theater as we mostly know it, or even in performance art. Or that the theater as an institution will ever again have the presence of the other media in our lives.

It is only to say that there's not much substance to theater that doesn't occur in the space of indeterminacy between what's tangibly there, or appears to be, and whatever images of mediatized representation are there as a supplement to (the absence of) the real. It may be that we'll eventually encounter some protovirtual version of what Richard Schechner calls Rasaesthetics, opening up performance to the whole sensorium; as if inspired by the *Natyasastra,*[17] the technological virtuosity of virtual reality may, in the desideratum of embracing cultures, eventually program synesthetically some aromatic and emotional fusion of proprioceptive experience, bringing it instantly across continents to the entire world. But since—however and wherever the sensorium is expanded—it will still be occurring in anthropocentric terms, the ancient problems of knowing remain, with issues of identity and otherness too. And a major question still to be responded to is the one asked years ago by my KRAKEN group, in a work called *Crooked Eclipses* (derived from Shakespeare's sonnets), its initiatory image of a suspended gaze, mirrored in the moment: "What is your substance, whereof are you made, / That millions of strange shadows on you tend?" (Sonnet 53). What, for all the resources, doesn't exist on film or the electronic media is anything like those shadows, the ghostings, which exist all the more in performance when—whether or not encroached upon by filmic or video images with more seeming presence than the bodies on stage—their presence seems most suspect.

Long before our consciousness of the media, or of mediated consciousness, this paradox was apparent at the outset of Büchner's *Woyzeck,* which dramatizes what was, in Leipzig in 1821, the equivalent of a media event: "What a murder! A good, genuine, beautiful murder!" as the Policeman says at the end about what started as a strange sensation: "Quiet! . . . Can you hear it? Something moving! . . . It's moving behind me! Under me! . . . Listen! Hollow! It's all hollow down there!"[18] And so it is in Beckett's *Endgame,* when Hamm is pushed by Clov to the wall, something dripping in his head ("A heart, a heart in my head")[19] that, when push comes to shove, you can never get on film—even the film of Beckett's *Endgame.* As for the liveness in that drip, or the hollow, whatever it is that's moving, it can't be remediated (or, as we used to say, represented) because, moment by moment, right before your eyes in the becoming of theater (even if you could hear the heartbeat), it's inevitably something less.

NOTES

1. See Jon McKenzie, *Perform or Else: From Discipline to Performance* (New York: Routledge, 2001).

2. John Cage, "Experimental Music," in *Silence: Lectures and Writing* (Middletown, CN: Wesleyan University Press, 1974) 8.

3. Herbert Blau, *The Audience* (Baltimore: Johns Hopkins University Press, 1990) 218.

4. Michael Fried, "Art and Objecthood," in *Minimalist Art: A Critical Anthology,* ed. Gregory Battcock (New York: Dutton, 1968) 116–47. *"The success, even the survival of the arts,"* Fried wrote in 1967, *"has come increasingly to depend on their ability to defeat theater"* (139). While disdaining Cage as well (in quality, relative to Elliott Carter, no comparison) Fried's animus was directed mainly against visual artists (Donald Judd, Robert Morris) who were undoing the epiphanic "presentness" or "single infinitely brief instant" that—for Fried, to this day—is grace (146–47).

5. Samuel Beckett, "Breath," in *Collected Shorter Plays* (New York: Grove, 1984) 211.

6. Philip Auslander, *Liveness: Performance in a Mediatized Culture* (London: Routledge, 1999) 54–55.

7. Margaret Morse, *Virtualities: Television, Media Art, and Cyberculture* (Bloomington: Indiana University Press, 1998) 196. Of the various books proliferating in this hyperactive scene, this is the most sophisticated that I've come across—and the most evocatively written—in its own mediation between what media artists are doing, from "telematic dreaming" to virtualizing physical space, and the shadowy means required to do it, the "algorithms and abstract symbols in an imperceptible realm of data" (5). To negotiate its seemingly endless prospects, cyberculture demands a lot of imagination, and Morse respects it when it's there, while keeping a jaundiced eye on its transcendent fictions and not losing sight of those who, in the globalized here-and-now, still have next to no access to the profusion of worlds online.

8. Quite recently we've seen the equivalent of this in the universe of video games, which are deploying their newest technology for an increasing realism, while warding off abstraction and its arbitrary rules. It may be that the credibilizing effects are achieved by numerous buttons, triggers, and toggling switches, and the computer keyboard, but the irony is that the most sophisticated technology, by Xbox or Nintendo today, is drawn upon for games with an animus against technology or with a sort of primitive reflex, as if before technology, which—in the regulated intricacy of its puzzling or fantastical worlds—departed too much from the real, with its muscular sensations or plain old blood and guts.

9. Bertolt Brecht, "The Literarization of the Theater," in *Brecht on Theater: The Development of an Aesthetic,* ed. and trans. John Willett (New York: Hill and Wang, 1964) 44.

10. Alice Rayner is especially perceptive on the rhetoric of telepresence that, promoting it, fails to recognize that it usually occurs in the language of theatricality ("Everywhere and Nowhere: Theater in Cyberspace," in *Of Borders and Thresholds: Theater History, Practice, and Theory,* ed. Michal Kobialka [Minneapolis: University of Minnesota Press, 1999] 278–302). Thus, while the community of telepresence is all over the place, or could be, in a global culture, the desideratum is a sense of here and now, the materiality associated with an actual theater space, which remains just that, a "place for seeing," even when the enveloped space of wings and flies, and the binary of stage and audience, is amplified or otherwise transformed by slides, films, video clips, whether for purposes largely scenic or caption-like, or as a kind of dialectical image-source for the actors or the drama. Whatever the apparent dispersal of the event, through the media or, prospectively now, by way of the Inter-

net, most of what presumably occurs in cyberspace is there with an institutional referent and in the "language of dimensionality" (281).

11. Herbert Blau, *Take Up the Bodies: Theater at the Vanishing Point* (Urbana: University of Illinois Press, 1982) 299.

12. "Cyborgs at Large: Interview with Donna Haraway," in *Technoculture,* ed. Constance Penley and Andrew Ross (Minneapolis: University of Minnesota Press, 1991) 16.

13. See Mark Dery, *Escape Velocity: Cyberculture at the End of the Century* (New York: Grove, 1996) 11–12.

14. For many artists and social theorists, if sluggishly so in the theater, the emergence of a global economy, projecting itself on the Web, requires a radical and unprecedented "upheaval in our historical perceptions of society and the subject. If behavior at local levels has not quite caught up with the revolutionary prospects of a net-based economy, much of what's happening in the art world seems to be focused there. "Net art, from physical local installations to world-wide network computer games, has become the forum in which many of the emancipatory hopes of the historical avant-gardes are being rephrased. Web art is a form of art to which great political hopes are linked" (Peter Weibel, "The Project," in *net_condition: art and global media,* ed. Weibel and Timothy Druckrey [Cambridge: ZKM Center for Art and Media / MIT Press, 2001] 19).

15. Richard Sandomir, "In These 'Live' Olympic Games, It's a Matter of Timing," *New York Times,* February 22, 2002, C20.

16. August Strindberg, "Author's Preface" to *Miss Julie,* in *Strindberg: Five Plays,* trans. Harry G. Carlson (New York: Signet, 1984) 53–54.

17. Richard Schechner, "Rasaesthetics," *The Drama Review* (T71) 45.3 (2001): 27–50.

18. Georg Büchner, *Woyzeck,* in *Georg Büchner: Complete Plays and Prose,* trans. Carl Richard Mueller (New York: Hill and Wang, 1989) 111, 137–38.

19. Samuel Beckett, *Endgame* (New York: Grove, 1958) 18.

TWENTY

Auto Archive

MEMORY SEEMS TO BE DOING DOUBLE DUTY these days, since I've been working on an autobiography, and quite recently, for a conference in St. Petersburg, I gave a keynote on "The Emotional Memory of Directing." The conference was held at Meyerhold's theater, the Alexandrinsky, but if the title defers to Stanislavski, by way of *An Actor Prepares,* the emotional memory was mine—or, with irrepressible subtexts, a composite of mixed emotions—about having worked with actors for just about half my life. Adventitiously, just before St. Petersburg, I was in Dublin, having been invited to reflect, for the Abbey Theater's centennial, on "Memory and Repertoire," the memory again mine, as reassessing the Abbey's history summoned up from my own what, years ago in the theater, seemed a vain ambition. What I talked about, in cultural contrast, was trying to evolve a repertoire, and a company with continuity, in a vaster, diverse country, where there was only what used to be called (by the old yellow-covered *Theater Arts*) "Tributary Theater," with everything coming from Broadway, as if in rivulets to the outland, and with everybody paying tribute, the actors dreaming of it. Nor was there anything even remotely like the conditions for a national theater, neither the semblance of a burgeoning unity nor an apparent mythic tradition—whatever the illusions there—that William Butler Yeats invoked when he founded the Abbey Theater.

While those who invited me had particularly in mind The Actor's Workshop of San Francisco, which Jules Irving and I founded in 1952, they were unaware that Yeats was one of the two major figures (the other T. S. Eliot) in my doctoral dissertation, which I was writing as our theater started for the English Department at Stanford. Nor did they know that the first play I ever directed—in our loft above a judo academy (with rat shit below the stairs that I'd clean up before rehearsal)—was *Playboy of the Western World.* But that was a relatively conventional choice in what became, quite radically at the time, an innovative repertoire, the first or early productions of now canonical playwrights: Brecht, Beckett, Genet, Pinter, Whiting, Arden, Dürrenmatt, Frisch, and, among those utterly unknown, Maria Irene Fornes. Moreover, out of a discouraging context, the Workshop did manage to develop and sustain a company, from eight actors in that loft to (including the technical staff) considerably more than a hundred, performing in two or three theaters simultaneously. With our theater a major force in the San Francisco Renaissance, it was a shock to the city when, in 1965, some of us went to New York, as Jules and I took over the directorship of the Repertory Theater of Lincoln Center, replacing Robert Whitehead and Elia Kazan. That, sadder to say, was hardly a major success, and I've reflected on it before, as I have on much of this, in one or another book. As my dear friend Ruby Cohn said, in her characteristic way, when I told her I was working on an autobiography: "What are you doing that for, you're always writing autobiography." Well, maybe so. But if memoirs are now in, that was—and compellingly long before—more like a habit of mind that, not unlike performance, exists at the nerve ends of thought.

As to how it all came to be, my initiation in the theater and the perspective emerging from it, I've not yet dealt with in the autobiography, no less the radically altered vision in the work of my KRAKEN group. But if you were to look at the first chapter, about my growing up in Brooklyn, on the streets of Brownsville (now prefixed with Ocean Hill, with or without the prefix as bad as a neighborhood gets), you'd see that the prospect of my being in the theater, no less writing about it theoretically, was about as inconceivable as my eventually being a dean. The fact is I wanted nothing more than to be a ballplayer. That was my real ambition, all through high school and even into college, but as it turned out I was a dean, twice, and a provost, though even more anomalously in over half a century of teaching (still unretired), I did have that parallel career in the theater, but *outside* the university. And when I've taught, it's not been in drama departments, but—except for CalArts, which I mostly conceived as founding provost, while also dean of the School of Theater—in English and comparative literature. There were periods when, exhilarated beyond exhaustion, I was working full-time directing and full-time teaching (four courses per semester, two in freshman comp), all the more anomalously because my first degree was in chemical engineering, which I really liked, was very good at, and intended to pursue—having finished at NYU, going on to MIT.

And I might very well have done that had it been more theoretical at the time. But in those days, gearing up for the war effort—and particularly the Manhattan Project, for which chemical engineers did the fluid mechanics—the stress was on problem solving. I had no trouble with that, though there was another kind of problem. In thermodynamics, for instance, I could work with the function of entropy, $dS = dQ/T$, but I never quite knew what it meant until, as I wrote in *The Impossible*

Theater (a chapter called "Growing Up with Entropy"), I began to think seriously of certain dramatic figures like Orestes or Hamlet, who in his "ratiocinative meditativeness" (as Coleridge called it) is a measure of the unavailable energy of the universe. Which, of course, along with the post-Brechtian critique of tragedy (see Derrida on Artaud and the fate of representation, which remains, despite all desire for closure, the representation of fate), they're now trying to ameliorate or redeem in terms of chaos theory. Speaking of chaos, however, my veering into the theater was, to begin with, far more accidental than theoretical, and had much to do with my realization that I was not going to make it as a ballplayer, not at the highest levels, in either basketball or football (my two best sports). While I was shifty, tricky, heads-up, smart, I was not big enough or fast enough to compete.

Before saying what came, however, from what nearly drove me crazy, let me reflect for a moment on what I still owe to sports and—however perverse or overreaching, hopefully heads-up, smart—that abiding desire to compete, or perhaps I should say excel. For it had the residual virtue of bringing into my theater work, as to my writing and teaching as well, an impatience with imperfection, excuses, bullshit, faking it or goofing off, which you can't get away with in sports (all doping scandals aside) at "The Limits of Performance." That's the title of an essay in my most recent book, *The Dubious Spectacle,* and those limits were the theme of a conference at Stanford, perhaps the best I've ever attended, with Olympic medalists, Olympic prospects, Jim Ryun (who first ran a four-minute mile), Bill Walsh (with three wins in the Super Bowl), most of the Stanford coaches, as well as a Nobel Prize surgeon, a clinician who monitors the marathon runners from Kenya, and a world-class ophthalmologist. I was the only one speaking of performance in theater, but they knew what I was talking about, not only the coaches, when I remembered those moments at some threatening edge of inquiry, where in a sort of double vision I've seen what I was doing as next to immoral, urging the actor toward some physical or psychic danger—I mean s/he could really get hurt!—though with a certainty of revelation, eliciting the extraordinary, a performance beyond itself, if I didn't back off or relent. The ophthalmologist remarked at breakfast, relative to what I'd said, that with doubt at the sticking point, wanting to withdraw, if he wavered a millimeter he could easily ruin an eye.

The subtitle of *The Dubious Spectacle* is *Extremities of Theater,* which are still linked, no doubt, in my own eye to what—in that early, notorious book, subtitled *A Manifesto,* with its assault on the American theater—I had called the impossible. And since I began to see the theater as nothing but (the) impossible, or nothing much without it, the extremity led inevitably, not only to certain productions at The Actor's Workshop, their spectacular excess, about which I'd say we were "risking the baroque," but then, with the self-regarding scruple of a solipsistic contraction, the unnerving "ghostings" and "burrowings" in the methodology of KRAKEN, which became the heuristic datum of all my subsequent theory. "This book is the remembering of a theory": thus, the opening of *Take Up the Bodies: Theater at the Vanishing Point,* in which, as KRAKEN itself was vanishing (impossible to continue, for financial reasons), I tried to transfer its performative energy, psychophysical but cerebral, elliptical as it was, to the written page—where I said, in describing what we did, that if the work never existed, if I were simply making it up as I went along, the theory derived from it would be no less true. I can't rehearse the process here, its ideographic complexity in an almost manic obsessive, ceaseless movement of thought, but when I say that the work was cerebral, I mean just that, not only that the actors could perform standing on their heads (and they could), but more importantly, that it was a matter of *taking thought,* and with similar permutations also *taking time.*

"*Take* thought," I'd say to the actors, "take *thought*"—and they, whatever their other talents, had to be willing to think. (You might otherwise be a fine actor, and by then I'd directed many, some famous, some not, but if you didn't like ideas, forget it, this was not for you.) And if during the course of inquiry—into which without cessation every impulse was absorbed, and with hieroglyphic siftings turned over again in thought—there was some inhibiting reflex of psychological acting, like "I can't do this, I don't feel it," I might erupt into what, as theorized, was itself a reflex of method: "*I don't give a damn what you feel! feelings are cheap, I only care what you think!* What we're doing here is *thinking,* we're trying to understand"—that is, whatever the investigation, understanding what, without impassioned thought, we probably never would, and even then remembering, "whatever way you turn you have not even *started* thinking." (That's an epigraph from Artaud to my book called *Blooded Thought.*) As for the actors' other talents, they were considerable, in a group that included Bill Irwin, Julie Taymor, and others like Linda Gregerson, a superb actor, who refused to continue in theater, however, when that work unfortunately stopped. (She started to write poetry instead, took a Ph.D., teaches Milton and Spenser, and recently won, for a new book of poems, the biggest prize in the country.) That the thinking assumed feeling, powerful feeling, which accrued in the process of thought—over our years together, they brilliantly understood that. "But, ah, thought kills me that I am not thought. . . ." They also had to deal with that, which comes from the best manual of acting I know, Shakespeare's sonnets, from which we made a theater piece, with a teasing specularity, the impacted *Crooked Eclipses.*

Speaking of which, back now to the unexpected deviations that brought me into the theater. The School of Engineering at NYU was up at University Heights in the Bronx, with a liberal arts college adjacent (much better then than the one in Greenwich Village). As a way of sublimating my thwarted passion for ball-playing, I went over to the *Heights Daily News* and soon became its sports editor. This was the first time any engineering student had been on its editorial staff, and that's really when I started to do some writing. I should say that with the advent of World War II, in order to expedite the training of engineers, they discontinued all courses in the humanities, and had I not gone to Boys High, one of the elite schools in New York, I'd have graduated virtually illiterate, and as it was I was hardly well read. I continued writing, however, when I went into the army and became, after volunteering for the paratroops, one of the editors of the Fort Benning newspaper, which had the double benefit of keeping me alive, since it was the 82nd Airborne, my outfit, that having jumped behind the lines in Normandy for the D-Day invasion, was still endangered till war's end. I jumped out of planes and had my trooper's wings, but otherwise I was writing, sometimes about jumping, and that was it, except that it made me realize even more that I *could* write, and about things other than sports. When I left the army, I went back to NYU, and while finishing up my degree I worked again on the newspaper, and became its editor-in-chief.

As it happened then, the previous editor, Leonard Heideman—who later became a fairly successful screenwriter, though better known for the TV series *Bonanza*—was about to go into the playwriting program at the Yale Drama School. Up to this time I'd never gone to the theater in my life. Going to see a play was a nonexistent reality for anybody in my family, or any of my friends. One day, however, Lenny showed me the play he'd written that got him accepted at Yale, and after reading it, I said to myself, I can do that. So I wrote a couple of short plays (one actually in verse, called *When Death Is Dead*), and showed them to Lenny, who was impressed. And he urged me to send them, as he'd done with his, to Yale and Stanford (the two major drama schools at the time), on the good chance, he thought, that one or the other would offer me a fellowship. So I sent the plays, for kicks. Sure enough, both of them offered me fellowships, and it then occurred to me, why not? I've just been in the army, I'll be getting my degree, I can do that for a year, and then use the GI Bill to go to MIT. But which one meanwhile, Yale or Stanford?

As it happened, too, Jules Irving, who eventually became my partner for over twenty years, was the head of the Green Room Players at the liberal arts college, and I knew him slightly because he'd come over to the newspaper to ask for publicity. I'd also heard that he'd been a child actor on Broadway, and indeed he had, in *The American Way,* with Frederic March. As I was thinking where to go, I met Jules one day on the steps of Gould Hall, the library, and asked him what he thought—whereupon another coincidence: he had been at Stanford during the war, in a language training program, studying Russian, and was going back there, into the Drama Department. "Why don't you go to Stanford," he said, "it's like a country club." And indeed it was when I went, those golden hills behind the campus, the groves of eucalyptus on Palm Drive, and for a mile each side of the entrance, before El Camino Real was developed, rows of fruit and vegetable stands (I'd never seen an avocado or artichoke before) in front of a fence of roses. For me, except for the Borscht Circuit, never out of New York, it was utopia. But before I actually went, as the prospect came upon me, I was suddenly frightened. I'd still not seen a play, nor had I read any plays I could remember, except Lennie's, and *Julius Caesar* in high school. So I went quickly, first on campus, to see Jules in *The Hasty Heart,* then to a show on Broadway, *The Moon Is Blue,* with Barbara Bel Geddes, and next—because Burgess Meredith was in it, and I'd seen him in the movies—*Playboy of the Western World,* which some years after was the first play I ever directed.

Meanwhile, too, during my final semester at NYU, I asked everybody who might know what I should be reading, and that's when I started on Shakespeare, the Greeks, much of Ibsen, Chekhov, O'Neill, and others like Clifford Odets and Elmer Rice, while pretty much ignoring my courses, which I managed to get through without studying. Still feeling unprepared when I did get to Stanford, and in the graduate program, it took a while to realize it, but I'd read more—since I kept reading, and *about* the drama too, Barrett H. Clark, John Gassner, Joseph Wood Krutch—than most of the students there who'd presumably been majoring in drama, though many were there for acting. And some of them, indeed, were very talented, with a certain maturity among the men, those back from the war on the GI Bill. Aside from the course in playwriting—taught by Hubert Heffner, godfather of the American Theater Association (now the ATHE)—I was fascinated by Development of Dramatic Art, my first course in theater history, though I soon found myself puzzling over curious things, like the Romans invented the curtain, which they called the *auleum.* That was it. As to *why* they developed the curtain, a rather strange phenomenon when you think of it, or the open-air theater at Epidaurus, with nothing hiding the stage—why in the world, by what accretion or perversion of value, would you want to separate the seers from what's to be seen, when it hadn't been done before? But when I'd pose a question like that, it made me feel a little peculiar, because nobody wanted to talk about it.

Nor did they want to talk about a book like Eric Bentley's *Playwright as Thinker,* which went against the grain of what they taught about the drama of modernism, though modernism itself as a concept was not, as I remember, talked about at all, no less anything like the modernist avant-garde. (Nor did I ever hear of *Ubu Roi,* which caused Yeats to say when he saw it, "After us, the savage gods.") And while I loved watching rehearsals or even the technical setups in the theater, and was much enamored of actors (and the lovely women among them), sometimes seeing them in a production over and over again, I was perplexed when I tried to discuss the play itself that I was getting little by way of response. And it soon became apparent that Bentley was onto some instructional fault when he wrote about a production of Ibsen at Yale, in which the students there would talk about the lighting, the costumes, the sets, the acting—everything except what the play was about.

And then, there at Stanford, this included my own plays, which were soon on the stage of the Little Theater, where a few years ago Martin Esslin and I, just before he died, gave talks in a retrospective on the theater of the Absurd. Had any of the playwrights Martin had included in his seminal book, Ionesco or Adamov, or even Beckett, come on the scene at Stanford when I was there, most of the faculty and students wouldn't have known what to say—the more likely thing being that the plays wouldn't have been produced. As it was, when we first did such things at The Actor's Workshop in San Francisco, Stanford—like other university theater departments, which one would have thought should be leading the way (as in medicine or physics)—was still doing a conventional "season": *a* Shakespeare, *a* Shaw, *a* musical, and maybe *a* (safe) new play or *a* Chekhov, who was (would you believe it?) still considered avant-garde. As to when and whether the absurdists were being discussed, and to what extent (no less distinctions between them and Beckett or Genet, also in Esslin's book), I can't say; it was certainly true, however, that by the time theory surfaced—preempting the idea of performance, or colluding with performance art—the department was still behind, though I've talked again there recently, and surely there's been a change.

I was so disenchanted at one point, even after I'd won the Margery Bailey Playwriting Prize, that I left Stanford and went back to live with my parents in Brooklyn, still intending anyhow to return to engineering. There had been, however, one major contribution that the Drama Department had made to my life and career, for it was at Stanford that I met Beatrice Manley, who eventually became my first wife. She was there as a visiting actor from Broadway in what was, as I recall, the first artist-in-residence program in any university. Glamorous as she was, five years older, experienced in more than theater, I could only fantasize dating her then, while I ran the lights on *As You Like It,* in which she played Rosalind. But she was very gracious to me when I'd ask her a question, and seemed to think I was bright. And so I dared to call, when I was back in Brooklyn, and she had returned to her apartment in Greenwich Village (next door to W. H. Auden), driving over the bridge to see her in my father's car.

It was she who, in New York, introduced me to various theater people, like Teddy Post, who with Sidney Lumet headed a group of actors that at the time rivaled the Actors Studio. I went to plays with Bea, and through her eyes, began to see more in the acting. It was Teddy who showed one of my plays to Erwin Piscator, who critiqued it at his Dramatic Workshop, where I first encountered the ideas of Brecht, as well as one of his *Lehrstücke.* Meanwhile, they were still doing my plays at Stanford, and when Heffner induced me to return, to complete an M.A. (I refused to take any more courses, and they virtually gave it to me), Bea and I kept in touch, and soon she came out too, giving up her career in New York. She was there when they did my thesis play (designed by O. J. Brockett), by which time I had already gone over to the English Department to take a course in poetry.

The curmudgeonly man teaching it stood behind a lectern and literally read his own essays, with some mumbled metacommentary, but it was the first time I'd ever felt in a classroom that this was a matter of life and death. Each idea was a moral issue, and you found yourself at risk if you didn't take it seriously. I hadn't the faintest notion who he was, but it turned out to be Yvor Winters, one of the great New Critics, with whom I did my dissertation, after the head of the department, Richard Foster Jones—with whom I took a seminar in (of all things, and I'm not sure why) Ciceronian rhetoric—came up to me one day on the quad, and said, "Mr. Blau, would you like to teach?" How he become aware of my background in engineering, I don't know, but he wanted me to do a freshman course in Scientific Writing, which I did, with the very best students at Stanford, in chemistry, physics, neurology, some preparing for medical school. As for a Ph.D., I didn't even know what that was until I started teaching.

When I decided to go ahead with it, it was because of Winters and Wallace Stegner, with whom I first studied Henry James. We had to do a paper every week, and for the one on James, by an accident of what was on the shelf in the library, the book I chose to write about was *The Golden Bowl.* It dazzled as it baffled, and I'm still most drawn to things that arouse me by confounding. What's more, if there's any notable influence on the way I've come to write (some speak of it as "density," others "opacity," in my various books) it's the prose of "darkest James," where nothing is but what materializes in a sort of perceptual slippage, with its dilatory, circuitous, parenthetical (have I really said it? or even vaguely seen it?) delaying of predication, requiring an interjection, because you want to say it all, in a syntactical anamnesis, before you come to it (what *it*? "it all, it all," as Beckett would later say) though it wouldn't be what it *is* (it wouldn't even exist) if I didn't say it as I did. Or as Wallace Stevens would say, in the highest modernist vein, poetry is words about things that wouldn't exist without the words, a notion I found exhilarating, as with other new directions. While sorting out an aesthetic in the reading I was doing—hardly able to believe to this day that they pay me money to teach it (all those good books!)—I chanced upon a job in the Language Arts Department at San Francisco State, with Jules already there in the Theater Department, and his wife Priscilla Pointer (they had performed together abroad, entertaining the troops) also on the scene.

When Bea and I moved up to the city, she became almost immediately the most desirable actor there, but while there were various "little theaters" around (that movement still alive), there was no professional work except with a poorly directed, so-called Repertory Theater, in which she became the star, though in short order very dissatisfied with that. Whereupon, fearful that she was getting restive, and I might lose her, I suggested to Jules that we start our own theater, and when he, and Bea, and Priscilla, were skeptical—they were all, and how not?, still oriented to Broadway—I would naively draw upon my reading of theater history and literally say things like: two guys sit down over a tacky table in Moscow, talk for nineteen hours, and create the Moscow Art Theater—why can't we do that? They may have laughed or condescended but eventually went along, at least with the idea of a workshop for actors, and I'll abbreviate this archive now by saying the rest is history.

I didn't direct at first, Jules did, and I was a sort of undesignated dramaturg, gradually commenting on what was done, or not, which sometimes troubled me—choice of plays, absence of method. If ignorance is not exactly bliss, it does have certain advantages, and that was certainly so in the theater, and in our own theater as much as any. Had I known what some there thought they knew, because they'd been in the theater a good deal longer, we'd have never done what, when it was celebrated, they forgot they had resisted. And they resisted, some of them, almost every innovation, not only the audacious plays in the repertoire, or even the *idea* of a repertoire—the constitution of meaning as we moved from play to play, and the stylistic implications—but also experimental tendencies in the staging, the collaboration with other artists, formed by abstract expressionism or happenings or the Action events of the time, or the anticipatory genres of installation art. After learning all I could about the theater, seeing everything around, I realized there was far more to learn from the other arts about what might be done in the theater. And even today, when I do go to the theater, it still tends to confirm that, belated as it mostly is, even when experimental.

One last word about resistance: what was true in the theater was also so in theater studies, as one can see in the history of *Theater Journal* itself (to which I may very well be the oldest living contributor, having published my first essay there, "The Education of the Playwright," in 1952, the same year the Workshop started). When poststructuralism first came on the scene—appropriating as it did, in the opacity of its prose, the idea of performance—it was not among theater scholars. As for the emergence of performance studies, that came, if theoretical at all, out of an anthropological inclination, differing from my own, which (in memoriam) tends to be ontological, trying to see in what's forgotten—the actor dying in front of your eyes—the materialization of theater from whatever it is it is *not,* life? the Real? or, in its (dis)appearance, is it life as a dream? "What is the theater," I wrote in *Take Up the Bodies,* "but the body's long initiation in the mystery of its vanishings." But here I am on autopilot, obsessed even more with the vanishings, while aging into the mystery, with an archival habit of mind.

Publication History

"Relevance: The Shadow of a Magnitude," *Daedalus* 98.3 (1969): 654–76.

"The Faith-Based Initiative of the Theater of the Absurd," *Journal of Dramatic Theory and Criticism* 16.1 (2001): 3–13.

"The Soul-Complex of Strindberg: Suffocation, Scopophilia, and the Seer," *Assaph: Studies in Theater* 16 (2002): 1–12.

"From the Dreamwork of Secession to Orgies Mysteries Theater," *Modern Drama* 52.3 (2009): 259–78; also in *Modern Austrian Literature* 42.3 (2009): 1–18.

"Performing in the Chaosmos: Farts, Follicles, Mathematics, and Delirium in Deleuze," in *Deleuze and Performance,* ed. Laura Cull (Edinburgh: Edinburgh University Press, 2009) 22–34.

"Seeming, Seeming: The Illusion of Enough," in *Against Theater: Creative Destructions on the Modernist Stage,* ed. Martin Puchner and Alan Ackerman (New York: Palgrave/Macmillan, 2006) 231–47.

"Who's There?—Community of the Question," *PAJ: A Journal of Performance and Art* 83, 28.2 (2006): 1–12.

"The Emotional Memory of Directing," *Theater Research International* 30.1 (2005): 1–12.

"The Commodius Vicus of Beckett: Vicissitudes of the Arts in the Science of Affliction," *Journal of Dramatic Theory and Criticism* 18.2 (2004): 5–19; also in *Beckett after Beckett,* ed. S. E. Gontarski and Anthony Ullmann (Gainesville: University Press of Florida, 2006) 22–38.

"Among the Deepening Shades: The Beckettian Moment(um) and the Brechtian Arrest," in *Where Extremes Meet: Rereading Brecht and Beckett (Brecht Yearbook)* 27 [2007]: 65–81.

"Apnea and True Illusion: Breath(less) in Beckett," *Modern Drama* 49.4 (2006): 452–68; also in *Beckett at 100: Revolving It All,* ed. Linda Ben-Zvi and Angela Moorjani (London: Oxford University Press, 2008) 35–53.

"Art and Crisis: Homeland Security and the Noble Savage," *PAJ: A Journal of Performance and Art* 75, 25.3 (2003): 6–19.

"Thinking History, History Thinking," *Theater Survey* 45.2 (2004): 253–62.

"Why *WHAT* History?" *Modern Language Quarterly* 70.1 (2009): 3–10.

"Auto Archive: Herbert Blau," *Theater Journal* 56 (2004): 253–62.

Index